SHIMMERFROST

Shimmerfrost

Swordbane Book II

Paul Joseph Santoro Emerick

Copyright © 2024 by Paul Joseph Santoro Emerick.

Library of Congress Control Number:		2024902812
ISBN:	Hardcover	979-8-3694-1358-6
	Softcover	979-8-3694-1357-9
	eBook	979-8-3694-1599-3

All rights reserved. No part of this book may be reproduced or transmitted in any form or by any means, electronic or mechanical, including photocopying, recording, or by any information storage and retrieval system, without permission in writing from the copyright owner.

This is a work of fiction. Names, characters, places and incidents either are the product of the author's imagination or are used fictitiously, and any resemblance to any actual persons, living or dead, events, or locales is entirely coincidental.

Adobe Stock images depicting people are used with their permission and for illustrative purposes only. Certain stock imagery © Adobe Stock.

Print information available on the last page.

Rev. date: 02/01/2024

To order additional copies of this book, contact:
Xlibris
844-714-8691
www.Xlibris.com
Orders@Xlibris.com
849919

Contents

Acknowledgments ix

Chapter 1	An Unexpected Reunion	1
Chapter 2	In the Pursuit of Adventure	4
Chapter 3	Ambushing the Pursuer	9
Chapter 4	Shedding Blood in the Forest	11
Chapter 5	Entering the Portal of No Return	15
Chapter 6	A New Life After Death	26
Chapter 7	Searching for Answers	32
Chapter 8	A Son's Mourning	37
Chapter 9	Fighting for a New Survival	40
Chapter 10	Arrival in Hell	45
Chapter 11	A New Commission	50
Chapter 12	Paying Final Respects	54
Chapter 13	Stepping into the Light	60
Chapter 14	To Find a New Infernal Purpose	68
Chapter 15	Discerning among Friends and Foes	73
Chapter 16	Finding the Way to Shimmerfrost	80
Chapter 17	Seeking an Audience with the Overlord	85
Chapter 18	An Infernal Reunion	89
Chapter 19	Doire na Cairn	94
Chapter 20	Portent from the Past	105
Chapter 21	Fear and Warning in the Darkness	110
Chapter 22	Infernal Lovers	115
Chapter 23	Revelation in the Lord of Punishment's Lair	123
Chapter 24	New and Familiar Encounters	126
Chapter 25	Summoning Divine Wind	131
Chapter 26	Trial of the Wailing Golden Valkyrie	137
Chapter 27	Channeling Hell's Fury	148
Chapter 28	Bracing the Cold Onslaught of Dyr Valley	154

Chapter 29	Nature's Ill Omen	159
Chapter 30	Summoning Nature's Fury	162
Chapter 31	Plotting and Counterplotting	171
Chapter 32	Infernal Ambush Reversal	173
Chapter 33	Infernal Humiliation and Imprisonment	177
Chapter 34	Beginning to Forge a New Peace	180
Chapter 35	Promising Developments and Unfortunate Tidings	189
Chapter 36	Ambush Reversal	193
Chapter 37	Surviving the Onslaught	202
Chapter 38	To Raise and March an Army Through Hell	207
Chapter 39	Young Dark Lord's Deliverance	214
Chapter 40	In Pursuit of Darkness	220
Chapter 41	Prize of Torment	225
Chapter 42	A Titan's Path to Chosen Vesselhood	228
Chapter 43	Discovery From the Vast Blue Yonder	232
Chapter 44	Unleashing the Primal Beast	240
Chapter 45	Sacrificing Light to Purge Darkness	247
Chapter 46	To Court and Find Deception	258
Chapter 47	Settling a Final Infernal Old Score	265
Chapter 48	Delayed Showdown	277
Chapter 49	A Cunning and Deadly Proposition	281
Chapter 50	Battle of Abhainn Gainmhich Mawr	287
Chapter 51	Unleashing the Winter Death Witch's Wrath	299
Chapter 52	Mutual Pursuits of Vengeance	303
Chapter 53	Triumph of the Lord and Lordess of the Infernal Plane	316
Chapter 54	Nebelheim under Siege	323
Chapter 55	Communing with the Infernal Lord and Lordess	336
Chapter 56	Battle at Jotunn Gate	344
Chapter 57	Final Showdown at Jotunheim	362
Chapter 58	Roadmap to Reunification	382
Chapter 59	Finding Closure	391
Chapter 60	A New Dark Ascendance	395

To my late friend and one of the biggest fans of *Swordbane*, Brandon Michael Hunt. Also, to my three children, Leonardo, Lorenzo, and Aelia. Without them listening to my rated G—PG bedtime story version of *Swordbane* and now this book, I honestly don't know if I would ever make it this far in writing. They were also among the biggest fans of the fantasy world I created. Thank you, kiddos. I'm blessed to be your dad.

Acknowledgments

A special thanks to Brina Borges Boyle for collaborating with me and making the awesome maps as a reference for my readers. Brina, you are truly a mapmaker! Also, special thanks to Tim Hearon for being the beta reader of this book and providing relevant feedback to help me improve the overall storytelling. Lastly, special thanks to one of my friends, Paul Timmerman, for passing along the idea of the *Banesmen* in response to the release and promotion of my last book, *Swordbane*.

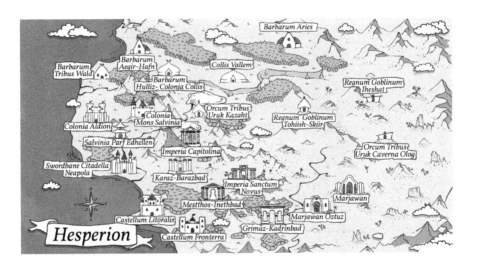

Chapter One

An Unexpected Reunion

A lone figure soared high above the air in the near pitch-black sky. A majestic yet terrifying fortress estate lie below, next to the flowing river of burning magma amid a landscape of charred brimstone. The lone figure gave loud enough shrieks. Inside the fortress, in the throne room, a werewolf seated on the throne stood up and called for one of his servants. This werewolf had a black and grisly appearance and stood about six feet tall. He was the lord of the domain he claimed for himself in the hellish plane of Hadao Infernum. It was in this plane that the divine spirits condemned him after he perished in a duel as a mortal. In his previous life, mortals knew him by both his former title and name respectively as Dux Decius, the chosen vessel of the respective patron deity spirits of death and war, Calu and Laran. He was also once the dux, or acting regent of Imperium Sanctum Novus. No longer among the living after being condemned to hell ten years ago, this dark warlord still embraced his ambition to become an overlord and conquer and rule over the domain he was in just like he had once sought to do in the mortal plane world of Terrunaemara. He would use his supernatural powers occasionally to disappear from this unforgiving plane while transforming into his ghost avatar. From that point, Decius could teleport in his spectral form and return to the mortal plane of Terrunaemara for a short time. He could do so only to commune and converse with the living after they had performed the religious ritual of libation and incense offering to Decius's patron deities while calling upon his name.

Decius's bid to become the lord of hell created a division that its current ruler, Orcus the Lord of Punishment, struggled to maintain control while ruling this eternal place of condemnation. Orcus considered this new upstart rival as a threat to his power as Decius swayed many of the hellish denizens to his cause. Decius claimed to bring an era of new change to Hadao Infernum wherein its denizens would no longer suffer under the sadistic leisure of Orcus, the latter of who made a habit to enjoy torturing while sending his minions to take any of the condemned by force to bring forth to Orcus's presence.

Reclusive and hiding to avoid potential foes while studying his surroundings, Decius knew this dark and fiery plane well enough to explore more openly while using his known titles, his frightful appearance, and his powers to his advantage to convince many of Orcus's servants to join Decius in seeing him as a more pragmatic and powerful rival to challenge Orcus for ruling over all of hell. The servants at first were low-ranking flying red imps that looked like goblins with both having pointed ears, jagged teeth, and a short stature of three feet. Yet, these imps also had red wings and two small protruding horns from their front cranium.

The second group of denizens that joined Decius's cause included the succubi, individually known as succubus. These were flying female demons that took the form of attractive women yet also had a pair of horns, jagged flying wings, and a tail. They were also considered to be demonic sirens, in which they had an alluring yet also very haunted tone of voice. There were known to be at least seventy-two of these female demons. Decius had used his powers and his recent gathering of imp followers to defeat these demons one by one or a couple at a time. He convinced them to join his cause rather than end their lives.

It was only about three years ago, after capturing the last succubi, that Decius launched his attack, planning to use his converted imps and succubi to keep the forces of Orcus at bay while Decius confronted and fought Orcus to claim the throne of condemnation. However, as Decius gained the upper hand, all the succubi turned against him. They sought to get rid of him as an offering for Orcus in exchange for being pardoned from their betrayal by allying with Decius.

Decius, angered by the betrayal, barely escaped with his remaining forces of imps to retreat far from the fortress of Orcus. He decided instead to bide his time while ordering the imps and the subjects of the realm of condemnation who swore fealty to Decius to address him by his former title as dux and build him a grand fortress estate. The imps obeyed by addressing their overlord with his preferred title and completed their construction after a year of labor that still stood nearly two years later.

At the moment, Decius, seated in his throne room, was vaguely familiar with that shriek as he had heard it from the succubi before though not knowing which succubus it was, anticipating a possible preemptive invasion by Orcus against him.

When one of the imp servants came before Decius's throne, the servant reported that there was a lone flying succubus who sought his presence and wished to join him. It surprised the dux and made him suspicious, not believing it to be true, knowing that all the succubi had betrayed him before. He would hear what this succubus had to say. However, the dux intended to kill this succubus and satisfy his desire for revenge against the betrayal. Before granting an audience to the succubus, Decius inquired out of curiosity, about the identity of this succubus. The imp shrugged, showing its uncertainty.

Not caring as much to know about the lone succubus's identity, Decius motioned with a hand to let the succubus enter. The imp acknowledged the command. The dux went back to his throne but prepared to strike the succubus when he felt like doing so.

When the chamber door opened, a lone figure walked in. She was a succubus, but one Decius did not recognize. She approached Decius slowly while kneeling, stopping a few paces from the throne. Decius's jagged werewolf jaws dropped in awe at what he saw. She was not one of the seventy-two succubi that had betrayed him. Rather, upon seeing her face and recognizing her, he realized she was someone he knew before in his last life. He saw this person again, noticing that her form had changed to that of a succubus. Decius could not hold back, unleashing a loud howl that startled all his loyal denizens who were close enough to hear with curiosity and fear.

Decius then quickly kneeled next to the lone succubus. He could not hold back an expression of remorse and sadness at seeing this person again. She was the last one he expected to see. In his soul, searching for understanding, he could not help but almost ask her why she was in Hadao Infernum. Somehow, he did not need to ask because, in his heart, he already knew the answer.

Chapter Two

In the Pursuit of Adventure

Nearly a week earlier, just east of Swordbane's northern coastal settlement of Colonia Mons Salvinia on a bright early spring midday, a dark spot was moving on the canopy of gray pine, cottonwood, and various oak trees. Far above the shadow, loomed a lone flying skyship that was of a wooden caravel design secured with a harness assembly of a ballast hot-air balloon. This unique contraption was being crewed by four people who were on the top deck of the floating ship while searching all about the forest and grassy terrain below.

Among these four figures included a slender average-height wood elf, a ranger also trained by his mother in the lock-picking arts of the rogue. He was known by others as Linitus. He had sharp brown eyes, distinct narrow pointed ears, snow-white skin, and short raven-black hair except for a noticeable topknot that he displayed. His face was youthful, slim, and chiseled. The elf ranger wore a brown leather armor cuirass crafted in the elven linothorax design over a white tunic. Linitus wore leather gloves and decorative elven mail boots and pauldrons. He wielded an elven composite bow and had a quiver full of various types of arrows. The elf ranger carried an exotic silver elven-style long sword that had a slight curve, which was secured in an exquisite scabbard with a dragon relief on his back. This sword he could wield with either hand or with both hands. It was a special sword gifted to him by his father-in-law, King Ascentius IV, in recognition of this ranger's heroic deeds, playing a pivotal role in saving the United Kingdom of Swordbane (or simply known as Swordbane) during the war against the secessionist faction, the Imperial Remnant, led by Dux Decius ten years ago. The war was over, and peace was brokered with a treaty where both the United Kingdom of Swordbane and the Imperial Remnant had an uneasy agreement to coexist. Linitus however, along with another figure that stood next to him on the top deck of the ship managed to defeat and slay Decius before the last battle that ended the civil war.

The other figure was the elf ranger's fellow companion and endeared wife, known as Princess Marin, a human knight in the order of the Eternal Flame known by her nickname as the Princess Knight. Her title in part was attributed to being King Ascentius's daughter. She was a human with features reflecting both her Citadellan and Nordling backgrounds. She was slightly taller than Linitus but still of average stature and somewhat noticeably more of a muscular build compared to him. Marin had golden-brown hair that could pass as bronze or dark blonde. She had warm fair skin. She also had blue eyes and her facial display tempered yet still confident knightly stature. She wore a combination of half-plate mail armor, protecting her vital areas that overlapped the underlying hauberk chainmail that she also wore. Her armor stood out from the rest of the knights of the kingdom, being noticeably bright and vibrant transition violet-azure dye coloring. She wielded a flaming long sword known as Sol's Fury, and she also carried a small round shield that bore the emblem of a dragon sigil with the respective animal representing the symbolic totem of the kingdom. Marin, like her elven lover, played a pivotal role in the defeat of Dux Decius which led to the treaty that ended the civil war, and their fame spread throughout the kingdom and beyond. Together, Marin and Linitus stood on the bow of the ship and took turns using a spyglass to look about for a particular human trafficking convoy.

Behind the two lovers, at the aft deck of the ship, manning the steering wheel stood a young halfling wizard who was roughly half the height of Linitus and Marin. Those who knew him throughout the kingdom called him Wyatt the Spellslinger. Wyatt attained his reputation for casting various spells with speed, such as flaming balls of fire or bolts of lightning. He had long flowing dark hair that fell just below his shoulder. He wore a dark gray robe and a black cloak with blue lace embroidery. The wizard also wore a pointed dark gray hat and wielded a small silver wand to cast his magical spells.

Next to Wyatt stood another figure nearly of the same height but plumper. He was a dwarf who was rounded though muscular and had fair skin and a gray beard. In the kingdom, they knew him as Smokey Peat. He was a dwarf warrior who served as a former captain of King Ascentius's bodyguards before eventually crossing paths and teaming up to adventure and fight alongside his three companions. This warrior dwarf bore a heavy two-handed war hammer made from dwarven steel, and he wore segments of forged dwarven armor, including pauldrons, gauntlets, and boots that were distinguished also with the same azure color as Marin though with a gold embroidered color offset. Peat also had a strapped carrying assembly behind his back that mounted two explosive barrel bombs. The dwarf had a short temper when fighting enemies. He became even more feared of his penchant to resort to using explosives to demoralize his enemies. He also enjoyed putting them down quickly and destructively. Peat, along with his three companions, had earned their reputations during the civil war ten years ago. It was during that time they formed an elite order known as the Comradery.

Though the civil war was over, these four warriors still decided that rather than disbanding to instead repurpose themselves in serving the kingdom in various ways. Chief among these was aiding and assisting those in need, exploring and seeking adventures, and patrolling the skies for any potential threats to the kingdom. The most prominent of their foes included bands of bandits that sought to organize and prey upon the kingdom after it was weakened by the civil war with the Imperial Remnant ten years ago. Now it was a particular case of banditry or, rather, child trafficking in which the Comradery was recently in full pursuit of a trafficking caravan.

As the floating skyship continued its course, soaring in the air, Linitus had spotted and pointed with his hand below to the subject of interest that they were seeking. A mysterious caravan of young males led by two cult members escorted them across the border region that separated the boundaries and domain between the Kingdom of Swordbane and the Imperial Remnant. This mysterious caravan was part of a rising cult, a group of extremists founded by Dux Decius's many followers after the civil war. These cult followers became radicalized and took to their hearts Decius's divine-like figure. He gained this cult following after his death when he learned to transcend the boundary between death and life by projecting his specter into the world of the living whenever he was summoned by his devoted followers.

Many of these cult followers spread this emerging religion of Decius as the dark lord who would bring order through destruction and death. Several of these adult cult leaders and followers even moved freely across the borders of Swordbane and the Imperial Remnant to spread the influence and message of this religious cult. As they did so, they also recruited adolescent male boys from the Citadellan coastlands and interior forests. These adolescents would join the dark lord's cause and would be trained in the ways of war and find a worthy path of attaining prestige and glory. Additionally, the cultists provided financial incentives for their recruitment efforts. The parents of the recruited male youths were paid a modest but acceptable amount by the itinerant cult recruiters for the services their sons would provide the Remnant. Once recruited and trained, the young male youths would fight for the Imperial Remnant against the enemies they were in conflict with. This included a kingdom known as Marjawan in the low desert in the southeast of the Remnant's border and the coastal forest barbarian Nordlings living in the northwest of the Remnant's border. This particular group of Nordlings (unlike their fellow barbarian mountain brethren) broke off from the Remnant's control after the civil war when the Remnant was no longer strong enough to assert control over this many of the Nordlings.

Only the Nordling tribes in the northern interior were still loyal and were under the control of the Imperial Remnant. They were willing to still do so in exchange for its leaders being granted by the Imperial Remnant titles of ownership to their barbarian brethren's coastal settlements while the Remnant attempted to reconquer these resisting Nordling tribes. However, even after nearly ten years, the battles between the Imperial Remnant and its allied mountain Nordling forces against the other Nordling tribes along the northwest coast proved unproductive and resulted in this prolonged stalemate. The Imperial Remnant was determined to change that by seeking recruits from the Citadellan coastlands to undergo arduous training at a young age like Decius did under his wizard mentor, Agaroman. By doing so, the Imperial Remnant would have a new generation of multitalented soldier officers to lead and conquer in reestablishing a new envisioned empire based on the ancient Lupercalian Empire, eventually destroying Swordbane once and for all when the time was right.

However, unbeknown to Agaroman, the four heroes of the Comradery started to notice what was happening. The Comradery was determined to put an end to it despite not knowing the full-scale intentions and plans of the Remnant. Linitus and his comrades at arms that followed under his leadership were attempting to track and follow the cultist caravan to discover where their base of operations was located. They would also set about retrieving the indoctrinated adolescents from the cult members. From there, the Comradery would return the adolescents to their homes with pledges from their families to never sell off their sons again. If the families refused or showed they could not be trusted, then the Comradery would surrender the trafficked youths to the nearest monastery-ran orphanage. From there, they would be made wards of the kingdom while being trained in adulthood to serve among several professions in service to the royal crown, including priests, wizards, and craftsmen, or to pursue becoming knights in one of several elite orders.

The heroes tracked this caravan that slowly but gradually made its way near the southern end of the Great Azure Lake. However, this interior lake on the leeward side of the Great Coastal Mountains was heavily forested. Linitus had a hard time following the caravan under the thick forest cover while staying undetected. Eventually, the heroes would have to decide whether to continue pursuing the caravan from the air or let Wyatt teleport them below in the hopes of Linitus being able to track them with his insightful skills of the outdoors and detecting the scent of the cultist caravan while following on foot. Ultimately, Linitus decided for Wyatt to teleport him, Marin, and Peat into the forest before the canopy obscured the last direction that they saw the caravan still southeast from the lake shoreline.

Wyatt cast a teleportation spell with his silver magic wand. With a bright flash, the wizard's three comrades disappeared and then reappeared on the forest floor. Linitus made sure upon teleporting that Wyatt would do so by placing his comrades a few hundred yards away from the caravan. This would make it easier for the elf and his companions to track their target undetected. However, unbeknown to the adventuring heroes, the pursued apparently had also taken notice of their presence.

Chapter Three

Ambushing the Pursuer

The cultist caravan was only a few hundred yards away when someone among the group noticed they were being followed. Emerging from one of the black robes of one caravan cult member was a dark brown clawed hand with fur that reached out with a raised palm. He had called the caravan to halt. This figure removed its hood to reveal his werewolf's head.

He was Lucianus Canus Anicii Diem. His followers knew him as Lucianus Canus. He was the son of Dux Decius Anicii and Duchess Lady Lucia Diem. At only about ten years old, he had been traveling in the past year as part of the caravan escorts with his trusted advisor and instructor, the wizard Agaroman. Agaroman previously served and mentored Decius into becoming a warlord and dark lord in his quest to become a chosen vessel of the divine spirits and bring about a new envisioned empire based on the Lupercalian Empire in the ancient days of old.

Since Decius's passing, Agaroman trained Decius's son and successor. This time Agaroman sought to do so by teaching Lucianus more than just honing his skills in melee like his father had done. This time, the wizard instructed the young dark lord successor in mastering the ways of wizard magic. To Agaroman's admiration, Lucianus had been very proficient in the art of magic. This made the young werewolf formidable. He also was adept at utilizing his natural canine-like abilities. He could detect an array of scents and was very receptive to various ambient sounds, even from a distance.

Lucianus turned to Agaroman and stopped the caravan. Agaroman was at the head of the caravan, also wearing a hooded cloak. The action perplexed the wizard mentor at first into stopping. He knew Lucianus though a young werewolf and in his adolescence was still as skilled as anyone else to notice trouble. The wizard looked at his disciple's face. Lucianus nodded when asked by his mentor if they were being followed. Agaroman, with a stern face, instructed Lucianus to proceed and unleash his abilities to call upon and summon their allies. The young wolfling youth nodded again. Lucianus immediately unleashed a frightening howl heard throughout the woods surrounding the Great Azure Lake.

Within moments, a wave of howls sounded throughout the forest in response to Lucianus's howl. Three large packs of wolves emerged from several nearby dens and startled almost everyone in the caravan. Lucianus however was not surprised. He had summoned them after all. Agaroman was also unsurprised as he had seen this done before by Lucianus and his father before him.

All three packs of wolves huddled with Lucianus. The feral canines growled while standing in an obedient postured form for who they considered their pack master. Lucianus pointing his hand toward the west while howling again had prompted the packs of wolves to understand and obey while turning abruptly and charging in that direction. The wolves would hunt down their master's pursuers until either they were slaughtered to the last wolf, or they had killed the last person following Lucianus.

Meanwhile, the cultist caravan resumed its course at a much faster pace. They stopped once again when another pack of dire wolves appeared. This wolf pack carried a band of mountain raiders on their backs. They reached Lucianus's path, ready to answer their summoner's call. Upon recognizing Lucianus, the goblins with their mounted dire wolves knelt in submission to his overlordship. The goblin bandit leader came forward to ask what they may do upon receiving his summons. Lucianus pointed his hand again toward the west while instructing them to find and eliminate whoever was pursuing them. The goblin bandit leader nodded while raising his jagged sword for the rest of the mounted pack to follow his lead. Once again, the cultist caravan resumed its double-paced march. They would not stop until they reached their destination several miles away. They would use the cover of the trees to obscure their path from being followed as much as possible.

Chapter Four

Shedding Blood in the Forest

A few hundred yards away, Linitus was following the scent. He paused, and his face showed his fear. At first, he thought he was following the group of humans' trail. Soon he knew there was much more to discern. The elf ranger noticed human footprints on the ground. He also recognized one set of footprints that surprised him more than anything else. A series of wolf-like footprints on the ground followed along with the human footprints of the caravan. His shocked look had garnered Marin and Peat's attention. Marin asked her elven lover what was wrong. He pointed at the wolf-like paw prints. Marin's face shuddered in the same sense of shock. She wondered if Decius, the heavens forbid, had returned to the world of the living in his bodily form. As she wondered, she and her comrades heard distinct howls coming from the direction the heroes of the Comradery were following. This cultist caravan was not alone. The howl, though alarming, was not one Marin and Linitus recognized. They still remembered the howls Decius could make. This one, though terrifying, was different and not as powerful in being projected, though still intimidating.

The three comrades reacted by drawing out their weapons to bear in hand while still taking several steps eastward to pursue the caravan. Moments later, Linitus, hearing and then seeing with his sharp eagle-like eyes, spotted several packs of wolves converging on his company. The elf reacted and called out to both Marin and Peat to ready themselves. He motioned with his head and eyes to the advancing packs of wolves that he was ready to confront them should they challenge him. The elf ranger took out one of his sabot arrow barrage canisters. He deployed the canister after he pulled back and let loose the bowstring. The canister propelled forward and dispersed multiple arrows that struck an entire pack of wolves save two. Marin, the Princess Knight, grabbed two sharp plume darts she had used to hold back her hair and threw them. It struck one dire wolf while the Princess Knight blocked the other oncoming wolf with her shield as it charged at her. She plunged her flaming blade, Sol's Fury, at the attacking wolf in its abdomen before making a final swift strike at its neck while it went down at the first inflicted wound.

Peat meanwhile pulled a latch that released one of the explosive wooden barrels secured to the dwarf's back via a back-strapped pack assembly. Peat rolled the barrel to the ground toward another oncoming pack of wolves while calling out for Linitus to shoot the barrel. Linitus turned toward his side as Peat motioned for the elf to set off the barrel bomb. Linitus pulled out a spark-ready flaming arrow from his quiver. He let loose the arrow from his bow after pulling back the bowstring just at the right time as the second pack of wolves came. The deployed arrow the elf shot struck the explosive barrel several dozen yards away. This strike set off an explosion that enveloped the oncoming pack of wolves. None of the feral beasts were left standing. So far, the three heroes thought they were in good standing.

The sense of mood however changed when the third pack of wolves tried to envelop them by swarming from different directions. Linitus shot two arrows to take one down. Marin struggled with fighting two wolves that charged at her. Peat wielding his war hammer also faced one. The dwarf struck it down while evading and went to Marin to assist her by downing the remaining two wolves. After doing so and surveying the blood that they shed by downing the wolves, all three companions took a breath. Peat stretched his hands and told his two comrades that they should enjoy taking a trip to one of the hot springs that was not too far from one of his dwarf kin settlements of Grimaz-Kadrinbad in the low desert afterward.

However, a stray arrow darted across the air and struck the dwarf in the arm. Peat reacted in pain while groaning and cursing. Marin and Linitus turned in the direction they believed the arrow came from. Several dozen yards away, a fourth pack of dire wolves came. There were goblins mounted on the dire wolves. These goblins were armed with swords, spears, and bows and arrows.

The Comradery realized they were in greater trouble than expected.

The wolves and goblin riders wasted no time and charged right toward the three of them. Then sudden bolts of lightning pierced across the air, striking six of the dire wolves and their mounted goblin riders. Only half of their contingent remained. The surviving goblins mounted on their dire wolves turned toward the wizard. The beastly creatures were shocked and angry. They charged only a few feet away from Wyatt. By that time, the wizard had cast a teleportation spell and teleported right next to his comrades. Peat motioned with his other uninjured hand for Wyatt to teleport his bomb to the confused wolf-mounted goblins. The wizard did so with haste. Linitus then reacted without hesitation, shooting one of his spark-ready flaming arrows at the explosive wooden barrel as soon as it emerged right next to the remaining goblin enemies. Just like before, the barrel exploded upon impact, taking out the remaining enemy ambush party.

Linitus, along with the other members of his party, looked for any remaining possible sightings of enemies lying in wait to ambush them. They each conceded that it was a safe moment for them to take a sigh of relief. Linitus shot a flare-like arrow high in the air at a slight angle going toward the direction that they were pursuing the escaping cultist caravan. He then commanded Wyatt to teleport them to the skyship to regroup and recover. Wyatt nodded in acknowledgment. He then teleported himself and his comrades back to the skyship.

Upon arrival on board the skyship, the young wizard used several surgical tools, including pliers, to remove the arrow shaft from Peat's arm. Upon doing so, Marin came to Peat and tended to his wounded arm using her divine power of healing. She chanted while casting a greenish-blue orb that emanated from her hands and went outward to embody the affected area of Peat's wounded arm.

Linitus looked ahead for any signs of where the caravan they were pursuing might have gone while referencing the arrow flare that emanated bright sparks, which he fired off earlier. Pointing in that direction, Wyatt changed the course of the skyship as it soared high above the forest canopy that surrounded the Great Azure Lake. The most noticeable landmark the elf ranger would have surmised that the cultist caravan would have ventured off to would be a mountain mine entrance from a mountain range on the south end of the lake rising above the forest. This mountain mine was declared neutral territory. The Kingdom of Swordbane and the

Imperial Remnant agreed that neither side would occupy the mine and extract mineral resources from it.

The elf ranger, knowing the ambitious nature of the Imperial Remnant, surmised they did not intend to honor the agreement. He surmised that this mine could have very well been used as a possible staging point by the Remnant to hide inside while trafficking adolescent youths from the Kingdom of Swordbane into the Imperial Remnant's side of the border. It seemed at this point if the Comradery could prove that it was indeed the case, then they had to address it now. The elf ranger was determined, as were his companions, to stop the trafficking once and for all. They intended to return the trafficked youths to their homes within the settled boundaries of the kingdom. However, Linitus decided perhaps it would be more prudent, after surviving the ambush of the dire wolves and goblins, to be more cautious when intercepting the cultist caravan. The elf ranger instructed Wyatt to teleport him and Marin to higher ground with a rock formation above the mountain mine entrance that would obscure them from being seen.

Marin thought carefully with consideration just like her elf ranger husband. The Princess Knight suggested waiting in the sky above for a while longer and having Wyatt use his magic to shroud the skyship from detection. Linitus thought about his lover's suggestion and agreed. They then both speculated about the loud howl they heard earlier. The elf ranger and Princess Knight knew and ruled out Decius from the sound of the initial howl. Perhaps it was a similar type of werewolf as what the dux had last become in his mortal life. Regardless, they would lie in wait and observe the mountain cave mine. They would intercept the caravan the moment it emerged from the forest's canopy to make their way to the mine entrance. They did not expect however the cultist caravan was still as patient as them, waiting long enough for nightfall before infiltrating the mine.

Chapter Five

Entering the Portal of No Return

At dusk, hiding within the dark shroud of trees, various figures covered in black robes from the cultist caravan proceeded to their destination. They darted out from the forest. They made their way to the nearby cave entrance. It was at the base of the mountains, south of the Great Azure Lake. The cultist caravan believed that whoever was pursuing them was no longer alive. Their pursuer might have survived and given up or even may have lost track of the caravan's whereabouts. The caravan team was far from suspecting the actual truth. They were still being followed.

Linitus looked below from the top deck of the skyship. The elf ranger used a special pair of goggles that Wyatt had invented. It enabled the wearer to see in the darkness, a special sort of night vision. It enabled the elf ranger to spot the caravan emerging from the forest on its way to the cave mine entrance. Outside the mine, there was a small warband made up of six goblins and orcs carrying torches and guarding the mine entrance. Linitus motioned to the rest of his comrades that he had spotted their target. The elf ranger instructed Wyatt to teleport them a few moments later to the right side of the cave entrance, next to some large boulders. They would do so to avoid detection.

The evening went by quietly. Linitus picked the right time to make their move. He gave the cue to Wyatt with a motion of his hand. Wyatt teleported himself and his companions to the entrance, using the cover of the rock boulders to avoid detection. The rock boulders obscured the right side facing the cave entrance and made the Comradery's presence unnoticeable.

The unsuspected orcs and goblins stood guard outside. They chattered near a small fire pit. Linitus caught the enemies by surprise. The elf ranger, still wearing the special night vision goggles, began shooting arrows one by one. Three of the six in the goblin-orc warband fell in rapid succession. The other three guards were startled and brought up their weapons. However, it was too late for them to raise the alarm. Within moments, Wyatt had teleported his three comrades. Right behind the three remaining enemies guarding the entrance, Linitus, Marin, and Peat struck singular mortal blows on the remaining goblin-orc warband. It was a risky but swift and well-delivered calculated move by the Comradery to infiltrate the mine without causing alarm. It had paid off. Wyatt teleported himself near the fire pit next to his companions. They were ready for the next phase of the plan to intercept the caravan by entering the mine, proceeding unnoticed and undetected.

The Comradery proceeded through the mouth of the cave mine, which was supported by a horizontal beam and vertical post frames made of timber. The mine itself, however, was not lit by any fixed torches. Linitus and his company knew that more than likely, the cultist caravan went inside the mine, carrying their own torches. The elf ranger took the lead in his party to follow the path of the mine. He would do so wearing his night vision goggles. The other members held their torches ready to set alight. They did not do so. Instead, Wyatt used his magic to create a special floating dim light above him. It would make it easier for Marin and Peat to follow and stay close to the halfling wizard. Linitus stayed several paces ahead. The Comradery all knew how to take advantage of the element of surprise with the least risk. They would do so by letting Linitus stay far enough in the front with no signs of illumination by Wyatt's magic. They would also not light torches to give away their presence to the caravan that they were being followed.

Meanwhile, less than a mile away, the main tunnel passage deep within the mine, there was a large open hallway. The hallway itself was impressive. It had a decorated carved stone altar with ornate stone column pillars behind the altar, and between the stone column pillars was an ancient marble stone arch. It was a Lupercalian ancient temple shrine dedicated to the deity spirit of Calu. Now the group of cultists occupied it. They revered Decius as the chosen vessel and heir successor to Calu, the god of death, and Laran, the god of war. They had used the makeshift altar to conduct a libation and incense offering ritual to summon their venerated dark lord.

Among the cult members wearing black robes, one slender figure approached Decius's son, Lucianus, and Agaroman, who had also walked up to meet the other figure. Upon being a few feet away, the mysterious hooded figure removed the cloak to reveal herself. The figure was that of a Citadellan woman with sharp, chiseled features. She had olive skin, dark brown eyes, and dark wavy hair. Lucianus had embraced her while kissing her left cheek, then her right cheek, acknowledging her as his mother. This was Lady Lucia, the duchess of the Imperial Remnant and widow of Dux Decius. Lucia returned the same greeting while smiling and telling her son and Agaroman how pleased she was to be reunited with her son. The duchess was glad to see him safe with the recruited young male Citadellans from the coastal and interior forest regions who joined their cause.

Lucia turned to thank Agaroman for ensuring her son's success and safety. She next turned to the recruited young adolescent soldiers to let them know they had chosen well by making the first decision to serve the ultimate cause. They would restore society to a new age of prosperity and order that they had not seen since the ancient Lupercalian Empire. By giving their lives to such a worthy cause, they would be martyrs for the Imperial Remnant. They would receive their promised reward in the next life.

The new cult converts responded they would live and die for the cause and glory of reinstating this new envisioned form of the ancient Lupercalian Empire. They hailed Lucia as the reverent consort of the dark lord and reverend mother of the dark lord's successor, Lucianus. Pleased, Lucia turned to Agaroman and Lucianus to tell them they had done well in finding these new devoted converts. Agaroman replied that these converts were convinced to follow their cause after seeing Lucianus. He was the first werewolf Lupercalian to be seen in over a millennium. The wizard followed up that it had been a wise calculation on Lucia's part to grant his request that her son take on a direct role by learning how to recruit future soldiers. Lucia nodded. Recomposing herself, she stated it was time to conduct the ritual. The duchess wanted to reinforce the recruited cultists' conviction and zeal to follow her husband's cause. She wanted them to bear witness to his power after death. Agaroman nodded while preparing the incense under the brazier that he then unpacked and placed upon the altar. A moment later, as the incense was burning, the wizard drew from his satchel a small bottle of Citadellan red wine. Agaroman poured it over the burning incense while calling out Decius's name and his title as the chosen vessel to both Calu and Laran.

Within moments, as everyone present observed and the cult converts were in awe, a bright flash emerged with a spectral, translucent werewolf ghost. It was Decius. The werewolf specter turned and looked at Lucia and their son Lucianus. Decius, in his spectral form, realized that, as scheduled, they had raised a new small group of Citadellans to join the Imperial Remnant's military. The new recruits froze in awe at seeing the late dux in his new form. It was revealing to see firsthand. The stories were true. Decius defied the rules of death and the afterlife. He returned to the mortal world as a specter. The recruits recomposed themselves as instructed. They gave salutations and hailed Decius as their eternal dark lord, and they did so while kneeling and placing a clenched fist against their chest. Decius nodded and gave an extended arm raised in the air with a dark, translucent spectral blade that had emanated out of his hands. He told the new convert soldiers to rise and remember this occasion as marking their first day of giving their fealty to the dux. They would be generously rewarded as long as they served him with unwavering loyalty.

After giving his speech, Decius turned to Agaroman and asked if the portal gate was ready to open to receive more recruits to their forces that would wage regular skirmishes with the Nordlings on the northwest coast. Agaroman nodded, and Decius commanded the wizard to open the portal gate. Agaroman did so after motioning with his wooden staff. Within moments, a flash of energy came from the portal gate in which the mine cave wall behind the gate from staring at it was obscured by a glowing translucent sphere of energy. A portal connected to a faraway place had been revealed.

Within moments, figures not native to Swordbane and its neighboring regions emerged. Among the figures included a large white apelike beast covered in thick white fur. It was a snow troll. Behind it emerged several other exotic creatures not native to the Swordbane region, including a group of small dwarves wearing deer skull masks and with their faces painted. They wielded large spiked wooden clubs. There was also a group of cave orcs who only wore waist-sized furs and wielded primitive wooden spears with obsidian blades.

Agaroman revealed to the young cultist recruits to behold other fellow new servants of the dark lord dux and his heir, Lucianus. These new creatures hailed from the faraway land of Shimmerfrost, which was further north than the known northwest forest coastland of the Nordlings that bordered the Kingdom of Swordbane to the south. Agaroman informed Decius that these recently arrived forces were a small token of what Helskadi, nicknamed the Winter Death Witch, was offering as a gesture of goodwill to her new prospective ally, the Imperial Remnant. The Winter Death Witch commanded a large army though not as organized as the Imperial Remnant's. Her forces from Shimmerfrost also lacked the more advanced blacksmithing techniques for weaponry and siege craft to dominate the entire region of the cold far north. However, news had spread even as far north as Shimmerfrost of Decius's exploits as a chosen vessel and dark lord before his mortal downfall. Upon hearing of the news, Helskadi developed an immediate fondness for the Imperial Remnant's reputation for relishing order and power through commanding forces of darkness. Helskadi felt compelled to seek a common alliance in dominating their spheres of influence with her to rule supreme in the far north and for Decius's heir, Lucianus, to rule the rest of the western continent of Hesperion, south of Shimmerfrost.

Impressed at the sight of his first wave of unknown forces that would subdue the Nordling barbarians in the northwest coastlands, Decius in his spectral form, told Agaroman that he would agree to it provided he would meet with this prospective associate. Agaroman expected as much and let Decius know it would be done. Stepping forward before them among the crowd of dark forces that emerged from the portal was a goblin shaman from the Shimmerfrost region. He brought a crystal orb forward. The goblin uttered several words and tapped the orb with his staff. The orb activated and emanated a bright flash of light. The light projected a translucent image inside the orb. It was a female figure.

This figure appeared to be a tall human-like female giant. She had blonde hair, pale skin, and blue eyes rimmed by dark black eye circles. She also had four horns that protruded from her head. She wielded an exotic spear-like wooden staff. The weapon possessed a sharp stone point at the head of the spear and a sharp curved pointed object made from animal bone at the bottom of the spear. This figure wore a set of leather and fur armor, including hand bracers, boots, a corset, and a large white bear's fur cowl. She wore a white midriff dress of a material, not animal hide and fur, but likely linen or some other fabric made from plants. She also had on various pieces of gold jewelry.

Her appearance became known from the orb that the goblin shaman held. The figure also took notice and recognized Decius in his spectral form. The figure from the orb introduced herself as Helskadi, the Winter Death Witch and ruler of the dark forces of Shimmerfrost. She greeted Dux Decius and his inner circle. Decius acknowledged her salutation. He inquired to confirm with her if what his wizard advisor had revealed was indeed true, that she wanted to become allies with him and his Imperial Remnant forces. Helskadi nodded. She told Decius that by helping her secure absolute control of Shimmerfrost, she would spare more of her forces to aid a fellow lord of darkness. Decius nodded and grinned with his jagged canine jaw before stating that he would aid her to their mutual benefit.

Meanwhile, as this dark alliance was being revealed, several figures were hiding in the shadows. They peered from the corner of the tunnel's corridor that connected it to the open hallway where the chapel shrine was located. The hidden figures began to eavesdrop and listen to these startling revelations. They went unnoticed. One of them, Linitus, used his camouflage cloak to shroud himself while, several feet away, Wyatt had quietly cast a spell that rendered himself, Marin, and Peat temporarily invisible. They were unsure how long they could listen to the conversation without being detected. However, after Decius had cemented his alliance with Helskadi, the Comradery was relieved to know that both the images of Helskadi in the orb and the spectral ghost of Decius bidding farewell to his soulmate and wife, Lucia, and his son and dark lord's heir, Lucianus, disappeared. After Decius's image faded, Agaroman notified the present company by stating that they would leave the cave at a moment's notice.

Linitus motioned to his comrades that it was their cue to press the advantage, having the element of surprise, to attack first before Agaroman could cast a teleportation spell. The elf ranger used another of his sabot barrage arrow receptacles, holding two dozen arrows, and let loose toward the snow troll, who was far away from the risk of the arrows striking the youth that were being recruited into Decius's cult and Remnant forces. Within moments, they heard a flurry of sound emitted from the arrows whistling through the air of the silent ambient cave. All heads turned toward the sound to see a barrage of arrows being deployed in midflight from the dispersed receptacle. Almost all the arrows struck the large snow troll. The towering creature, though superimposing, fell in pain.

Lucia, reacting instinctively, told the present company to draw their weapons and prepare for combat. The duchess removed her robe and drew a long pair of exotic, jeweled decorative twin daggers. She wore her iconic warlike infiltration garb that included a black split-joint, half-sleeved jumpsuit. Her son, Lucianus, followed suit and removed his robe. He revealed his furry body, wearing a red tunic and an ornate segmented black-stained cuirass made of steel. He wielded a short sword. Agaroman sensed the source of the attack and knew who it was. He called out to the rest of the Remnant forces to be ready, including the new recruits.

Linitus knew this battle would be difficult. The dark forces outnumbered his group by at least ten to one. This was excluding the fallen snow troll and the abducted recruits the Comradery wanted to avoid fighting with. Many of their newfound adversaries included two dozen cave orcs and goblins from the Shimmerfrost region, as well as a dozen exotic pale-skinned dwarves wearing deer skull masks, bone armor, and red-and-blue war paint. Marin and Peat could not help whispering a few expletives. A tense life-or-death battle was about to unfold. As a consolation, Linitus whispered sarcastically that, at least, they did not have to worry about the snow troll he slayed.

Another fleeting moment went by. Agaroman commanded the new allied forces from Shimmerfrost to proceed cautiously while seeking the intruders. The wizard pointed toward the general direction the heroes of the Comradery hid. Peat could not help letting out another expletive. The middle-aged dwarf swore he had an explosive barrel bomb. He would take down the whole cave mine if he and his comrades should fall in combat. Linitus shook his head, not agreeing to the impulse of his dwarven companion while Marin reminded him that they came to retrieve the youths. Peat nodded. He deferred to his comrades regarding the plan. The first wave of enemy forces from Shimmerfrost holding torches fanned out and made their way toward the tunnel the Comradery was hiding in. Linitus instead used his sticky silk bulbs in which he attached strands of strong hemp twine and shot a cluster of these arrows close together to the surface.

Moments later, the first wave of Shimmerfrost cave orcs tripped over each other. They struggled to stand up because of the adhesive silk bulb substance clinging to them. Wyatt cast a huge fireball that enveloped the small group of orcs burning in pain while startling their other fellow cave orcs. Soon the rest of them, including the goblins and the exotic

Shimmerfrost snow dwarves, rushed to attack their unknown enemies. The fighting soon picked up in the narrow tunnel and made an effective choke point in limiting Linitus and his companions from being overwhelmed as much while fighting with bow and arrow, sword and shield, war hammer, and spell-casting magic against these newfound enemy forces.

As the fighting intensified, Lucia called her son Lucianus and asked if he knew how to cast a special type of inscription magic that would set off a furious explosion. Lucianus nodded but cautioned that it could cause the cave mine to collapse. Lucia nodded and told him it was what she wanted should their attackers not fall by any other means. She caught her son by surprise and embraced him, giving him a kiss on both his cheeks. She stated, holding back her tears that she always loved him. She was proud of him for following in his father's footsteps to be the dark lord's heir. Since Lucianus had to take the new cult recruits along with Agaroman to escape out of the cave mine, Lucia would hold off the Comradery for as long as she could. Lucianus nodded with reluctance. He used his magical abilities while wielding his short sword. The young werewolf cast an inscription spell on the center of the hallway. It was set to explode the moment someone entered the hallway.

Lucia next turned to Agaroman. She looked at him, saying no words as the wizard observed and knew her well enough to discern her intentions. The wizard told her that despite his initial reservations about her when they first met, she had proven worthy as the consort and duchess of Decius. The wizard vowed he would continue to do everything possible to train Lucianus as Decius's successor. Lucia nodded and replied that she knew he would.

Later, Agaroman cast a teleportation spell. He would depart with Lucianus and the recruited youth cultists to a secret chamber in the cave mine complex. This chamber would lead them to a hidden exit out of the cave mine on the other side of the mountain.

Upon arriving at the secret chamber, Lucianus sealed access to it from the hallway by pulling a lever that caused a vertical stone slab to move down. He, Agaroman, and their recruited cult followers made their way to the other end of the secret chamber. It would lead to the other entrance that was more concealed and guarded. From there, they would set out to ride forthwith and make their retreat sixty miles northeast to the Remnant's next major settlement, Orcum Tribus Uruk Kazaht.

Meanwhile, still deep inside the mine hallway, Lucia looked on.

She recognized her foes from a distance as the fighting persisted. They were Swordbane's very own heroic Order of the Comradery. They fought fiercely, dispatching the forces from Shimmerfrost. The duchess decided she would take a life-and-death gamble by using the assassination skills she learned since her last encounter with the Comradery ten years ago. It was during that time they both negotiated talks to end the Great Civil War (also known as the War of the Chosen Vessels) started by her husband Decius. It was that time she forced the Comradery and the Kingdom of Swordbane to the bargaining table after she led the Remnant forces to victory, destroying most of what was left in a war of attrition against Swordbane's skyship forces that sailed toward the Remnant's capital, her home city of Sanctum Novus.

Ten years later, the four members of the Comradery were still as formidable as she knew them to be. They however most likely did not know how deadly she had become, training under the Marjawan's exiled sisterhood order of Surashi assassins eight years ago.

Wasting no more time, the duchess drew from her satchel a light dark cloak like a shroud that she covered herself with. It camouflaged her from being nearly undetectable, especially from the human eye. She strolled toward the tunnel entryway that connected the main tunnel to the chapel sanctuary shrine. Upon seeing the adventurers, she drew several throwing daggers from her belt. She waited for the critical moment to hurl them at the Comradery when they exposed themselves while fighting what was left of the Shimmerfrost warriors.

Linitus could see the daggers hurled in the air. He called out to the rest of his companions to take cover. They ducked. Marin used her shield to block one of the thrown daggers. Wyatt, with haste, cast a large enough shield globe that enveloped both him and Peat. The shield globe caused two of the thrown daggers to bounce off. The dispensed blades fell harmlessly to the ground. Linitus heard the footsteps moving back to the main hallway sanctuary despite not locating where the attacker was. The elf ranger pointed that out to his comrades while following with caution in that direction. He raised his bow and arrow and aimed at the area where the footsteps were heard while Marin walked alongside her elven lover and companion to use her shield to block the next attack that would be unleashed by their hidden camouflage target.

Walking closer to the center of the chapel hallway, only a step away from the etched magical marked imprint that her son Lucianus had planted,

Lucia, surprising the heroes of the Comradery, removed her magical shroud to give away her presence more overtly. Linitus and his other three comrades did not expect her to give away her presence. They noticed her son, Agaroman, and the new young cultist recruits were already gone at this point. She remained however. The Comradery still looked taken aback at the thought of confronting her. They had not seen her since their last encounter a decade ago. The rumors from the hearsay traveling tales about her alleged transformation as an assassin were true. She was formidable enough to keep them alert and their adrenaline being at a constant high.

Linitus motioned for Marin to strafe with him going around Lucia and be ready to attack her from the end of the chapel hallway closest to the shrine altar and portal gate while Wyatt and Peat would attack from the direction that connected the tunnel entrance to the hallway. They surrounded Lucia while Marin proclaimed to the duchess that it was over, and it would be time for her to discuss the terms of surrender, including the return of the abducted adolescents who were lawful subjects of the Kingdom of Swordbane.

Lucia gave a brief surprised laugh. She retorted that it would be over for them as much as for her. She would not allow them to retrieve the abducted youths.

Linitus, taken aback by her somewhat cryptic response, wondered what she meant or whether she was in denial as the odds of her prevailing over them were low. He noticed, however, her glance at the floor next to her and what appeared a small lit flaming series of markings on the ground. He shouted again for everyone in his company to move back and take cover.

Lucia took a step toward the etched explosive markings on the ground. The duchess reflected in a brief stream of thought about her life. She intended to save her own son's life from still being pursued while taking out as many of these adventurers as she could in the tunnel. She would also have her revenge for the loss of her beloved husband, Decius, who fell in combat at their hands more than ten years ago. To her, this sacrifice was well worth it.

In a sudden moment, a loud explosive burst emanated and consumed her body. The explosion shook the cave tunnel and the hallway sanctuary. Marin used her magical round shield to cover both her and Linitus while, on the other end of the hallway, Wyatt cast another enveloping globe to shield him and Peat from the large cave rocks and hallway chapel carved stone architecture that fell and collapsed from the intensity of the explosion. The chain reaction and partial collapse ended with dust rising from the air.

Linitus and Marin stood to see that the cave mine was still shaking. A vibrating series of bursts and noises emanated as the rest of the cave mine and hallway sanctuary still seemed to be poised to collapse. Linitus saw no way out. Then he looked back. He saw the portal still flashing with energy. The portal connected to Shimmerfrost was unharmed and still intact. It was their only way out. The elf ranger took Marin by her hand and told her to follow him. Marin nodded, trusting Linitus and his judgment. She regained her composure and sense of the surroundings after seeing much of the hallway covered with fallen stones blocking the path to the tunnel. They went closer to the portal. Marin then pondered and realized what this meant. She asked Linitus if they should go through the portal. Once they did so, they would be far from home. Linitus told her it was their only choice before the hallway collapsed and trapped them. Marin nodded again, showing her understanding of her companion lover's reasoning.

They continued walking through the aura of energy of the portal gate, but the ceiling above them collapsed with a piece of carved ceiling stone striking one of the pillars, which fell. Linitus noticed and pushed Marin out of the way. He also tried to leap out of the way. However, the column rolled, and Linitus's foot was caught and wedged in. He groaned in pain and struggled on the ground to free himself. Marin got up and realized that Linitus saved her by sacrificing himself. She saw her elven lover's leg caught by the fallen pillar. Mustering all her strength, Marin used her body and shield to help pry his foot free from the pillar. It worked. Linitus could move his foot back. He still groaned in pain, struggling to get up. He limped as he started to walk. Marin turned to notice. She came over to him, gravely concerned. The Princess Knight placed his arm around her shoulder and used her body as a partial crutch to help him move with her while walking toward the glowing portal that was still intact. They walked in just in time and disappeared through the portal as the chapel sanctuary completely collapsed.

On the other end of the tunnel, with his view obstructed by falling debris, Peat could see something bright flash in the portal. Wyatt motioned to the dwarf that it was time to fall back. They would fall back to the same tunnel they entered earlier. Peat nodded reluctantly. He hoped wherever his other companions were, they could escape this grave peril as well.

Chapter Six

A New Life After Death

In what seemed a fleeting moment flashing before her eyes, Lucia, lying flat, woke up startled as she saw herself naked without any clothes on. She wondered what happened while seeing for herself that all around her was an empty white void. Unsure at first, she then recalled what had happened. She realized she had indeed perished after setting off the explosive marker to take out her enemies. She hoped her efforts would be enough to protect her son from being followed. She still felt compelled to say aloud, asking where she was.

Another moment later, something flashed before her eyes. It was a pitch-black orb emanating a mist-like dark black smoke aura appeared. This mysterious being called out to her using her name, surprising and scaring her even more by knowing who she was. She responded by asking who it was. The mysterious orb-like being replied that he is the deity spirit of death, also known by many humans, including her Citadellan kind, as Calu. Calu altered his shape to that of a large translucent mist-like figure posing as a pitch-black werewolf. This creature stated that perhaps in this iconic image, Lucia would be more familiar with recognizing. Its image was that of the Lupercalian werewolf species. Many regarded the species as the totem of symbolic images associated with Calu.

Lucia then stood upright and became more alert. She recognized the deity spirit and knelt before it. The duchess professed her devotion to both Calu and the other deity spirits, especially Laran, the deity spirit of war. Calu, in his spectral werewolf form, grinned while acknowledging her reverence and worship of him. He confided to Lucia his admiration after her passing from the mortal realm into her next life that she still exhibited worthiness in practicing her faith and devotion. Calu also professed that she had exemplified the product of her faith in being charitable toward her subjects during her mortal life. He declared that her faith and following through with her faith merited her to receive the afterlife reward of paradise since being judged.

Lucia was grateful, knowing that her faith and following through with it allowed her to pass through paradise to be with her ancestors. Still, her thoughts lingered in her mind about her departed husband, Decius. She asked the deity spirit of death about him and if she would see him in the next life of paradise.

Calu looked down while searching for the best words to explain to her so that Lucia could understand. The deity explained that she displayed admirable devotion to him and walked a careful path for his cause. Still, her departed husband's path differed from hers. Both Calu and Laran were pleased to recognize Decius as a chosen vessel during his mortal life after he caused so much bloodshed. Decius merited the attention of Calu and Laran after dying and going to the afterlife. This was due to him violating the boundaries as a chosen vessel. He had done so by opening a portal from Hadao Infernum. This allowed the demonic denizens to be unleashed against the mortals of Terrunaemara and cause death and destruction. This cycle of warring and inflicting death had nourished the energy from which Laran and Calu drew from and yearned, yet it was fleeting and came at a price. Decius would pay the ultimate mortal price for his actions. His punishment included being condemned to the hellhole of Hadao Infernum after falling in combat against the Comradery near the end of the Great Civil War.

Lucia looked down. The duchess gained both sadness and a sense of defiant resentment. She paused and processed what he said. The duchess then looked up at Calu with firm conviction and utter surprise. She told the deity spirit that she refused to enter and live in paradise, known in the Citadellan tongue as Caelum. Instead, she insisted on being sent to reunite with her departed lover, Decius. She would follow him and his path even if it meant condemnation inside the realm of darkness and hellfire.

Surprised, the deity spirit emanated unsuspecting mists of energy. Calu responded to her request with curiosity. Calu stated that in all of existence, no one who had received the award of paradise asked to be sent to a dark place of condemnation and suffering instead. Calu understood, however, knowing that much about his chosen vessel, Decius. He and Lucia were devoted to each other. All the deity spirits knew this, even the ones who despised Decius. Taking a moment to ponder, Calu called out two words or names in the void. The Citadellan religion and lore knew those names as Vanth and Charu. They were Calu's messengers and escorts (even if by force) of those passing from mortal life to the next stage of the afterlife.

A moment after the summons, two flashes of energy appeared in the white void. Two figures then appeared upon the flashes of energy dissipating. Both figures appeared to be of average human-like height, with a paired set of bird-like wings attached to their backs. One figure, Charu, was an exotic blue-skinned male demon with orange hair and a full beard. He also had a pair of small twin horns protruding from his forehead, and he carried a long bronze war hammer. He wore a red tunic with two vertical white stripes and a pair of exotic leather boots.

The other figure, Vanth, was a slender fair-skinned female demon. She looked much more human in appearance with brown eyes and chin-length brown hair. She, like her male companion, had a pair of small twin horns protruding from her forehead. Vanth wore a short rolled sleeveless dress that looked like a tunic. Her attire was an uncommon form of dressing for women in the mortal realm of Terrunaemara to wear except for those identified as outdoor huntresses. She also wore exotic leather boots and carried a hand-length bronze flaming rod and a lit torch.

Calu briefed and consulted with the two summoned demon messengers to weigh in on his current predicament. Perplexed as much as the deity spirit was, both Charu and Vanth understood the attachment Lucia had for Decius. The two demon messengers considered their own pairing. They also knew couples who would be tempted to defy being separated in the afterlife. This was especially true if they were as adamant as Lucia was about being reunited with her departed husband. However, no departed spouse they ever knew before Lucia went to the extent of demanding to be in the same hell as their beloved counterpart when she was offered paradise and to be with other loved ones. Charu and Vanth both recommended that Calu let Lucia have her way and be reunited with Decius. The messengers also cautioned that she was condemning herself to be in the infernal realm of Hadao Infernum for eternity. Calu agreed and briefed Lucia one last time. The deity warned her to be aware of where she wanted her soul and new body to be sent.

Lucia nodded without hesitation. She replied she was aware. The duchess further asserted she would overcome any obstacle that stood in the way of reuniting with her soulmate.

Calu nodded, replying with admiration at how devoted she was to his chosen vessel. The deity spirit offered her powers and features similar to Vanth and the succubi of Hadao Infernum to assist her in her journey. By doing so, it would better position her survivability in that realm. Calu also again warned her that this realm would offer no means for a person to live again after dying there. Lucia nodded once again, still insisting on her devotion and determination to be with Decius. She declared that if such a gift would aid her in her efforts, she would take it.

Calu, still impressed, confirmed her wishes and granted it. The deity spirit raised its dark, ethereal, and translucent werewolf claw and chanted several words. Soon a sudden burst of energy emitted from the deity spirit and was transmitted to Lucia. It enveloped her like a cocoon of shadows until, moments later, it exploded.

Lucia emerged from this black paintball. The duchess became a figure similar to but different from the succubi of Hadao Infernum. She was still of moderate height and was slender with wavy dark hair that went past her shoulder. Her eyes were yellow and black, like a cat. Lucia could see her naked body though her skin this time appeared to be of vermillion color. She had a pair of protruding black horns that that protruded from her hairline. These horns were sleek and somewhat longer than those of Vanth's and Charu's. This newly spawned female demon had a pair of black-and-vermillion batlike wings. The wings protruded from her top back shoulders along with a black and vermillion sleek curved tail with a sharp pointed tip. Her lips were also of a pitch-black color. When she realized this mysterious transformation had happened, she still could not hold back from asking what happened.

Calu waited a moment for the transformed figure to reaffirm to her she was still the same person. She was still Lucia Diem, as they knew her in the mortal realm. Her transformed body bore a resemblance to the winged sirens of Hadao Infernum. Legend and lore knew them collectively as succubi.

Lucia became fascinated when she looked at her own features. She was overwhelmed by the transformation she undertook. This was true even after Calu created a reflection mirror for her to see herself and come to terms with her new body and form. Her appearance still carried most of her features as a mortal. In fact, her new form was actually a blend of her human features and the defining features of the wicked sirens from Hadao Infernum.

Lucia still felt uncomfortable with her new form while still being aware that she was also exposed. Vanth and Charu laughed mildly. They both pointed out to Calu. Calu was fully aware. In response, the deity spirit acknowledged and offered Lucia various sets of armor and clothing to wear in addressing her insecurity in being bare.

The duchess was uncertain at first of the clothing assortment or armor pieces to choose from. Still looking, one stood out in contrast to her new vermillion skin appearance, which Lucia liked. The attire comprised a set of exotic black clothing and light armor made from an indescribable lightweight material. The clothing itself was a black corset laced with gold (leaving an exposed midriff) and a short black miniskirt also laced in gold. It included an attachment set of long boots with gold-and-red laced leg guards. The attire was attractive and seductive in reflection of the profile of her new succubi form.

Lucia pointed at selecting her new attire. Calu nodded and enchanted a brief series of words, only to cause the selected clothing articles to disappear. The attire then reappeared with Lucia wearing it. Lucia was astounded.

Vanth and Charu were amazed as well. Charu could not hold back his immediate thoughts. The messenger of death said aloud that upon arriving in Infernum, Lucia would easily incite the jealousy and wrath of the succubi. It would bring a new level for the demonic sirens to compete with her in seducing and hunting prey in the condemned infernal realm.

Vanth gave a sigh of displeasure at her colleague's remark. She admitted that her fellow messenger companion was likely right. The succubi would react in jealousy and resort to violence and eliminate Lucia. They would see her as new competition in seduction and slaughter.

Lucia heard. She was uncertain how to react. She interpreted the postmortal messengers' comments as being a two-sided omen. It was both a compliment and an ominous portent regarding her newfound demonic and seductive form.

In another moment, Calu asked Lucia if she was ready to be transported with Vanth and Charu as escorts to her next destination in the afterlife. Lucia nodded without hesitation while replying in the affirmative. Calu then motioned with his hands and summoned a bright, round portal bordered with flames. Knowing what to do, Lucia walked through the portal while Charu and Vanth followed. After walking through, they appeared on the other side. They entered the fiery realm of hellfire and suffering.

Chapter Seven

Searching for Answers

 Outside the other secret mine entrance, Lucianus, Agaroman, and their new cult converts made their escape. They encountered over two dozen goblin and orc wolf riders and their dire wolf mounts. These wolf riders acted as sentry guards of the secret mine entrance. Lucianus issued new orders to the wolf riders. They were to switch places with the cultist caravan. The cultist caravan would ride these wolf mounts back to Orcum Tribus Uruk Kazaht. As Lucianus instructed his followers, a sudden loud explosion went off in the cave mine.
 Then suddenly there was a large quake. The escaping cultists in the caravan heard the explosion and the aftershock. They could feel the ground shaking. They knew the cave mine had collapsed. Lucianus said no words but stared at his wizard mentor. Agaroman could discern the other's expression. The wizard sighed with sadness and shook his head in reply concerning if Lucia was still alive.
 Both Lucianus and Agaroman knew Lucia was determined in her stand. They knew she would at the expense of forfeiting her life against the heroes of the Comradery. In doing so, her sacrifice ensured her son's well-being. With her no longer acting as regent, Lucianus was poised to be named as the next dark lord successor to her beloved departed husband.
 Lucianus however felt an uncontrollable flurry of emotions from sadness and anger. He could not hold back, unleashing a loud, horrifying, yet mournful howl at the loss of his mother. He did not want to accept such an outcome. Lucianus however knew as much as Agaroman. There

was little to no chance of survival. Part of him still doubted and wanted to still believe that his Citadellan mother was alive somehow.

Agaroman understood and sensed the young werewolf's pain. Agaroman assured Lucianus that they would direct the present goblin and orc guards to investigate and find his mother or at least her remains no matter how long it took. When Lucianus and Agaroman arrived at Uruk Kazaht with their new cult recruits, they dispatched more of their forces to aid the current guards in investigating. They would eventually find out the fate of his mother.

Lucianus nodded, knowing that this was the best outcome. By refraining from risking himself at a confrontation with Swordbane's deadliest elite heroes, he knew he had honored his mother's last wishes. She sacrificed herself so that he may return to his fortified settlement in Uruk Kazaht and decide how to move forward while being better guarded by his forces. He would make her sacrifice count by avenging her death and fulfilling his father's dream of becoming the next true dark lord.

Lucianus followed Agaroman's advice. He tasked the guards to investigate the mine and determine the fate of his mother and his adversaries. The goblin and orc guards bowed to their master's wishes and set forth to do their task immediately.

Lucianus next gathered the new cult converts to mount the dire wolves like him and Agaroman. They would make their journey to the nearest major fortified orc-goblin settlement, known as Uruk Kazaht. The settlement was sixty miles away and well within Imperial Remnant territory. Under favorable conditions, Lucianus's caravan could expect to arrive there in two days. Upon arrival at Uruk Kazaht, Lucianus would dispatch more of his forces to redouble his efforts in finding his mother and possibly his enemies, or at least their remains.

The dark lord's heir would also discuss with Agaroman on how to find additional recruits to replenish their Citadellan forces that formed part of the Remnant's army. Previously, their forces had steadily declined over the years after a brief war against Marjawan and the ongoing back-and-forth skirmishes with the Nordlings on the northwest coast. Lucianus and Agaroman knew they needed to replenish their standing army.

Meanwhile, deep inside the networks of mine tunnels, two figures covered in dust emerged from the mine collapse. They brushed the dust off their faces while coughing. The next moment, they looked at each other to process and assess the situation in which they had survived. One of them,

Peat, looked at Wyatt, who was still brushing off his pointed dark gray wizard hat. The dwarf looked about. Peat asked his halfling wizard friend if he was okay. Wyatt nodded while also looking about. They both noticed that the tunnel that they came from was clear of obstruction. They walked out the same way they came in. Wyatt used his magic wand to cast a spell of a small illumination glowing orb to emerge at the tip of his wand. The halfling wizard noticed the other side of the tunnel. The same one they had fled from leading to the religious shrine hallway. A wall of debris, mostly rocks and dirt, blocked the passageway. There was no way they could return to the hallway shrine to reunite with their comrades, Linitus and Marin. Even worse, both Peat and Wyatt feared the prospect if their companions had perished from the collapse that Lucia triggered.

Peat still could not help but ask his wizard companion if he thought their two missing comrades could have survived. The dwarf guardian wanted to know if there was any way they could reunite with them. Wyatt, in one of the few times in his life, felt uncertain about how to resolve a solution to what they saw as a dire problem. He knew that there was no way anyone, even those considered as chosen vessels like Marin and Linitus, could survive. That is unless they escaped to the other end of the hallway shrine. The wizard considered the layout of the hallway shrine and the exits, which were limited. All these routes would have collapsed at the same distance of proximity as they had on their side tunnel. Wyatt concluded that Marin and Linitus might not have even made it that far after recalling their earlier battle. Still, he thought there had to be a way to escape.

Peat also took time to retrace the steps their companions could have taken to escape. Only one possibility came out when Peat and Wyatt shared their thoughts about how their companions could have escaped with their limited options. It was unlikely. Yet Peat, mentioning his description of the layout, described the noticeable places his companions could have hidden for cover if they were to survive the cave mine collapse. Peat ruled out the stone slab altar and mentioned the portal as the next noticeable object in the hallway.

Wyatt snapped his fingers. He reacted excitedly and optimistically. There was that possibility. He realized that their companions very well could have taken the portal to escape. This could have been the case, as the then-new arrivals from Shimmerfrost left the portal gate open when the battle ensued in the hallway shrine. The wizard thought that if there was anyone who would take the opened portal as a last-ditch option for escape, Linitus would be among the first. He would recognize that as a viable option and take it to escape with Marin.

After Wyatt pointed out his agreement with the observation and speculation Peat made, the dwarf guardian warrior nodded again. Peat then wondered where the portal led to. Wyatt knew from recalling when he and his companions eavesdropped on the conversation between Lucia's party, Dux Decius, and the mysterious group of new arrivals, along with the magical projected image of that strange, pale female giant queen. Wyatt recalled it and then snapped his fingers. He said in an ominous voice the one word of the place he had heard about where this mysterious envoy group came from. It was the faraway region called Shimmerfrost.

The obstructed tunnel was beyond Wyatt's powers to remove the debris without risking further collapse in order to verify whether their companions did indeed take the portal to Shimmerfrost or were buried in the rubble. Peat knew as much. He motioned to his wizard companion that it was best for them to report to King Ascentius at the coastal metropolitan capital of Citadella Neapola. Once there, they would inform the king of the latest developments. They would also recruit several teams of miners, both human and dwarven, as well as some gnomes, to search this cave mine. The mining teams would clear out the debris and verify who perished and who remained either alive or missing. Wyatt nodded with reluctance. He regretted the situation for what it was while having a solemn face. He wished there was more he could do. Still, he would not risk using his own magic to put himself or Peat at peril.

Peat sensed Wyatt's frustration. The dwarf put his arm around the halfling wizard's shoulders, assuring him again they would do everything possible to find their comrades no matter how long it would take. They would convince the king to use as much manpower to clear the rubble. If their companions were not there, then no matter how far the distance, they would travel wherever they had to go to reunite with their companions even if it was Shimmerfrost in the far frozen north where few had even ventured even among the northwest coast Nordlings.

Wyatt nodded again. Mourning, he turned to look one last time in the direction his comrades, Linitus and Marin, last stood before the cave tunnel collapsed. He took a moment to compose himself, then he turned to Peat and nodded that he was ready. He was ready to fall back to the cave mine entrance with Peat. There they would teleport to the skyship and travel to the capital to deliver the news to the king of what had transpired. The wizard hoped that somehow King Ascentius would have an answer in helping their friends. Marin was his daughter after all. Linitus was also the closest the king could ever call a son as his son-in-law.

Chapter Eight

A Son's Mourning

Peat and Wyatt returned to the skyship to enact their plan to get more aid and support in finding their companions. Meanwhile, over sixty miles to the east, a small convoy of dire wolf riders on their wolf mounts were charging at full pace. They made their way across the open prairie and high basin sparse with trees and surrounded by mountains. Soon they approached a large fortified settlement known as Uruk Kazaht. It was the main goblin-orc settlement east of the Great Coastal Mountains. The settlement grew over the past decade to become the second most populated settlement of the Imperial Remnant. It was second only to the faction's capital, Imperia Sanctum Novus (also known as Sanctum Novus) to the south in the high desert.

As the mounted wolf riders approached, they came to a sudden halt over several dozen yards away from the settlement's reinforced wooden barricades. The leader of the mounted riders removed his hood and unleashed a terrifying howl that caught the attention of the settlement. Nearby orcs returned the call with an acknowledgment in their own guttural language. Within moments, the settlement's reinforced gate opened, and the dire wolf riders rode in at a steady but slower pace.

The leading wolf rider dismounted from his dire wolf upon reaching the main entrance of the settlement. He proceeded through the main entrance. This entrance led to a central pathway that had a large makeshift fire pit next to two large tents. The tents belonged to the settlement's leading goblin shaman and orc war captain. Before the settlement stood its many denizens. They froze and were impressed by this leading wolf rider's aura of command. Only the goblin shaman and the orc war captain slowly approached him with greetings in acknowledging his title and authority as the dux's heir apparent. Despite him being ten and still considered an adolescent by many, Lucianus was hellbent to ensure all that served under the Remnant would acknowledge and respect his authority. He would wield and exert this authority while he sought to follow in the footsteps of his late father and be recognized as the next dark lord.

Agaroman stood by Lucianus's side after dismounting. The two of them briefed the goblin shaman and orc war captain of the settlement about their current predicament in which they escaped unscathed but at the cost of Lucianus's mother, Duchess Lucia. They explained how the duchess risked sacrificing her life and likely may have perished from her presumed last stand. Lucianus, still angry, did his best to maintain his composure while ordering a large retinue of goblins and orcs to follow him back to the cave mine sixty miles west. There he would see to it his deployed forces would find his mother and, if necessary, recover her remains.

The goblin shaman and orc war captain complied. The war captain summoned the settlement's best wolf riders to prepare to ride out with Lucianus to find his mother's corpse. Agaroman tried to dissuade Lucianus from going back while reminding him of his mother's sacrifice that ensured his escape. Lucianus was still insistent, however, in wanting to be part of the search party he dispatched. Agaroman persistently dissuaded Lucianus by offering to ride in the young dux's stead.

Lucianus spent no time contemplating. His thoughts centered chiefly on his mother. They were very attached, and their bond was practically inseparable as mother and son. Lucianus, however, gave a counteroffer and asked Agaroman to return with him. Agaroman could watch over him.

Agaroman paused and considered before nodding. Later, after preparing the forces to be dispatched, two retinue groups of wolf riders came forthwith along the dirt road outside of Uruk Kazaht. Lucianus's retinue would follow him to the cave mine. Upon arriving, the deployed forces would use makeshift tools they had in their possession to clear the collapsed mine of any debris and recover Lucianus's mother, alive or not.

The other dire wolf cavalry rode south toward the Remnant's high desert capital. Upon arriving, the newly Citadellan youths would be trained and indoctrinated into the ways of the Remnant's military and would be trained as the next generation of soldiers for the Remnant.

Lucianus and Agaroman trekked westward with his cavalry to the long dark evening route pathway that led to the cave mine. The dark lord's young heir thought of summoning his father and alerting him about Lucia. However, Lucianus reconsidered his course. Instead, he waited until he had more information regarding his mother's fate before summoning his father to inform him about his mother and ask for advice. Lucianus confided this to Agaroman. The wizard agreed. He knew Decius well enough. His old disciple would not take this matter lightly, especially without conclusive evidence of Lucia's fate.

Chapter Nine

Fighting for a New Survival

A dozen figures gathered around a fire pit in a cold, damp ice cave. Besides their snarling sounds, shouts, and clamoring, the cave was otherwise empty, quiet, and dark save for the fire pit and the shimmering reflections from the ice. Less than twenty yards away stood the only distinguishing decor in the entire frozen cave. It was a large pillar with an arc connecting it to the two ends of the pillar.

Suddenly, a loud burst of sound came from the portal gate. The noise was followed by a large electrical type of conduit field in which two figures emerged from the portal.

Linitus and Marin, these heroic adventurers took a moment to observe in awe. They realized what had just happened. They had teleported from one dark cave mine collapsing on them to this surreal ice cave. This cave was unique compared to the ones they had seen before. It glimmered with various ice stalagmites, and icicles, as well as frozen columns of ice and ice extrusions. Only a bright flame from a fire pit within twenty yards of the distance stood out. Various dark figures huddled around it. Eventually, they turned and looked at the two new intruders in shock. However, these creatures perceived the intrusion as a hostile act, crossing into their domain. These cave dwellers shouted instinctively and wanted to kill the unknown intruders.

The menacing figures moved away from the fire pit. They furiously charged at Marin and Linitus. The two looked at each other. They knew, despite what they went through, they would have to endure and persevere to survive. It was daunting and tiring. Regardless, they were of the same mind. They resolved to be the last ones standing. Marin and Linitus assumed their combat stances. Marin told Linitus to stay behind her and keep his distance when engaging their foes. She knew he was still injured from saving her while escaping the collapsed cave mine from the other side of the now-defunct portal. Linitus nodded while instructing his lover to fight with patience and try to control the rhythm of the combat. Marin nodded. She waited for the first group of new enemies to make their first move. When they did, she would be ready to parry and strike back at them.

A few paces away, Marin and Linitus could tell who they were after getting a better view of the enemies when Marin's flaming sword illuminated the surroundings. These were the same type of creatures they fought earlier. They were cave orcs. They wore waist-sized furs and wielded primitive weapons, including wood and stone war clubs and wooden spears with black obsidian spear points. These cave orcs differ from their southern brethren. The former had a light yellow skin tone while the latter had a grayish-blue skin tone. These cave orcs also had their hair growing long behind their heads to their shoulders. Like their southern brethren, the cave orcs of this region, Shimmerfrost, also had jagged fang-like teeth protruding from their lower mouth. They had large muscular build bodies with heights of six to eight feet. The sight of them would intimidate any adversary they came across. However, the human female knight and male elven ranger proved themselves the exception. The two gazed at the cave orcs with a will to fight them head-on. They would not hold back. They would not let the cave orcs intimidate them.

This took away the element of fear the cave orcs were inclined to have when charging toward their opponents. Instead, with calm and methodical calculation, Marin evaded and parried. She then counterattacked with her flaming blade. It was clear the cave orcs underestimated her ability and resolve to hold her own against them as the battle became intense.

Meanwhile, Linitus used his bow and shot one arrow at a time as quickly as possible at the other approaching cave orcs. The elf ranger aimed at the ones that were furthest from Marin without her being in Linitus's line of fire. One after another, the elf ranger slayed at least four of them. By that time, Marin had struck down the first two cave orcs. She was poised to face the one closest to her. That cave orc prepared to engage her in melee combat.

Soon only six cave orcs remained. After quickly assessing their casualties they decided to retreat. It was not worth risking for the rest of their group to lose their lives against a realized set of formidable enemies. One more cave orc fell in combat. It was the one who engaged Marin in single combat. Despite her adversary's efforts to overpower her, Marin, using the skills and tactics Linitus had taught her in their earlier adventuring years, tripped the cave orc and let his imbalance cause him to fall onto the floor. Marin then dealt the final blow, impaling him with her burning blade.

After turning again to brace the next enemy to strike, Marin before looking and assessing, had her blade raised high in the air ready to strike downward at the next orc only to halt herself in midstance while staring motionless at who she realized she was about to impale. It was Linitus. He evaded the strike by stepping back. He then raised his hands and told his lover to calm down.

Marin stared for another moment before processing and realizing how close she was to being caught up with her emotions and nearly struck her elven lover. She dropped her blade and apologized to her elven lover. She realized she had nearly lost her discipline and almost gave in to her anger without thinking and being in a state of utter anxiety.

Linitus embraced her as she fell into his arms. He told her to take several deep breaths to calm down while assuring her she had caused no offense other than reacting as he might have from being at an elevated level of alertness with a high emotion in trying to survive.

All these years, there was one strength of her lover that Marin appreciated more than any of his other qualities. He possessed the ability to understand. He empathized with others who went through the most dire and stressful times in needing someone to listen to them and for them to be heard. For her, it was endearing to be heard by someone who understood and accepted her for who she was.

With her composure regained, Marin turned her attention to the situation, assessing her surroundings and Linitus. She noticed that he still limped. His recent injury took a toll on him despite his subtleness and dismissiveness in showing his pain. Marin placed her hands on him. She told him to lie down next to the fire pit. Although cold, the heat from the firepit and the nearby surface created enough warmth for Linitus to lie down with his head resting on Marin's knees as she knelt. Taking a moment before concentrating, Marin focused her mind on several words of incantation. A bluish-green orb emanated from her hands and began to expand and envelop her and Linitus. The orb's properties began to mend and heal Linitus's wounds in moments.

Linitus was healed. Still, he felt somewhat weary. The elf slightly staggered to get up. Marin held back her hand on his shoulder and told him not to. Instead, she told him to lie down and rest. They felt safe for the time being. There was no telling how long it would remain that way. Both Marin and Linitus knew at least that much. Still, she wanted to comfort him. She wanted him to place his trust in her ability to assess the situation while scouting the nearby surroundings of the ice cave, including finding a way out. She assured her lover and companion in arms that she would. Linitus trusted her to do so before he nodded and closed his eyes to rest briefly.

As Linitus rested, Marin, using her flaming sword as a guiding light, walked around the ice cave. She paid keen attention to any foe that lurked at any crevice or obstructions of the ice cave that would expose her to being ambushed. She found no enemy. The search took her several minutes to find a narrow corridor that seemed to be the way out of the cave. She contemplated whether to explore it further or to hold back, at least until Linitus has fully rested.

Marin used caution with the same level of discernment her elven lover had exhibited through the years that she had known him. In contemplating the possible outcomes including the risks, Marin decided to suppress her urge to further explore the passageway and go back to where her lover rested. She would stay by his side until he woke up. Together they would face the unknown sights and encounters that await them. She knew at least that if they explored together their chances of prevailing against any enemies and surviving were far greater than being separated and ambushed apart from each other. If there was one thing that was known to them, it was that they were on the other side of the portal after teleporting. They knew they had to be somewhere in Shimmerfrost.

Though Marin had never traveled to Shimmerfrost before until now, she had heard a fair share of tales about this land from her late Nordling mother Gretchen during childhood. Shimmerfrost was a land considered the coldest, harshest, and farthest one could trek northward. Survival was not impossible but very difficult, especially during the long winter season. This was a brutal and unforgiving land full of monsters and creatures with bad intentions. It was a land considered by some as the long-lost homeland of her earliest peoples, the Nordling side of her ancestry. Though many of the Nordlings migrated southward, including some in Marin's family line, she recalled her mother saying that many Nordlings from Shimmerfrost still chose to stay behind. Those who did still called this dangerous land their home.

Marin did not know what to expect of the dangers they would encounter. Regardless, she still recalled most of what she had heard about this mysterious land. It was a place of great mystery and suspense that her late mother described vividly through stories. Marin was surprised realizing how much of Shimmerfrost and its inhabitants were made up and how much was real from the childhood folk stories she remembered. It was those stories that both intrigued and scared her. She knew when it was time to explore more. She and Linitus would find out which folk tale was far from being made up. Regardless, her hope centered not so much on the matter of discovering an unfamiliar land. Rather, she wanted to find a passage back home.

Chapter Ten

Arrival in Hell

In the dark yet bright burning plane of Hadao Infernum were many caves. The air felt sultry though still tolerable to live in without the flesh burning from air contact. The scent smelled of phosphorus. Deep inside, in one of the southern reaches of a desolate plateau, lay a dark, exotic carved stone portal. It remained sealed for entrance or exits, unless its operators used it. Suddenly, a loud, high-pitched blast sounded then a large energy field appeared in the portal gate. Three figures emerged from the portal. The first to come out was Charu. He was followed by Lucia in her new succubus form. Vanth came behind Lucia. Upon seeing the dark and fiery landscape of the cave, Lucia was mesmerized. To an understandable extent, she was also frightened though she tried to conceal it.

Looking about while still amazed, Lucia turned to her post-mortal escorts to find out what to do next. She wanted to know where to find her soulmate, Decius. Vanth and Charu looked at each other sarcastically. They told Lucia she would find out for herself and that she was on her own. They told her she would have to struggle to survive at her own peril.

Vanth and Charu also cautioned Lucia to be wary of the denizens of this condemned place of the afterlife. Nobody in Infernum could be trusted without the risk of being betrayed and to pay the ultimate price of dying a last time in the afterlife. Once that happened, there would be no reprieve left for the affected soul. There would be no other plane or station in life left to be assigned to. The soul would be extinguished permanently, like a burning flame put out.

Lucia shuddered slightly. She now knew that whatever she might have not realized before. She had made an immense sacrifice for the one that she truly and deeply loved. She resumed her focus and displayed a calm expression, focusing on the matter at hand and the reason why she elected to be here. Lucia would find Decius no matter what the obstacles were. She would traverse the greatest lengths if she had to. No matter what, Lucia would find and reunite with her long-lost lover. There was no turning back, and she would not have changed her mind if she rethought her decision from before.

Lucia nodded and gestured to acknowledge the advice Charu and Vanth gave. She gave a simple salutation of goodbye, knowing that they would never see each other again. The two messengers or escorts of death returned the gesture and salutation before departing, stepping through the portal once it was reactivated.

Lucia recollected her thoughts as she continued to absorb what she had seen. She stood on a platform with a series of stone steps with jagged rock edges, separated from the distance by a lava river. From behind and above, the platform and portal gate pierced through a bright natural opening or mouth of the cave from which to exit. Lucia looked with caution. She became frustrated seeing how tall the opening was. She would have difficulty scaling it.

Lucia took a moment to ponder. The duchess reflected with the eager realization that she now had her succubus powers to use. She could use her demonic batlike wings to hover and fly out of the cave's opening. At first, she had trouble experimenting with and realizing her abilities. Lucia adapted herself to her new powers, hovering and circling higher and higher above the cave opening. Eventually, she was clear and able to move in the air to land outside the cave entrance. Upon landing and looking about, the sight shook her more internally upon realizing how harsh and unforgiving this new environment she has resigned herself to live in.

Much of the landscape was flat. The notable exception were the jagged cliffs several miles away that were towering above. There were more cliffs in the opposite direction, towering over the central mesa of this hell. Each layer or plain separated by the cliffs represented a level or layer of hell where the condemned lived in. The lowest was reserved for those condemned for the most severe offenses. They were without the faith of the various benevolent deity spirits to follow and practice their ways during their previous mortal lives.

Decius once lived at the lowest level for violating the covenant of the chosen vessel. As a mortal, he had opened the gates of hell to join the mortal realm of Terrunaemara. He was also considered suitable to this realm for the other crimes that were committed on behalf of Calu and Laran. However, he escaped the lowest level with his chosen vessel powers and teleported easily to the higher planes. Eventually, Decius ascended to the highest plain of Hadao Infernum to build his citadel, Sanctum Infernum.

Lucia familiarized herself with this hellish landscape ten years after her late spouse first had. Lucia looked all about and continued to take in and make sense of Infernum. Wherever her lover was, she knew he would make an impression, including to be known among the denizens of hell. From a distance, she sighted above a layer of cliffs a jagged and sleek rectangular prism compound. It stood above next to a flowing river of lava that fell down the cliff as a burning waterfall. This structure was impressive, and she knew Decius was there.

Lucia used her bat-like wings to take flight again. She heard a loud screeching noise behind her. She looked and turned. Only in a sudden moment, she could evade. Lucia moved over to her side while the attacker darted past her. This female demonic creature swung a large double-bladed ax and missed as Lucia evaded her attack. The attacker bore a similar resemblance to Lucia's new demonic appearance. This figure had bat-like wings, cranial horns, and a curved pointed tail like Lucia. The figure wore somewhat similar clothing to Lucia. This figure wore a dark maroon corset with long black leg guards and a similar short black-and-maroon skirt. Even from a quick glance, Lucia could tell this figure was one of the dreaded succubi Vanth and Charu had warned her about.

The duchess turned around to face the flying demonic creature. Lucia emanated with her powers from one of her hands a magical whip, or more specifically a cat-o'-nine-tails. This enchanted weapon was known as Nine Sufferings.

As the attacking succubus made another pass, Lucia dodged again in midair while hurling her multi-tailed whip. It struck the demonic female creature, causing her to fall to the ground, screeching in pain and struggling to move. Her ax had fallen next to her and was out of her reach. Lucia used her mind and focused on calling out her whip as if feeling it had been part of her body and essence. Her weapon flung back toward her while Lucia landed on the ground next to the bladed ax. Though she was prone to showing mercy, she knew she would not receive any, especially from a creature like this. This other female succubus stared at her with utter hate while wincing in pain. Not withholding, Lucia demanded that the creature explain herself. Lucia wanted to know why the creature attacked her. The duchess wanted to know if this creature knew the whereabouts of Dux Decius. The creature did not respond other than to screech in a curse-like manner at Lucia.

Not wanting to show any signs of weakness, Lucia used the ax that belonged to the creature and severed her arm with one fell swoop. The creature shrieked in pain. Lucia waited a moment before calling to the creature again, demanding she explain herself, why she attacked her and to disclose the whereabouts of Dux Decius. Lucia threatened she would continue to deliver the same punishment as she had just done if the creature would not comply.

Once the creature complied, Lucia would end her misery with a quick death. The creature cursed at Lucia while the latter became more creative with her torture, taking the bladed ax and severing the adjoined wings of the succubus. Once again, the creature screamed in agony while Lucia waited for a moment. The creature, though spiteful, recognized the futility of further resisting; it no longer wished to receive further torture. The succubus finally confessed to Lucia. The succubus confided she attacked Lucia out of jealousy. The creature saw how close the duchess was, even from a distance, to seek the one she says they call Decius. The succubus did not know who Lucia was. The creature was jealous of her as a new arrival and contender among the remaining seventy-two succubi (including that creature). This creature wanted to have the honor of trying to slay the one they called Decius and rise to prominence from her current position in this dark realm. This succubus and her other fellow succubi, if given the opportunity, would hand over the desecrated corpse of Decius (upon slaughtering him) as an offering to their reigning lord of hell, Orcus, also known as the Lord of Punishment.

Upon hearing the succubus's confession and feeling raw anger and fear at the prospect of losing her eternal lover and soulmate, Lucia had heard enough. The duchess unleashed a loud shriek while using the ax of her new nemesis to sever her head. In an instant, the severed head rolled from the motionless corpse of the succubus. Lucia dropped the ax and picked up the severed head by the hair before flying off into the distance to the faraway structure she presumed would be Decius's fortress. Though she did not know what else would lie in her search for her lover, she did not care, nor would let it stop her. Lucia would fly as quickly as possible to reunite with him. The duchess had waited long enough and sacrificed everything to his will. She would wait no longer and sacrifice only the blood of their enemies to be with Decius again. She was bound even in hell to make sure that, this time, they would be inseparable from each other after they were reunited.

Chapter Eleven

A New Commission

Less than a day after the cave mine collapsed, the lone skyship that Peat and Wyatt had continued to sail high above the sky. The skyship loomed over a cloudy late midday sky on the coastal sparkling metropolis of Citadella Neapola. It was the capital of the Kingdom of Swordbane. Though the city had been severely damaged ten years ago after the disastrous and costly war against the Imperial Remnant, it had long since rebuilt. Not as prominent as before, the city still stood as a bright beacon of hope. The optimism and determination of its inhabitants seemed poised to bring back the full prestige that the city once had. Some of the urban dwellings were rebuilt over different intervals. They were white and majestic as before. These dwellings surrounded the city's famous monuments. The monuments themselves were as majestic as before the war. Some of them were the Great Amphitheater of Swordbane, the Grand Circus, the Great Basilica of Sol Invictus, the Royal Curia of the Senate, and the Royal Crown Palace.

As the skyship approached deeper above the city, its course was fixed to the Royal Crown Palace. Both Peat and Wyatt would teleport below and seek an audience with the king, Ascentius IV. The two adventurers arrived in front of the courtyard. They informed the king's guards they urgently needed to have an audience with the king. The guards found it odd that the two had returned without Linitus or Princess Marin. These guards, however, knew that the sense of urgency Peat and Wyatt conveyed was important to find the king at once.

King Ascentius granted the dwarf and halfling adventurers an audience at once. The monarch sat on his royal throne while waiting for Wyatt and Peat to approach him in his throne room. The king's appearance was prominent as much as it was intimidating compared to his previous human form. That was at least before his bodily transformation toward the end of the Imperial Remnant's uprising and civil war against Swordbane ten years prior. Ever since, he had assumed the anthropomorphic form of a green half-dragon, half-man. Consequently, many of his subjects indirectly referred to him as the Dragonman King. Ascentius however was also reincarnated in a unique way. He was infused with both his soul and part of the essence of the deity spirit of Sol Invictus.

Upon seeing two of his loyal subjects bow before him, Ascentius motioned and told them to rise. Though he did not know the exact circumstances, he knew that the halfling wizard and dwarven guardian came with dreadful news. Ascentius knew that something had happened to Linitus and his daughter Marin. They needed no exchange of formalities. The king simply took the direct approach. He asked Wyatt and Peat what had happened. What happened to his son-in-law, Linitus, and the king's beloved daughter, Marin?

Peat composed himself as best as he could before responding. He let Ascentius know that the two had disappeared when the cave mine near the Great Azure Lake collapsed. Peat explained the result of the collapse transpired from the fight they had against a deadly new alliance. It was an alliance they uncovered between the Remnant and a strange new faction led by the Winter Death Witch, Helskadi, from the mysterious northern region of Shimmerfrost. Peat continued his account of what had happened. He mentioned to the king that Marin and Linitus might have escaped during the mine collapse through the portal gate and were teleported to that strange faraway region. However, Wyatt and Peat were unsure of where to search for their companions' whereabouts. They thought it best to consult with Ascentius. The dwarf and halfling felt compelled to let Ascentius know before they took action.

Ascentius bemoaned in disappointment and looked down at his lap. He lamented the dangers his daughter and son-in-law would face. The Dragonman King however resolved himself with a strong sense of resolution and conviction. He knew that if anyone could survive that dreary and unremittingly cold place, it would be those two. He knew even with the divine spirit of Sol Invictus in him that Linitus and his beloved Marin were still alive. He could sense their life force was still in the mortal realm of Terrunaemara.

The Dragonman King stood up from his throne with his reptilian tail whipping behind. He gave a sudden dragon roar before directing his attention to Wyatt and Peat. After recomposing himself, Ascentius looked at the two and charged them with a new set of orders, or rather a commission. The two members of the Comradery would go and find their companions in the faraway lands of Shimmerfrost.

Peat and Wyatt still looked somewhat puzzled and asked where exactly north. They also asked if there was a way the king could use his powers to find his own daughter and son-in-law.

Ascentius lowered his reptilian head and gave a sorrowful expression. He was constrained from directly interfering and using his chosen vessel powers. He could do so only in certain extraordinary situations, including when it violated both the natural and divine order of various planes. The most prominent example was when Decius opened the portals of hell upon the mortal realm of Terrunaemara during his uprising ten years ago. Though the deity spirits had allowed Ascentius to stay in the mortal world of Terrunaemara to assume his duties as king of Swordbane, he could only rule in terms of decision-making and managing his kingdom. He could not use his divine superpowers and act directly in various manners or predicaments, including the one in which his daughter and son-in-law had found themselves. Only in rare and extreme cases such as an unnatural disturbance in the mortal realm could Ascentius personally intervene.

The king again lamented. He wished there was a way he could directly go to his daughter and son-in-law's aid and bring them home. Still, he knew that, at the very least, he could offer advice and clues to help Wyatt and Peat.

As Ascentius explained, he told the halfling and dwarf to use the skyship they had after replenishing it to make their way north. They would travel to the large friendly settlement of Aegir-Hafn, in which they would find help on their quest to retrieve their allies. The king also informed Wyatt that he would know if his missing companions were there when they gazed upon the talking stone. Though puzzled by his use of words, Wyatt, perceptive as always, picked up on the king's words and knew that Ascentius was referring to the wizard's ward stone. This magical stone could sense similar stones and would vibrate more intensely as they came closer into proximity. This could be used as a means for Wyatt and Peat to track their companions when close enough and if Linitus and or Marin had their own ward stone.

After advising the halfling wizard and his dwarven companion, King Ascentius motioned with his hand in a commanding manner to set out as soon as their skyship was replenished. Wyatt and Peat kneeled before the king, vowing to do everything to find the king's daughter and son-in-law, their comrades in arms. The king acknowledged replying that he knew they would and that they would return home with Marin and Linitus.

Soon Wyatt and Peat were on the skyship. They looked down and spotted several supply crates. The supplies included food and water. Wyatt teleported the supplies on deck along with the porters who would help the two members of the Comradery stow the provisions onboard the skyship's cargo hold.

After replenishing the ship's supply, the king's porters wished the two good luck on their adventure. Wyatt and Peat thanked them. At sunset, they departed north in their skyship past Aldion, one of the kingdom's fortified northern settlements. Once they reached Aldion, the two adventurers would cross the border to the coastal northern forest frontier of the Nordlings. After a day or two, they would reach the largest known coastal forest settlement of the Nordlings, Aegir-Hafn. They can only imagine what advice the local Nordlings of the settlement would give them. If they were fortunate enough, the settlement may even provide a guide familiar with Shimmerfrost.

Chapter Twelve

Paying Final Respects

A day after Lucianus Canus and Agaroman went back to the cave by the Great Azure Lake to find Duchess Lucia's remains, they returned to the Remnant capital, Sanctum Novus. Flying above the desert city, they stood on the top deck canopy of the skybeast. Looking down at the city, it stood as majestic as it always had. It was a harmonious mixture of date palm trees, tall and pointed yucca palm trees, and cypress trees that dotted the urban landscape of desert sandstone and marble buildings in Citadellan architecture complete with columns, arches, and domes. The most impressive structures of the city could be seen at once from high above, including the local amphitheater, the local capitol building, the Great Temple of Laran, the dux's palace (also known formally as the Imperial Ducal Palace), and perhaps unique compared to the coastal Citadellan cities, the Grand Colonnade (or series of columns) that followed along the southern gateway entrance along the main city road to the central plaza, or forum.

From below to those unaccustomed that could catch a clear view, the skybeast was equally impressive to stare at. However, it was also a terrifying, massive flying contraption. It was a vessel made of blackened metal. It had an elongated shape. The vessel's wings were that of a large bat. The forward bow and cockpit formed the head of a menacing wolf.

For the residents of the city below, it was a sight familiar that they revered. It was a sign that the ruling family had returned. Things were different this time however. The city's population would mourn upon realizing that only one had returned alive. The other had not.

Upon teleporting from the skybeast using both their magic, Lucianus, and Agaroman arrived with a company of the strongest goblins who carried the wrapped corpse of Lucia in an ornate ceremonial litter. The goblins attached the ornate litter to an luxurious designed wagon. A chariot pulled by a pack of dire wolves led by Lucianus and Agaroman towed the wagon.

Lucianus and Agaroman then began a slow and solemn procession of Duchess Lucia's remains, making their way to the main city plaza. Agaroman took additional measures to dispatch a town crier. The crier announced to the public in a loud voice that the duchess had died, giving her life to the Remnant's cause.

Crowds quickly assembled, including not only Citadellan humans but also goblins and orcs who lived in the city. All paid their respects and prayers while shouting in mourning. The procession stopped once it arrived at the heart of the city's plaza and forum. They stopped right at the steps of the rostra, a raised platform for orators. They used it for those prominent in giving public decrees. Here, Agaroman announced loudly on top of the rostra that Duchess Lucia had died, sacrificing her life for the greater cause. She had allowed her son, Lucianus, the dark lord's heir, to escape and survive during a perilous encounter.

In reaction, the public mourned. They cried out and chanted Lucia's endearing Citadellan name of Domina Patronessa Matria. It meant the lady patroness mother for they saw her as that. They knew and recognized her role and capability to serve their interests as a caring maternal patron and ruler.

As the mass grew in number, Agaroman ordered several priests from the temple of Laran to prepare a makeshift altar on the rostra itself. These priests displayed the symbols of Laran and Calu on top of the altar. Lucianus would lead those in observance to take part in the incense offering and wine libation ritual to the two respective deity spirits. Upon conducting the ritual, the young dark lord's heir would call upon his father, Decius, to appear in his spectral form.

Meanwhile, as Lucianus made preparations for the ritual, a lone person emerged from behind the rostra while calling out Lucianus's name. Lucianus turned to see it was his maternal grandfather, Senator Diem. As the old senator slowly walked closer to his young werewolf Lupercalian grandson, Diem noticed that something was not right. The senator did not hear the earlier announcement when he stepped outside from his estate. He did not know the occasion for the impromptu elaborate procession.

Looking deeply at Lucianus and receiving a solemn stare in return, Diem knew what happened. No words needed to be said. The senator came forward and hugged his grandson. Lucianus held back his tears. He only held his grandfather firmly and spoke slowly in a stern yet soft voice that he was sorry. Diem held back his tears also. He knew his grandson felt genuine guilt for the death of his mother.

Diem also felt the same remorse, for he wished it was him and not his daughter who died. Even so, the senator wished he could have embraced his beloved daughter just as much as he cherished embracing his grandson.

The senator found consolation that Lucianus was alive at least. Still, Diem could not hold back mourning and sadness, expressing how much he missed his daughter. He wished this day would never have come while he lived. Senator Diem cherished all the moments he had with Lucia. Their bond was strong as father and daughter. He knew in his own Citadellan psyche and belief system, piety compelled him to still persevere in life without her, as difficult as it was. He would wait for the day he would reunite with his beloved daughter in the heavenly abode of Caelum. Diem would not know until later his daughter's fate in the afterlife. He believed without a doubt she was in Caelum. Her faith and charity were renowned for the divine spirits to recognize her as being deemed worthy to enter paradise.

Diem paused, looked, and noticed that a chariot with the wrapped remains was in a litter. It was his daughter, and he knew his grandson intended to burn his mother's remains in the ceremonial funeral pyre. After observing some more, Diem also knew that from the altar being set up that his grandson intended to summon the spectral spirit of his father, Diem's son-in-law, Decius. Diem did not object, only saying that he wished to be the one to hold the torch to light the pyre. It was his daughter and his duty, his place to do this one act as a form of closure. It was his way of paying respects to the one he loved and cherished as her father.

Lucianus consented to his grandfather's wishes. Diem, out of respect for his grandson's wishes, also agreed to wait and summon Decius and notify him about his wife's passing. After Lucianus finished the summoning ritual, Decius appeared in his dark-blue, pale translucent spectral werewolf projection of himself. The dux looked somewhat perplexed, trying to make sense of the staged impromptu procession that he saw.

Eventually, he realized, after seeing the wrapped body that was transferred from the ornate chariot towed litter to a high prestigious makeshift funeral pyre that something had happened. Something important and pressing had transpired for his presence to be called. He knew, seeing everyone close to him as a mortal present except one, his beloved Lucia. Decius could see the lowered and saddened face of his wolfling son Lucianus and the saddened but stern face of Senator Diem. The senator stared at Decius's ghost in a way in which Decius could make out and read his father-in-law's thoughts to know the time had come for Lucia's mortality to end.

Just as before with Diem and Lucianus, Decius and Diem needed no words to explain what happened. They all could read each other's faces and physical expressions. Decius, angered, unleashed a deafening howl. His gesture elicited other nearby wolves to howl in tandem. Decius then remained quiet while motioning for the general crowd to follow suit.

Soon Decius signaled to his son Lucianus, who was carrying a lit torch in his hand. Lucianus nodded solemnly and then handed the lit torch to his grandfather. Senator Diem set alight the base of the makeshift pyre holding his daughter's remains. All present observed in silence as the flames quickly enveloped the entire pyre, burning everything to ashes. No words were said except for Decius in his spectral form, looking at the crowd and telling them to remember Lady Lucia as their spiritual mother, who had cared and nurtured them in her capacity as a stateswoman and patron who provided for all their needs.

Decius paused and reflected again about the stately affairs in which were left at hand that Lucia had previously managed. The dux knew his duchess had prearrangements that were in order to be implemented for the day she was to pass on to the next life. Decius motioned for Agaroman to obtain Lady Lucia's will. Agaroman had already expected this, dispatching a small detachment of Citadellan knights of the Order of the Black Wolf to accompany one of Lucia's trusted attendants to fetch her will. It was secured in a locked chest in the main chamber of the dux's palace that, aside from Lucia, only Agaroman, Diem, and one of her most trusted attendants had access to.

After receiving Lucia's will, Decius ordered for it to be read before the public. Agaroman nodded and unsealed the envelope holding the will. He then read the document, declaring that her written will affirmed her son Lucianus as the rightful heir to be named Dux of the Imperial Remnant and that her father, Senator Diem, would serve as regent until Agaroman deemed Lucianus of age to assume full military and political duties as the next dux to formally succeed his father, Decius.

For the immediate physical property of her estate, Lucia instructed through her written will to be transferred solely to her son, with her father assuming custody until, again, Lucianus was deemed of age by Agaroman to assume full duties as the next dux. Lucia knew that while Agaroman would not hesitate to bypass her father as a possible perceived rival for the course of how he wanted to guide Decius's son to rule as the next dux and dark lord, the wizard was still rational and of sound mind that he had to wait until he knew Lucianus was capable and ready at an age to lead. Possibly, at the age when Decius was in his prime. It would take still several more years, as they considered Lucianus an adolescent, not fully ready to lead.

Finally, Agaroman read the last part of Lucia's will. All of her monetary wealth, aside from her estate holdings given to Lucianus, would be donated equally to every citizen and serving soldier in the Remnant's army. Her accumulated wealth was vast. She gained much of it over time through various means. Among them included the material wealth her deceased husband, Decius, previously gained in appropriating from the expelled clergy over ten years ago, as well as from trade and the spoils of various wars over the last ten years. Every citizen of the city and every serving soldier, including among the nonhuman creatures like the goblins and orcs, by best estimates, would have received ten coins of silver and one of gold.

After another moment of quietness, multiple voices broke out in the crowd to give chants of praise and reverence to Lucia with many bringing personal items that they added to the burning pyre. Lucianus at first was astonished and unsure if he should order the guards to take action though Decius motioned with a ghostlike hand not to. He explained to his son that the citizens were honoring Lucia as best as they knew how to give back an allotment of their own possessions as a reciprocation of their affection toward Lucia.

Lucianus nodded and understood. He stared as the flames on the pyre grew steadily larger from the various objects that city locals had thrown on top of the burning pyre. It was a rare moment Decius and Lucianus shared, mourning the wife and mother they loved. Behind them, Agaroman and Senator Diem considered mutual collaboration and trust when working together. They both knew despite their periodic odds with each other that it was necessary to put their differences aside to ensure that the Imperial Remnant government stayed stable under Diem's management. Meanwhile, Lucianus would still be trained in statesmanship and warfare. However, understanding Diem's wishes to pay his final last respects to his daughter, the wizard agreed to defer the matter of their arrangements for collaboration to another time. For the moment, Diem would have that space and time to solemnly pay their final respects to Lucia, together with his son-in-law and grandson, before the burning pyre rendered Lucia's remains into ashes.

Diem put his arm on his grandson's shoulder. Looking at the ghost of Decius, the senator told his grandson that they would honor her memory and continue the work of making the Imperial Remnant the rightful and prosperous successor to the past Lupercalian Empire. Decius and Lucianus both nodded in agreement.

For a little longer, Decius's spectral presence would remain in the mortal realm. Eventually, his ghostly form would depart from his son and his father-in-law to disappear along with his consciousness back to the hellish domain from where he lived. By that time, it would be nightfall. The city would continue to observe the pyre until the early morning.

Chapter Thirteen

Stepping into the Light

Only a day after their arrival in Shimmerfrost via a portal, Linitus awoke. He felt well-rested after his wounds were healed by his lover, Marin. She stayed awake the entire time to keep a lookout for lurking enemies. However, she also lay prone next to her elven lover, holding him. They stayed warm in each other's embrace and by being near the burning fire pit.

Marin felt a movement. She became alert, realizing that her elven lover was awake. She asked him how he felt and if he was ready to continue finding their way out of this dark, frozen cave. Linitus nodded, telling her that before they left, they should scout around the cave. They should look for any clues as to where they were, including any possessions that their slain enemy may have that they may find useful.

Marin nodded. The Princess Knight told him she had scouted a path leading out of the cave. She admitted, however, she had not ventured that far. Marin pointed out that they had limited vision, along with a lack of illumination given that the cave was dark. She could see only within a limited range with the aid of her flaming sword, Sol's Fury. Linitus nodded while taking a small bundle of silk bulb arrows from his quiver. Without having to tell her, the two lovers could read each other's mind just by looking at each other's facial expressions and from being well attuned to each other from all the years they had shared adventures together. Consequently, Marin took her flaming sword and set alight the bundles of arrows. The two walked close to each other, surveying the corpses of the cave orcs.

From a distance, next to a wall, Linitus peeked to see that there were two chests with different engravings. He walked forward and motioned for Marin to follow carefully behind him. There were no traps, so he prepared to get his set of lockpicks and skeleton keys. He used his lockpicking set to unlock one of the two chests. Marin then recognized the symbols of the writing that were from her mother's Nordling native language. She interrupted Linitus while cautioning him about the words that she had deciphered. The chest the elf had opened had symbols that, according to Marin, in Nordling meant "fire breath." Linitus still could not make sense of it until Marin told him it was possibly a trap. Meanwhile, she deciphered to the best of her knowledge of Nordling's written runic language regarding the other chest. She deciphered the words as being "path of knowledge."

They both believed that, most likely, the other was not a trap. Linitus turned his attention to that other chest and slowly and carefully picked its lock. The elf ranger, or rogue ranger as he was sometimes called, became known for his versatile skills, including lockpicking. He learned from his mother, who was a former rogue in lockpicking and lock making and worked as a domestic servant at the household of a noble elven family in Salvinia Parf Edhellen.

After Linitus released the lock, he opened the chest. Inside the chest, Linitus found a round a small cylinder barrel with a fuse that somehow lit presumably as soon as he opened the chest. Linitus quickly closed the chest while dodging and telling Marin to take cover. Marin reacted with haste. She used her shield and placed it before them. Within moments, the chest erupted in a burst of explosion. The impact of the blast, however, was not significant. The two adventurers retreated far enough to avoid the effects of the blast. Marin also used her shield to deflect some of the debris and shrapnel that came in their direction.

As another moment went by, Marin raised her shield and glanced at her surroundings. She sighed in relief, knowing she and Linitus were alive. They turned to each other and realized that that chest was a trick that would cause the unlucky opener to believe it was not the decoy explosive trap in which it was. The two companions and lovers could not hold back in this realization. Marin asked who in their right mind would take such a deceitful and reckless approach to disguise the chests in such a fashion. She wondered if the cave orcs could even tell the difference and not be lured into the same trap. Linitus understood the bizarre danger that almost cost their lives. He cautioned that they had to both be careful next time. They were in a dangerous land that they knew little about and had not even had the time to understand.

Marin nodded. She could not help but say with irony that they had not even made it outside the cave yet. Her lover nodded. He looked at the other lockbox. Linitus left nothing to chance as he carefully used one of his lockpicks slowly to unlock it. This time though he knew as soon as he had unlocked it, that a mechanism inside had made a snapping sound. Once again, he told Marin to take cover. They maintained the earlier posture and braced for impact. The chest also exploded and as before had not affected the hero companions.

Marin lowered her shield. She could not withstand herself from feeling paranoid by how this was a ploy for them or any other unsuspecting individual to be at risk of being blown up either way. The Princess Knight cursed at how psychotic anyone would be to do this. She could not help but wonder if the person who planted the explosives in the treasure chest considered to give a prior warning to the cave orcs about this deadly contraption lest they would fall victim to it as well. However, both she and Linitus realized again that they had to use caution as they were in a dangerous, unwelcoming environment. Taking a moment to let her catch her breath, Linitus motioned for Marin to take the lead. Marin would guide as she retraced her steps from the path she followed earlier in the cave that she presumed would be their way out to the surface.

As they followed the path, natural light began to pierce through the darkness. It became brighter and clearer as the two adventurers continued making their way along pathways leading out of the cave. Marin and Linitus were in awe when they saw the mouth of the cave that opened to the outside world. They could see from a few dozen yards away the bright sunlight shining down upon a stream of water that emerged from inside the cave. The flowing water bled outside from the cave while embracing the warmth of the sunlight. The banks of the water stream on either side met with various small, jagged rocks. Beyond those rocks was a steep green field with terraces that would become jagged cliffs. Beyond that, they would see the cliffs descending vertically downward into the ocean, circumventing the long narrow body of ocean water. This would be the legendary southern fjords of Shimmerfrost.

Eager to leave the darkness of the cave, Marin walked forward. Linitus quickly grabbed her arm and pulled her back gently. He motioned to her with his hands that they were not alone. Shocked and dumbfounded while looking at the path ahead, Marin then asked quietly in a whisper how he knew. Linitus said to look at the reflection of the water. At first, Marin saw nothing, but looking intently, she noticed a small rising smoke in the water's reflection from a distance. It puzzled her how they could see that without a flame appearing in front of them.

Linitus understood his lover's expression and astonishment. He told her that they were likely enemies emitting that smoke. It is possible they were positioned above the mouth of the cave and poised to ambush them.

Marin nodded after thinking and understanding the logic her elven lover had in suspecting such a possibility of ambush. She asked in a low voice what they should do. They did not know if the enemy lying in wait outnumbered them. They also were at a disadvantage since the enemy had the high ground and was positioned above the mouth of the cave.

Linitus thought the same. He thought of the many ways they could evade the enemy while staying alive. The elf ranger devised a plan. They would share and use his camouflage cloak. He had never used it before to share it at the same time with another person, including Marin, despite all their adventures together. Marin even gave a look of expression in questioning the practicality of using the cloak for two people. She knew it was made to fit one person.

Marin had another idea. She suggested that Linitus use the cloak first to sneak quietly out of the cave in the likeliness of being undetected. She would follow behind after a few minutes. If there were any ambushers, they would only suspect and notice her. Marin could distract their attention long enough for Linitus to make the first strike before they could attack her since they would not be able to detect the elf ranger.

It was risky, and Linitus did not like the plan. He knew that his beloved wife would risk her life to make this gamble so they could escape and prevail against their enemies. Linitus indicated his concerns.

Marin however interjected. She put her hand on his mouth and kissed him. She told him how much she loved him and that this was perhaps their only chance, if not their best chance, for survival.

The elf ranger nodded with reluctance. He returned with a brief and subtle kiss. Linitus told her to do everything to stay alive. He told Marin to be ready to fight as fiercely as ever should the enemy before them be formidable.

Marin nodded then motioned with her head to Linitus to use his camouflage cloak and walk out of the ice cave. Faintly, she could hear his footsteps as he walked near the rocks to the side of the emerging cave stream.

A few minutes later, Marin composed herself and then slowly walked out to the cave. The Princess Knight took a few steps outside the cave mouth and turned to look both up and back. She saw staring straight back at her four cave orcs and three ugly, bloated creatures. These three bloated creatures were nearly as tall as the white troll she had seen before when she and her companions fought in the cave near the Great Azure Lake. These strange, bloated creatures were bald and had thick, humanlike skin. They were extremely muscular, even for their size, despite being bloated. One of the three had an armament that included a combination of chain mail overlapped by partial splint mail chest armor, a large triangular shield, and a large spiked club. The other two had skins with a slightly yellowish tint (just as the first did). These two creatures wielded simple wooden clubs. They wore worn brownish loincloths along with heavy chains slung around their shoulders. Marin remembered hearing tales about these grotesque creatures, thinking they were only figures in children's stories. Little did she expect to find that these creatures, called ogres, were very real indeed. For Marin, it was almost intimidating to face off against three of them who no longer existed within just the confines of horrifying fairy tale stories. They were very much real indeed.

Meanwhile, the creatures noticed her after looking downward from where they stood at the top of a rocky overlook above the mouth of the cave. The cave orcs present were the same ones who fled the fight. This time they were joined by three ogres. They all looked at her in a menacing manner. Marin, in return, pointed her flaming sword at them and goaded them to come and challenge her in combat.

One particular ogre, wearing the combination mail armor, ordered the rest of these beastly creatures to attack Marin as he pointed his spiked club at her and yelled loudly. The other creatures also gave their own war cries and started making their way down the steep overlook. Marin quickly sheathed her sword and pulled out her two weighted ornate hairpins that tied her hair together. Then she hurled her hairpins at the cave orcs. At least one of her hairpins struck one of the cave orcs, causing the creature to fall to the ground in pain. Meanwhile, the other hairpin missed.

As the three remaining cave orcs approached her, two arrows whistled through the air, striking two of the cave orcs, leaving one for Marin to contend with, which she did so quickly, unsheathing her sword again. Meanwhile, the two ogres who were still scaling down the top of the cave mouth were in disarray. They turned and looked towards the direction where the arrows came from where their ogre leader stood. The armored ogre leader was also startled. He turned around only to realize it was too late as a sharp slightly curved long elven blade had cut across his neck severing his head from the rest of his body. Behind the decapitated ogre stood a slender elf ranger of moderate height wearing an exotic ornate green cloak who had revealed himself while seizing the element of surprise.

The other two ogres were furious. They were in shock at what they observed. This lone elf ranger and the human female clad in metal armor quickly disposed of most of their warband in short order. Regardless, the ogres went in separate directions. One of them scaled down the top of the cave entrance to engage Marin in combat. The other ogre went back up to engage the elf ranger. Linitus wasted no time. He readied an arrow from his bow and let loose a shot that struck the ogre straight through his neck. The creature dropped to the ground, dying in pain.

Meanwhile, Marin had already finished defeating the last of the cave orcs before turning her attention to the remaining ogre who shouted viciously as it charged toward her. The Princess Knight took her shield and threw it and hit the abdomen of the ogre. She struck the beast directly, causing it to moan in pain long enough for Marin to charge toward him. She used her momentum to run and kick upward toward the ogre, causing Marin to leap up in the air above his head. As Marin leaped high, she raised her flaming blade and struck the head of the ogre fiercely. Her strike connected and dealt a mortal blow to the creature. He fell motionless with Marin's blade stuck in his head.

Even from a distance, looking down from atop the cave entrance, Linitus could not help but be impressed with his lover's technique of taking down the enemies she fought. She never stopped to amaze him from time to time in how she deployed her own manner of fighting prowess. She was formidable and among the best. Linitus would not hold back acknowledging even for her to see with a nod of his head. Marin nodded back while scaling up to reach the top of the cave. Linitus helped her up with his hand. After catching their breath for a while and surveying their surroundings, Marin noticed a satchel from the ogre leader Linitus slew. She opened it to find several items, mainly ornate gems and pieces of gold.

However, she also saw, tucked in the chest, a folded parchment. Marin opened it with great care.

Linitus stared intently as his lover revealed the content of the message on the parchment. Linitus noticed it was a map marked with runes. Marin identified it as being written in the Nordling script. She took her time to decipher the symbols while reading out loud and trying to make sense of the map of a piece of land with a long, jagged peninsula that jutted out to the ocean in the south, and in the north was a ring of mountains. The map had various locations marked.

While reading and making sense from the map, Marin found their suspicions were true. The map had identified at the top in large runic writing as the regional name of Shimmerfrost. She pointed to the marked spot being the likely location in which they were at the south end of the jagged peninsula that was full of fjords. She had let her elven lover know they were at a famous ice cave near the coast of Storr Aegir-Hellir. Marin pointed at the nearest settlement on the map. It was a Nordling coastal settlement, shown in the map to be at the northeastern end of the peninsula. The settlement was named Nebelheim. On the northwest part of the peninsula depicted from the map, there were also many drawings of exotic longhouses with a label indicating they were villages of the dyr folk.

Linitus said it looked promising. At least that they somewhat knew where they were currently at. Then the elf next asked which of those two places would be the best place to go and which were friendly enough to receive them. Marin contemplated, showing her uncertainty, as she only knew about these from stories her mother told about Shimmerfrost. She also wondered whether they would be welcomed as guests or treated as enemies to be hunted depending on where they go. She could not help expressing this uncertainty to Linitus. She indicated that, either way, they would have to take a chance and venture out to at least one of these settlements to befriend and seek aid to return to their home. Linitus agreed and told her that perhaps it would be best to follow any path leading to Nebelheim and choose a location first since it was identified by Marin as a Nordling coastal settlement. The people there would understand in communicating with Marin in basic Nordling about their predicament and seeking vessel passage south to their home. Marin nodded and agreed.

As they looked about once again, they could not resist sharing their mutual admiration of the scenery despite being in a cold, faraway northern land. All about them they could see the vast ocean of the south hugging against the fjord cliffs of the landscape while prominent glaciers jutted out from several of the fjord cliffs and majestic snow-capped mountains hovering over the landscape from the distance.

Looking again at the map, Marin and Linitus followed the path that seemed to be the best direction. They would head north by northeast to Nebelheim. However, after noticing several partially covered footprints in the snow, Linitus looked back. He realized that something was not right. Marin looked at him, puzzled while putting her hand on his shoulder to ask what was wrong. He told her they had slain four of the orcs outside the cave beside the large ogres. Marin shrugged in uncertainty, asking why that would startle him. He told her that inside the cave there were six who had escaped, indicating something that Marin then realized as well with some concern. It was evident to her, as much as to her elven lover, that two of the cave orcs had escaped. Marin told Linitus with resolve that they then had two cave orcs to hunt along the way to their destination.

After taking a moment to catch their breath, the two adventurers marched side by side at a faster pace. Linitus used his tracking skills to locate the two remaining orcs along the way. They did not know how long it would take them to reach their enemies or their destination. But they were determined as ever to survive together in this frigid and harsh land and return home.

Chapter Fourteen

To Find a New Infernal Purpose

Lucia soared through the air amid the backdrop of darkness and burning flames hovering above the landscape. The duchess could see the large, jagged rectangular fortress. It stood atop large black cliffs where a large waterfall of flaming magma flowed down. If her lover was there, she would be eager to reunite with him. Nothing would stand in her way, she thought to herself.

However, only a few hundred yards from the jagged cliffs, a series of loud shrieks sounded. The duchess could hear it coming from behind her. She turned her body and wings in midflight only to see several hundred yards away a swarm of small reddish-purple flying imps hurling themselves at her. They carried small axes and spiked clubs and spewed small balls of flames from their mouths. Lucia reacted quickly and evaded. She flew in a constant strafe formation. She turned more and more in a serpentine-like manner as the small yet intimidating creatures tried to catch up and overtake her.

Her fear heightened. The imps could sense it. They fed on her fear. At that point in the pursuit, the duchess saw another swarm of flying imps who appeared more reddish. Many of them bore a black tattoo of a wolf. These creatures also swarmed toward her and were much closer. She closed her eyes, only to suddenly realize that this swarm of imps was not seeking to harm her. Instead, they engaged in combat with the other swarm of imps. She counted on her divine blessings with whatever trick of fate had led her to be spared.

Then the duchess watched the ensuing yet turbulent fight between the two groups of imps. They seemed to hate each other more than anything. They were just as consumed with hatred as the succubus Lucia fought and prevailed against earlier.

Regardless of the reason for their circumstances to fight each other, Lucia looked about and decided she had to take cover. Several of the first swarm of imps continued to pursue her. She decided, after looking at the distance, to take cover in an odd-looking cave. She saw it hidden in the jagged cliffs below. Lucia would hide there. She would seek refuge for the time being. Then she would continue her path to the original destination of interest. Once there, Lucia would investigate the large, jagged fortress.

Lucia entered the narrow cave. The narrow passage became a long tunnel. Lucia slowed down to avoid scraping onto the hard, sharp rocks. The narrow passage opened into a gigantic cavern. This cavern was deep within the bowels of the mountainous cliffs. Inside the cavern, in the vastness of open air, stood a large hill plateau with a traversable path that led to this plateau. At the height that Lucia hovered above, she could see hundreds of odd-looking rectangular structure buildings. They were made from cave stone. She did not know what else to do other than to use the surroundings to her advantage and outthink the remaining demonic pursuers.

Lucia hovered high above in the cavern. She looked in the direction she emerged from to see that the narrow opening of the cave tunnel was not unique. She realized she was in an open-air cavern with a large network of tunnels. With the advantage of being in a higher position, Lucia waited for the pursuing enemy imps. A group of six of them still soared straight into the cave, staring at the lone hill with the eerie city landscape featured above the hill from a distance. The creatures shrieked and looked at each other, confused and wondering where their target was. Giving a loud shriek of her own, Lucia descended on them while she whirled her demonic cat-o'-nine-tails against them. Her fast-charging strike in the air succeeded in knocking down two of the hostile imps. They plummeted to the base of the cave. Meanwhile, the other four imps directed their focus at this strange new succubus they had not seen before. The remaining four imps shrieked back and spat small balls of fire at Lucia which she evaded and continued to move toward the odd-looking cave settlement.

Lucia continued to soar through the air. She narrowly evaded another series of fireballs spewed out by the four remaining imps as she made her way closer to the lone settlement. It looked abandoned from a distance. However, after approaching it from above, Lucia saw various slow-moving bodies. They numbered in the thousands. They were humanlike but were charred and pale. Many of them wailed in agony and suffering. These tormented souls were known as the condemned. They had been sent to this hell in condemnation for their lack of faith and for living a life of habitually committing evil deeds as mortals. They were deemed by the deity spirits, especially by Calu, as unworthy of the paradise of Caelum. Lucia had not yet understood who these condemned were or how they ended up in this open cave network. She troubled herself to not ponder while keeping in mind there were still several deadly imps pursuing her. She wondered whether she could hide in one of the rectangular stone buildings that had a second-story patio and room covering. Upon doing so, Lucia waited until the imps still in pursuit lost track of her. She saw hundreds or thousands of walking zombie-like denizens below. The imps instead took their fury upon the local population, spewing fireball after fireball, setting aflame the various humanlike creatures.

    Lucia hid at first. Though she thought her chances were safer to survive in waiting out the pursuing imps, she soon changed her mind. She still had a sense of empathy and compassion for those who were more vulnerable in society. She remembered her human life and how she used her own resources, her own means, and her own resolve to help others.

    This time her own moral convictions had stirred Lucia into action. She compelled herself to respond again, even in the plane of condemnation that she was in. Emerging from the second-story building with a roof patio, Lucia expanded her batlike wings and flew quickly toward the four imps. She shrieked loudly while using her deadly multi-tailed whip to hurl at one of the imps. The targeted small demonic creature fell while the many walking condemned inhabitants looked at the fallen creature lying helpless on the charred ground. The condemned inhabitants took their revenge on the attacking creature while surrounding the imp and ripping apart its body and wings.

    As the three remaining imps looked about, Lucia flew and charged furiously at them. She grabbed one imp by its wings and whirled it around before slamming it against another imp. The collision caused the two imps to fall to the ground of the cave city as well.

    Once again, the local denizens grabbed these imps and ripped them into pieces, taking their revenge against them for the harm they caused to their condemned neighbors. The last remaining imp retreated. It feared for its life after realizing the deadliness of its newfound adversary. The imp would remember the strange exotic, yet also beautiful red-skinned succubus. The retreating imp was determined to survive and report what it witnessed to his infernal master.

Lucia considered chasing the remaining enemy imp, but instead, she opted to tend to the condemned below. These denizens cheered in their haunted voices at this newfound succubus benefactor. When Lucia came down, she was cautious in seeing how these denizens would treat her after seeing them retaliate viciously against the imps once they were on the ground. However, she could tell they would treat her differently. The condemned all knelt before her. Lucia nodded to accept their newfound form of respect toward her. She commanded them to rise while she surveyed the damage the imps caused the denizens. In part, she felt guilty. Despite coming to their aid, she had seen herself in some sense as the source of the cause of their losses. Had she not gone to their settlement, it was likely they would not have suffered such losses, a half dozen or more. But she knew she had in her own conviction made the right course of action to intercede in their behalf.

Lucia walked about and saw one of the local condemned creatures in agony. She placed her hand on its charred forehead as it wilted in utter pain. It spoke in its decrepit form. It begged for her to end its agony. Lucia nodded with reluctance. She wished she had some way to heal it instead. It pained Lucia that she did not. The duchess did not have some way to transfer pain to her. As soon as Lucia had taken one of the fallen imps' axes, she asked the condemned creature what his name was. The creature spoke in pain, telling her in an unfamiliar language. Regardless, Lucia understood what he had said. She nodded and replied that she would remember him even if he ceased to exist in another life. The creature thanked her while nodding and closing his eyes. The other condemned creatures moaned and turned their heads away while Lucia felt a sense of guilt and hesitance. She raised the small ax and took a deep breath. Then, finally, she compelled herself to strike swiftly, severing the condemned creature's head from the rest of his charred-looking corpse. She shrieked in a mournful tone before turning and realizing that it was done. This condemned creature was no more. His suffering had ended permanently, but so also his last life.

Lucia only had his name to remember and pass on. She would say his name aloud. Lucia told the rest of the condemned denizens she would remember his name and commanded every one of them to do the same. The duchess then told each one of them with a compelled sense of morality to say aloud one by one their names so she would remember them and alas she would tell them her name so they would know her as well.

When the duchess did say her name aloud, some of the condemned responded familiarly from knowing her in their previous lives. These were dead, fallen humans, orcs, and goblins. Many of them had done unspeakable things in their previous lives. Some of them were condemned after they sought to further the cause they fought for at the side of her late lover, Decius, at the time of his rebellion ten years ago.

Those who recognized her proclaimed her as their new patron lady of the condemned. They picked her up while convincing the other condemned who did not know her before to accept her as their leader.

Lucia acknowledged their acceptance. She realized that despite electing to be in this place of condemnation in pursuit of her lover, she now had another meaningful purpose. She would lead the condemned in hell and serve as their matron, just as she had done for her subjects and fellow citizens of the Imperial Remnant before. Lucia would find Decius (wherever he would be) and offer him the allegiance of these newfound followers as a gift of their infernal reunion.

Chapter Fifteen

Discerning among Friends and Foes

Three days and two nights had passed since Linitus and Marin had stepped out into the light and left the ice cave near the fjords of Storr Aegir-Hellir. They were dozens of miles north and drifting northeast. They were uncertain how many more days it would take them to reach Nebelheim, but they were close to reaching the northern fjords of Nebel Bay. They were both sure that they could reach their destination in three days if the weather was calm despite it being cold even in spring. It was at least colder than what the two of them were accustomed to in Swordbane.

They rested while traveling to see the fjords from the distance from atop a clear hill scattered with a few forest thickets. They both could not help but again marvel at the beauty of the nature they saw with waters clear enough to reflect the cloudy sky. At sunset, Linitus returned after catching two fish. Marin had prepared a makeshift fire pit after collecting some nearby fallen wood. They ate their fish while using their leather costrels (or flasks) to drink water they collected earlier from a nearby stream.

There were moments that the two would find themselves all alone, depending on each other's survival, while finding time to catch up and reminisce about their earlier years together. Linitus admitted to Marin that, of all the times he had used his various skills to aid them on their quests, it seemed this time from his vantage point the tide had turned in which he was depending more on Marin in this unfamiliar land. Marin laughed also while agreeing. She admitted that as hostile as this land was to them both, perhaps her familiarity with her mother's culture from folk tales and even her knowledge of the written Nordling runic language would aid them in their quest to return home. She comforted her lover, putting her hand on his shoulder. Marin told Linitus that even if he was not accustomed to relying more on her than the other way around, at least they both could understand each other's perspective that much more. Linitus nodded while confiding to her his inward appreciation to the deity spirits that at least they were together. They still had each other, even if alone from everyone else they knew in this cold forest and mountainous land. If he had to choose the one to spend his life in such a way, it would be with her.

Touched by Linitus's admission, Marin said no words. Instead, she gave him an intimate look and stared deep into his eyes. She locked her mouth to his and gave him a deep kiss. He accepted it and returned the gesture. After the two lovers exchanged deep kisses, they both were tempted to forget their surroundings and fall into their feelings and passions to be intimate with one another. However, they both stopped after several kisses and agreed the moment would have to wait when they knew they were in a much safer place.

After breaking off, Linitus told Marin that just like the night before, he would stand watch, so she could sleep throughout the evening as he stood guard. They both knew there were at least two cave orcs that had evaded them in the ice cave. Marin and Linitus would have to be alert. At least one of them had to stay awake in case the two cave orcs found them and attacked or, worse, found reinforcements to attack them.

Linitus offered Marin to use his camouflage cloak to stay warm and to stay shrouded because of its magical effects. Marin, however, thought of another idea. Thinking as creatively as she had learned from her lover, she suggested instead that she sleep without the cloak. She proposed using herself as bait. Linitus would use the cloak to hide himself and lie in wait. He would alert her and attack at a moment's notice any enemies ambushing her, not suspecting that her lover was hiding and lying in wait to catch them.

Linitus acknowledged the potential merits and ingeniousness of Marin's idea. Linitus was, however, somewhat reluctant. He told Marin when asked, he said he feared putting her, the person he loved, in harm's way. Marin told him that if they wanted to have any chance at baiting the cave orcs or any other enemies while having the greatest chance of success, this would be it.

Sighing and contemplating, Linitus finally agreed. After a few hours of implementing Marin's idea, Linitus stood hiding a dozen yards away, looking at Marin as she slept near the lit fire pit atop the hill.

Not long after, shadowy figures moved about and made a noise. They grunted and snarled while talking among each other. The figures soon became visible to Linitus when they emerged from the shadows and went near the fire pit. There were two cave orcs (the same ones Linitus recognized) and a small warband of green goblins armed with spears. Among the goblins, one goblin stood out. He wore an ornate headdress and wielded a spiked club. This notable goblin appeared to be the shaman of the warband. Behind this goblin shaman appeared also two small humanoid figures wearing bone armor, including the skulls of deer and leather armor. They wielded jagged wooden clubs and spoke a dwarven dialect that Linitus could hear but did not understand. He could see Marin's eyes lit up while keeping her head down and quenching her sword in her scabbard. She could make out what the two figures said and knew as much as Linitus surmised that these figures in the warband were an unfamiliar type of dwarves, perhaps native to this part of the world.

Locking eyes from a distance toward where Linitus was last at before he used his camouflage to hide from plain sight, Marin nodded and winked. This was her cue. She was ready to get up and strike the enemies without hesitation, having the advantage of surprise, with them not knowing that she was awake and poised to fight them. She got up in one fluid motion, turning back and unsheathing her sword. By then, three arrows whistled through the air and struck three goblins that were close to each other. Marin was surprised, thinking her life would pass before her eyes if she had been the intended target before realizing that it was Linitus who made the first strike and, as usual, surprised her as much as their enemies.

Shocked, Marin looked in various directions where the three arrows had come from. The warband of goblins, orcs, and pale dwarves were startled and then enraged. They unleashed loud war cries. Marin then pressed the advantage by striking one of the two cave orcs. The other cave orc fell back and called for the warband to retreat, fearing once again that their newfound adversaries were deadlier than the forces they had mustered and were sufficient to prevail.

The other members of the warband answered their dark brethren's call and retreated. Linitus had already revealed himself after removing his cloak to shoot arrows with his drawn bow. He acted with haste and gave chase to the enemies. The elf ranger unleashed one arrow after another and struck them down. Marin also pursued them on foot but relied on her ability to charge and strike her enemies down as soon as she could catch up to them to whittle down their numbers. However, following the enemy became more difficult for Linitus and Marin to not lose their location. Added to the list of uncontrollable variables also, nightfall made it harder to track the enemy warband even with Marin using her flaming sword as a source of light and Linitus using a sticky silk bulb arrow as an improvised torch after setting alight on the makeshift fire pit.

Within moments, another series of loud war cries sounded. These war cries were different, and from hearing the voices Marin, though surprised, was also somewhat relieved and excited to recognize. These cries were by Nordlings who were on the lookout. They were hunting the same enemies.

Marin and Linitus approached. They could see the figures carrying torches and various melee weapons. These warriors hacked away at the remaining goblins and fearsome pale dwarves. These figures were tall, bearded male Nordling warriors. They wore various types of leather and fur. Some wore intricate horned helmets and deer bone helmets like the ones worn by the dwarves they slew. Linitus and Marin still had their weapons ready. They still did not know if these Nordling warriors would treat them as friends or foes. Marin and Linitus wanted to avoid the chance of making new enemies and causing unnecessary bloodshed. Marin called out the word for "friend" in Nordling to tell the Nordling warband they were not enemies.

Upon her call, the members of the Nordling warband looked and turned to them. At first, they still showed fierce looks, and their posture did not adjust to one of benevolence. However, suddenly the group leader responded with the same word Marin had said in the Nordling language. Marin returned the call of the same word. Linitus used his instincts to trust Marin in not perceiving this warband as an immediate threat. The elf ranger slowly lowered his bow at the same time Marin lowered her sword and shield in a gesture of trust and goodwill. They hoped these Nordling warriors would respond in kind and do the same. Their gamble proved to be right.

The presumed warband chieftain, who wore an ornate horned helmet, called for the rest of his company to lower their weapons, which they did as well. The Nordling warband chieftain approached Marin. He gave his name by uttering one word: "Arik." Marin motioned with her hand to herself. She said her name aloud while pointing to Linitus and saying his name aloud to identify him as well. Linitus, speaking to Marin, decided that perhaps it was as good a time as any since facing hostility at each turn in their journey to ask the way to Nebelheim. Marin agreed and spoke two words as a question to ask the whereabouts of Nebelheim to Arik. The Nordling chieftain understood and could tell that they were strangers. He was intrigued why Marin knew some words in the local Nordling language and presumed her to be of Nordling ancestry based on her appearance.

Marin had inherited many of the physical features from her mother's Nordling ancestry. This included her fair skin, blue eyes, and her hair being blonde (though it was darker compared to many other Nordlings that had lighter shades of blonde hair). Marin in fact had golden-brown hair that many would consider as being dark blonde. This was attributed to her background being a mixture of Nordling and Citadellan ethnicities (as Citadellans on the other hand were known to have dark brown or black hair). Regardless of her distinct appearance it would not be hard for many of the local humans in Shimmerfrost to assume she was a local herself save for the foreign clothing and armor she wore. Even her physical disposition of behavior was reminiscent of how Nordling women would behave in being headstrong and even assertive at times. However at times she also acted with a Citadellan form of etiquette from her paternal side of culture that seemed more formal compared to the Nordling manner of behavior that lacked formalities and in which many Citadellans would consider unrefined, barbaric, and uncivilized by their standards. Marin, however, had no such prejudices and understood the differences between her mother's and father's sides as simply differences between cultures. She understood very well like her father had in being fond of her late mother during his first major political visit to Nordling territory in the coastal woodlands of the northwest, still far south of Shimmerfrost.

Being an adult, Marin felt she could understand on a deeper level what her father went through in being acquainted with those from cultures considered foreign and remote from hers and his. She was eager to become familiar with the people of this land while she and Linitus sought a way home to the warm temperate southwestern coastlands of Hesperion.

Arik motioned with his hand for Linitus and Marin to follow him and his warband back to Nebelheim where this group had come from. Though Marin understood basic Nordling and could make out Arik's pronunciation of some words that sounded somewhat different from the Nordling dialect of her mother's land, it was sufficient for the two to communicate.

After surveying the carnage that Arik's warriors had caused, Marin complimented the warband. She stated she would sing songs of glory to them as a gesture to better befriend their newfound acquaintances. Linitus meanwhile appeared somewhat surprised and concerned. It was so apparent that both Marin and Arik took notice and asked what was wrong. Linitus told Marin, which she later translated to Arik, that though Arik's warriors slayed many goblins and all the fearsome dwarven barbarians, there were two unaccounted for among the slain. They had escaped, the goblin shaman and a cave orc.

Despite their escape, Linitus could still pick the cave orc's scent with his experience in tracking, not to mention that he had secretly planted one of the magical ward stones on the cave orc by flinging it at him with a small glob of sticky silk adhesive. This ward stone was one of several he took with him from Wyatt's skyship before they had departed that fateful day for the cave mine near Great Azure Lake. Linitus used another matching magical ward stone. This one hummed and vibrated a low tone to the other one planted on the cave orc. The one Linitus had would continue to hum and vibrate increasingly louder as the elf ranger drew closer to the other ward stone planted on the cave orc.

Linitus's genius once again impressed Marin and still made her somewhat jealous. She felt she had just outdone her elven lover in thinking cleverly ever since arriving in Shimmerfrost only to see he was still one or two steps ahead of her when she least expected it. Marin both envied and admired this quality of Linitus and she aspired to be like him in her own way. The Princess Knight surprised him and planted a kiss on his lips while complimenting him on his cunning.

Arik and the other Nordling warriors did not understand until Marin mustered what few words she knew in her mother's Nordling tongue to translate what Linitus said, so they could understand Linitus's plan. Amazed by the elf's cunning, the Nordling warriors also complimented the elf despite their mild apprehension and distrust toward him. They still regarded him as somewhat of an outsider that they would tolerate in part only for his relationship with Marin, whom they were freer to accept as their own fellow Nordling.

Linitus could see this invisible and subliminal barrier of prejudice and preference. He let it be while hoping that, in due time, they would come to see and recognize him as a genuine friend and that they could trust him for his own merit and not by his relationship to Marin. He also hoped they would rethink their impression of others different from them.

Marin knew this also and spoke to her lover, telling him she could read his mind and understand that he knew how to put others and their differences before him, even when giving them time to remove barriers from building common understanding and respect. She admitted it was a quality that she admired and loved about him, his empathy. To her, he was a miraculous gift that came to her life from the deity spirits as a blessing in disguise to learn from. Linitus, humbled and appreciative, nodded modestly, and Marin kissed him once again.

Her attachment to the elf ranger also struck the Nordlings of this region as odd. With few exceptions, the Nordlings in Shimmerfrost did not become accustomed to nor thought it acceptable for those of different sentient races or species to have relations with one another. Regardless, they would display no outward objection. They accepted what they saw without comment, practicing their own limited form of tolerance despite not being exposed to this unique aspect of relationships between different races or species in their own native lands.

Though they wanted to make camp, Marin and Linitus pressed their newfound allies onward, using the ward stone and pivoting to the direction that it seemed most noticeable in vibrating and humming while giving off a light faint translucent blue coloration. The cave orc and the goblin shaman had a good head start. However, as much as they could run and hide, Linitus eventually would catch up by tracking them using the ward stones.

Chapter Sixteen

Finding the Way to Shimmerfrost

A lone skyship stood out against the cloudy and rainy sky as it hovered over the canopy of alder, fir, and maple trees. The floating vessel approached a large coastal settlement. The settlement comprised of dozens of crafted wooden longhouses. There were also several large wooden docks. These docks jutted out from the coastal inlet. Inside the vessel, two figures looked below in awe of the mesmerizing and serene forest landscape that hugged the coastal bay and surrounded the settlement. These figures, Wyatt and Peat, departed from Citadella Neapola only less than two days ago. Now, they finally arrived at the Nordling settlement of Aegir-Hafn. Like the Kingdom of Swordbane and its capital, the Nordlings of the various coastal woodland settlements rebuilt their homes and lives. They too endured savage brutality brought by Decius (when alive) and the Imperial Remnant forces more than ten years ago. However, the tall and sturdy Nordlings were as resilient and determined as the various peoples of Swordbane in rebuilding their homes.

The skyship circled several times above the main building of the settlement. That building was the chieftain's hall. It was a tall five-story wooden longhouse. Onboard, Wyatt and Peak looked down. The dwarf pointed at the settlement's leader, a female Nordling chieftain. This leader was a tall Nordling woman of strong stature. The chieftainess had fair skin, sunflower-blonde hair, and blue eyes. She wore an elaborate headdress of fur, animal bone, and amber. She wore a mix of linen, wool, and fur clothes. This chieftainess also had on various pieces of jewelry. These pieces were exquisite and made of gold and amber. She was the renowned Nordling leader Helga. She was also Marin's aunt on her mother's side.

Helga had just stepped out from the chieftain's hall. Behind her stood an elite team of Nordling bodyguards. It was Helga who looked at the sky. She noticed the arrival of familiar guests. Helga then noticed a flash lighting up the skyship as she continued to gaze above. Her surprise increased when she noticed another flash of light a few yards away. Wyatt and Peat had teleported with Wyatt's magic. The quick teleportation caught Helga somewhat by surprise and in awe. She had not seen that done in many years since she last saw Wyatt and the rest of the Comradery.

Helga, though delighted and honored to welcome Wyatt and Peat, was surprised to notice that Linitus and her niece, Marin, were not in their company. She asked the two members of the Comradery where the other members of their order were. Wyatt frowned, his dark gray pointed hat pointed down. Peat hesitated for a moment. He stomached his apprehension at answering with a stern voice in explaining all that had transpired, which led to the disappearance of their two comrades. After hearing the dwarf's account of what had happened, Helga frowned. She became visibly concerned. She hoped that Marin and Linitus survived by escaping through the portal. Helga believed the two lovers would persevere and survive. She also expressed her faith in Peat and Wyatt that they would find Linitus and Marin.

Wyatt and Peat continued to explain that they were headed north to find their missing companions. They exclaimed that they also stopped at Aegir-Hafn to follow King Ascentius's explicit instruction. They were to seek Helga for aid.

The Nordling chieftainess mulled over the matter. She wanted to rescue Marin and Linitus as much as Ascentius, but like the Swordbane monarch, she too had her reservations. Helga knew her presence was still needed by her people for the continued rebuilding of the settlement. She also did not want to risk being seen as an invader by their Nordling brethren in the far north should she dispatch too many of her own warriors. Not to mention, she also needed to retain as many of her warriors as possible for the settlement's defense. Helga wanted to be ready at all times in case the Imperial Remnant ever decided to invade again like they did over ten years ago.

Last in her reasons of contemplation for providing aid, Helga had only heard stories about Shimmerfrost while growing up. She had no personal experience of giving the adventurers any specific directions when traveling to the far north region. Only a handful of visitors come from Shimmerfrost to visit Aegir-Hafn. The same could be said that only a same small number of visitors from Aegir-Hafn that had ever ventured to Shimmerfrost and returned home with amazing stories to tell.

In fact, there was one elderly man in the village who had been there before. He came forward to explain that he took part in several whale hunts and other fishing ventures along the coastlands of Aegir-Hafn and Shimmerfrost. The elder Nordling explained he could no longer muster his own strength to row one of the expeditionary long boats. Still, he had longed to venture far north and see Shimmerfrost once again. He offered his services as a guide to show Wyatt and Peat the way to Shimmerfrost, even from the sky.

Wyatt and Peat agreed to hire this elder Nordling as part of their expedition team. The two companions, however, had no difficulty convincing him to join their company free of charge. The elder Nordling only requested that his clients make time on the journey to go fishing off the coast of Shimmerfrost. Wyatt and Peat agreed without hesitation. Peat was excited to share pastime stories with the elderly fisherman. The dwarf grew tired at times of Wyatt's company in performing magic tricks. The wizard's performances included mildly humorous ones at the dwarf's expense. Peat, however, did not always find these tricks funny, especially when Wyatt teleported a beaver on top of Peat's horned helmet and another one that managed to fit inside his helmet when he wore it.

Before Wyatt and Peat departed, Helga still wanted to assist them in finding her niece and nephew-in-law. Though not able to provide an official retinue of her own Nordling warriors to assist them in finding their comrades, the Nordling chieftainess offered an alternative solution. She gave the mercenaries in her settlement the chance to travel and adventure onboard the skyship by joining the halfling and dwarf adventurers on their quest.

After hearing Helga's impromptu decree, several mercenaries came forward and volunteered. There were twelve of them, all tall and strong Nordling mercenaries. They belonged to an elite berserker class of warriors. They wore various types of leather and fur armor, including a large coat and cowl made from bear skin. They also wielded various types of weapons made of wood, iron, and steel. These mercenaries were part of an elite fraternal company Peat was familiar with though vaguely. The dwarf heard of them from passing stories at several mead halls and bars in the Nordling district of Swordbane's capital. The Nordling locals knew these berserker mercenaries as the Brotherhood of the Banesmen, or simply the Banesmen.

This elite fraternal group attributed that name to their being hired for taking on the most dangerous quests and vanquishing the most dreaded foes in the lands of the Nordlings. They sought both wealth and fame. They would be sure to gain enough gold from their adventures and spend it in the mead hall while listening to the songs of praise and the glory for their great deeds.

Peat and Wyatt accepted the offer of the Banesmen. Meanwhile, Helga offered to pay the Banesmen's services on Peat and Wyatt's behalf as a small token gesture of gratitude toward the Comradery for their services and deeds in the past. Helga had not forgotten that the Comradery, including her niece Marin, with the other forces of Swordbane came to her people's aid more than a decade ago when Decius and his Remnant forces ravaged the coastal lands of the Nordlings, including Helga's own settlement.

The Nordling chieftainess also offered Wyatt, Peat, and their newly formed crew to stay and rest overnight at the chieftain's mead hall before departing. However, the newly formed crew respectfully declined the offer. Peat spoke to Helga on behalf of this newly formed crew that time was of the essence to find his comrades as they did not know what dangers Marin and Linitus likely faced far north.

Helga understood their reasoning and nodded. She sent them her blessing to make haste in departing. However, she offered, as a concession, for the skyship crew to take as many provisions as they can carry, including mead and beer. Peat, with an enormous grin on his face, gave his immediate approval of that gesture of Nordling hospitality.

Wyatt, however, shook his head and frowned in disapproval at seeing some of the extra provisions. At least the alcohol, was unnecessary. The halfling wizard was concerned that such provisions onboard could increase to indulgences in partaking alcohol and possibly worse in leading to drunken brawls when the skyship was sky-bound.

Peat, seeing the wizard's apprehension, tried to ease his concern as consolation by stating the dwarf himself would take only as many provisions of alcohol as he could fit in the captain's cabin. He would lock it up and take charge of distributing modest small allotments to the rest of the Nordling crew for consumption. Wyatt rolled his eyes and responded with the expression in indicating that this was exactly what he was afraid of, leaving the dwarf in charge of the alcohol.

The halfling wizard doubted whether his dwarf companion could refrain from overindulging. Wyatt knew well enough that Peat enjoyed drinking as much beer and mead as the dwarf also did when it came to smoking and brawling. In order to for the dwarf to stay true to his word and exercise moderation strictly, Wyatt made Peat agree that the moment he had gone astray by overindulging, the halfling wizard would teleport all the alcohol into the ocean to feed the Hafn salmon or other wildlife below. Peat nearly collapsed at the thought of the wizard doing such a thing but knew that Wyatt very well could and would do so. The wizard at least had a way to ensure the dwarf's vested interest in wanting to keep to this arrangement. If he did not, then Peat would get rid of all the alcohol. At that point, he would not only blame himself, but the thirteen Nordlings who joined the skyship's new crew would also be upset.

Finally, the last arrangements were made and the provisions transferred to the skyship from Aegir-Hafn through Wyatt's teleportation magic. The skyship prepared to depart. The floating vessel had set its sails to take a course north by northwest. In less than a day, Wyatt and Peat's newly crewed vessel departed from Aegir-Hafn before sunset. Many of the townsfolk and the chieftainess below cheered and waved farewell. The elder Nordling guide onboard informed Wyatt and Peat that with steady, fair winds, they could reach the nearest major coastal settlement of Nebelheim within a week.

Chapter Seventeen

Seeking an Audience with the Overlord

Two days passed since Lucia arrived at the strange hidden settlement of Caverna Necropolis and only a day passed since she left that locale. Lucia soared through the complex cave network deep inside the cliff basin. She planned to find a passage leading outside atop the highest plain in Infernum. She had gained limited information from the denizens of the settlement, as they had never found a different passage to the cave other than the one she used when she first entered. Lucia flew fast and switched to different tunnel passages several times. Some passages she navigated in led to dead ends. Despite feeling despair, Lucia still did not give up. No matter what, she would reunite with her long-lost lover and soulmate. She and Decius would become one in union again. At some point, she found a passage that led to a vertical shaft opening. It was a cave pit that would provide a means to exit to the surface.

Lucia flew swiftly outside. The duchess sighed in relief as she felt the heat becoming more noticeable. It was this sign that she knew she had made it back to the surface. While looking about and keeping an eye out for any potential enemies, she spotted from a few miles away the same jagged and rectangular fortress she saw earlier from looking upward while in the lower plain of this infernal realm about two days prior. She realized how close she was to reaching her destination. Lucia knew she could make it there without interruption in a matter of minutes. At least she presumed that would be the case if no other demonic being lay in wait to ambush her and set her back from reaching her destination.

But Lucia also realized immediately that in her current location, she was surrounded by several towering structures. She could not tell whether these structures were natural rock formations or if these were made by some expert stonemasons carving preexisting rocks. At least, a dozen of these towering structures lay next to each other. Each one had a menacing hole, almost like an eye. Lucia would later find out that this ominous locale came to be known as Sanctum Oculi Malum. However, for the time being, these many menacing towers were still a mystery to her.

On the ground of these towering structures were vents where gas rose a few feet from the surface. A few rectangular structures also lay in front of these structures. Lucia looked about with caution but did not see any inhabitants from a distance. Still, she reminded herself that she could not discount the possibility that some dangerous denizens with designs to harm her or any bystander might lurk behind or inside those structures.

The duchess flew lower, closer to the steam vents, which provided some cover from potential stalkers. She darted ahead, intending to make her way past these strange eyelike cave towers. Lucia was still determined to reach the strange, large fortress in the distance.

When Lucia was close to exiting the high towers area, she hid behind the statue of a large and hellacious beast that was dozens of feet tall and then surveyed not only the lone fortress from afar but also the swarm of menacing red imps that soared in the air and was approaching her unaware that she was there. Lucia looked behind her shoulder as they soared past her. She took note that she was not the object of their attention. Instead, it was a different group of flying imps with a violet-maroon color that emerged from one of the eyelike openings of the tower mountains. Both groups of imps were then locked in combat. They tore at each other in a vicious display. It amazed Lucia to see the intensity of the fight. She became bewildered as to why these two groups from the same hellish kind were fighting each other.

But as she remained puzzled at the violent spectacle, she realized that the statue she clung to moved. It was no statue. Rather, it was some beast that apparently woke up just then. The beast opened one eye that was under its protruding horn and above its strangely jagged head. Its head also had two additional horns that protruded horizontally and a winged crest at the back of its head. Both were startled at the sight of each other. Lucia quickly vaulted and soared away from the creature while it let out a deafening roar. This creature then gave chase, only to stop as it was closing in when it reached the bank of the river of lava.

Lucia sighed while looking back and then turned her attention to the jagged fortress ahead. She knew it was now or never. She could no longer hide or hold back. Lucia would face any remaining opposition head-on or die trying. It was time to find out if her lover was there or if she would have to search further to reunite with him.

Alone, Lucia with her batlike wings soared higher and higher in the black sky that intermittently flashed brightly from the eruptions from distant volcanoes. The duchess looked down while still flying. She could not help but marvel at the terrifying yet majestic fortress. It was surrounded by a moat filled with flowing lava and burning magma that came from a nearby perpetually erupting volcano. Lava flowed like a waterfall. It cascaded to the next basin in the lower plains of Infernum.

Lucia instinctively felt she was close to her soulmate even though she could not see him. Still, she in her own innate way, called out in loud shrieks that could be heard. If he was there, she wanted him to know, just like before in their previous mortal lives when he gave a large howl sound similar to a wolf.

Eventually, a swarm of dark red flying imps covered with the black tattoo flew to her. They did not attack her like before. Lucia would take the risk that these creatures, at least these types of imps, though cautious and deadly had reasonable dispositions and could assess unknown entities they encountered. Lucia, in the form of a succubus, was different from all the other succubi these imps were familiar with. They did not know what to make of her. These imps hesitated to take any action until they could determine what course would please their overlord.

Lucia, being perceptive of their natural behavior, made the next move in giving the next indication of their assessment of her while seeing how they would react while both parties still hovered in midair. Lucia expressed her intentions in her Citadellan tongue. She demanded they take her to their leader. She said that by doing so, they would be well-rewarded. One imp, able to speak in the same tongue was familiar with her words. The imp found it strange that he found another creature that spoke the same language as their master. This imp believed her but still asked how they would know that their master wanted her.

Lucia responded with confidence and authority that they were soulmates separated by his death, but they longed for each other and to be reunited in the afterlife. She also threatened them that if they did not escort her to see Decius, she would let him know eventually when she found him. She would see to it they would be hunted down for challenging his consort's authority.

The imps all at once became terrified. They evaluated her words with care. They knew that the risk of reward, even if she lied, far outweighed the risk of doubting her and incurring their master's wrath. The speaker of the imps nodded, telling her discretely to follow them. Lucia nodded. After descending to the main fortress gate, Lucia followed behind the swarm of imps. Upon entering the courtyard of the jagged fortress, which was surrounded by a series of charred, bloodstained black-and-red columns, Lucia followed the instructions of the leading imp and waited until he had informed his overlord of her arrival and of her request for an audience. Moments later, the doors to the fortress opened. She could enter.

Chapter Eighteen

An Infernal Reunion

The lone shriek was loud enough to be heard inside the fortress. Decius could hear the noise from within his throne room. He knew this had to be a succubus of some sort. The dux stayed composed and seated on his throne.

For several years, Decius strove to elevate himself as the supreme overlord of hell. All the more while he contested the remaining entirety of the infernal domain with the incumbent adversary, Orcus, the Lord of Punishment. Orcus was the original and uncontested overlord of all Infernum. That changed once Decius arrived.

Decius once had been determined to rule over his domain when he was a mortal in Terrunaemara. For the past ten years, he was determined to do the same in hell. Only when he was in his spectral form could he project his avatar and commune with those who summoned him from the mortal realm. For most of his time, he was in his regular physical form gathering his forces in Infernum and turned against Orcus.

Many of the imps switched allegiances in favor of Decius. They saw him as being a more worthy and more calculating leader, worthy to become Infernum's overlord. Unlike Orcus, Decius exhibited a darkness and evil that was orderly even if it was violent. For the converted imps, it was a welcomed change to Orcus's form of control, which was devoid of order in preference for sheer enjoyment in torture and punishment. Orcus represented chaos without purpose. It was a form many imps saw as too excessive and unnecessary.

Meanwhile, many other imps remained loyal to Orcus. Those imps preferred the status quo that Orcus represented. Because of the division among the imps since Decius's arrival, hell had been in a constant state of perpetual war ever since. It was a war that many other denizens, especially the condemned original mortals from Terrunaemara, preferred to stay out of. They clung on surviving and living out their miserable form of a last life as long as possible. The condemned believed that the best form of survival would be to congregate in scattered communities. They sought mutual protection in numbers while trying to avoid giving away their presence by loitering around the open plains of the Infernum. They kept a low profile as much as possible during this infernal war. Their lives were still in danger however as Orcus would frequently order swarms of imps led by his succubi to raid their settlements. These raiding parties would bring back prisoners for Orcus's enjoyment and torture. Orcus relished his role of seeing that the condemned suffered.

As for the succubi and their role in the infernal war, these alluring sirens of demonic and mysterious origin with protruding horns and batlike wings had also initially joined Decius ever since his arrival to this hell. The demonic sirens, however, would later betray Decius in his last standoff with Orcus. It was a betrayal that Decius would never forget, and he swore he would exact his revenge against the succubi.

It was then that Decius realized, after hearing the succubus's voice, outside that he had an opportunity to exact this revenge for their betrayal. Still, he became captivated by the tone of shriek. Decius could not recall which succubus possessed such type of sound when shrieking.

Decius took some time to ponder who this mysterious succubus could be. He wondered what her motives were for disturbing him in his domain in the infernal realm. A swirl of several more thoughts came into Decius's head. He considered that this might be an attempt to deceive him. Decius thought to himself, perhaps this succubus sought to entice him. He suspected she would attempt to lure him away from his well-guarded domain. Perhaps she intended to lead him with an enticing opportunity. Perhaps to gain the upper hand against Orcus, only to find himself surrounded and ambushed by a larger enemy force loyal to Orcus. This was one possibility that Decius became suspicious of the unknown succubus in his small, fortified domain. Decius also expected to be besieged and attacked in his fortress by Orcus, while this succubus kept Decius distracted. He knew either way this succubus would attempt to take advantage of the dux for her gain to court favor with Orcus.

Regardless of the unknown succubus's intentions, Decius was still invigorated by an ever-growing curiosity about her. An imp servant then entered Decius's ornate throne room. The imp bowed before Dux Decius while announcing that a lone succubus had sought him out and wished to join in union with him.

The dux in his dark, menacing werewolf form could not hold back his astonishment and dubious suspicion. He considered that this may be a trick by this succubus to lure his trust again. Decius took that into account after he recalled being betrayed once by the succubi. The dux granted the request. Meanwhile, he planned to be ready. He would slaughter the succubus as his revenge for the past betrayal in his unsuccessful bid for absolute rule over the entire realm of hell.

However, with a persistent afterthought of curiosity, Decius asked the imp which among the succubi out of the seventy-two by name it was that wanted the dux's audience. The imp could not hold back in being uncertain while shrugging. Regardless, Decius motioned with his claw-like hand for the imp to proceed in granting the succubus an audience with him.

Decius returned to his seat as the imp carried out his order. The dux was intent on catching the suspicious succubus by surprise in a somewhat prepared posture in which he would be ready to rise and strike at will.

A moment later, the chamber door opened and a winged creature made her way toward the dux. Decius was curious. He could not fully make out which of the seventy-two succubi she was even to the point of not withholding in asking the lone demonic siren aloud. He did not recognize her until she paused. Decius, startled and unsure if this was a deceptive attack, quickly rose from his throne, only to realize she had kneeled before him a few paces away. Decius's disposition shifted to being in awe. His werewolf jaws dropped at what he saw.

He realized that this succubus was not one of the seventy-two succubi who betrayed him. Rather, she was that one being who was most devoted to him. Upon seeing her face and recognizing her, he became perplexed. She was his soulmate in his previous life, which he could recognize with shock despite her slight change of appearance as a succubus.

Decius lamented. He could not restrain himself from howling furiously and uncontrollably. His howl became so loud that it startled his loyal denizens who could hear him within his infernal fortress palace compound. He kneeled next to the lone black-haired, red-skinned succubus while expressing both remorse and sadness at seeing her again.

Of all the people he knew as a mortal, she was the last one he imagined being here with him. It pained him to see her condemned with him so much that he could not hold back but asked inquisitively why she was there. However, he knew the answer, and both he and the succubus knew he did not need to ask even though he still did. Even more so, they shared gazes while embracing each other. The two of them did not care how different they looked in their own post-mortal forms. They both knew what each other was thinking. They could read each other's expressions and feel from each other's aura how they felt.

Lucia, in her somewhat emotional but impassioned voice, finally spoke. She told him she meant it both as mortals and this time in their post-mortal life that they were soulmates. She intended one day to reunite with him no matter what it would cost her. Lucia continued to tell Decius she loved him with all her heart. Not even being granted divine admission into the paradise of Caelum would sway her from being with him even in hell. She would not change her mind no matter how many times to enter the realm of condemnation and suffering and be with him. She would do whatever it took to be with her lover and her eternal soulmate.

Decius knew from her words and actions that it was true. It stirred emotions within him. He embraced her more firmly, planting a kiss with his snout. He nodded and told her he knew. Decius wept while telling Lucia that she deserved better in her station than being assigned to this realm in the afterlife. Lucia placed her hand gently near his jagged mouth while interjecting that she was content and that she, in fact, received far beyond what he considered better. She got exactly what, or more correctly, who she wanted. She had found again the one person she loved more than any other in her previous life. This time she swore nothing would keep them physically separated like before for so long. They would live together, and though this infernal realm was still surreal and strange to her, she would make sure that they would rule it together. She would aid him again in their post-mortal lives as she had done in their mortal lives in Terrunaemara. They would be physically together again as a couple destined to rule all the domains—this infernal realm and possibly beyond.

Decius nodded while gradually letting go of Lucia. He told her that there was much to discuss about the past ten years since he had been condemned to Hadao Infernum. Before, he had only a fraction of the time as a ghost when summoned to the mortal plane to tell her about his experiences in the infernal realm. This time was different. He could share his experiences with her more directly in this condemned place where they both live together in actual union. He could directly rely on Lucia again as his consort and work together. Only this time, they would conquer all of Infernum.

Lucia intended to advise him as much as she could, including her limited and recent experiences in this hostile realm. They could conspire to end the current ruling occupant's domination of this realm once and for all.

Chapter Nineteen

Doire na Cairn

They were days into their pursuit and took only a few hours of rest at nightfall to reach their next destination. Linitus, Marin, and their befriended Nordling company led by Arik arrived at a strange sight at midday. They found themselves deep inside a green forest filled with ferns and various pine trees. They arrived at a clearance within the serene forest.

Inside the clearance (which had some fern vegetation overgrowth) lay an assortment of menhirs (also known as megalithic standing stones). Some of these megalithic stones included ones that appeared to be made of granite with carvings of flowing spirals, cairns (stacks of stones), and dolmen (two megaliths supporting a horizontal slab of stone). There was also a large stone mound at the center. Just behind the megaliths stood a prominent small grove of large yew trees bearing beautiful but poisonous red berries. These trees were decorated with various hanging ceramic ornaments carved with woven patterns. It was a strange yet awe-inspiring sight. However, the company kept their silence. They spotted before this site their two targets: the lone cave orc who evaded Marin and Linitus from their earlier cave encounter and the goblin shaman that had aided him.

Marin whispered to Arik, curiously asking him why these two vile creatures stopped at the sight of these stones. Arik, in Nordling, replied in a low and cautious voice that they were likely trying to summon a creature known as Wendigo and that they were at an ancient sacred site revered by a mysterious people, the dyr folk, who were enemies. Arik stated that these dyr folk called the site Doire na Cairn, which translated to "Stone

Mound Grove." However, when translating what Arik said to Linitus, Marin still had a somewhat horrified look. Linitus became curious about who Wendigo was and why that name horrified Marin the most.

Marin remembered the list of legends and mythological stories from her late mother when she was a child. Wendigo was the most terrifying creature. He was known to haunt ancient long-forgotten sacred sites, including the one that they were at. Even at this moment, Marin could not compose herself and turned to look at Arik. She asked the Nordling company leader if it was true that Wendigo existed. Arik, sensing that she was familiar with the name, nodded solemnly in confirmation. He told her that Wendigo was no myth and that they had to hurry and disrupt the goblin shaman before completing his summoning.

The company unsheathed their weapons after they spotted the goblin shaman performing the ritual before the main stone mound next to a granite altar with a small dead snow rabbit being used as the sacrifice. Arik and his Nordling company charged forth toward the center of this strange stone grove site. They were ready to strike at the goblin shaman and the cave orc that stood next to the goblin shaman. The goblin shaman took notice along with the cave orc. Using his magic, the goblin shaman emanated a strange-looking bubble aura barrier around the cave orc. This shield made of a visible green aura prevented the attacking company from having any effect on striking the cave orc. Not even Linitus arrows could pierce through it.

Meanwhile, the cave orc attacked the warriors. Two of the Nordling warriors received fatal blows before the rest of the company could fall back in a defensive posture, raising their weapons and shields to block the cave orc's attacks. Marin used her powers to concentrate and hurl a spear of light at the cave orc. Her attack however had no effect. The glowing, translucent shield still protected the creature against retaliatory attacks. Linitus became frustrated and sensed that his beloved soulmate was in danger. The elf ranger realized that his only chance of diminishing that creature's protected power rested in the source of the shield aura's creation, the goblin shaman.

Driven by instinct and by devoted love not to lose Marin at any cost, Linitus acted with paranormal instinct. He pulled back his bowstring and began preparation to hurl forth with all his strength a magical arrow of searing light. He somehow could tap into his innate power to create a projectile, just as Marin had been able to with her divine-like powers to create her spear of light. This bright, searing arrow took shape out of the elf ranger's thoughts. He released the bowstring, sending the enchanted arrow at unimaginable speed to pierce through the goblin shaman.

The goblin shaman who received the strike from Linitus could no longer sustain the energy shield protecting the cave orc. The shield barrier diminished. The goblin shaman, despite being mortally wounded, still attempted to summon Wendigo. The shaman finished his last words of incantation that he uttered faintly before dying.

Rising near the dolmen were black clouds. There soon emerged a haunting, jagged pitch-black creature in the shape of a skeleton. It had the features and head of a terrifying deer-like beast with protruding antlers. Arik could not help saying aloud that he hoped was not Wendigo.

Arik and his fellow Nordling warriors backed away in full fleet toward Linitus. Meanwhile, Marin used her innate powers to emanate with her hands another enchanted searing spear she hurled toward a dark necrotic creature. However, a swirl of dark mist formed a shield-like barrier, shrouding and absorbing the searing spear. The creature unleashed a haunting wail-like voice while glaring menacingly at Marin. For a moment, the creature's glare stunned Marin. She stood almost frozen as she could not believe she was facing off against one of the most fearsome folk tale nightmares from her childhood dreams.

Linitus watched and feared losing his lover in this battle, who still stood frozen and in a state of fear. The elf rogue ranger yelled in a frantic tone while charging and unleashing the same rare divine-like energy that Marin had used. Only again, this energy came as an enchanted arrow emanated from Linitus's hand, which the elf ranger let loose the magical arrow after drawing his bow. The soaring enchanted arrow, though powerful, was also absorbed by the creature's dark, mist-like shield. Meanwhile, the strange shadowy creature turned its attention toward the elf ranger. It had teleported itself using its strange shadowy mist only appearing a few feet before the elf.

Marin came to her senses and composed herself. She had the same urge to take action for fear of losing her elven lover. She ran toward the elf ranger and the creature known as Wendigo. Marin with the same paranormal instinct channeled her innate power in a new way to emulate Linitus's ability to summon whirlwinds. This time though it was a unique form as well.

Channeling her thoughts to emulate this innate power, Marin yelled with all her energy and emotion in a loud, defiant voice of power. A small whirlwind echolike pitch immediately emanated from Marin's mouth. Her voice produced a powerful blast of sound that targeted Wendigo. Wendigo somehow was affected by this defiant voice of nature and reacted in a debilitated and evasive manner. It was weakened by the powerful blast Marin had somehow used.

Next, the strange, exotic, dark creature unleashed a horrible shout that startled everyone. Then, the creature vanished in a dark mist within the ancient megalithic site. It was nowhere to be found. The last known link to the unknown dark force disappeared. The only other connection that came to mind was Linitus and Marin realized while taking a moment to pause and breathe. They both replied aloud to each other about the lone cave orc. This creature vanished before their sight.

Following the scent of the cave orc, the Nordling warband led by Arik closed in. The cave orc ran frantically past pine trees and ferns, holding his primitive but deadly obsidian spear. This foul creature knew it had to decide to either find a place to hide or stand its ground. The cave orc knew his enemy Nordling pursuers would overtake him if it kept running.

The cave orc turned and unleashed a loud war cry while poised to hurl or lunge his spear toward the first approaching Nordling barbarian that would engage in combat. Only a sudden whooshing noise interrupted him as he felt a sudden plunge and jolt through his abdomen. He was in immense pain from being able to turn. The creature realized he fell at the hand, not by one of the enemy Nordlings, nor the elf ranger or the clad armored female knight, but by someone else.

From a dozen feet away an exotic creature charged at full speed. It was someone Marin and Linitus caught a glimpse of. This female being had the torso, arms, head, and face of a human female and a pair of brown antlers protruding from her head. The lower half of her body had a pair of forelegs with hooves. This creature's appearance also stood out. She possessed the surreal beauty of her kind. This creature had long braided red hair and an ornate crown of flowers. She also wore a green-and-black plaid checkered tube top mid-shirt and dress. This creature ran to the fallen cave orc. As this deer-human hybrid approached at full force, she reached and yanked free the decorative aquamarine spear from the slain cave orc.

When she turned, she noticed the band of adventuring Nordlings with weapons drawn confronting her. They called out the name of this creature, which Marin was as familiar with as the mysterious Wendigo. She was called a dyr, the Nordling word for the hybrid of a deer and a human.

This creature wielded her spear, assuming a defensive stance, ready to engage against any of her potential Nordling attackers. The Nordling warriors' prejudice, resentment, and distrust of outsiders were on full display. They heaped various insults at the female dyr. Marin and Linitus were still at a loss and amazed at what they were witnessing. The two newcomers in this strange northern land could not comprehend how this unfamiliar but also potentially friendly creature who had slain a common enemy would receive the same hatred from their company. What could have caused such antagonism between this warband of Nordlings led by Arik and this strange yet beautiful dyr?

As Marin and Linitus watched the tense standoff almost unfold into further bloodshed, Linitus asked the question he and his companion lover had: Why were they fighting each other? The elf pointed this out, considering both parties have a common enemy. Arik turned, and though angry, he was willing to overlook what he considered the newcomers' ignorance about their lands and histories. He told both Linitus and Marin that this creature was a dyr. The dyr folk were the mortal enemies of the Nordlings of Shimmerfrost for ages.

The dyr beast meanwhile spoke and used her magical abilities with her left hand to cast a sparkling teal aura of energy onto herself. Her spoken words became instantly and magically converted into the native tongue of both the Nordlings as well as Marin and Linitus's common Citadellan tongue. All of them understood her. The dyr seemed eloquent. She refuted Arik's last statement. Her people's relationship with the Nordlings of this region was not always hostile. Her people were only hostile as they had to defend themselves from the periodic slaughter that Arik's people waged against hers.

Marin and Linitus were stunned while looking toward Arik and asking if this was true. Arik replied in the affirmative, nodding without hesitance. He expressed with no resentment and confirmed what she said was true, but only after a member of the dyr caused death, destruction, horrible nightmares, and horrid witchcraft upon his fellow Nordlings when they initially welcomed a member of the dyr folk. According to Arik, the only way his people believed they could end the suffering was to hunt every dyr down, including the one that they saw earlier, the dreaded Wendigo.

It was then that Arik said, and affirmed by his Nordling colleagues, that Marin used surreal powers. It showed to them she was the destined helper of their people in this fight against Wendigo and his minions. Marin was then proclaimed by Arik and his warband of Nordlings to be the divinely chosen shield maiden under the title known as the Golden Valkyrie.

The Princess Knight was familiar with the Nordling legend of the Valkyries. They were described by her mother as beautiful young adult maidens assigned by the divine spirits in Nordling mythology to retrieve the worthy among the fallen warriors. The Valkyries then carried off the fallen warriors and brought them to the halls of celebration and feasting in the afterlife. This afterlife of paradise was called Val-Hifinn in the Nordling tongue.

Marin, however, was uncertain why Arik gave her that title. She did not come to retrieve fallen warriors to deliver them to the warrior's paradise in the afterlife. She asked Arik how that would be the case. According to Arik, with his Nordling companions nodding in agreement, while referring to ancient Nordling folklore and prophecy, only a living and divinely chosen female warrior or shield maiden with the powers Marin possessed was worthy to be called Golden Valkyrie. She possessed the powers of light, and she chose to stand up to confront Wendigo, the perceived source and cause of death in the lands of Shimmerfrost. The Nordling warriors recognized this in particular, which Arik pointed out after seeing the power of golden light being projected by Marin based on her enchanted spear summoning powers and her ability to use her new innate power of wailing to choose to stand up to Wendigo. Wendigo, according to Arik, was a symbol of death itself. For someone to cause the dark creature to tremble and flee in fear, which Marin had done, was no small trivial recognition. This, according to Arik, had warranted Marin this special recognition of the title.

Arik and his warband Nordling followers kneeled before Marin. Arik pointed the handle of his blade toward her. He beseeched her to lead them, their Nordling people of Shimmerfrost, against Wendigo, against his master, and against his allies, of which, Arik again accused, the female druid priestess was one.

The dyr priestess, who had been patient, protested against Arik's earlier accusations about her and her people being in league with Wendigo. She admitted she held distrust and disdain toward the Nordlings as utterly stupid, barbarian brutes. Still, she pointed out as refuting the accusation

Arik made based on what Linitus had stated earlier. She asked the same question as the elf had about why she would ally herself to Wendigo or his master when she had just killed one of Wendigo's minions.

Arik shook his head in denial, refusing to believe that this dyr was a genuine potential ally and did not pose a threat to his people. The Nordling warband leader responded that though this dyr druid priestess spoke eloquently, her words were the same as that of her intention. It was a deception in Arik's view. Linitus and Marin, however, had a hard time believing that. They both sided with the dyr, pointing out that she had given no sign of being their enemy other than an age-old blood feud between Arik's people and hers.

Marin recognized Arik and his warband followers' willingness to be under her leadership, so she decided it was best to use that to her advantage to help this strange dyr escape her current predicament of being against an overwhelming force of Nordlings that outnumbered her at least ten to one. Marin turned to Arik while looking at Linitus with a smirk and witty look that her elven lover was uncertain what she was up to or about to do, though he had an idea that she was going to press the advantage.

Calling upon Arik and inquiring about what he mentioned earlier, the Princess Knight demanded to know if it was true that Arik and his followers were willing to recognize her as their divinely appointed shield maiden or Golden Valkyrie. Upon all the present company of male Nordling warriors nodding their heads with Arik confirming, Marin confidently issued her first order to them. She commanded them to lower and sheathe their weapons before the dyr priestess and to let this strange but beautiful creature state her case in being heard along with seeking a potential new ally in this still unfamiliar and hostile land of the far north. All the male Nordling warriors along with Arik followed her orders though with some reluctance.

The dyr lowered her spear and expressed her gratitude to Marin. Marin nodded while returning the welcome and asked who this creature was. The dyr introduced herself as Alani-Aki, though she also went by being addressed as Alani. Alani indicated she was the druid priestess (also called a druidess) of a dyr village, called Aki, on the other side of Dyr Valley, north and northeast of the fjords of Shimmerfrost. Marin and Linitus were unfamiliar with the area but knew enough to know that she was not too far from their current location and that it lay somewhere to the north.

Marin and Linitus introduced themselves, explaining briefly their dilemma and how they ended up in Shimmerfrost. Alani-Aki told the two that just as much as this warband of Nordling adventurers believed Marin to be a divine savior, the dyr druidess also believed that these two strangers perhaps were predestined to be sent by the divine spirits to help bring peace and stability in this very hostile and turbulent cold region. Alani heard the wailing voice earlier in the woods around Doire na Cairn while she was undertaking a spirit quest to be in harmony with nature and undertake a pilgrimage to a nearby shrine dedicated to Cernunnos. Cernunnos was the anthropomorphic antlered deity spirit worshipped by the dyr folk and also associated with nature and wild animals (similar to how Citadellans of the southwestern lands of Hesperion associate with their nature deity spirit known as Silvanus). She came to investigate the source of the noise before finding the cave orc Alani slayed. The dyr druid priestess asked if it was true. She inquired whether Marin used her powers to emit the loud, wailing voice to cause Wendigo to flee in terror. Marin and Linitus both nodded while Marin spoke to confirm it to be the case.

After Marin's admission, Alani-Aki's facial expression turned to one of unsuspected rejoicing. The dyr priestess proclaimed it as Arik had earlier. Alani declared that these two newcomers, Marin and Linitus, were divinely sent to purify the lands from the forces of darkness and that Marin was the Wailing Banshee of Light told by the druidic folktales of Alani's people.

Marin and Linitus could not hold back their reservations of uncertainty and some skepticism. It was a lot for them to take in, especially Marin being elevated to two predestined roles after they arrived in Shimmerfrost in barely a week. Marin had a basic familiarity with Nordling lore about the Valkyries, but she knew even less about what a banshee was. That became clear when she said the word aloud with uncertainty.

Linitus was vaguely familiar with such lore. He told Marin that he had heard vague tales of women, known as banshees, who mourned as a portent of the impending death of loved ones. The elf ranger explained these tales, not to mention the worship of Cernunnos, were common beliefs among the halflings and Collis people of the high basin plains. Apparently, like the deviation from the familiar role and tale of Valkyries, the banshee title seemed to have also been adapted to become a heroic defender of Shimmerfrost. Linitus and Marin wondered if there was a cultural connection between the dyr folk of Shimmerfrost and the halfling and Collis peoples of the high basin plains. It seemed to be the case, just like the Nordlings had a clear, traceable connection with those in Shimmerfrost and the other Nordlings in the coastal forest and mountain lands south of Shimmerfrost.

Regardless, the elf ranger and Princess Knight were both apprehensive about their elevated roles, particularly Marin. The last thing they wanted to do was be caught up in filling roles with unfamiliar, predestined, fatalistic prophecies. However, these prophecies also seemed to revolve around preventing a catastrophe from happening or saving humanity and civilization at its last hour when heroes were usually called to step up and protect the innocent and all that stood for good.

Marin and Linitus had already been through that experience of being selected as chosen vessels of the divine spirits to protect their cosmopolitan kingdom. It was a big enough task, and they struggled to preserve what was left of the Kingdom of Swordbane against Decius and his rebellion. Marin and Linitus were exhausted. They wanted to return home at a moment's glance if they could wish upon the heavens for the deity spirits to take them back home.

However, the elf ranger and the Princess Knight realized that this was a task they could not turn their backs on. As much as they both longed to return home, Marin and Linitus knew it had to wait as their presence and actions would make a significant difference. They both felt compelled to at least know the full scope of the region's predicament then considering what aid they could give to both the Nordlings and the dyr folk against Wendigo and the other forces of darkness that he commanded. They knew, fatalist prophecies and title roles aside, they would have to do the right thing and become champions of the forces of light and what they saw as righteous if the situation was that dire with so many innocent lives at stake. Even if it meant going along with the titles and prophecies that were being heaped upon them, specifically Marin. She would do it. Marin and Linitus gained an understanding, though still limited, that Shimmerfrost was not all what it seemed. Before, they had relegated the land as entirely hostile and almost devoid of any innocence and goodness. The two newcomers realized that, from their limited but increasing exposure to the inhabitants of this region, this was not entirely the case. It was a struggle between light and darkness. It was the same type of struggle Marin and Linitus dealt with ten years ago during the Great Civil War between their Kingdom of Swordbane against its emerging secessionist rival, the Imperial Remnant.

While Marin and Linitus decided to stay in this land longer, Alani-Aki had already sensed that the lovers had the essence of divine spirits within them. The dyr priestess invited them to follow her and return to the sacred megalith grove known as Doire na Cairn several meters away. They were about to find out the truth that lay within the engraved standing stones.

Marin and Linitus, though apprehensive about finding the truth from the great unknown, agreed to the female druid's request. They both felt and sensed that this dyr seemed to be genuine, and these could very well provide greater insight to them and Arik's people by having a greater sense of this land's deep history and mysteries.

Later, after returning to the sacred rock and forest grove, Alani-Aki motioned to one of the engraved stones for Marin or Linitus to place their hand on. They must concentrate on the engraved symbols that had the power to subliminally communicate with them. Marin and Linitus looked at each other again. Though still somewhat apprehensive, each nodded while placing one of their hands toward one of the engraved stones. As they followed Alani-Aki's instructions concentrated on the engraved stone and opened themselves to what messages it might reveal. A light suddenly flashed. Alani-Aki, Arik, and Arik's warriors all covered their eyes from the brightness.

In a moment, the light disappeared. Linitus and Marin stood nearly frozen like the rocks in the grove about them. Their thoughts and faces showed the instant mental preoccupation that the two non-native strangers had been caught in a vision or a spirit quest into the spirit world as Alani-Aki explained to Arik and his companions. They would not awaken to their present surroundings until they had concluded their vision.

Arik, angry and suspicious, accused Alani of treachery. The druid priestess, also angry, denied doing such a thing. She insisted that as much as he had considered Marin as Nordling people's chosen Golden Valkyrie, her people too thought the two strangers were conferred by the great natural and divine spirits as worthy of completing their spirit quest. Alani further stated they would know this also by examining Marin and Linitus's understanding of the enchanted power of visions and the history of the dyr folk recorded in these engraved stones.

Arik nodded with reluctance but agreed. Despite his people's animosity toward the dyr folk, he and Alani-Aki knew these strangers had the potential to break the curse of evil and darkness that befell their two peoples. Perhaps it would be these two strangers who would hold the key to their future in being free from the torment that Helskadi and Wendigo posed against their two peoples. Only time would tell as these two strangers embarked on their divine, enchanted, and mysterious spirit quest.

Chapter Twenty

Portent from the Past

Deep inside their minds, their vision was clouded at first. Then it cleared. What was unknown to them before became known regarding Wendigo, his origins, and the long, bitter enmity between the dyr species and the Nordlings of Shimmerfrost.

Linitus and Marin stood next to each other in bright but faded-like form. They observed all the major events streaming before them. It was fast, turbulent, and saddening. They had seen it unfold again and again.

Marin and Linitus had seen a vision from thousands of years ago in Shimmerfrost. The elf ranger and Princess Knight saw before them a group of humans. These humans, based on their plaid clothing and light-skinned appearances, resembled the Collis people of the high basin plateau south of Shimmerfrost and northeast of the coastal heartlands of Swordbane.

This group of humans gathered around the spot near Linitus and Marin at Doire na Cairn. These humans were unaffected or unaware that the elf ranger and Princess Knight were watching them. These humans surrounded each other in a circular pattern. They invoked a strange series of incantations during a ritual enactment. When the ritual was completed, there was a bright flash, and the transformation took place. This group of humans morphed into creatures that were sentient and anthropomorphically was a combination of a human and a deer. They had become the species known as dyr.

In a separate scene to their right, Marin and Linitus saw a different series of events occurring through time. These dyr species at one time had amicable relations with other humans. These were the Nordlings from Shimmerfrost who had not been transformed. The two species interacted and traded in peace. However, their harmonious relationship changed when Linitus and Marin turned again. This time behind them, they saw the next series of events unfold. They had seen the relationship between the Nordlings and dyr folk. Then one Nordling woman in particular had relations with a dyr male druid priest. The two separate communities had at first been welcoming of it. However, things tore the two people apart the moment the Nordling woman was about to deliver her child.

It was at that moment Marin and Linitus tragically saw that the Nordling woman died while giving birth. Miraculously, the child had survived though it appeared to be born prematurely. The child was not expected to live, even though the creature had. The male dyr druid mourned the loss of his beloved human wife. He became protective of his surviving son. The Nordlings of that village, however, became hostile, killed the dyr druid father, and left the son (who would later become known as Wendigo) for dead. They blamed the dyr druid and his son for causing the death of the Nordling woman despite being the former two's wife and mother. The Nordlings took the woman's death as a dark omen in seeing this tragedy personified as being a larger representative threat to their survival as a human species. They saw the child and his dyr species as being the symbolic collective sin of the Nordling people for having amicable relations with the dyr species, even to the extent of intermarriage. As a result, this group of Nordlings in the spirit vision resolved that their only recourse for addressing this perceived collective sin was to both banish and hunt down every dyr creature that came before their presence.

Ever since, as Linitus and Marin had seen the second to last viewing of this vision, these two societies, Nordling and dyr, had been in a perpetual state of hostility and distrust toward one another. Before their vision had ended, Linitus and Marin had seen what had become of the unfortunate and condemned creature known as Wendigo. It had been left to die, isolated and filled with an ever-manifesting hatred toward nearly every living thing. It had hated the Nordlings of Shimmerfrost even more than they had shown their hatred of him. Even the dyr people gained Wendigo's scorn and hatred, for the former were wary and shunned his presence among them in what they considered a deformed and mutilated example of their species that had no place among them.

It was in that final viewing Marin and Linitus had seen what that creature's fate had become. The grown Wendigo was still an outcast. He had trekked to a massive rectangular stepped and multi-towered structure with several enormous towers looming over amidst a background surrounded by a ring of cold frozen clouds that surrounded a chain of snowy mountains. That creature had made its way to the lair of Helskadi. Linitus and Marin became shocked at what they saw. This treacherous, vile witch took advantage of and manipulated the condemned creature, the latter of which kneeled and pledged itself in service to Helskadi.

Before they could see more, the vision had ended, and a flash before their eyes exploded. Within a moment, they had awakened with their eyes wide open. Both Linitus and Marin looked about, realizing a strange set of staring looks about them from both Arik's group of companions and Alani-Aki. When Alani-Aki realized they had awakened from their spirit quest and slowly returned their consciousness to the mortal world, she could not help herself as much as the Nordlings in wanting to know what Linitus and Marin had seen. Alani-Aki had asked both Marin and Linitus to confirm what they had seen while tapping into the mysterious power among the carved etched megaliths of Doire na Cairn.

Marin and Linitus blinked their eyes and realized they had ended their deep trance and vision. They both had already returned to consciousness to realize they were in the present time amid the surroundings of the megalith sacred grove. They looked at both Alani-Aki and Arik with utter anger and disgust to realize the origin of their current people's hostilities. Marin, perhaps more so in not withholding her anger, pointed the finger at Arik and his companions after giving a quick and less mild look of disappointment toward Alani-Aki. The Princess Knight blamed them both as representatives of their respective people for their ancestors' past actions and in the present for why they do not get along as they once did. Marin confirmed to Alani-Aki that everything she and Linitus had seen was enough to know the source of their problems and what led to them. She was disgusted by how both their people changed for the worse and treated those who were different. From Marin's perspective, the tragedies that unfolded were misdirected and misguided signs of fatalism. Marin condemned their actions and behavior to justify and attribute their superstitious beliefs to impose violence and neglect toward others.

Alani-Aki and Arik, at this point, felt ashamed and a deep sense of guilt. Despite their previous animosity toward one another, they agreed to set aside their differences and could not hold but look at each other with irony. They both realized that now Marin, this part Nordling stranger from the lands further south, had more anger toward them than they had toward each other.

Linitus, despite also feeling the same initial feeling of anger, had tempered his emotions and reaction. He observed and realized that Marin overreacted. He noticed it as she had continued to blame Alani-Aki and Arik as the representative sources in bearing the collective blame of their people. The similarity resonated with the elf ranger just as much as he and Marin had witnessed from their spirit vision quest the respective ancestors of Arik and Alani-Aki's people blaming other individuals, including Wendigo and his dyr father, for the natural death of Wendigo's Nordling mother while giving birth to Wendigo. The elf ranger could not help but point out the irony to Marin. He asked her if she and, by extension, himself (based on his initial feelings), were any different from the people who had rejected Wendigo from so long ago in having so much anger to blame individuals for the actions of others based on shared collective ancestry.

Marin was dumbfounded at first. She took a moment to process what her elven lover had said. Her expression changed from pure anger to one of sadness. She realized the point Linitus had made. He was right. She went to him and embraced him while apologizing to him, and then she apologized to Alani-Aki and Arik. Marin admitted she would be no better than Alani-Aki's and Arik's ancestral people by being misguided and attributing individual and collective blame toward others through no fault of their own.

Taking another moment, Marin and Linitus, in rotating turns, shared more details with Arik and Alani-Aki about their shared vision experience that they had. This included what they had seen in different phases of a historical chronology of the history between the dyr folk and the Nordlings of Shimmerfrost, especially as it related to this dark creature, Wendigo. Alani-Aki and Arik were both captivated by the accounts of Linitus and Marin's spirit quest they had heard. They both agreed their people had to work together as they once did and put their differences aside. Arik and Alani-Aki also felt even more convicted in their beliefs that Marin and Linitus would be the ones destined to help them realize a new era of peace to build on the ashes of their peoples' past animosities.

How they would go about it, Alani and Arik each had their different resolutions. They nearly came to blows until Marin came to a compromise with them. She would follow Arik to the nearest large populated

Nordling settlement, Nebelheim, along the northeast fjords of the Bay of Shimmerfrost. She would serve as an emissary of the proposed alliance between the Nordlings and dyr folk and have Arik vouch for her legitimacy to assert her leadership and claim as the Golden Valkyrie.

Meanwhile, Linitus would travel with Alani-Aki to the nearest dyr settlement that lie northwest of Doire na Cairn and just west of a valley passage called Dyr Valley that was next to this sacred grove of megaliths. Like Marin, Linitus would serve as an emissary to propose the alliance between the dyr folk and the Nordlings with Alani attesting to his legitimacy in fulfilling the spirit quest as well as him displaying his limited supernatural powers over nature if needed.

Alani-Aki and Arik each nodded and agreed with the proposal while both commending Linitus and Marin for showing what they both saw as a promising sign of these two newcomer arrivals being the ones to help forge a new peaceful future between the dyr folk and the Nordlings in Shimmerfrost.

Before departing, Linitus and Marin embraced each other while pledging to one another to persevere and stay alive until they would next reunite. If all goes well. Linitus would bring a delegation of dyr folk with Alani-Aki to rendezvous with Marin, Arik, and Arik's company at Nebelheim to assemble their forces in uniting and bringing Shimmerfrost to a more controlled state of peace and order.

Chapter Twenty-One

Fear and Warning in the Darkness

Nestled deep within a circular chain of snowy mountains north of Dyr Valley stood a tall snow-covered ziggurat with several tall vertical towers that rose high above at different sections of this massive structure like a ziggurat. Only a narrow, jagged, and snow-covered road connected this complex to a path that led in descent southward eventually to Dyr Valley.

Looming above the surreal frozen landscape was a ring of massive frozen storm clouds that obscured the night sky save only the eye of this frozen storm which revealed the darkness of the sky and the countless many stars that shined above. This cold and frightening locality of Nordling legends that included the ziggurat complex itself was called Jotunheim. It was the domain of superimposing pale giants who went by several names including jotnar or jotunn folk or simply jotunn, as the Nordlings called them.

On that night, a dark vertical mist came down to the center of the ziggurat complex. This mist left a large vertical trail. All those denizens in the vicinity who had seen it knew who had arrived. Deep inside the tallest tower adjoined the ziggurat building lay the throne room of this giant kingdom's ruler. It was a large open room made of stone. It was large enough to hold the jotunn giants that stood inside. There were four of them, including two guards by the entrance to the throne room while another one stood as acting chief guard to the reigning giant monarch that sat on her frozen stone throne. She was Helskadi, the unofficial ruler and claimant of a divided Shimmerfrost. She was a jotunn and one of the few known female giants of her kind. She also earned the notorious nickname which she embraced as being the Winter Death Witch.

Now deep within her throne room, the same mist that had made its way from outside and descended to her multi-tower palace complex, this dark clouded mist had enveloped the center of Helskadi's throne room before her presence. A dark figure emerged after it took physical form as a jagged skeletal dyr creature. It was Wendigo. The creature could not speak in the same way the Nordlings or jotunn folk could. It communicated in variations of shrieks and screams. Only Helskadi understood its form of communication.

The Winter Death Witch became startled with a sense of concern. She called forth the creature, addressing it by its name, Wendigo, to ask what had happened. Helskadi wanted to know what troubled it. The jotunn queen placed her frozen pale hand upon the creature's jagged pitch-black deer skull forehead while asking it to let her read his thoughts. Wendigo nodded while shrieking. Able to read and see Wendigo's thoughts, Helskadi made sense and her face became pronounced with fear while also screaming. It had startled two giant guards and her chief guard known as Fornjotr.

Helskadi then rose from her throne and picked up her long magical three-pronged spear staff. She had motioned her hand with it while uttering several words in jotunn tongue toward a crystal ball that she had next to her throne. Within moments, a figure emerged within the same crystal ball, and she could view who it was. The figure, a bald Citadellan dark-robed figure, responded in acknowledging that she had requested his audience via teledistant conversation. Helskadi nodded with a sense of urgency and anger while affirming and calling out the other figure's name, Agaroman.

Agaroman sensed the concern. He could tell based on her tone of voice that Helskadi had bad news to report to him. He was prepared to hear it. The Winter Death Witch would deliver it to him but wanted to consult with his leader, Lucia. The Citadellan wizard frowned while he informed Helskadi that Lucia had passed away into the afterlife after sacrificing herself to save her son and her late husband's heir, Lucianus, from a perilous ambush they had in the cave tunnel complex after they last spoke with Helskadi. Agaroman went further to mention that consequently the only paired set of portal gates that connected their two realms in Terrunaemara were out of commission after the ensuing ambush led to the collapse of the cave mine near the Great Azure Lake.

Within the throne hall chamber of Helskadi's fortress, the jotunn female monarch became enraged. She had not known about this. Now she realized that the same two strangers whom her most powerful and deadly follower, Wendigo, had encountered and retreated from after fighting them, were likely the same two strangers that she presumed had a role in Lucia's death. She would not put it past her and presumed that they very well could have taken the same portal gate she sent a retinue of her forces to supply the Remnant's forces as a gesture of goodwill while obtaining an alliance with the Remnant. It made sense to her, after all. As of late, she had not heard about any recent developments from any of her forces south of Dyr Valley and deep into the Shimmerfrost peninsula save for Wendigo.

Within the image of the crystal ball and behind Agaroman peered out a young werewolf adolescent. It was Lucianus. He observed and interjected during the teledistant conversation that it had to be indeed the same ones that Helskadi mentioned. The new young dux of the Imperial Remnant suggested he would help deal with them as revenge for the death of his mother. Lucianus still planned to send a large shipment of weapons, armor, and siege equipment weaponry to assist the Winter Death Witch in dominating the region. The young dux declared he would also find a way to hunt down both the elf ranger and the Princess Knight when he made his trip to Shimmerfrost to deliver the shipment to Helskadi. Helskadi became impressed by her ally's offer. Still, she inquired with him how he would suggest doing that since they could no longer use the portal gates that they had used before.

Lucianus responded that he and his wizard advisor would see that the skybeast vessel would be packed as much as possible to deliver powerful siege weapons, siege munitions, personal armament, and other war materials and equipment to Helskadi. Agaroman became impressed and complemented Lucianus with his shrewd thinking. Helskadi also became further impressed with his proposal. The Winter Death Witch had been familiar with seeing the impressive and terrifying flying vessel made of dark steel on one occasion when she met the Remnant's diplomatic delegation that included Lucia and Agaroman several years ago when they sought to recruit like-minded dark forces throughout Terrunaemara that would be interested in allying with the Remnant. It was during their surprise visit they encountered Helskadi and her diverse army of various minions, including her fellow jotunn warriors, cave orcs, snow trolls, goblins, and the pale evil dwarves of Shimmerfrost that donned various sets of animal bone armor. It was still an awe-inspiring first encounter meeting to remember. Now, from the perspective of the present Remnant delegation, both Lucianus and Agaroman knew they had much to gain from this meeting. They intended to secure a sizable portion of Helskadi's forces to serve as mercenaries for the Imperial Remnant in return for a massive weapons shipment.

Now, though Lucia was gone, Helskadi had seen the same potential of the duchess' werewolf son. He seemed keen and savvy enough to know how to maximize the use of his forces and resources. Helskadi believed the dark alliance she had with the Imperial Remnant would still benefit her, even after Lucia's passing.

Helskadi returned her thoughts to the moment at hand. She nodded and complimented Lucianus on having the same shrewd potential of statesmanship and logistics as his parents. Lucianus nodded while acknowledging with gratitude and determination that he had no other purpose than to aspire to emulate his parents' example. He was hellbent on leading the dark forces of Terrunaemara while aiding common allies of the forces of darkness to triumph over the forces of good. Lucianus also had a personal grudge against the forces of light, especially the Kingdom of Swordbane and its heroic Order of the Comradery. The young werewolf adolescent swore a personal oath that he would avenge the loss of not only his father at their hands but also recently the loss of his mother.

Helskadi next asked how soon Lucianus and Agaroman could make the arrangements and deliver the weapon supplies to her. Lucianus still relied on the expertise of his wizard mentor. He turned to Agaroman for an answer. Agaroman sighed while thinking to himself how much time they needed to produce and deliver a large weapons shipment to fit in the skybeast vessel as well as how long it would take to arrive at their destination in Shimmerfrost. The wizard advisor estimated they could do it within a month. He would need at least a week to make the order with the various weapon smiths in both the Remnant capital of Sanctum Novus and the fortified goblin and orc settlement of Uruk Kazaht. They would need another week to outfit the skybeast vessel with as much of the weapons as it could hold as cargo to deliver to Helskadi's forces. At least two weeks would be needed for the skybeast to travel to Shimmerfrost to deliver the weapons to Helskadi at a slower speed when factoring in how heavily weighted the floating behemoth of a vessel would be in requiring it to travel at a speed comparable to a traditional floating skyship.

Helskadi did not see this as being ideal. She wanted the superior weapons for her forces ready as quickly as possible to address the perceived threat of these new unknown visitors in Shimmerfrost. Regardless, she still considered this arrangement acceptable for the time being. Her forces would hold off and distract these new visitors and whoever would ally with them in Shimmerfrost until her forces received the weapons shipment. The Winter Death Witch's forces would use these superior weapons against their various enemies in the region to tip the balance of power in her favor.

Helskadi nodded and confirmed to Lucianus and Agaroman that they had reached an agreement. She would receive the promised weapon supplies, and in return, she would provide another retinue of her forces for Lucianus as the new dux could use to supplement his forces and further wage war against the Nordlings of the northwest coast that his father once conquered. Lucianus and Agaroman both nodded and excused themselves while their image departed from the crystal ball that Helskadi peered through in her throne room.

Helskadi next turned to Wendigo and ordered the creature to return from which it came to the ruins of Doire na Cairn to keep a distance while spying on their guest newcomers and report back to her on what it had learned. Meanwhile, she would prepare a large raiding party among her forces once Wendigo had reported on their guests' whereabouts. This raiding party would overwhelm and destroy the newcomers before they caused any further trouble within her domain of Shimmerfrost. If these newcomers did survive then Helskadi would still leave it up to Lucianus and Agaroman to use their means to get rid of them once and for all.

Chapter Twenty-Two

Infernal Lovers

Awakening from a pleasant rest, the first in over a week, Lucia turned to see her body rested against Decius's body. She found herself in a strange bed made of an exotic dark stone with an exotic layered covering of some silk-like material on which she rested her body. She saw one of Decius's large werewolf arms wrapped over her as she felt her infernal lover's warmth. Lucia had waited over a decade for the day they would be physically together. Before she wanted to be intimate as they once were. She wanted to wake up next to her dux wherever they were. The longing she felt after being away from him ceased to exist. She was content and strangely despite being in this infernal hell, she was at peace. Lucia was by Decius's side. She felt they were truly a couple in the physical sense just as they had been before. They would be together, forever building an empire as rulers with an unmatched ambition to surpass all those before them.

Only a moment later, Decius awakened after sensing his lover's slight change of movement next to him. With his dark protruding wolf-like snout, he nuzzled it against her face as a gesture of mutual comfort and contentment in being next to her. He could read her expressions even from her somewhat different-looking reddish demonic yet still attractive face. She thought the same thing as he did which he knew and pointed that out to her.

Lucia blushed and gave a slight nod while acting seductive in rubbing her slender red feet against his clawed black feet. Decius rubbed back while the two embraced each other and exchanged kisses. They still remembered each other as who they were in their past mortal lives. This was clear to them despite the obvious awareness that they had changed in physical form compared to when they first met during their mortal lives as humans.

Only another moment in passing did Decius gently and casually let go of Lucia while rising from his bed. The dark werewolf creature donned himself with his armor. It comprised a set of dark shoulder pauldrons and a dark red waist tasset that covered his waistline to the length of his upper legs and regalia. Lucia became awakened and looked on to observe. She rose and assisted him while perching her lips against the side of his cheek. Decius turned and put his clawed hand over her hand that rested on his shoulder while nodding.

After donning his armor and regalia, Decius turned to Lucia noticing she barely covered herself. She had only worn by this point a black loin cloth along with an upper black breast cloth bikini top. Lucia's face blushed. She knew he took notice of her. He was still attracted to her appearance in this afterlife as much as her previous mortal life, despite her being a red-skinned succubus. The two embraced once again before Decius broke off subtly. He told her how grateful he was for her choosing to share their fates. He vowed he would always be loyal to her as she had been with him. Lucia acknowledged telling him she knew he would as he always had been in their previous mortal lives. She expressed her gratitude that Calu, along with his lieutenants, had allowed her to be with Decius as persistent as she was to insist it would happen.

As the two thought about being together, Decius told her to follow him in leaving his room and proceed downstairs back to his throne room. Lucia nodded. On their way to the throne room, several of Decius's red imps stood guard both outside the doors of his chamber and to the throne room entrance. Decius and Lucia both held hands while they continued to make their way toward his crafted dark stone throne. As Decius took his seat, he motioned toward one of his imp subordinates to see that another throne seat would be crafted and provided next to his. The dux then gave a glance toward Lucia and he informed her that this additional throne would be for her as his reigning infernal duchess. Lucia blushed and expressed her gratitude toward her soulmate. Meanwhile, the imp, eager and earnest to serve, could not help but turn to look at Lucia with curiosity after the imp acknowledged his infernal lord's command.

Lucia broke from decorum and gravitated toward her caring nature to open up to wanting to know her subjects more personally. She thanked the imp lieutenant while asking what its name was. The imp told her he did not have a name. Lucia was surprised. She asked how it was that they had no names, especially to discern from one another. The imp replied that for whatever reason they somehow just do.

Lucia turned to Decius. She saw the opportunity with his consent to make her first reform as his consort. The duchess bid him to grant this creature and all other imps like it to be given personal names even for a modest token of recognition. Decius turned with admiration and profound realization by his lover's genuine concern. The dux saw no conflict between his way of ruling over his demonic subjects while considering her recent request. Decius nodded to Lucia stating that he would grant her wish. He also conveyed to the imp and all other imps present as witnesses while introducing Lucia formally to them. Decius announced she would co-rule with him and that her authority would be second only to his authority.

Taking another moment to think, Decius realized that they needed to notify his followers in the mortal realm of his infernal reunion with Lucia. He wanted to confirm to them that this recent revelation of her defiance in the afterlife to be with him was a testament to not only their eternal bond but also that of the reign he would share with her to rule over Infernum. The most important on Decius's list was notifying their son, Lucianus, Agaroman, and Lucia's father, Senator Diem. It was not before long however while Decius sat on his throne that he received a libation and incense summoning ritual. Decius felt an aura like a blue flame around him brightening.

Standing up from his throne and channeling his deepest thoughts, Decius in his mind focused on widening the surrounding aura while telling Lucia to hold his hand. The same aura like a blue flame enveloped her as it did Decius from which it originally emitted around him. Lucia, though apprehensive at first, trusted her lover and held his hand while moving closer to his side. Decius instructed her to focus her thoughts on him. Lucia told him she did not know how. Decius assured her to think out of desire. He told her to think as he had in concentrating and commanding her thoughts along with his. They both wanted intently in their minds to be at the same place that had summoned them. She nodded while closing her eyes. Within moments the aura, which was a portal of energy, had enveloped them. The aura flashed and closed in a bright ball of flames soon to be self-extinguished.

Decius and Lucia's bodies disappeared and transformed into spectral transparent images of themselves. For Lucia, it was surreal to witness the first time in her experience this incredible transformation. When she opened her eyes, she could see Decius and hear her lover's voice. Like Decius, Lucia became a spectral ghost of her bodily form. Now they had 'awakened' one might say or rather teleported in their spectral form to the mortal realm. She had realized she was in the main chamber room of the dux's palace in the desert metropolis of Sanctum Novus. Before her and Decius was an altar table of a Citadellan lararium with religious totem items. One totem represented Laran as a miniature upright sword above a fixed stand. The other represented was a miniature black wolf statue representative of Calu. Also at the center of the altar table was a brazier of lighted incense. Next to it stood an empty chalice once filled with wine that had already burned upon being placed in the brazier.

To her and Decius's left stood several figures responsible for summoning Decius and unknowing to them by extension in summoning Lucia as well. The figures' expressions were in awe and almost on the verge of collapsing by what they had seen. Among them included Lucianus in his werewolf adolescent form wearing military regalia iconic with what his father once wore though without the breeches. Next to him stood Agaroman and Senator Diem along with several elite black wolf order knights, and a representative goblin shaman as well as an orc war captain. The latter two were the Remnant's coalition representatives among the beastly races.

Lucianus unleashed a frightening howl upon seeing the sight of not only Decius but also what Lucianus presumed and rightfully knew was his mother. Decius could not help but grin with his werewolf-like snout at what he saw. It was perhaps the most frightening coming-of-age howl he had heard from his son in all his years of knowing him. He could tell Lucianus was close to Lucia and mourned his mother's mortal passing. Even Senator Diem could not help but quench his fists and kneel while asking if it was her. Lucianus interrupted and replied sharply but also respectfully that it was indeed her. He knew his mother's face well enough even if she had taken on a unique form in being a succubus. He knew that this was Lady Lucia, former duchess of the Imperial Remnant. It was his mother. He called out to her, asking for her forgiveness.

Immediately, Lucia noticed and still processed the surreal experience of seeing the mortal forms and the physical surroundings that she once knew. She could not help but be moved by her maternal instincts. She moved in a drifting transparent manner toward her wolfling son. She tried to caress his head with her narrow yet delicate sharp hands. However, she realized upon having this ghostly apparition form she could no longer physically touch or hold on to things in the mortal realm. She could not hold on and embrace those she cared the most. It pained her. She wept while telling her son Lucianus to rise and know that there was nothing to seek forgiveness on his account. He had done his part in surviving and leading the remaining forces with him out of the cave mine. She had done her part to assure that it happened even if it meant sacrificing her life to pass on to the afterlife and seeking to reunite with his father.

Lucianus followed his mother's instruction and nodded while rising from the kneeling position. Decius interjected and let those present know that Lucia had indeed rejoined him in Infernum while triumphing over the initial will of the deity spirits to assign Lucia to the paradise of Caelum. It was a bold proclamation even with two priests (one representing Calu and the other Laran) being present to hear what Decius had said. However, all those present believed in what the dux said after seeing Lucia in a spectral form like their infernal dark lord. Everyone nodded while chanting various praises in hailing both the dark lord and his dark duchess consort in being united even in hell.

Senator Diem showed disappointment and reservations. If he had his way, his beloved daughter he knew and shared countless memories would be with their ancestors in the paradise of Caelum. Alas, he accepted as everyone else that, somehow, she would prevail over the divinely intended destination of her mortality in how she believed and lived as a faithful, pious worshiper of the various deity spirits. That was even apparent when she sought her path to being compatible to perform acts of charity even under adopting the notorious title of consort to a dark lord the likes of Decius. It seemed incomprehensible the two of them were compatible with each other when comparing how different they were.

However, Lucia had always been drawn to Decius from the first moment she saw him when they were still mortals. She knew how to always make their differences work out effortlessly without conflict between her and Decius both in their mortal lives and now apparently in their post-mortal lives. Diem knew she loved him and would do anything, including willing to change the course of her divinely intended destination. He lamented that his daughter chose her fate to be in the realm of condemnation, torment, and eternal fire. However, Diem knew also strangely and correctly that she somehow would be content in being reunited with Decius even in such a terrifying place to be residing in such as Hadao Infernum. In his mind, he only hoped as some consolation that whatever happiness and content she would find with Decius, that her son, his grandson, Lucianus would at least be with him and his ancestors in the paradise of Caelum. Diem had developed a deep bond with his grandson, just as he had with his daughter Lucia. Still, Diem doubted his grandson based on his current trajectory would strive to want to join many of their ancestors in Caelum when it would be his grandson's time to one day depart from the mortal world of Terrunaemara. Lucianus after all sought to emulate in every aspect of being a dark lord as his father did before during his previous mortal life.

Meanwhile, Agaroman, also in awe, kneeled before the shade spirits of Decius and Lucia while addressing them by their previous mortal titles as dux and duchess. Decius, in his blue spectral form, nodded while unleashing a minor howl and told Agaroman to rise. They had much to discuss, and time was a deterrent as there was limited time. Decius could not sustain maintaining his spectral form and now Lucia's spectral form to project for too long.

As they briefed Agaroman, Decius and Lucia alternated in explaining their reunion. Lucia explained much of what transpired since her passing and last recollection of her mortal life in the collapsed cave mine outside of the Great Azure Lake. She continued further to explain her surreal transformation as an alluring red succubus after contesting with the deity spirit of death, Calu, over her assignment of residence in the afterlife. After Lucia's explanation, Decius instructed all those before them that after witnessing their infernal reunion, they would now pay reverence to both he and Lucia when being summoned. Their family and followers would continue to give libations and incense offerings still calling out his name and as well as now Lucia's name. All those present in the palace chamber room nodded in obedience while still being amazed and renewed in their conviction. Decius to them was an immortal dark lord and one that was still worthy to be considered as a chosen vessel for Calu and Laran even in the infernal realm of the afterlife.

Decius next returned to the next order of business at hand. He inquired with the present company for the reason they had summoned him and to brief him on the current ongoing developments.

Lucianus depended on Agaroman or his late mother Lucia (when she was alive) to brief his father on the purpose of their daily libation summoning of him. Now however the wolfling dark lord heir and successor took it upon himself to brief his father directly. He wanted to do his part to show as a potential sign of his leadership that he was capable and worthy of being a newly ascended dark lord to further his father's aims for the Imperial Remnant. Lucianus responded with confidence to the latest developments, including his most recent situation in receiving communication with their allies in the far north of Shimmerfrost, namely the Winter Death Witch, Helskadi.

Lucianus apprised both his late parents that according to Helskadi's suspicions and based on one of her top servant's firsthand reports, their mortal enemies, the Princess Knight, and the elf ranger had somehow teleported from the cave mine and ended up in Helskadi's domain of Shimmerfrost. Helskadi now wanted the Remnant to expedite the weapons shipment to deliver to her forces should these two outsiders to Helskadi's realm unite the various forces of good against her including the Nordlings and the dyr folk.

Decius and Lucia's expression, even in their ghostly form, became equally alert and enraged. Decius howled. He raised his voice that the Remnant must do everything possible to ensure such an outcome does not become realized by his sworn enemies. Lucia inquired with Agaroman if he had devised a plan for finding an alternate means of shipping the weapons to Helskadi in Shimmerfrost. She suggested for him to use the skybeast. Agaroman replied flatly, though with some confidence that this was already being done by the initiative of her son, Lucianus.

Surprised and impressed, Lucia and Decius both grinned while praising their son for seizing the initiative to devise such a plan. Decius even went so far as to extol praise upon Lucianus for being worthy to be recognized as his ascending successor to lead the Remnant as their dark lord and dux. Lucianus replied humbly while kneeling that he learned to emulate by example in indicating his father and predecessor, Decius.

Lucia next inquired about the details of how they would stock the provisions and supplies. Still familiar with the skybeast vessel's schematics during her mortal life, she wanted to ensure that the flying war behemoth was optimally managed in transporting various items that she wanted to consult both her son and Agaroman. Agaroman replied that during the next summoning, they would consult with her but that for now they were making an increased quota procurement from the various blacksmiths in both the Remnant capital and in Uruk Kazaht. Lucia became pleased, and both she and Decius expressed their gratitude. Lucianus followed up by notifying them in exchange for their shipment delivery the Imperial Remnant would receive various creatures serving in Helskadi's army to use for raiding enemy Nordling tribal villages along the northwest forest coastlands.

His foresight and planning, despite being an adolescent wolfling, had seen its course in being well nurtured and recognized by not only his parents but also Agaroman. The wizard over the last few years had devoted his time and effort to teach Lucianus not only the dark arts of casting magic spells but also with his grandfather, Senator Diem's tutelage, in shaping Lucianus to be astute in the ways of military strategy and empire building. Truly, before all those present among the senior-ranking leaders of the Remnant, Decius's heir was shaping to be fully ready to take over his father's position even if it was considered a trial by fire. They saw Lucianus as being a competent leader and dark lord despite being thrust into this current predicament with his mother no longer acting as regent in the mortal realm.

Only a few more minutes would last before Decius along with Lucia would have to return to their infernal abode in their postmortal, corporeal form. Their ethereal ghost form they projected their appearance and consciousness as would eventually dissipate completely. Before departing however, Lucianus dismissed all those present except for his grandfather, Senator Diem, so that he and his grandfather would at least have their own time alone for the few remaining moments with his parents and Diem's daughter and son-in-law even in their ghostly apparition. At least they would be together and catch up with the time they still considered important to share as a family. There was much to discuss but both Diem and Lucianus were content to feel as if they had seen some consolation in knowing that Decius and Lucia were reunited while still having a way to interact as a family. They mutually missed each other yet no longer felt in many respects separated as they did a week prior. Even when Decius and Lucia did eventually disappear in their ethereal form, Lucianus and Senator Diem found solace to know and look forward to being reunited again with Decius and Lucia each time that either Lucianus or Diem performed the summoning ritual.

Chapter Twenty-Three

Revelation in the Lord of Punishment's Lair

Opposite of Decius's fortress in Hadao Infernum stood erected from the mount of volcanic rock, a central bastion fortress surrounded by walls and tower fortifications. It was located on the lower plains of hell next to a series of cliffs that separated the charred landscape from an endless ocean of burning lava. This place came to be known as Sanctum Orcus. It was the lair and keep of the infamous Orcus himself, a demigod considered from ancient legend to be the founding patron of the orc race itself.

Loud screams of anguish sounded deep within the bowels of this demigod's central keep. It was in this vile despotic place that Orcus made as not only his place of torture but also as his throne room. Several deformed humanlike figures were imprisoned inside cages that swung while alternating between rising and lowering before hot burning coals placed below. As the imprisoned human figures screamed in agony, a lone large and very muscular figure rose from his throne of human skeletons. He laughed in a sadistic delight at the pain that his victims felt while being tortured. This vile figure stood over eight feet tall and had a reddish skin hue along with two large prominent golden horns protruding from his head. He also had a broad forehead, flat broad nose, pointed ears, and tusks protruding from his lower jaw.

Many denizens of hell called Orcus the deity of torture and punishment (especially for those who broke their oaths in their former mortal lives), despite being a demigod with only partial divinelike powers. Regardless, before his presence, he made sure all who addressed him would do so as Lord Orcus. Failing to do so would incur his wrath that many of the denizens of hell knew all too well that they would prefer to avoid except one. This one earned his strongest ire. Orcus sought to make an example of this one being defiant to his authority as hell's sovereign. This one considered a relative newcomer at least when measured by decades, became known in his prior mortal life as being called Dux Decius.

Since his arrival by a mere decade, Decius had challenged Orcus's claim to hell. The newcomer and challenger brought about half of Orcus's hellish forces to his cause, including for a time all the succubi. It was only until Orcus convinced all of the succubi out of fear and temptation for a further reward that these demonic sirens switched sides back to him. His forces had beaten back Decius's efforts to depose this demonic hell lord. However, Orcus could not get rid of Decius once and for all. They were at a perpetual standstill. For now, Orcus was content to have his forces harass those loyal to Decius from time to time. It was enough to cause Decius to fall back to the furthest remote and ascending parts of hell that Orcus had little to no interest until now.

As the demigod continued to torture his condemned human victims, a stray imp announced before Orcus a most disturbing report that this imp had witnessed firsthand while escaping. It had reported to its demonic hell lord that it had escaped from a new looming threat that had just arrived at Hadao Infernum. This threat came as a succubus, but not one of Orcus's original seventy-two known demonic siren succubi. Even more shocking, this lone new succubus arrival had even killed at least one known succubus.

The imp finished his report while it displayed a large amount of fear in not knowing how Orcus would take it other than becoming visibly upset and finding someone to serve as the object for him to inflict pain while he dispensed his anger. His imp servant was correct as Orcus shouted in a surprised fit of rage and frustration at the troubling news. The report infuriated him even to where he withdrew a large two-handed cleaver-like blade. Orcus dispensed his rage in a sudden motion toward his present company of tortured victims. The demonic demigod with his large broad cleaver slashed and severed the cords holding the cages in place. Within moments, the agonized tortured prisoners fell along with their encased cages at the burning hot coals while screaming in further agony. Orcus hurled various curse-like expletives while swinging his broad cleaver-like blade toward one of his helpless victims before moving on to the next. He would end their torment brutally and most unpleasantly until he reached the last of his tortured victims who lay motionless. It was a horrific sight, but one that his followers came to be accustomed to seeing their hell lord create, especially out of pure anger.

Orcus breathed hard for a moment before he turned toward the imp that had given him the message. The demonic demigod instructed the imp to gather the other denizen servants in his palace. He would order all of them to find all the surviving succubi to report back to him at his fortress. Orcus would see to it in briefing each of his demonic sirens of the new threat that posed both against him and his control of hell or at least the great expanse that he still possessed outside of Decius's sphere of control.

The demonic demigod also became suspicious of the succubi. He still had not forgotten their former betrayal before they renewed their allegiance with him. Orcus would see to it to inspect and inquire with each one of them to ensure they remained loyal to him. He would do so while having them witness him torturing one condemned denizen just as he had a moment before several of his prisoners in full view of his loyal imp informant.

Chapter Twenty-Four

New and Familiar Encounters

In opposite directions from where they departed near the sacred grove and megalith site of Doire na Cairn, Linitus and Marin had now been further apart from each other than they had ever been for several years. Linitus traveled westward along with the female dyr druid Alani-Aki to her native dyr village several dozen miles west of the sacred grove and west of Dyr Valley. Marin meanwhile traveled with Arik and his company of Nordling adventure followers east to the nearest major seaport settlement, Nebelheim.

Upon arrival at Nebelheim, Marin became immersed in awe and familiarity with the seaport's architecture. It had reminded her to a degree of the Nordling settlements to the south along the forest coast, including Aegir-Hafn. Nebelheim had large wooden longhouses with either vertical, slanted overlapping roofs or roofs that resembled Nordling longboats positioned upside down. The seaport town was ideally situated near the confluence of a river that bled out into fjords along the eastern divide of the Shimmerfrost peninsula. Even approaching the seaport from the opposite side of the bank of a small delta, Marin noticed several large longboats that floated around the coastal waters surrounding Nebelheim.

There were also several prominent landmark features of this circular wooden walled settlement. One of them included a large wooden dock near the river confluence that jutted out toward the ocean. The other notable landmark could be seen even from outside the walls. This landmark was near the center of the enclosed settlement. It was a prominent tall Nordling building that had several corner posts, or staves, and its framework was made of timber. The wall planks of this landmark rested on sills. Marin would presume this building was the chieftain's hold and mead hall. Arik confirmed with her it was upon Marin inquiring. Arik also explained to Marin that the Nordlings addressed their local chieftains by the title called jarl. The jarl's hold and mead hall was a tall slanted Nordling building, and according to Arik, stood just over a hundred feet tall above the base of a hill on which it was erected.

However, what was more surprising that Marin caught notice while looking above was a lone skyship that hovered in the sky above. It was a caravel design. She could make out the insignia of the ballast balloon and the sails. It had a blue dragon perched on top of a sword. To her realization and delight, without holding back her joyous expression that caught Arik and his chosen warrior companions by surprise, Marin declared aloud that they had arrived. Her fellow members and companions of the Comradery have finally arrived. If only she could give a signal from where she stood to alert her companions that she and her newfound friends were approaching them from below. They were approaching the coastal settlement where the skyship had gracefully soared and left its small shadow from high above.

Then Marin realized she had the newfound power of the voice of what Alani-Aki called a wailing banshee. Marin could unleash it high in the sky. It may or may not work, but she knew she had to at least try. After briefly explaining to Arik and his company that the skyship above were her friends, she motioned for them to step a few feet back while Marin concentrated and thought earlier on how she first unleashed her newfound power. Marin channeled her mind into the same sense of intuition she had done before. She focused her thoughts and quickly transferred her state of mind to what she wanted to say, what she wanted to unleash and hurl toward the sky. In another moment, she did. Her voice screamed out in a loud and repetitive wailing that overtook all other ambient noises. It could be heard from nearly everywhere within sight and beyond.

Within a few moments after pausing, Marin looked up after catching her breath and noticed that the lone skyship suddenly changed course and moved toward her. It worked. Even Arik and his fellow warriors were impressed with how loud her voice was despite all of them covering their ears when Marin had signaled earlier for them to do so.

The lone skyship approached Marin and her Nordling warrior company from above. The latter were still again on the other side of the river confluence just outside the wooden walls of Nebelheim. A bright flash emanated from high above and then below on the surface, right in front of them. A small splint mail armored dwarf and halfling wizard in black and blue robes approached Marin. Arik and his company prepared to raise arms in a cautioned and guarded stance. However, they refrained from doing so when Marin motioned for them to stand at ease. She assured Arik that the teleported arrivals were friends of hers.

Within a moment in what seemed memorable and iconic, Marin ran toward the two figures as they ran mutually toward her. She embraced her familiar friends, Peat and Wyatt. Marin took a breath before she asked them in a humorous tone what had taken them so long. Peat without restraint and being of his own stern dwarven sarcastic nature replied that he and Wyatt did not want to ruin Marin and Linitus's tenth-anniversary honeymoon. Marin laughed mildly while replying to her dwarven comrade that she was sorry that she interrupted him in his time to find a prospective spouse of his own. The dwarf laughed back while stating that he had already found his. He gestured while wielding his large war hammer. Marin gushed with laughter as did Wyatt as well.

Perhaps it was too much for them, but Peat followed up by asking what they were waiting for. He declared that he had a honeymoon of his own in wanting to take his war hammer out to war against any would-be foes that stood in their way while adventuring.

Marin felt overjoyed in her reunion with her comrades. She could not help however after hearing Peat's words in mentioning her and Linitus being together. She felt saddened to be away from her lover's presence. They had been apart from each other for several days. She thought of Linitus and hoped he had fared as well as her. Linitus was on a separate diplomatic quest in traveling with Alani-Aki to meet with her dyr people and convince them as much as Marin would with Arik's people to set aside their differences and form a common front against Wendigo and ultimately Helskadi.

Peat sensed that Marin's mind became somewhat occupied and distracted. The dwarf guardian noticed Linitus was not around her while she had a company of Nordlings that stood behind her and appeared to be native to this landscape. The dwarf asked her where their comrade, Linitus, was. Even Wyatt, quiet as he almost always was, expressed a similar gesture of curiosity.

Marin let them know with a brief explanation that they had parted ways to fulfill what she and her elven lover felt compelled to do. They both vowed to help the innocent people of this strange yet dangerous foreign land. It was as inhospitable to them as newcomers as it nearly had been for any of the local creatures that called Shimmerfrost home. While telling Peat and Wyatt there was much to still discuss which she would along the way, Marin informed them that she had to speak with the local settlement's chieftain to discuss the looming dark threat that the Winter Death Witch posed along with her minions and their clandestine deadly alliance with the Imperial Remnant. The Nordlings had to end whatever feuds they had with each other and with the dyr folk throughout Shimmerfrost.

Peat, however, interrupted and let her know that while he would stand by her side and be eager to stop this threat, he did caution about her father's desire to find her and, ultimately, bring her back alive with Linitus. Marin sighed and moaned slightly. She was not surprised that her father would find out about her and Linitus missing, and she knew that her comrades, Peat and Wyatt, would go to her father, the king, to consult and receive guidance in following his orders to find them. However, she felt also torn, and she imagined it would put Swordbane in a difficult place in possibly being positioned to enter a long far away war if her father Ascentius found out she was involved and would risk putting his forces in a position that would weaken the Kingdom much in the state it was in after ending a near two-year prolonged war with the Imperial Remnant over ten years ago. He would not risk it, but she knew her father well to have someone go out to find her and Linitus.

Now that Peat and Wyatt had found Marin, she would imagine how angry her father would have felt if she decided to stay longer and not return. She could not hold back from indicating the dilemma she was in while confiding to Peat and Wyatt. The two of them understood and pondering with her in that same sense of emotional conflict, they came to the same resolution she had before, the same one that Linitus already had the day they encountered Alani-Aki and had that mystical trancelike vision at the sacred grove of Doire na Cairn. They had to do something, especially in their position when they could help and use their fighting skills. The values of the order of chivalry required them to defend the weak and those most vulnerable from the forces of darkness and evil. They could not simply turn back and say this was not their war to fight even being so far away from home. They knew that they had to always answer the call when lives were at stake.

While they talked and came to that understanding, Peat looked at Wyatt and Marin while asking with curiosity what they would do next. Marin grinned slightly while turning back to introduce Peat and Wyatt to her new companions being led by Arik. Arik slowly approached the dwarf guardian and halfling while motioning his hand in a welcoming salutation to bid them peace.

Peat motioned back while admiring Arik's double-bladed ax that he had strapped back to his back. The dwarf could not hold back but to compliment him on his choice of weaponry. Arik, caught by surprise in mutual appreciation, complimented Peat back in the Nordling language in stating how impressive the design was with the war hammer he wielded. Peat thanked the Nordling while stating aloud before Marin and Wyatt that finally he found someone in the last several weeks to have a meaningful conversation with besides the old Nordling fisherman who served as a guide. Marin and Wyatt laughed along with Arik's companions.

Marin indicated it was a good sign among hopefully many in due time that they would have in their new journey to unite Shimmerfrost. She quickly told Wyatt that it was time to depart and teleport back to the skyship along with her newfound Nordling companions. Wyatt nodded and another moment later they flashed and disappeared from the surface while a new flash emanated from the deck of the lone skyship. Once onboard, they resumed the skyship's course to the neighboring settlement of Nebelheim. Marin's next itinerary would be to arrive at the settlement itself and beseech its local ruler to the newfound call for unity and putting aside past differences. She had hoped that while doing so Linitus would have as much luck in persuading the dyr folk.

Chapter Twenty-Five

Summoning Divine Wind

About a hundred miles away to the east by northeast of Nebelheim, where Marin and the other members of the Comradery had reunited, Linitus being escorted by the dyr druid priestess Alani-Aki, had arrived at their intended destination. They had arrived at one of the main dyr settlements. It was a settlement of multiple birchbark houses within a clearance among a large surrounding forest of birch trees and other trees. The trees stood as high as fifty to sixty feet tall and flooded the settlement with a measurable amount of shade when it was sunny. The birch trees themselves had shown signs of some of them being harvested with a sticky amber-brown sap. This was an edible commodity the local dyr folk had used after extracting from the trees. They extracted the substance using intricately pierced pike contraptions with holes through the pikes that bled this sticky sap into wooden buckets to collect the sticky sap. There were also dozens of dried sockeye salmon cut nearly into half except for the fish tail, and hung over wooden drying racks.

Approaching the settlement, Linitus looked in awe of the various exotic dyr folk who also looked with peculiarity at him. Linitus noticed that they also appeared with the same physical type of appearance as Alani-Aki. The dyr folk had a human's upper body and that a deer's lower body, but they still walked on two legs as they only had two legs. They also had antlers that protruded from their heads and wore plaid clothing.

From the dyr folk's perspective, the elf stood out also, as they had never seen one before. However, they were not as alarmed as they would have been had he been a Nordling, given the dyr folk's long-time feud with the Nordlings of this region. Linitus also noted the various birch wood longhouse structures covered in thatch. Linitus became impressed also after seeing several exotic totem poles. They were intricately carved with various shapes and patterns resembling animals of the region, including bears, deer, salmon, eagles, and wolves.

As Linitus walked next to Alani-Aki, the dyr druid priestess announced to the village folks that she had arrived with a special stranger who had befriended her while confronting Wendigo. The villagers' reaction changed into a celebratory mood. They cheered in jubilation that one of their druids had now found someone who could save them from the various evils that haunted them. They thought among themselves if this strange humanlike creature with pointed ears had been an enemy of Wendigo and lived to tell about it with one of their dyr druid priestesses, then he very well could be the one they had prophesied would end the Great Long Hollow.

Linitus, still under the effects of Alani-Aki's spell in being able to understand and speak with her people, was surprised and concerned about what they meant by the Great Long Hollow. Alani-Aki explained to him it is a period of dark times that continues to plague her people today. Linitus said aloud upon the realization that this had to be about the strange vision he and Marin had near the sacred grove. Alani-Aki nodded and confirmed to him it was and now it would be Linitus and Marin who would help her people to end these dark times. Alani acknowledged, however, that she and Linitus would have to find some way to convince her people that to realize this new era of peace they would have to put their differences aside with the Nordlings of Shimmerfrost. They would have to work toward building a new future together against common foes like Wendigo, Helskadi, and other dark evil denizens that seek to harm and exploit them for their gain.

Linitus nodded but pondered how they would do so. Alani-Aki told him it was simple. She had seen him use his powers to an extent. She told the elf ranger he must call upon his powers to show her people he was one with nature and also had the power to command it. Linitus nodded again. He realized that Alani-Aki's people were indeed in harmony with their natural surroundings. If there would be any way to convince them to follow what Linitus and Alani had advocated in seeking common ground and unity with the Nordlings, Linitus would be the one to do it. He would convince the dyr people that he possessed the ability to command the forces of nature that they were in tune with. In doing so, it might be enough to command the dyr folk's respect and trust toward Linitus in agreeing to make a pact with the Nordlings. This would be the first crucial step to unite against the forces of darkness that seek to divide and conquer Shimmerfrost.

Upon greeting one by one the high-ranking clan leaders of the dyr tribal village would allow Linitus, with Alani-Aki vouching support for him, to demonstrate a trial to gain their trust and follow him. This trial would be one the elf would show that he had indeed the power to control the forces of nature.

At nightfall, once again various members of the settlement's clan elders met with Linitus and Alani near the village firepit that was set aflame. Linitus would concentrate while chanting several words to summon a small whirlwind. He wanted to make sure that, unlike the previous whirlwinds he summoned, this one would be relatively small and harmless. Upon doing so, it impressed the various inhabitants of the village, including the clan elders and Alani-Aki. His miniature whirlwind centered on the firepit created a cylindrical wall where the flames rose straight up while circulating with the wind. Somehow, as frantic and fierce the rising became, it still stayed within the fire pit. The flames gradually weakened and ceased to rise to the heights that it had before. Instead, the flames returned to their normal position a few feet above the base of the fire pit.

After they huddled and consulted with each other, the dyr clan elders agreed this elf had indeed shown from this trial his worthiness in controlling the forces of nature. The clan elders agreed that their village, along with spreading the word to the other dyr villages, would follow Linitus's leadership. They would put their differences aside with the Nordlings to find common causes against Wendigo, Helskadi, and the other forces of darkness. The next morning the clan elders would dispatch dyr messengers on foot to call upon the other villages about what they had witnessed. The other dyr villages would be instructed to follow suit in pledging their obedience before this strange yet also divine chosen elven newcomer.

However, as it was still well into the evening, Linitus noticed something peculiar behind a thicket of trees that surrounded the village. The elf ranger looked intently and noticed a set of dark gazing eyes had watched him. It had stalked him ever since he had used his unnatural powers to use the forces of nature and summon the divine wind. He looked back from the distance and stared intently and in an almost telepathic way, trying to affix his thoughts in communicating to this creature. He both sensed and knew what it was. The creature knew it also and, being alarmed that the elf had sensed it, it fled deeper into the forest, deeper into the darkness. Linitus knew it was afraid. He knew also that the creature for the first time sensed that someone other than Helskadi had finally begun a way to understand it and tap into its feelings.

Alani-Aki noticed the elf staring at the forest and could not help but ask what she had sensed also if it was Wendigo. Linitus nodded. Alani proposed pursuing the beast to track and find its lair. Linitus however shook his head and told her it was best to let it go. When asked why by Alani, the elf ranger told her it was misunderstood.

For once Wendigo had now realized that someone had perceived it for what it was while not treating it as a threat and that perhaps if not, at some point, Wendigo would change. Linitus expressed his hope that this creature would no longer be a creature of darkness and hostility that fed into the violent thoughts and fears it preyed upon. Instead, the elf ranger prayed that this creature would instead channel its mind into a new unknown; a new beginning to let go and accept peace and contentment.

Alani laughed somewhat mildly. She expressed her skepticism in thinking that a creature like Wendigo, which had caused so much trouble and had been born into evil and sin, could know anything other than to project the same malice it had endured. She thought after all, how could it change? After so much hate and vile it had endured and sought to cause as retribution? What other course could steer it differently from its path of fear and destruction?

Linitus responded simply that it would take time. It could change. The elf pointed out that only recently did Alani and her people change into reconsidering their previous hostilities with the Nordlings while being open to building a new future together. Alani admitted it was true. She said it had to be so because the divine spirits had sent him and Marin into their lands and that it was different since the two newcomers had so far passed the trials and prophecy in seeing and understanding the evil that tainted this land. The evil that came into being as Wendigo. It was he who symbolized the original sin and strife between her people and the Nordlings.

Linitus however challenged Alani. He told her to consider the strife that occurred between her people and the Nordlings was not so much from Wendigo itself, but in how her people and the Nordlings responded in their behavior and capacity (or lack of it) to the hardships that fell upon them while shifting the blame to someone else to be used as a scapegoat including Wendigo. Was it merely a continued cycle of suffering, fear, and misdirected violence by those who were prone to accept it without calling into question that change on their part was needed to end that cycle? The elf posed this question to her and without letting her ponder for too much longer; he gave the answered; he told her everyone could change, including in their ways, and that her people had the same capacity to change and seek a better future to build along with the Nordlings of the region. Alani, examining her own beliefs while questioning what the elf presented before, responded that the change her people and she believed in was because of prophecy and that those who came and demonstrated through divine trial their worthiness would bring forth that change for her people and the Nordlings to follow.

Linitus understood her response. He knew it was enough for him and Marin to undergo these trials and use their unnatural powers to perform what seemed to the local inhabitants as being a phenomenon coated in the words of prophecy in order for the dyr folk and Nordlings to change their ways and work toward a better future. Linitus would accept it and imagine Marin would also. However, he told Alani as much as he believed it to be sufficient with her reasoning; it did not have to take him nor Marin to be here and demonstrate their supernatural powers as a trial to convince them to change. If they had realized earlier, it only required them to want to end their feud and put their past behind them while seeking harmony.

Alani understood and despite being initially angered by being challenged to think differently while listening to the elf ranger explain his point of view, she conceded perhaps it was true what he said. Still, she wondered if she, her people, or the Nordlings of the region would think and come to believe otherwise if he had not been here to explain his point of view. They had not changed in all these years their hostilities with the Nordlings until recently with the arrival of Linitus and Marin. These two newcomers were considered the deciding force that caused them to change regardless of what they could have done differently before and chose not to. If the dyr folk and the Nordlings of Shimmerfrost were to change it would only happen because of his arrival along with Marin. The two had introduced them to the possibility of a new beginning.

Alani was correct, and Linitus nodded in conceding as well. The dyr folk and the Nordlings of Shimmerfrost would change but only because of his presence and Marin's as well as their demonstration of supernatural abilities. Linitus only wished the dyr folk would change and cease hostilities with the Nordlings and build a prosperous future together by their intuition without his presence or Marin's.

Still, it was enough for Linitus to accept that he and his wife would undertake prophetic roles if that was what it would take to build this better future. He only hoped that at some point the dyr folk and Nordlings would not become too dependent on him or Marin once they established peace and purged the darkness of Helskadi in these lands. He wanted both the dyr folk and the Nordlings to learn to rule among themselves and live peacefully without his presence and Marin's. They wanted to help, but both he and Marin knew it was not their place to rule in this faraway land. They both wanted to return home to the Kingdom of Swordbane, the place where they belonged and had their responsibilities to protect as well. Linitus would dwell and reflect on this for some time around the fire pit before he would eventually go find rest.

Meanwhile, after resting overnight, by midmorning while being well provisioned with food rations including several kinds of tree nuts and fruit berries, Linitus along with Alani and a small delegation of dyr warriors led by one of their clan elders would depart the village to make their way back toward the same direction from which Linitus and Alani came, east toward the Nordling coastal fjord settlement of Nebelheim. From there Linitus would reunite with his lover, Marin, and the two would help cement the forging of a new peaceful beginning in building a bridge of mutual defense between the dyr folk and the regional Nordlings of Shimmerfrost.

Chapter Twenty-Six

Trial of the Wailing Golden Valkyrie

On the other side of the region of Shimmerfrost, the eastern side, east of Nebelheim and its bay near a river that bled into the ocean with another series of fjords, stood a few miles inland, a lone notable cave of ice. It was nestled against a small ring of mountains. Outside the ice cave, a small shadow moved across the adjacent river and cold, grassy, and partially snowy landscape only a few miles inland from the eastern fjords. As the shadow neared the ice cave, a bright flash from above emanated, only to flash again on the surface. Seven lone figures had teleported to the surface from the lone skyship above.

The figures made their way to the entrance of the mouth of the ice cave. They looked at each other for mutual consultation before entering the darkness of the cave itself. One figure unsheathed her long sword with flames wrapped around the blade. It was Marin holding her blade, Sol's Fury. She turned to the other companions that bore witness. Each of them blushed in awe at her new appearance that differed from before. It caused Marin to feel embarrassed, and she detested undergoing this trial. At the insistence of the chieftain known as Jarl Harleif of Nebelheim, Marin, with reluctance, had adorned herself with the armor and regalia of the legendary Nordling war maidens. In particular, Marin wore the armor said to belong to the original Golden Valkyrie. The origin of the armor is said to have dated from before history was recorded in writing, and such legends became passed down through oral tradition. The armor was also said to be passed down between succeeding generations of Nordling nobility in

Shimmerfrost. Jarl Harleif had been considered the last custodian to keep this legendary armor as part of his inherited treasure hoard stored within his chieftain stronghold. The respective war maiden attire consisted of a somewhat revealing unitard combination of black and turquoise etched leather being superimposed with a gold set of breast, thorax, and waist armor pieces. Along with that armor set, Marin had also adorned shoulder pauldrons of the same vibrant gold color. She also wore a pair of metallic bracers displayed in the same gold overlapping silver metallic offset style as her pauldrons. Her legs and feet were covered with a paired set also of gold and metallic silver greaves and sabatons with the greaves running up almost midway to her thigh.

The most unique item that Marin wore was an enchanted neckband that attaches to the back of her neck. The neckband kept the wearer warm even while wearing the somewhat revealing armor that Marin had on while being exposed to the cold elements. Last, the most artistic piece of this Valkyrie attire was a gold helmet. The helmet covered only the forehead and the side of her face with the helmet's cheek guard. From the top sides of this ornate helm above the top of the cheek guard behind Marin's ear were a series of small gold metal angelic wings. This was an indication of the female wearer according to local Nordling lore as being one of the legendary Valkyrie, though Marin in her deepest heart had no such belief or had intentions to claim being one of the fabled war maidens as part of her Nordling heritage. For her, it was a matter of necessity to appease the Nebelheim chieftain in conforming to this prophecy that he and others in the region seemed hellbent on believing. Marin went along with this superstition. She would give them what they wanted only for a cause that she believed was of the greater importance: to unite the various innocent folks of the land, including Nordling and the dyr people to make a stronger common front against the common forces of darkness led by Helskadi. In doing so, she hoped to provide new peace and prosperity to the region before she departed with her companions to the place that they called home in the Kingdom of Swordbane to the south. If she had to go along with this role in giving them hope even in dressing as a mythic female figure that she would consider as being too provocative looking, she again would do it just to get this over with. Still, being surprised, she had to admit to herself the armor was lighter than what she wore before, and she could maneuver with greater ease. It perhaps gave her an advantage in combat, which she was not as accustomed to as much while preferring to wear the heavier plate mail armor set that provided her greater protection. It would take time to get used to wearing this lighter armor, but she felt up to the task for the time being.

The armor she wore however also courted distraction. Marin could not help but turn around with a mild expression of anger at everyone else who still looked at her with awe. She swore before them that as soon as she completed the task for this trial, she would be returning in wearing her regular plate mail armor. Peat could not help but joke that if Linitus saw her in her current state, this might arouse the elf to blush and turn redder than Marin's angry face.

Only then, after a brief pause and moment in thinking, did Marin burst into laughter while agreeing. Her former dwarf mentor and companion had a point, she thought to herself. As much as she thought this form of war armor attire was awkward in not only being provocative as well as being impractical for many to imagine wearing in such cold weather, but it also had an alluring feel. She even contemplated after the trial to still wear it just to see her elven lover's reaction. Marin took another moment from pondering on such a thought. She nodded while affirming that once the trial was over, she would consider still wearing this attire in front of Linitus just to see his reaction. Her remark had given her enough content to elicit a surprised reaction from Peat and Wyatt. They did not think she was serious about still wearing it after this foray, but knowing Marin, she was up for challenges to see other people's reactions.

Arik, meanwhile, and his three Nordling chosen warrior followers were also distracted and somewhat mesmerized by Marin's beautiful appearance. Still, with a reputation as Nordling warriors, they did their best to act indifferent in noticing Marin, though she could tell she had their attention as well. Regardless, Arik and his fellow Nordling warriors cared more about the role Marin would play for their people. She would be the one that they believe would help deliver them to a new era of prosperity while ridding the region of Helskadi and her dark, evil influence. It was enough for them to see her dress like a mythic war maiden since they believed she was one and that she would be up to the task as their chosen liberator. The four Nordling warriors would follow behind Wyatt, Peat, and Marin into the darkness of the cave to bear witness that Marin had the prowess to pass the trial that was assigned to her by the Nebelheim chieftain. She would prove her ability to cleanse the tainted darkness by uncovering one of the ancient Nordling tombs which had along with other Nordling burial grounds been defiled and compromised by the dark forces of magic by one of Helskadi's most powerful servants, Wendigo, the necromancer.

Deep within the bowels of the cave awaited a dark creature fueled by the powers of Wendigo. This creature was asleep, or rather in a hibernated state in its tomb, awaiting any would-be tomb plunderer or unfortunate adventurer that may disturb it while seeking its prizes. This buried creature had pale, decaying mummified skin that looked almost skeletal in being, though not quite. It was adorned in ancient Nordling armor while also holding in its arms a large double-bladed two-handed ax. In its past life, the human spirit that inhabited this once mortal and pre-undead body was known as Vonkarl, the original king of the once ancient United Kingdom of Shimmerfrost. It was during his reign that he united and ruled over the various Nordling chiefdoms of the far north including Nebelheim, Shimmerheim, and Frostburg.

Marin used her flaming sword as a makeshift torch and lit the torches of her companion followers who followed behind her deeper into the mouth of the cave as the outside light began to dim and give in to the prevailing darkness of the cave. The adventurers soon realized while traversing that this cave was a cavern network of tunnels that had large burial niches on both sides of the cavern tunnels. Marin, along with Peat and Wyatt, could not help but turn to Arik with questions about where they were at exactly.

Arik however could read their minds just by seeing their visible expressions next to the lit torches without them yet saying any words. He could make out what they wanted to know. Arik explained to them that this cave or rather cavern network was the burial place of not only the first king that united the various major Nordling settlements of the far north but also the resting place for many of his loyal thanes, or noble warriors, that served the king in return for several plots of land and a small portion of the king's wealth. Marin could not help but reply in a sarcastic tone about how comforting it was that her trial would not be alone with just the present living company. Peat chuckled while brandishing his war hammer and responding (in Nordling which he knew almost fluently as a dwarf) that the more company they would have the merrier they would be. The dwarf then out of curiosity turned to inquire with Arik if they could partake in combat against any of these corpses should they become awakened and hostile or if they had to leave it to Marin contending alone to demonstrate her worthiness from the trial. Arik nodded while specifying it was fine for them to partake in combat if they left Marin alone to duel against the king of the undead creatures, or draugs as the Nordlings called it.

Peat grinned almost sadistically in his dwarven-like demeanor while indicating his delight at how good of a day this trial was going to be, and he would see that great songs of their deeds would be sung from this day. Arik nodded and agreed, saying that he was happy to find an outsider who relished in conquest and glory against the forces of darkness as much as he and his warrior followers did. He even told Peat that when it was over, they should celebrate at the great chieftain's hall in Nebelheim. Peat could not hold back in grinning while asking if they had plenty of beer at the chieftain's hall. Arik nodded while stating as much as to his content. Peat, losing his composure, shouted aloud with expletives in his eagerness to get this trial done and over with. Marin sighed while taking note and replying with irony that despite her being part Nordling, Peat would adjust better to Nordling culture than her. Peat laughed again while stating that perhaps there was a common ancestor between his dwarven kin and Nordlings. Marin shrugged while stating in a low voice that no one would ever know unless they were alive back then or had visions of the past that would reveal it. Peat laughed loudly again while nodding in agreement.

Suddenly, however, the loudness of his voice was enough to sound off their presence as intruders. Slowly pushing up against the heavy caskets and tombs, the undead draugs had awakened from their slumber. Marin, Wyatt, Arik, and Arik's warrior followers all looked at Peat, wondering why he could not wait until later from his eagerness to give away their presence. Peat, realizing this, gave a quick apology while telling them to make a run for it while he held off the closest draug who were close to bursting out of their caskets and stone tombs.

Marin had a better idea. She told Wyatt with haste to use his magic to cast a special explosive fire enchanted marker on the ground that would cast upon impact from any creature that touched it. Wyatt nodded while chanting and motioning with his hands and magic silver wand to emanate a flurry of fire-like energy that traveled near his hands to the floor surface between them and the nearest set of caskets. Upon doing so, Marin told all present in her company to make a run while instructing Wyatt to continue to cast one magical fire trap marker after another. The halfling wizard did so and stopped along the way at intermittent intervals to cast the same spell after every couple of tomb markers. The process would continue until a few hundred feet and after over a dozen tombs had been passed. Soon the first magical trap marker had been triggered after two of the ancient undead Nordling warriors had broken out of their encased tombs to confront the force that had disturbed them. Upon detonation, these undead warriors fell. The same pattern happened a few more times over with the other set of explosive trap markers Wyatt cast with his magic.

Meanwhile, the cavern tunnel had ended, with a large chamber entryway being revealed. Marin proceeded while noticing a large burial tomb in the center of the chamber along with several chests of treasures. She had to wonder why no one had taken the treasure despite the tomb itself being uncovered. Soon she would find out why. Marin turned to her side. She saw a horrifying undead bearded figure with pale blue eyes adorned in ancient Nordling armor wearing a helmet that had two diagonal protruding spikes along with a central third spike emanating above the helmet. This figure wielded a two-handed double-bladed ax and unleashed a large strike toward Marin.

Marin reacted fast enough to evade by ducking. She raised her shield and in an offensive manner, smacked her shield toward the skull and helmet of the undead adversary. The draug groaned in pain before recomposing himself and speaking in ancient Nordling, which Marin could make out in the creature challenging her boldness to disturb the corpse of the former first great Nordling king of Shimmerfrost. Marin, shocked while speaking what few words she knew in her native maternal Nordling tongue, challenged the creature to identify itself, saying that while it had possessed the corpse of the first Nordling king of Shimmerfrost, it was not the spirit of the former one. The possessed body laughed terrifyingly while nodding and identifying as an undead servant of Helskadi. Marin, still in dismay, asked how it was possible.

Marin somehow knew it was possible however and with a mild shocked reaction uttered his name only for the undead creature to grin. It was Wendigo and his dark magic that truly made this possible. It was this spiteful creature that could be capable of using its supernatural powers of necromancy to possess the corpses. Though she did not know exactly how it had done so, she now knew why the Nebelheim chieftain had given her such a daring trial, which at first seemed trivial and far from what she expected. Now, she understood. If she had demonstrated her worth by defeating these corpses possessed by darkness, it would show the measure of her claim of being worthy to gain the allegiance of the Nordlings throughout the region at her behest.

As her stream of thoughts processed in her mind about all of this, Marin knew she could not lose her composure over a possessed corpse. However, she feigned for a moment. If she could give the impression that she lowered her guard, it may give this creature enough time to also lower his guard by preparing another slow but powerful strike. It had done so, only for Marin to sidestep and trip the creature from behind and knock it hard with her shield again. The possessed draug fell hard to the floor but slowly picked itself up. Marin would have a hard time fighting it, but she decided to use her supernatural powers. She concentrated her mind while uttering several words that she then said faster and faster. Marin aimed her voice and released a fast-pitch wailing shout toward the creature. As she had done so, she could feel a small but powerful hurricane blast of sound projecting from her mouth. Her voice was the source, and upon realizing this, Marin moved her flaming blade toward her mouth. In an instant, the flames traveled forward in the same direction as her loud wailing. In another moment, the scorching flames made contact and scorched the corpse of the undead former king.

The possessed creature lost its composure and ran around frantically in pain. Marin, feeling somewhat drained, took another moment to compose herself before using her divine powers again to chant and create an elongated bright flashing spear. Then she hurled the enchanted weapon at the draug. The creature took the impact of the weapon and traveled a few feet across the air before landing hard on the ground. It still screamed in agony while it was still succumbing to the flames. Marin walked over to it on the ground and raised her flaming sword. In a swift downward motion, she struck and severed its head. The creature ceased to move and came to a standstill. It was over, or so Marin thought.

As she recomposed herself, she noticed from behind her that both Peat and Arik looked at her while being impressed. Peat could not help but boast to Arik about how he used to mentor Marin and taught several of her fighting stance moves. Meanwhile, Marin looked on and noticed Wyatt and Arik's three other companions forming a perimeter in blocking the other ancient Nordling draug warriors including the most superimposing berserkers that wielded two-handed axes like the one undead Nordling king that Marin just slew. Marin, composing herself, realized while not withholding in telling Peat and Arik that there were perhaps too many of the enemies to stand their ground.

Arik shrugged and asked Marin what she had in mind. Marin looked at Peat and noticed that the dwarf guardian had two explosive powder barrels attached to his back with a supportive apparatus frame. Marin told Peat to quickly unload the barrels and to give her a torch. Peat could not help but express mixed emotions, one in part of his admiration for his former protégée resolving to his manner of combat yet even the dwarf could not hold back and caution her in knowing what she was doing as this explosion would collapse the cavern and take them along with the undead draug warriors. Marin smiled while telling both Peat and Arik that she was counting on collapsing the cavern but that she had an idea of how to escape while looking at Wyatt. Peat became even more nervous, pointing out that as talented as the halfling wizard was in casting his magic as fast as he could, no one could escape by one teleportation spell with them being this far deep in the cavern tunnels. Marin smiled with confidence again. She told the dwarf to trust her while assuring him it would not be just one spell.

Peat nodded, while Marin turned to approach Wyatt. Tapping the wizard gently on the shoulder while calling his name to not alarm him as he cast several lightning bolts at the draug warriors, Marin told him of her new plan. At first shocked, the halfling wizard nodded when Marin asked if he thought he could pull it off. The wizard nodded. When Marin gave the signal and Wyatt nodded to show his readiness, the Princess Knight told Peat and Arik to gather around her, Wyatt, and the three Nordling followers that stood just a meter in front of Wyatt. Wyatt, looking around to make sure everyone was close enough to his proximity, looked to Marin, waiting for her to give the signal. Marin took another breath, thinking it was now or never, and then she nodded. Peat stated that he hoped Marin knew what she was doing.

With a few quick utterances and then motioning with his wand at the two explosive barrels placed in one corner of the ancient royal burial chamber, Wyatt quickly released a fireball spell while immediately turning and uttering as fast as possible with his hands including his silver wand that he held another spell. As he said his last utterance while motioning, a large flash emanated just as the moment of impact from his fireball spell occurred. A large explosive flaming burst shot outward and nearly reached them only to catch the emptiness of air as the flash dissipated again. Instead, the explosive flames continued to spread and engulf at least four ancient Nordling draugs.

Meanwhile, in another instant, Wyatt and his companions had flashed and teleported to his last track. He had cast a spell with an explosive tracking ward that detonated from earlier. They were far enough from the immediate radius of the explosion and the burst of flames. However, they felt the ground shake while noticing that the ice cave and tunnel network started to collapse as falling debris began to strike the surface. Marin motioned and pleaded for Wyatt to quickly repeat the spell. Wyatt already knew to do so and began casting immediately his next teleportation spell that would transport them to the next ward tracking point from his earlier explosive trap spell. He would repeat this process again and again while mustering all his concentration and energy to teleport both him and his six other companions. It was daunting. They only had seconds to spare as the tunnel network and ice cave were collapsing at an alarming rate.

Only after about half a dozen times of repeating this teleportation spell-casting process, the halfling wizard and his companions was able to teleport and arrive at the mouth of the cave. At that point, Wyatt was exhausted and could not concentrate anymore. Marin and Peat both knew this, and they both told Arik and his companions to make a run for it and leave the mouth of the cave. Peat carried Wyatt over his shoulder. The dwarf guardian ran as fast as he could, following closely behind Marin and their companions.

Within moments, a large thunderous noise emitted from the mouth of the cave along with falling large chunks of ice and a large veil of cold air that became visible almost like smoke. Only a few dozen feet away before turning back to realize, Marin looked at Peat to sigh in mutual relief. Though barely, they had made it. Arik took a deep breath while smiling and cheering along with his three companion followers who boasted of their escape from the clutches of certain death.

Marin nodded, consigning herself internally that this was indeed a rare moment to celebrate. She turned to Peat again as he gently put Wyatt down on the ground. Marin gave a concerned look, but Peat assured her the halfling would be okay and that he seemed to breathe well despite wearing himself down to utter exhaustion with his spell-casting abilities and concentration. Marin sighed in relief while stating that had Wyatt not been here with them, they would not have survived. Peat agreed but also retorted that had Marin not conceived the improvised means or plan of escape, they would not have survived anyway. He could not help but admit to her that her elven lover's ways had rubbed off on her in being as creative as Linitus would have been to pull this escape and victory off at the same time.

Marin nodded while thinking about Linitus after Peat had brought him up. Her thoughts became centered on her elven lover. It had only been a few days since they last saw each other and had been together. For her, it seemed like an eternity. It was the longest they had ever been apart from each other aside from when they first met as children, and they would not see each other until twenty years later right before the start of the Great Civil War. She did not want to be away from him even another day, though she knew she would have to.

Peat looked at her and even Arik and his men took notice. Peat knew that what he last said had struck a chord with Marin. He asked rhetorically if she missed her elven lover's company. He knew she had indeed missed him. Marin nodded. She could not hold back, letting go of at least one small yet visible tear. The dwarf, feeling for her sadness, wiped the tear away and assured her that soon he and the other present company comrades in arms would see to it that Marin would be united with Linitus as soon as possible. Marin nodded, telling him she knew, but first, she and they had to fulfill their responsibilities.

The trial was over, and Marin confided to Arik and his men that they would attest to the jarl of Nebelheim that she had completed the trial given to her. She had gone to the depths of the cave of Jokull-Hellir and vanquished in single combat the possessed corpse of Vonkarl, the first ancient king that united the Nordlings of Shimmerfrost. Peat asked squarely, out of concern about what to do if the jarl or anyone else of nobility would not believe them. Marin nodded while taking from a small bundled-up cloak she had secured with a small rope tied to her gold waist armor belt. Unfurling the bundled cloak, she quickly revealed a small, jagged jewel-encrusted gold crown which she took away from the slain corpse of the undead former king. Peat's face and dwarven beard widened proudly while boasting of his amazement at the feat Marin had executed. Arik and his men also nodded while heaping praise upon Marin. Arik stated to Marin that from this day he and his men would sing glorious songs about what she had achieved that day while leading them to victory against the forces of the undead darkness. Marin gave a solemn nod to acknowledge Arik's praise. She stated again; that she cared only to do what was needed while wanting nothing more than to reunite with her lover and eventually return home once this was over.

Another moment in passing, Marin quickly padded her hand over Wyatt's forehead as the halfling wizard awoke and gained full consciousness. Marin and Peat next to his side told their wizard companion that he did it. He had pulled off one of the greatest known escapes and spell-casting performances in the history of Terrunaemara. They told the halfling wizard to rest and recover as much as he needed until he was ready to teleport them again.

After a few more passing moments, the wizard had picked himself up. He looked about to notice that the ice cave they had entered was no longer accessible due to it being filled with snow, ice, and rubble. Wyatt then teleported himself and his companions onboard the skyship. Upon arrival, the halfling wizard turned to man the steering helm at the skyship bridge. The crew onboard would return to Nebelheim, where Marin would lay her claim in proving herself through trial as being worthy to unite the Nordlings and the dyr folk of Shimmerfrost against the forces of darkness that had divided and preyed against the good peoples of this far northern land.

Chapter Twenty-Seven

Channeling Hell's Fury

Flying alone and above the plains of hell, Lucia circled in and around the mountainous carved gazing towers of Sanctum Oculi Malum. She waited to see if her presence would draw out the attention of any hidden foes lurching inside one of the many porous holes of this strange series of near-identical and horrendous landmarks. To no avail did she catch any adversaries to lure into following her. Adopting a sudden change of course tactics, she uttered a loud demonic scream. It was one that she had delivered before. If her dark siren call had caught the attention of the denizens of this realm before, she knew it would work again.

Only a moment later did she hear a return call of horrid little beast-like screams and even several succubi screams like hers. They were succubi and with them a swarm of flying demonic imps loyal to Orcus. Returning the demonic scream in the same direction, Lucia then darted away. She soared through the air to the same familiar place she knew before. It was an open hole that led to darkness beneath the surface of the highest layer of hell that she was in. Upon entering the chasm, Lucia unfurled another demonic scream to catch her pursuers' attention. From the distance, she could tell and make out that her presumptions were right. With her eyes adjusting to the darkness, Lucia counted at least three succubi and numerous imps behind them that easily numbered in the hundreds.

Descending downward through the mouth of the open pit chasm, Lucia made her way gradually to just above the hidden cave settlement of Caverna Necropolis. She would float above the middle of this condemned city of the dead. From the surface hiding inside the burnt stone-like dwellings, the inhabitants of the settlement waited quietly and patiently until they received the signal to attack. They had nothing to use, except for piles of small molten rocks. They would hurl these lava rocks using makeshift slings made from the intestines of hellish creatures they had hunted near the perimeter of their settlement.

Meanwhile, hiding inside the dark corners and stalactites of this large cave, dark creatures with red glowing eyes waited until the same signal was also given to attack. These creatures looked intently at the two beings whom they would obey: the one lone succubus that flew in the air and the other one whom the succubus had considered her eternal soulmate. He was also the same one these creatures swore their fealty to. A demonic werewolf covered with ornate regalia and armor in the same fashion as the one he wore in his past life as one of the most feared Citadellans to roam the mortal lands during his former life. Regardless of the change from his past mortal life to his current infernal condemned one, he was still known by his title, Dux Decius. He made it a habit to ensure his name would live on in infamy, even in the afterlife.

Seeing the hundreds of flying imps descend toward the necropolis-like settlement, Decius waited. Eager to want to unleash his full fury, he tempered himself to wait with patience. He concentrated on channeling all the hate and rage he had. Somehow, he could telepathically feel and share the same aura with Lucia in channeling this fury and rage. Their bond had become strong. It was strong enough even in hell that nothing could separate it, especially when they were now united in the same plane or realm with supernatural powers. Their minds could feel and sense each other.

Within moments Lucia spotted the third succubus pass through the deep chasm. Lucia blinked while sending in her focused thoughts and feelings toward Decius. The message was clear. Now was the time to unleash all of his loyal imps waiting in the cave's darkness, poised to strike.

Decius sensed the feelings and thoughts of Lucia, with her adrenaline being heightened. The dux gave the order with a loud terrifying howl. All within the cave and necropolis could hear. The howl terrified both the three succubi lieutenants and their swarm of subservient imps loyal to Orcus. Upon hearing the howl, multiple swarms of opposing imps loyal to Decius ambushed and flung across the internal cave to collide against their mutual counterparts.

Despite the dispatched swarm of imps loyal to Orcus numbering in the hundreds. Decius and Lucia, however, had amassed enough in the thousands. The two of them did so to ensure that this battle would be a slaughter while taking as minimal casualties as possible. It was a masterful plan and a stroke of tactical genius that the dux wished he could have thought of earlier. Now he was grateful that his lover had not only united to be with him by his side in the afterlife but that she had also developed a tactical and strategic mind in combat surpassed only by her ability to manage and administer over the government that tended to her subjects and fellow citizens during her past mortal life. He complimented her, and he would do so following the immediate aftermath of the battle that lasted only a matter of minutes.

As the initial pursuing forces of Orcus dwindled at an alarming rate, the three succubi realized the quick turn of events. Their roles had been reversed from being the hunter to now being the hunted. They screamed to signal for the imps loyal to Orcus to fall back and retreat to the same chasm they came from. It was useless, however. Lucia made sure along with a cadre of Decius's most experienced imp warriors, to intercept and repulse any of the fleeing enemy forces from making their way out of the dark narrow vertical chasm. Lucia would make sure that none of them would escape. Decius at first before the battle contemplated leaving at least one survivor to serve as a lone herald to attest to his power, terror, and domination over all of Hadao Infernum. However, Lucia convinced him it would serve better to slaughter all of Orcus's forces while leaving no survivors to repeat the same tactic as many times as possible. It would leave Orcus's forces decimated gradually over time. In such a war of attrition, the numbers would at some point shift in favor of Decius to outright challenge Orcus once again for the title of being the uncontested lord of hell.

Through sheer determination and ferocity, Lucia's plan worked. None of the imps loyal to Orcus would survive along with their three succubi superiors. The three succubi changed course back down again to the surface of an open cave to desperately fly wherever they could escape. Several hundreds of Decius's imps blocked the other narrow chasm that lay before the opposite end of the cave. Fearing that their options were limited, the succubi along with a few surviving subordinate imps flew to find safety and shelter to hide among the edifices of the necropolis only to realize that thousands of condemned humanoids, mainly humans, that looked charred had stepped out from the structures. These condemned humanoids pelted multiple volleys of rocks toward the succubi and their imp followers. None of the remaining imps survived the onslaught and only two succubi still survived the initial volley. The two demonic sirens decided in a last resort of rage to fight the condemned denizens while flying and darting toward them. As they did so, Decius, in his large dark werewolf appearance, came from behind and charged at one of them. Decius mauled the fallen succubus viciously, ripping off her wings. He delivered a painful death, and he took delight in making it last as long as possible. He soon sensed the other succubus changing course and charging at him. Concentrating his powers, he teleported, causing the enemy succubus to come to a sudden halt before colliding with the corpse of her fallen comrade.

Hearing an audible scream that almost sounded like one of her fellow demonic sisters, the lone succubus loyal to Orcus turned, only to realize she was too late. She was struck in the air by a whip-like leash. She became weakened and temporarily paralyzed. As she looked up, though struggling, she saw the whip-like leash with multiple sharp strands gravitate back in the same direction from where it came to fall back into the possession of its owner's hand.

The struck succubus saw that her attacker looked like one of the succubus sisters, but she was not. She had a unique appearance. Her skin tone was a reddish tint that none of the other succubi had. The other succubi instead had a pale fair to pale ash-grey skin. This red-skinned female also moved and showed gestures that were more commonly associated with the condemned human species that the succubus was all too familiar with in this infernal realm. She had to be one of them, yet she was not. She had bat-like wings, a pair of horns, and attractive features like the other succubi. As the paralyzed succubus still pondered the identity of this enemy newcomer, the latter landed gently from the air while walking in a very human-like manner. She approached her defeated enemy while wielding her powerful weapon. She had asked the last surviving enemy succubus from the battle if she had any last words. The creature only asked who she was and what her purpose was.

Lucia nodded, telling her she would grant her a response before being dealt the eternal blow of non-existence that she thought this creature rightfully deserved. She told this creature that she was the consort of the dux, the true and rightful lord of hell. The defeated succubus was mentally stunned by this point as much as physically. The creature could not help but say what she had thought in her convictions that it was not possible, since Orcus was the true lord of hell. Lucia rebutted while raising one of her sharp black boots in the air and proclaiming that this was no longer true. It was Decius who would be the true lord. Another swift moment and a sharp boot plunged as hard as possible to crush the skull of the succubus. Lucia would make sure the creature was dead for good while stomping furiously several times.

Behind Lucia, a loud howl sounded. She turned. Decius clapped again while telling her that he could feel her anger and hatred as much as he knew she could feel his. The same satisfaction she had in slaying brutally her fallen succubus adversary, he could feel it pulsing through his body and being nourished by it. She felt it and realized it also while turning to see swarms of imps all about the air, as well as the condemned humanoids cheering on. They said her name and Decius's name. She had only introduced her soulmate to these condemned two days before to befriend them and make an alliance to enlist their aid in supporting her and Decius for his claim to ruling over all of hell in exchange for providing them mutual aid and defense while acting as their patron benefactor. Now, with the first battle over, the first of many, she had assured them that both she and Decius had made true to their word in keeping it.

It was an all too familiar symbiotic relationship that had worked well between the dux and the duchess in their mortal lives. Now in the afterlife, Lucia had helped her lover Decius capitalize on his bid for domination successfully, at least in this battle. She had given him an additional source of followers beyond his previous control of the many countless imps that were already swayed to his side against Orcus and his remaining loyal imp counterparts.

In time, Lucia planned to repeat the same pattern of building new clients loyal to her dux while depleting the forces of Orcus in a war of attrition and by swaying as many of his servants to change their allegiance to Decius. She and Decius would use them, all of them who chose willingly to follow. She was aware of it and while she pondered the moral implications, including what shred of humanity she still had left, Lucia assuaged those implications by internally telling herself it was justified. The inhabitants of this infernal realm of condemnation deserved better rulers. Decius and Lucia could not achieve that aim to fulfill that role if they did not use the denizens at their disposal. For her, they had to be used, but she told herself at least in doing so, it would have meaning. They would have a better future than their current state. The entire Hadao Infernum was resigned to accept in sorrow before Decius and Lucia's arrival.

For now, Lucia would revel in the moment along with her lover and their army of followers and new subjects. Eventually, they would use their fallen foes' remains for whatever purpose they could conceive, including as weapons. What scraps of enemy remains were left, Decius's forces would take and stack high outside near the entrance to the vertical chasm above the underground cave. They would burn those remains while Lucia would again use her unfamiliar presence to bait the next enemy swarm of ambushers to fall prey to the same trap again. This would be days from now. It was plenty of time to prepare, and for the moment plenty of enough time for her to embrace her lover and depart together back to his fortress until they would return to implement the next step in Decius's bid as uncontested lord of hell.

Chapter Twenty-Eight

Bracing the Cold Onslaught of Dyr Valley

After two days of travel, the dyr embassy composed of Linitus, Alani-Aki, a dyr clan elder, and several dyr clan warriors made their way through Dyr Valley. This region was one that the dyr folk were all too familiar with. Its namesake was given to them. However, it was also well known by the regional inhabitants as being a dangerous nesting ground for beastly races to settle down temporarily and raid any unsuspecting parties, albeit either dyr folk, Nordlings, or any prey worth hunting.

The valley itself had melted snow and damp grass at the lower elevations along with thickets of hemlock, birch, and spruce trees. The higher elevations still had plenty of snow on the surface that had not fully melted. The weather seemed fair at first considering that it was still the early to middle part of spring. Things however quickly changed by the time this diplomatic embassy was well into the middle stretch of the valley. A sudden small but notable snowstorm appeared unexpectedly. The elf rogue ranger turned to confirm his suspicion with the dyr druid priestess about this sudden and drastic change of weather. He inquired if either Helskadi or more likely her chief minion, Wendigo, had caused this. Alani-Aki nodded while insisting that despite the harsh weather being in their way, they had to persevere. With luck, they could still make it out of the valley even with a few more days of delay.

Linitus nodded while inquiring with the druid priestess and the dyr clan elder about their lore of Shimmerfrost, and more immediately, about the valley itself. They both agreed the easiest way to traverse would be out in the open, as there would be fewer thickets of trees to block their path. They could also look at the valley hills and mountains from a distance to scout any threats that may loom from the coverage of the boulders and trees in the hillier parts of the valley. Linitus was complacent to trust their better judgment but still wondered how they would know if any threats lurked before it was too late to be ambushed. Alani-Aki turned to the elder clan druid, smiled, and then turned back to Linitus to explain to him that, like him, they too are a people of nature, and they can even channel telepathically and communicate with other creatures of the forest whenever the friendly creatures would let them know. Linitus nodded while telling her he understood what she meant as his elven people could also bond with the creatures of the forest. Alani-Aki smiled while letting the elf know she was glad he too could understand her people's bond with the forest. She expressed some remorse in how she wished others, including the Nordlings, would in due time appreciate nature as they both did.

 Linitus nodded in agreement. However, his thoughts upon hearing the word Nordling shifted to Marin. He wondered how much progress she had made with the Nordlings of the region. Though she was in large part on her late mother's side belonging to their culture, Nordling culture was in some respects as alien to Marin as it was to him. This was especially true in the case of Shimmerfrost. Marin had been familiar with her mother's Nordling culture to an extent. Still, she struggled to embrace it fully as she felt an awkward difficulty in navigating between that part of her background compared to her largely paternal Citadellan heritage that she considered herself more accustomed to identifying with. Even then, Linitus thought that because of her mixed heritage even for being fully human, it perhaps gave her a keen insight of both awareness and having an open mind of being exposed to the cultures of others, including his elvish culture. Part of this was normal to her as she grew up in a diverse kingdom full of subjects having various sentient backgrounds. Still, he thought about her openness and genuine desire to want to explore and understand the greater unknown. He thought that if she could understand the views of others who valued being more attuned to nature and their natural surroundings, anyone else, regardless of background even of human Nordling descent, could as well. Perhaps more so without even saying aloud to avoid provoking a negative response from Alani-Aki and the other small group of traveling dyr folk,

Linitus thought they also might appreciate and respect certain aspects of Nordling culture that they may not have fully understood.

Drifting deeper into a stream of thought, Linitus could not help but go back and still think of Marin. He missed her, and while he did not show it noticeably, Alani-Aki could tell from his subdued facial expressions that each delay would take longer for him to reunite with her seemed like a mental torment he wanted to escape. Still, he could not. He had his calling as he knew it just as he knew Marin had hers for going on their separate trial quests. Alani understood that much from observing the elf ranger. Regardless, the dyr druid priestess interjected to let Linitus know that, his lover, Marin, was safe and that he would see her.

Assured by Alani, Linitus nodded while seeking to press on at the front of the traveling embassy envoy. He thought as much and would tell himself the same thing each day. He and Marin were survivors. They both knew how to rely on their skills to survive. However, there were times, earlier in their reunited adulthood when his lover's life was in peril, and he saved her and even saved himself. This time he could not do it since he was not there with her to know. It bothered him and to an extent made him feel somewhat insecure. However, Linitus consoled himself to know that she would persevere even when he was not there with her. She had grown wiser and more mature since they were together. He knew she would prevail in her creative way whatever challenges came before her.

Linitus returned to the moment at hand while assessing their current state of slow but progressive travel in the now snow-filled valley. The elf rogue ranger suddenly heard loud screeching sounds from a hawk. He screeched back to summon it toward him. The red-tailed hawk heard his summoner's call. The bird descended toward Linitus before stopping and floating down to land on the elf's leather bracer on his left arm. Upon doing so, Linitus looked upon its expressions while studying its eyes. He could tell the hawk became startled by what it saw below. Though the elf was uncertain of what the source of its distress was, he channeled his thoughts into the creature. Telepathically channeling his powers of nature, Linitus summoned the creature to rise and ascend into the sky. As it did so, Linitus's focus was attuned to sharing the thoughts and senses of the creature. He could control its thoughts and actions by gaining the creature's trust to allow him to do so through his powers. As he did so, with the creature's vision, he could scout near the same area that it had surveyed earlier. He noticed clustered groups that hid among the high valley hill and low mountain tree line. It terrified Linitus. His body was nearly frozen on the surface, as Alani-Aki and the other present delegate company of dyr folk were alarmed and curious about what he had seen. They could tell that his facial expressions revealed a sense of shock and a slight sign of fear. The dyr escort company wanted to know what Linitus saw. They waited, however, until the elf broke his focused trance to release the hawk from his telepathic control and allow the creature to fly freely back to its instinctive destination due south.

Alani-Aki and the dyr clan elder both asked what he saw as Linitus composed himself and withdrew the bow he had slung earlier around his back. The elf replied they were being pursued from the north and that they had to veer southward toward the southern valley hills and low mountains. He knew there was not enough time to escape while being pursued as the enemies were closing in at a fast pace, but he thought to himself that if he could retreat with his present company to the cover of the southern thicket next to the hills and low mountains while the enemy pursued them by venturing out into the open valley center itself which had less cover, he could unleash as many arrows along with the few dyr that were armed also with bows and arrows. Perhaps by wearing down the numbers of the enemy without being exposed to how few Linitus and his present company numbered it may give them enough of an advantage to deter the pursuing enemy from following further and to fall back. At least that is what Linitus hoped.

Alani-Aki and the dyr clan elder, still curious, asked Linitus who their pursuers were. Linitus told them they were being followed by a mixed army of hundreds of goblins, dozens of cave orcs, a small group of snow dwarves, and several snow trolls. The worst part the elf ranger disclosed was that this army was being led by some strange, tall, brutish giant human creature. Alani-Aki was familiar with the description to identify to Linitus what he described. It was according to Alani-Aki, a jotunn, which was a pale giant. They were the tall folks from the high mountains of Shimmerfrost led by the Winter Death Witch known as Helskadi. Except for the image of Helskadi when eavesdropping in the mine cave by the Great Azure Lake, Linitus was unfamiliar with these strange giant creatures. He knew from possessing the hawk and its vision that even just one of these jotunns was presumably formidable and intimidating given their superimposing tall stature.

Meanwhile, alarmed by what Linitus had revealed from using his powers of sight vision with the hawk, the other dyr folk among the delegation followed suit along with Linitus. They withdrew their bows and arrows. Linitus led the way followed by Alani. They traversed away from the open valley floor while making their way to the southern tree line and ascended to the top of one of the low-lying hills. They continued to move westward toward Doire na Cairn. Eventually, Linitus had the delegation stop as soon as he found a hill high enough and open to look upon the lower valley floor.

Moments later, Linitus saw emerging from the north end of the partially snow-covered valley a pursuing small ambush army of dark forces. The elf quietly waited and aimed with his bow. He pulled back next to the bowstring while holding a cylinder sabot receptacle that would release a hail of cluster arrows. Still waiting patiently, the elf would let loose his deadly weapon barrage assembly as soon as the enemy ambushing army was within range and closing in on the southern end of the valley floor several hundred yards away from Linitus and the dyr delegation. Upon Linitus letting loose his shot, the other dyr warriors holding back their bows and arrows would do the same. Suddenly, the soaring arrows can be heard along with a terrifying screeching noise of the deployed arrow sabot receptacle that dispersed and scattered the many clusters of arrows across the open sky.

Within moments, the arrows found and struck several of the goblins and cave orcs that charged at the forefront of the dark ambushing army. Linitus knew that while they had taken out several of the enemies, many more would still close in to pursue him and his dyr allies. They were outnumbered by at least a hundredfold. Still defiant to strive to live and survive the odds, Linitus readied his bow with another sabot cluster receptacle. He had only two more left, which he had prepared while briefly visiting and residing at the dyr village. He would use one more of them while instructing the small number of dyr warriors to prepare one more volley before they would close in for melee combat. They would make their shots count while bracing for the cold onslaught of Helskadi's dispatched ambush war party.

Chapter Twenty-Nine

Nature's Ill Omen

For the second day, a lone skyship hovered above a dense, covered forest that surrounded a small plot of open land below. The small acreage of land below consisted of the ancient stone megaliths of Doire na Cairn. From the topside deck of the ship looking along the starboard side to the ancient ruins below, Marin waited for when her elven lover would arrive along with Alani-Aki and members of her dyr tribe. Marin's face stood still, but internally her eyes scanning about had revealed an impatient and concerned sense of feeling.

Peat looked across the ship from the aft while standing next to Wyatt. The halfling wizard manned the helm of the ship. Both he and the dwarf guardian looked about and could tell Marin's look of eagerness and concern. There was no hiding it. Peat knew the look from Wyatt's expression based on the dwarf's close affinity in knowing the Princess Knight longer. The dwarf knew he should be the one to comfort her while waiting for their elven comrade to return from his quest.

Peat slowly walked across the topside deck of the ship, before turning to put his arm over Marin's shoulder. Marin knew it was him and still had her eyes fixated on the ruins below. The dwarf guardian meanwhile told her that wherever he was, they would find him, or he would find them. If there was anyone Peat knew who could survive and overcome the odds of these harsh conditions, it would be the elf. Marin nodded with some comfort while taking in her former mentor and comrade's words. She admitted quietly that he was right, and she thought the same. Still, she felt something was not right. It was unusual for them to wait this long for Linitus, knowing that her lover was the first in typical fashion to outdo and outperform anyone. She had expected him to wait first, or at the very least to arrive by now. She had wondered what he had encountered if he was setback further in arriving as planned.

Only the screeching sound of a lone bird, a red-tailed hawk, that soared across the air making its way eastward and southward had broken Marin's fixture of the ruins below. She as well as everyone else onboard took notice. The elder Nordling fisherman that joined the ship's crew while Peat and Wyatt were stopping at Aegir-Hafn could not help but comment while observing. The elder Nordling indicated aloud how strange it was in this part of the spring season for a creature such as this to migrate southward to its winter home when it would have flown from the other direction during this time of the year when it was already spring season.

Marin, thinking about what she had pondered along with Wyatt and Peat, came to the surmisable deduction that something drastic had to have happened. She said aloud in questioning what other explanation would cause such a species to make this unusual change or shift in its migratory route of travel. She could not help but speculate that the source of this cause very well could come from the same direction from which the lone bird migrated. It could have come from the same direction her lover was currently in. She could not hold back but fear that this unusual notice of change was interrelated in affecting not only the lone hawk but also wherever her lover was. Fueled by this sign of nature's ill omen, Marin ordered that Wyatt change the ship's course. They would sail west by northwest toward the same direction from which this hawk emerged. Wyatt nodded and changed the ship's course while using his magic wand to steer the ship's helm remotely.

Meanwhile, Arik, being familiar with the landscape, informed Marin that by proceeding in that direction they would go through the rising elevated hills and mountains of Dyr Valley. It was through this valley that Linitus and his dyr allies would have likely used to proceed en route to rendezvous with Marin and the rest of their Nordling company.

As she gripped her hand with firm resolve on how to proceed, Marin told the crew to be ready for anything that they would encounter. Sailing away from the forest surrounding Doire na Cairn, Marin along with the rest of the crew took additional notice of the change of weather as they came closer to Dyr Valley. The wind became more turbulent and even snow appeared to cover the surface below from the cloudy sky. Eventually, they would be at the heart of what seemed like a near winter storm.

Chapter Thirty

Summoning Nature's Fury

Linitus fired the next salvo of arrows. He and his small party of dyr warriors were only a few dozen yards away from the still largely intact enemy army of Helskadi's dark forces. At least several hundred of them closed while scaling the increasing mountainous terrain. Linitus contemplated his options. He deliberated, though he knew he had to choose quickly. One option he considered included continuing to retreat to higher elevations. The other option would be to stand their ground while preparing one last volley of arrows to rain down against the enemy. The third option Linitus pondered was to charge forward while going downhill to fight off the many goblins, orcs, snow trolls, snow dwarves, and even this large mysterious giant human warrior they call a jotunn. Linitus called upon Alani, the dyr clan elder, and the dyr warriors to stand their ground. They would fire one last volley of arrows before preparing to engage the enemy in combat as they continued to close in.

Linitus prepared his final arrow barrage sabot receptacle loaded with multiple combs of arrows. The elf ranger let loose after aiming with his bow. The other dyr warriors, armed with their simple wooden bows and ash shaft barbed flint arrowheads, released a volley of arrows. Right afterward, they picked up their flint spears with six-foot-long wooden shafts to engage in combat against the dark forces of the Winter Death Witch. Linitus did the same as well. He slung his bow around his back and secured it. At the same time, in a steady fluid motion, the elf ranger unsheathed his sword while striking at the first cave orc that closed in. The cave orc fell along with his obsidian spear.

Meanwhile, several more cave orcs and goblins closed in. The rogue elf ranger, in a nearly effortless and natural sense of choreography, dispatched each of the enemies that charged toward him. While he did so, Linitus used his long slightly curved elven blade in a series of graceful parries, evasive strafes, strikes, and repeating the same cycle again and again.

The dyr warriors that fought alongside him fought fiercely while forming a defensive perimeter around Alani-Aki and the dyr clan elder. The latter two channeled their magical powers to summon several creatures to come to their aid. The nearby forces of nature answered that call with a sleuth of large brown grizzly bears that roared fiercely while charging toward the attacking dark army. The first to fall among the enemy at the hands of these summoned creatures were the grizzlies' natural rivals, dire wolves, along with their goblin riders. The grizzly bears mauled viciously at the charging goblin wolf riders and the dire wolves. The grizzlies quickly and effectively neutralized many of them that sought to outflank Linitus and his dyr companions.

Linitus and the dyr envoy still fought ferociously for dear life. They held their ground as firmly as they could while the first wave of Helskadi's forces crumbled. The few remaining cave orcs and goblins that stood on top of the snow-covered hills of Dyr Valley retreated to the valley floor. Linitus became uncertain if this was a feigning retreat. He told Alani and the other dyr envoy to hold their ground and not pursue. Instead, the elf ranger instructed the dyr envoy to use their bows and arrows again to shoot at any of the retreating enemies still within range. They picked off a few more of the goblins and orcs in retreat. Only a handful of the enemies' first wave of attackers survived, and they retreated behind the cover of the forest's low hill.

Celebrating what seemed like an initial victory, the morale of Linitus and his companions soon shifted into desperation again. A loud audible war shout could be heard from the distance by a large approaching snow giant or again jotunn as they are called by the Nordlings. This large jotunn was covered in large animal hide fur while adorning a large, spiked metal helmet that appeared to be made of some large animal bone. He flaunted one of his arms while wielding a large wooden club to signal for the rest of the attacking force to rally behind him. At once they charged again to overwhelm Linitus and the dyr envoy. Behind the large hairy, bearded, pale-skinned jotunn charged at hundreds more of the goblins, cave orcs, and several of the evil snow dwarves and snow trolls. The small sleuth of grizzly bears that came to the aid of Linitus's company earlier charged into the fray against the attacking forces. This time, however, the powerful allied creatures fell within several strokes of the jotunn warrior's large club. The fallen grizzlies managed before being slain to diminish a few more of the enemy warriors of this second attacking wave.

Linitus instructed the dyr warriors to let loose a volley of arrows before retreating a few paces. They would repeat the same process to harass the enemy forces at a distance while trying to maintain a gap between them. It would only last after several volleys. By this point, Linitus knew the enemy was still closing in fast. He ordered the dyr warriors to prepare to hold their ground again and switch their armaments to spears while engaging in melee combat. Alani-Alaki, however, knew that their chances of surviving were unlikely if someone did not take out the lone jotunn giant that was commanding this large raiding party. She told Linitus this and Linitus nodded. Alani used her telepathic-like powers. She could sense in this elf's mind that he was holding back his powers to command the forces of nature, and she knew why. He could cause enough destruction with his supernatural powers to harm himself and his companions and not just the enemy alone by being in proximity to each other. The dyr druid priestess, however, knew that he still had the potential to cause havoc and that perhaps it would not matter regardless. She said aloud for him not to hesitate and to do it. It was time for him to summon nature's fury even if it would come at a cost to them being so close. Nodding, Linitus prepared himself to say several words of utterance only for his thought of concentration to be disrupted as he heard a recognizable voice from a distance and high above.

Linitus looked up. To his surprise and relief, he saw a lone skyship with several faces from the distance peering down at him. One of them, Marin, screeched down from the highest low-lying snow-topped mountain in Dyr Valley. Her screeching became a deafening wail that caused a nearby mountain to shake uncontrollably. Within moments, a gigantic wave of snow broke away and descended in a rolling and cascading manner. It made its way to Linitus, the dyr envoy, and consequently, their enemies, which were only a few dozen feet from closing in. Immediately, a large flash of light emitted all around before Linitus and his dyr allies. Another moment they saw the snow and descending avalanche fade before their eyes in a sudden flash of light. After the next bright flash, they had arrived by teleportation aboard the lone skyship. They found themselves surrounded by familiar friendly faces, at least for Linitus, though less so for the dyr envoy.

All onboard the skyship looked below. They saw the large avalanche descend upon and bury the enemy raiding party. Many tried to flee. However, nearly all of them perished under the snow. Only a few goblins and orcs survived, including at least two goblin shamans who used their magic to safely teleport some of their comrades. Those few enemy survivors fled at once from the vicinity of the battle site. Everyone onboard looked in awe of what had transpired, everyone except Marin. She became fixated on Linitus, who she quickly came to embrace as soon as he appeared onboard.

Linitus returned the embrace. He focused his mind on two things: what had just happened and diverging his focus toward the one that mattered to him most, Marin. She missed him dearly as she pressed hard against him and kissed him. He held tightly toward her and returned the kiss while being interrupted, as she could not hold back the swirl of emotions from anger to fear of losing him. She missed him. Marin would do everything possible to make sure that he would not die before her eyes from the field of battle, at least if she did not die with him at his side. They were soulmates and to her, they were inseparable. Linitus knew that. Without her to utter more words than what was necessary to understand the gravity of how she felt, he cut his lover off to tell her he did everything he had to survive and to avoid an overwhelming force that was unavoidable. He could do no better to escape the danger that followed him while en route to rendezvous with Marin and their Nordling allies at Doire na Cairn.

Marin took a moment to absorb and process what he said. She nodded while understanding and expressing remorse, given the circumstances of what Linitus was up against. Her lover nodded while embracing her again for comfort and to let her know that for now, it was over. They had found each other, and they would live another day. It would be no different from the other days of adventure, or so he hoped to assuage Marin's concerns. In truth, they both knew this was the opposite since arriving in Shimmerfrost, or even before when pursuing the cultist caravan that led to their fateful encounter and miraculous survival in teleporting from the cave network near the Great Azure Lake. This adventure had become a test of survival like no other that they had faced before, or at least not since the days they first adventured together at the end of Swordbane's war with Marjawan over ten years ago and in the immediate aftermath of Dux Decius's rebellion and secession against the Kingdom of Swordbane. Things were dire and different now in a monumental way as they were then. They both knew it.

Marin nodded while Linitus found a diversion for them to channel their attention. The elf rogue ranger pointed back down again to let her know it was over while surveying the aftermath of the plunging avalanche. No one below survived, save again for the few goblins and orcs that managed to teleport away. However, as the occupants onboard the skyship celebrated their victory against the enemy. Alani mourned along with the dyr clan elder. They had sustained casualties among their party, with two of their dyr warriors falling victim on the surface. She lamented while expressing to everyone else on board that they had to wait until the unusual weather cleared up to cremate the fallen corpses, both friend and foe alike. Linitus asked why. Marin knew after battling in her trial against the ancient draug king of Shimmerfrost and his awakened undead company of bodyguards. The dark powers or magic of Wendigo could consume the corpses of the fallen if they were not disposed of and burned to ashes. She explained this to Linitus while Alani expressed her gratitude to Marin for understanding this practice by not only her people but also by the Nordlings, who adopted the same practice for many generations since Wendigo's dark powers haunted this cold and eerie region.

Alani acknowledged that they now had a dilemma. She and one of the dyr clan elders representing her people could not travel further to Nebelheim to bring peace negotiations with the Nordlings in a timely manner unless they abandoned the corpses of the fallen enemy and friend alike at the peril of Wendigo using his dark magic to resurrect the corpses to fight on behalf of Helskadi's army. Marin and Linitus acknowledged her concern and agreed in good faith something had to be done to neutralize the fallen corpses from being raised by Wendigo.

Linitus thought innovatively after taking a moment to ponder. Suddenly, he gave a slight grin after he conceived an idea in his head. He turned to Peat and asked the dwarven guardian if he had any explosive barrels on board the skyship. Peat became unsure of what Linitus intended to do, other than blow up the corpses to pieces. However, the dwarf realized Linitus's plan and smiled while shouting in a proclamation of excitement that the elf had finally come around again to understand Peat's level of thinking. Linitus knew that with enough explosive barrels, it could get the task done in disposing of the fallen corpses from being raised as undead by Wendigo. Still, he pondered how to get the explosive barrels deep within the snow that smothered the bodies because of the avalanche caused by Marin's supernatural wailing voice. Marin turned and proposed with a curious and insightful resolution of finding out if he could summon a large enough tornado whirlwind to uplift both the snow and the bodies under it while planting the bombs on the snow surface beforehand.

At first doubting herself if this would work, Linitus, impressed by his wife's creative suggestion, assured Marin that it was worth finding out. Peat nodded in agreement along with Wyatt, Arik, Alani, and soon everyone else on board, including Nordlings and dyr folk alike. They all thought at this point that this plan, strange as it may sound, had been simple enough to understand. However, to execute the plan itself was not as simple as it seemed.

Within moments, Linitus, along with Marin and Peat, were transported to the surface. Wyatt remained onboard the skyship to serve as a lookout from below. The wizard had planned to hurl multiple fireballs at the explosive barrels once they were in position. He even thought about teleporting the explosive barrels inside the tornado once Linitus summoned it. However, the elf rogue ranger ruled it out. Instead, he thought it best to scatter them on the surface to allow the explosive barrels to set off a chain reaction with a large enough blast radius. This became the preferred plan since it would be difficult for Wyatt to do since the halfling wizard could not teleport them all at once to different places.

Wyatt teleported the explosive barrels one at a time to the surface at different locations. Linitus instructed Peat, Marin, as well as Arik, and two of his Nordlings warriors to use the skyship's hemp rope to secure one of the open handles of the barrel explosives. Several of the barrels would also be carefully cut with a large incision near the top to later be used in disbursing leaked fuel for ignition once the plan was implemented. Over the span of two hours, an intricate weblike pattern was formed with the hemp rope that kept the explosive barrels secured at a fixed distance from each other. The elf hoped it would be enough to stay in place while it floated in the air along with the snow and fallen corpses once it was time for Linitus to use his supernatural powers to summon a massive whirlwind. Time would tell if his plan would work, but the elf and his companions were confident that it would, and they would be ready to depart by nightfall just in time before Wendigo would be at his strongest in creeping out from the darkness to use its powers in summoning the corpses of the fallen.

However, as Linitus and his assigned detail finished assembling the explosive barrels with the hemp rope and prepared to walk toward Marin and Peat, a gigantic pale hand appeared out from the snow. Steadily, the hand emerged along with the rest of a large hulking body. It was the lone jotunn warrior that led the raiding party from earlier.

Marin looked toward Linitus. Her face became visible with horror as her unsuspecting lover stood with his back turned toward the snow giant. Linitus however, with a keen eye, was close enough to look at Marin's facial expression and see the reflection from her eye to know something threatening and menacing was behind him. In a sudden flow of movement, the elf rogue ranger quickly leapt forward while twisting and leaning back to fall toward the snow. The snow giant swiped toward him but missed. As Linitus evaded midair, he quickly withdrew his bow. With his instincts and adrenaline being at its height, somehow, he concentrated on his thoughts and the flow of nature and energy around him. He could channel and harness it while projecting with his mind, spirit, and body to craft a bright glowing form of light that he aimed with his bow and bowstring to pull back and release. In a sudden moment, just before Linitus landed on the snow, he was able to let loose a lone bright streaking form of energy that was in the shape of an arrow yet looked like a lightning bolt.

This supernatural projectile flew dauntlessly toward the jotunn. It struck the giant's chest near his heart and caused him to stagger, only to receive another similar yet different form of lightning-like projectile that mortally struck and pierced into one of his eyes. The other projectile came from Marin, who also reacted as instinctively as Linitus in summoning and harnessing the forces of energy and light to craft a lightning spear that she hurled only a moment after Linitus first struck the jotunn.

The giant stood motionless after being struck by Marin's enchanted spare. Everyone else both on the surface and looking down from the skyship above were once again in awe from both the display of Linitus and Marin's uncanny divine-like powers. Linitus however, was in awe of Marin's fearless reaction while staring deeply into Marin's eyes only for his lover to express the same stare before the two embraced each other in being thankful that they still had each other.

After pausing another moment, Marin composed herself and returned her attention toward the dead body of the snow giant that had laid in the kneeling position with its back awkwardly sloping at an angle. Leaving nothing to chance if Wendigo could somehow resurrect this hulking beast in case the explosive barrels did not blow its corpse to pieces, Marin, the Princess Knight, unsheathed her flaming sword and with one mighty fell swoop severed the deceased giant's head from his body.

For Linitus and perhaps Wyatt and even Peat, her anger was savage and seemed to be more at home with what the local inhabitants were acquainted with. Marin took the dead giant's severed head and handed it to Linitus. The elf ranger was still in awe and unsure of what she wanted him to do with it. Marin knew from his facial expression while simply replying that he needed to display his kill to show to the Nordlings of Nebelheim and throughout the rest of Shimmerfrost the elf's worthiness as well as hers to lead them. Linitus took the severed jotunn's head with reluctance. He asked her however if she should keep the severed head as a token for the Nordlings to validate her legitimacy in leading them since she also slayed the giant as well as delivered the final mortal kill. Marin sarcastically smiled while responding that she already had her trophy to validate her legitimacy to lead the Nordlings. If they were to be led, she told her lover they would lead them together.

Linitus smiled mildly while nodding. Within moments of making sure the explosive barrel contraption was rigged and set to go, Wyatt teleported his companions from the surface back to the skyship. It was already sunset. Taking a moment to look at the view while not helping but to admire the beauty of the northern gales that picked up speed above the Dyr Valley, Linitus quickly channeled his thoughts and mind while quietly chanting several uttered words. In a matter of moments, a large circular whirlwind emanated near the center of the connected ring of explosive barrels. The swirl became tremendous and fiercer as it continued to pick up. Eventually, more and more of the snow was sucked into the whirlwind along with lifeless bodies of mainly the fallen enemy warriors which appeared.

The elf tried to hold his concentration for a few more moments as the whirlwind reached a steady speed of rotation. Wasting no more time, Marin called out to Wyatt to signal for the halfling wizard to enact his role in the plan. Wyatt nodded while holding the tip of his hat. He motioned several times with his hands and silver-tipped magic wand. Several large fireballs emanated and shot out from Wyatt's hands. The fireballs darted toward the divine-like tornado and eventually struck at least one of the explosive barrels. Immediately, a chain reaction took place while formulating an even larger explosion within the whirlwind that was also filled with explosive fuel vapor from several of the barrels that leaked. The gigantic explosion eviscerated everything within, the sight of which became an awe-inspiring spectacle as it turned into a fire tornado completely consumed by burning flames and ash.

From the distance, lurching behind a cluster of trees a few miles away, emitted a haunting scream that could be heard throughout the valley. It was Wendigo. Alani and the dyr elder were the first to react and recognize the loud and saddened voice. They both acknowledged that Wendigo became furious. The dark beastly creature had been denied the use of his powers to consume the corpses of others that would seek to do his will and the will of his vile queen, Helskadi. The corpses Wendigo wanted to possess were already consumed by the fire tornado and reduced to ashes.

As the sky got darker and the night set in, the lone skyship changed course to sail east toward its next intended destination. Within a day or so the crew onboard would reach Nebelheim to pursue diplomatic discussions for a new era of peace between the Nordlings and the dyr folk in uniting against the real menacing threat to their region. If there was any way that would convince the Nordling settlements' chieftain of that cause, Linitus and Marin would bear the tokens of their worthiness in pursuit of that cause including a severed jotunn head and the crown of an undead famous Nordling king.

For now, just as in their younger adventuring years, Marin and Linitus would enjoy each other's company while holding each other and staring at the bountiful, full moon sky glittered with countless stars and the rare, majestic sightings of several scattered formations of colorful auroras. It was a view which they would find some solace to cherish and marvel at the beauty from above in a land below that they still considered cold, harsh, and unforgiving. In time though they also came to find that this place could be called home by some who were willing to understand and warm their hearts to this region while making some effort to appreciate the balance of harmony and nature that existed. It was hardly a comfortable living to call a place such as Shimmerfrost, but still one perhaps that offered as much adventure and fascination as the warmer lands farther south.

Chapter Thirty-One

Plotting and Counterplotting

Deep in the bowels of the titular lord of hell's fortress, Orcus remained seated while quenching a fist and banging it hard on his jagged throne armrest. He became visibly angered. Still, he restrained and composed himself as a lone imp minion scout reported its fortunate survival by an army that had ensnared a sizeable portion of the lord of hell's forces. This army comprised many other imps in rebellion against Orcus's rule of Hadao Infernum. It also included a large settlement population that lived under one of the narrow cave chasms near Sanctum Oculi Malum.

The imp went further to mention that this rebellious army was being led not only by Orcus's contested rival, Decius but also by a mysterious female figure. The imp described this unfamiliar figure as someone who looked like any other succubus. However, this newcomer had reddish skin unlike the pale fair skin or pale ash skin of the succubi. She was also more fearsome and cunning than the other known succubi. The creature went further, saying it was a miracle it survived to count its fortunes in being able to report back to Orcus.

Orcus, however, stared menacingly. He remained fixated on all that he had heard. The demonic overlord picked up his large two-handed cleaver and hurled it at the lone imp survivor. All present in his throne room, succubi and imps alike became bewildered by what they had witnessed. The lord of hell got up from his throne. He paced slowly toward the fallen corpse of the imp to dislodge his weapon. He looked at his audience of subservient minions and shrugged while stating that this creature was too content in its station in the afterlife to still live under his service. Orcus reminded all those present how short the afterlife would be when he became angry. He wanted to remind them that the only cause worth living for was to serve him and fulfill his desires. The other creatures in his hellish royal audience understood the message and nodded in silence.

Orcus turned his back to his throne and sat down. He wielded his weapon in his hand and pointed it downward to the ground. The demonic overlord held his head with his other hand that rested on his jagged throne's armrest. He contemplated and mulled over what was revealed by the fallen imp's description of the battle. He realized that this strange new female creature was a formidable threat to contend with while she aided his rival, Decius. She had lured much of his army that tried to ambush her only for this strange newcomer to lead them to their demise in being hunted down from a reverse ambush deep in the chasm near Sanctum Oculi Malum. Orcus realized he had to devise an effective counterplot to neutralize the plotting that his enemies seemed to use with effectiveness against his forces. After some deliberation, the hell lord gave a fiendish grin while he pounded his bare fist hard against his throne armrest.

Orcus stood up and ordered six of the succubi in his audience to gather several dozen of his loyal imps. He told them to go to the demonic spider lairs of Caverna Lum to obtain their services. Caverna Lum itself lay southeast of his fortress. It was a cave that was deep within the chasms of the plateau ridges that descended deeper into the lower plains of hell below the plateau level where Orcus's fortress lay. The six succubi kneeled while nodding in submission before flying off and rounding several dozen imps to follow them. Orcus expected them to return in less than six days given the time to travel to and from the respective location. He also based the estimation on how long it would take the hell spiders of the cave to make and deliver Orcus's order as part of his master counterplan.

Chapter Thirty-Two

Infernal Ambush Reversal

A few days later, a lone reddish flying figure soared above the hellish flat plain of the highest level of Infernum. She darted as quickly as possible to lure her hunters toward the ambush that she would have in store for them only a few miles away. This demonic yet alluring figure known commonly as Lucia, along with her lover, Decius, continued to set up ambushes to further decimate Orcus's forces. She and Decius intended to leave no survivors to escape and report back to Orcus on the deadly ambush. She would lure the enemy just as she had done before. They would pursue her through the menacing eye towers of Sanctum Oculi Malum. On the other side, they would continue to chase after her through the chasm that descended to the cave of the condemned refugees, Caverna Necropolis. Once they descended, her hunters would find their roles reversed. Swarms of imps loyal to Decius would instead ambush them along with an army of the condemned that resided on the cave surface settlement below. Everything would work according to plan, or so Lucia thought.

Lucia made a pass through the first set of vertical mountainous eye-like columns. She noticed while in midflight that the gap between the pursuing imps led at the front swarm by three succubi and her had widened. They were not pursuing her as fast as she thought they would. It was strange and noticeable to catch her off guard while she passed through the second set of mountainous eye columns. Only a short distance to the third set of columns did she realize why their pace had slowed. She was about to pass through the third series of columns. However, Lucia noticed a wide, bright flashing net being suspended at the top of the two adjacent columns that she was about to fly through. Lucia tried to come to a screeching halt, but her speed was not enough to slow down and stop before it was too late. She had found herself caught in the net, which leeched onto her and shocked her with painful electrical discharges. As she struggled to break free, it only became worse as the net, or more specifically hell spider web, had small barbs that latched onto her body and wings to hold her into place.

The shocks continued in a stream of waves that jolted her body. It was painful enough. Lucia could barely tolerate the stinging pain she felt. She tried to resist losing consciousness, but a menacing succubus flew down to approach her. The succubus jeered at Lucia's state of distress and helplessness in being caught in the hell spider web. The succubus then paused, only to suddenly strike a painful blow to Lucia's head with a blunt mace. The impact was not lethal. It was hard enough to send Lucia into a state of unconsciousness in case the hell spiders' webs were not powerful enough to incapacitate her.

Upon delivering the painful blow, the succubus, assisted by her other demonic flying siren siblings and imp followers, carefully removed their red-skinned counterpart nemesis from the trap. They secured her with bonds made from the same material as the hell spider web. They would carry Lucia's slumber and nearly limp body to fly back to their master's fortress lair in Sanctum Orcus while flying west by northwest. They would arrive there in several days.

The succubi wanted to torture and tear apart to death their fallen foe out of jealousy and revenge for Lucia. They knew that she and her allies caused the deaths of several of their succubi sisters. However, these demonic sirens restrained themselves from killing Lucia. They did so out of fear of the repercussions if they failed to carry their master's orders. They were to bring back this strange red-skinned newcomer who looked like her succubus counterparts yet was not one of them. Orcus had heard enough accounts. He was curious about Decius's newfound ally. He would interrogate Lucia even through torture to find out about her. Ultimately, Orcus would decide what her fate would be. He would consider how best to use her as a tool to serve his purpose before discarding her to a painful death.

In what seemed forever as the hour passed, Decius hid under the cover of an underground cave settlement with a company of the condemned along with his swarm of imps. They waited patiently, but eventually,

Decius could sense in a telepathic way that all was not well. He could sense the pain, distress, and slipping into unconsciousness that his soulmate had felt. He knew his love, Lucia, was in trouble. The hellish werewolf motioned for his imp warriors to follow him to the surface to investigate why his love had not returned. Concentrating intently on supernatural powers, Decius managed to teleport himself to the surface as his imps rose upward from the chasm outside the vicinity of Sanctum Oculi Malum. He could see from the distance a large swarm of imps aligned to Orcus along with several succubi. Faintly though, he could make out that they were carrying Lucia, who was still unconscious and restrained by the hell spider web bonds that secured her hands, feet, and wings.

Decius became filled with fear and concern for his eternal love. He also became filled with hate for his sworn infernal enemies at what they had done. Decius unleashed a loud, frightful howl while ordering his imps to pursue and overtake the enemy that was falling back into their territory of hell. The imps loyal to Decius complied and unleashed childlike menacing screeches while darting at full speed in the air to intercept their adversaries while seeking to recover the dux's consort. However, as they did so while flying through the tower pylons with large, staring eyes, several contingents of Orcus's imps deployed the same type of hell spider nets to ensnare and slaughter many of their enemy counterparts. Decius's recovery efforts had faltered as he realized he had to pull back his remaining forces.

Decius swore he would pursue his enemy again when he had the chance. He would reunite with his soulmate no matter where they went or how long it would take the contesting dark lord to do so. He would howl one last time while announcing that vow before his surviving swarm of imps pulled back to follow him. Decius knew for now, he had to survive against the smaller but still formidable swarm of his adversary which dissipated out from the tower pylons of the horrid gazing rock structures. He would resort to the same tactic as he had done before, only this time leading the feigned retreat with his cohort of imps that trailed behind. Several of the small flying demons would carry Decius through the chasm back down to the underground surface of the cave settlement.

Meanwhile, the remaining imps loyal to Decius that were inside the cave would lie in wait to ambush the enemy that dared to go into the darkness of the open mouth of the cave pit. Just as before, Decius's hidden contingent of imps inside the cave would ambush their enemy counterparts from various directions while forcing the survivors to descend lower toward the settlement itself, only for the charred condemned inhabitants to pelt with stones and tear any apart that were within reach. It would work just as before.

Though Decius would ensure personally that this ensuing skirmish was still a victory, his immediate thoughts after the intense hard-fought battle quickly returned to his captured wife. He would rally all those who had sworn to follow him to the other side of hell. He knew the enemy would take his wife there. If they wanted to kill Lucia after apprehending them as early as they did, then he knew they would have done so and left her remains or part of her remains behind.

He knew they wanted him to follow them back to the lair of the current reigning lord of hell himself. Orcus would wait for him. Both he and Decius knew the latter would go after Orcus to rescue Lucia. If Orcus did not yet know who Lucia was, Decius was sure that eventually, Orcus would find out about her identity. Orcus would deduce that she had to have been close to Decius. It would only be a matter of time. Time was all that Decius had to contend with to make the most of his remaining forces to follow him to pursue Orcus's forces, save his wife, and possibly put an end to the dispute over the reign of hell once and for all. Decius consumed in his werewolf rage composed himself as best as he could but was determined to prevail and would muster as many of the denizens in hell that he could find to either fight by his side or die standing in the way of his path to end Orcus's reign of hell once and for all. There would be no quarter, no neutrality, no mercy. He would ensure anything and everything in hell that existed served him and turn against Orcus or cease to exist by Decius's own consumed anger.

Within a few hours, Decius's forces had assembled carefully outside away from Sanctum Oculi Malum and near his sleek, jagged fortress complex. In a large formation, they would swarm in the air while Decius himself would traverse the landscape below in his feral form. It would take him many days and possibly a few weeks, but eventually, Decius would catch up to reunite with Lucia. Orcus knew that much and would wait for their next violent showdown at Orcus's fortress stronghold.

Chapter Thirty-Three

Infernal Humiliation and Imprisonment

On the far side of one of the high plain valleys of hell stood Orcus's fortress stronghold. The stronghold was prominent as ever in rising above the scorched, rugged valley and promontory. On the walkway at the top of the tower, stood a red succubus. It was Lucia. She slowly woke up from unconsciousness while still moaning in pain. She could hear a loud laughing coarse voice from behind. Lucia could not turn herself to look as much as she tried to move. She had realized slowly from regaining consciousness that she had fallen in combat and now was being held as a prisoner in a strange type of pillory contraption made of an exotic metal framework. This type of framework was mounted on a stone post. Lucia's head and hands were secured through the tight holes of this contraption. Meanwhile, she could feel her feet being shackled by that strange numbing and sedative-like hell spider web.

As she still struggled to turn her head, Lucia sighed out of some frustration. The laughing figure stopped and used a leash type of weapon made from the same hell spider silk to whip her from behind toward her back. Lucia could not hold back and moaned in pain while letting out a shriek. The figure again laughed before walking in front of her. Lucia looked up with a face of anger and rage while staring at her presumed would-be capturer. She noticed this figure had red skin like her but looked like a large muscular and somewhat overweight orc-like figure with large golden horns. Lucia stared at him with her fierce eyes. She demanded that this figure identify himself at once and release her.

The large red orcish figure paused and laughed loud enough, along with a chorus of laughing imps and succubi that stared at her from various directions along the stronghold fortress ramparts. Several succubi also flew from above to spectate. The jeering was humiliating for Lucia to hear while she was still restrained and secured to this contraption that Orcus would refer to as the Pillory of Suffering. Lucia struggled once again sighing with anger and frustration at not being able to break free. She shouted in anger that she would have her revenge no matter how long it would take for her to be free.

As Lucia finished cursing at the spectators who laughed at her current state of imprisonment and humiliation, Orcus paced back around behind her and again struck her from behind with the whip only this time multiple times with more intensity. Lucia screamed in agony from the pain. After Orcus stopped, Lucia took a deep breath and gave a brief sigh. Again, Orcus paced around Lucia. The other spectators of imps and succubi looked on eager and delightful while relishing at the punishment and humiliation that their diabolical lord had dispensed. This prominent red orc then suddenly grabbed Lucia hard by her hair and raised her head to look at him. Lucia winced from the inconvenient pain as her torturer laughed and grinned. This tormenting figure spoke loudly and coarsely to Lucia that he was none other than the almighty lord of hell himself, Orcus. He told Lucia that she was in no position to make demands nor to command him. He stated it was Lucia who was in the dire position of having to beg for mercy for him to consider being generous enough to spare her life from further torment and painful death. Orcus then demanded that his prisoner tell him who she was.

Lucia, with a face of disgust, spitted toward Orcus. The reigning lord of hell laughed at her before he delivered a hard smack at her face in a sudden unexpected moment. The impact was hard enough to make Lucia pass out again into a state of unconsciousness. Orcus then shrugged while stating that it did not matter who she was. He presumed correctly that she must have been a love interest of his adversary. He would use it to his advantage.

Orcus turned toward his various minions who looked at what unfolded from various angles. The demonic hell lord ordered his succubi that were present to have their enjoyment out of torturing Lucia. They were free to do with her what they liked, so long as they did not cause her to bleed in excess or lose any parts of her body. When asked why, the lord of hell responded that he wanted Decius to see his lover in the same state she was in more or less before Orcus would deliver the final killing blow to Decius. Ultimately, Orcus wanted the hellish werewolf to be left with uncertainty in death by the fear and speculation of what further harm Orcus would cause in defiling and savagely killing Decius's lover.

One of the chief lieutenants among the succubi nodded while Orcus gave her his electrical whip and instructed that it was fair game however for the succubi to break the spirit of this newfound prize that they captured. Orcus's chief lieutenant succubus grinned demonically while taking the whip and turned to the mounted pillory that Lucia was still tied to. The demonic lord of hell took a few paces before turning. He waited a moment to observe and enjoy with sadistic pleasure at what happened next. It was just long enough to see Lucia return to consciousness while faintly moaning. The chief lieutenant succubi mocked her and carried out a slow on-and-off repetition of whippings of her red succubus adversary. Lucia struggled to keep her composure other than to quench her body and bite down from giving Orcus's succubus any satisfaction in the electrical shock pain that she dispensed to Lucia.

Orcus then made his way back to his inner lair sanctuary and throne. During his transit, he still enjoyed sadistically the audible moans and shrieks that his newly captured prize had exhibited. The lord of hell would take time to further plot how to defeat his rival adversary. Orcus knew his forces had led a noticeable enough trail for Decius to follow and be baited in seeking to rescue his new chief ally, one that Orcus presumed must have been his lover. Soon the demonic hell lord thought to himself, there would be a return to the natural order of Hadao Infernum once Decius was taken care of. Orcus reinvisioned in his mind that his authority and reign of hell would be supreme and uncontested just as it was before.

Chapter Thirty-Four

Beginning to Forge a New Peace

Only less than two days from departing Dyr Valley, the lone skyship at the command of Linitus and manned by his crew, including the dyr diplomatic envoy, had finally arrived at Nebelheim. The view below was spectacular as the Nordling settlement straddled the mouth of a river that bled out into the fjords and ultimately the ocean. It was midday and townsfolk of the settlement were out and about during the spring day to go about their business in various professions. Some were fishermen near wooden dock piers returning with their haul of local salmon. Others were manning several weapon forges and created fine works of heavy Nordling melee weaponry. Meanwhile, various other tradesmen and merchants sold their goods at an open central market. This market stood next to the chieftain's hold and mead hall at the center of the settlement. For the townsfolk, it was just another day like many others for this time of the spring season year. However, that was soon about to change as it had the first time when the skyship soared above the settlement nearly a week ago.

A flash of light emitted from the skyship above. At almost the same instant, below on the surface of the settlement's open square market in front of the chieftain's stronghold, another bright flash emitted. Upon fading, various figures had appeared before the local Nordling townsfolk. Many of the figures they saw had surprised them save Arik, his companions, Marin, Peat, and Wyatt. The latter two were a surprise to the town's folks a few days prior when they first laid eyes upon the dwarf and halfling companions of Marin. Now, the settlement's inhabitants were even more awestruck and somewhat cautious while gasping and murmuring at the sight of what lay before them. Now, there were several male dyr folk along with a female dyr who they could make out as being a druid priestess. Along with them also stood a lone slender and average height (though somewhat short of stature by male Nordling standards) male elf with dark hair. He wore an elaborate set of leather armor and clothing. He also carried a dark cloak slung around his shoulder along with his prominent bow, quiver, and sword sheathed in his scabbard. This elf shockingly carried while holding by the hair knot a large severed head of a jotunn.

Meanwhile, Marin, adorned in her Golden Valkyrie armor attire, walked beside her elven lover while holding in her own hand a large ornate ancient crown. The two of them walked in the front of this arrival procession. Arik and his men appeared to have motioned for the townsfolk to calm down and be at ease. As he was doing so, Marin turned to Linitus. She let Linitus know that if he had not mastered conquering his fear of being nervous before a crowd, now would be the time to do so. Linitus looked at Marin somewhat shocked and surprised. He realized though that perhaps they brought this upon themselves based on the less-than-subtle manner of their arrival. Still, the elf rogue ranger with inquisitive curiosity asked his human lover why.

Marin made a surprise move and quickly grabbed her elven lover's arm holding the severed jotunn head. She raised his arm in the air while proclaiming loudly for the people to behold the one who had defeated a fearsome, gigantic jotunn.

Linitus became even more visibly nervous from the loud cheers and the standing ovation he received from the local townsfolk crowd. Peat then turned to Arik while watching and pointed out to Arik that there was no use anymore for him and his chosen warriors to serve as crowd control. Instead, the dwarf decided to help Linitus return the favor with Peat, quickly raising Marin's arm and holding the crown of the former ancient Nordling king's undead corpse she bested in combat. Peat then proclaimed to the crowd to behold what they witnessed. They now had a second champion (along with Linitus) who had passed an ordeal by trial through combat in besting the undead former first regional Nordling king of Shimmerfrost.

The back-to-back surprise announcements at first caused the locals to murmur even faster while gasping before coming to a silent halt. Then suddenly, a loud burst of cheers erupted again with the Nordling town residents celebrating. They acknowledged and congratulated the two strangers, Linitus and Marin, who they had now seen as worthy defenders of their people against the forces of darkness.

Through the continuous uproar of rising chants and cheers of joy and celebration, Marin blushed while asking Peat if that was necessary. Linitus interjected while reminding her she did it first. At this point, the townsfolk had picked up and carried the two proclaimed heroes to the chieftain's stronghold and mead hall. As they approached, even the chieftain and his local guard could hear the loud ambient noise from inside his hall. The chieftain and his guard walked out to ascertain what sense of commotion had stirred the town with such excitement. Before the chieftain, he saw two figures being carried by the jubilant crowd of Nordlings. The first was the same half-Nordling woman that he recognized before, Marin, the Princess Knight of Swordbane. The chieftain, Jarl Harleif, saw Marin earlier during the first time she arrived in this settlement about a week prior. He revered her as the chosen champion to save Shimmerfrost as a whole from the dark forces after he heard about her brave encounter against Wendigo.

The second one that Harleif noticed was an elf being venerated next to Marin. This elf was unfamiliar to Harleif. The chieftain did recall, however, this elf being likely the supposed spouse and fellow adventuring companion of Marin that she had mentioned. He was well revered by her and said to have surpassed the skills of any warrior she had ever known. He was known as Linitus from one of the elven settlements in the Kingdom of Swordbane. The chieftain noticed while observing that the elf ranger held the severed head of a jotunn who was feared by various inhabitants of Shimmerfrost, including the predominant Nordlings themselves. To take down one of these massive imposing giants was no small task. The elf's renown had clearly seemed to be well founded and earned by the chieftain's esteem.

Marin noticed Jarl Harleif and introduced him to Linitus. She attested to the chieftain about the elf slaying the giant along with the proof of his prowess in holding the giant's severed head. Marin had used this display as proof to the Nordlings in Linitus being worthy to lead them alongside her against the forces of darkness. She wanted them by their Nordling traditions to recognize Linitus's worthiness to lead alongside her. He had proof after all. It counted just as much as Marin's victorious feat when she fulfilled her pledge of being worthy of a particular trial along with her proof in besting the undead corpse of the ancient first king of Shimmerfrost.

To Harleif and his settlement's subjects, it was impressive to see that on display each champion's respective tokens of trophy of their mighty valor and deeds. In fact, it was hard to believe at first. The chieftain even turned to verify and publicly ask Arik and his fellow chosen Nordling warriors if the presumed deeds were accomplished by these two newcomers. Arik and his followers nodded in loud affirmation. Then another round of cheers erupted among the growing crowd while they carried up Linitus and Marin.

After welcoming the recent arrival of the dyr folk envoy as well as Linitus and Marin's company, the day unfolded into the evening. Festivities and celebrations were held inside the chieftain's mead hall. The chieftain was seated at the center of a U-shape formation of tables. Alani-Aki and the dyr clan elder were seated to Jarl Harleif's right. It was a gesture of respect, which the jarl bestowed for the two dyr ambassadors in being his honored guests to be seated close to him.

To the chieftain's left sat Marin along with Linitus, Wyatt, Peat, and Arik. The mood throughout the evening feast was jubilant as much as earlier during their arrival. Much bolstering was still being given by Arik, his men, and even Peat to indulge alongside them about their latest adventures. The dwarf guardian drank much of his fill of Nordling beer in a large tankard. Peat continued to be very animated while holding a large boar's leg in his other hand to describe the great deeds he witnessed in Marin slaying the undead corpse of the ancient Nordling king. The dwarf then continued to gloat about the exploits he witnessed of Linitus and Marin later besting a frightening gigantic jotunn brute.

Marin and Linitus became flattered in receiving praise from Peat and Arik along with Arik's Nordling companions. Still, the two lovers could not help in wanting to finally have their own time together. Specifically, they wanted to be alone. They would eventually do so after receiving the chieftain's final celebratory decree.

Jarl Harleif lifted his horned goblet of mead. He announced his pledge to work toward forging a new peace with the dyr folk, which the dyr clan elder along with Alani nodded to acknowledge. The chieftain continued by also declaring that through Marin and Linitus's great deeds in passing their ordeals by trial through combat, their cause had been deemed divinely justified. The chieftain declared to lend his support to spare as many resources as needed to aid them and their quest to unify the forces of good in Shimmerfrost against those of darkness with ill intentions.

Jarl Harleif, however, cautioned with concern that their quest would be no easy feat. The two other major Nordling settlements, Shimmerheim and Frostburg, under their separate chiefdoms in the region were stubborn to submit to the leadership of outsiders like Marin and Linitus. It would not matter, according to Harleif, even if the two newcomers had proven themselves worthy by great deeds, or if Marin had partial Nordling heritage to sway the two other notable chieftains. Harleif explained further that one of these two chieftains, or jarls, was even suspected of secretly being a vassal of Helskadi herself. He was believed to do this in exchange for not being subjected to raids and siege assaults by the Winter Death Witch's dark forces.

Meanwhile, the other jarl, a cousin of the former, is believed to have actually formed a clandestine pact with Helskadi to allow her and her chief servant, Wendigo, to resurrect the undead fallen soldiers of his army by not cremating their corpses. Furthermore, these two jarls also became blinded by pride in waging skirmishes with each other in order to be the preeminent power among the Nordling settlements in Shimmerfrost. They both wanted to be recognized as supreme kings, or konung, as they called it in their dialect of Nordling.

After Linitus heard this, he vowed that he and Marin would seek to unite Shimmerfrost with or without these two regionally prominent rival chieftains. Marin seconded that while saying that if these two jarls would not submit peacefully then both she and Linitus would settle this the way that all Nordlings understood—through trial by combat with the prevailing victor to assert their claim.

The chieftain nodded while praising Marin for understanding the way of their Nordling peoples, which it might very well have to come to that should these two kings not listen to reason and submit their authority and domains to the leadership of Shimmerfrost's new champions. It was then that the chieftain stood up to proclaim before those in his mead hall while raising the arms of both Linitus and Marin as the region's bestowed champions chosen by the divine spirits. Gesturing for the two to rise and accept, Marin did so while Linitus followed suit though with some reluctance. The elf ranger was still not one to want to receive boisterous bestowments of public praise in front of large crowds, which Marin knew. Regardless, this was one of those times when Linitus knew inwardly that he had to acquiesce to the ways of Marin's maternal people. He had understood Nordling culture enough both from Marin and his limited interactions with them throughout both Shimmerfrost itself and further south in Nordling settlements such as Tribus Wald as well as the various Nordlings that settled yet partially assimilated to the Citadellan settlements and culture of the Kingdom of Swordbane.

Jarl Harleif lifted his horned goblet to symbolically cement this proclamation. The Nordling chieftain of Nebelheim clashed it against the tankards that Linitus and Marin each held as a form of cheerful salutation. The elf's uncertainty on his face in how to react afterward was enough for the rest of the audience in the hall to break into laughs swearing that he had his fill before drinking his first sip. Marin, drinking the mead from both her tankard and then taking Linitus's to drink, interjected as a defense that her elf lover only did so out of chivalry in being the greater warrior to give his share to her.

The Nordlings in the audience were impressed by the Princess Knight's reply and commended Linitus, the latter who again followed Marin's lead and nodded while stating that it was so. Marin, still wanting to find a reason for her and Linitus to finally be alone together, excused herself by proclaiming that because of his chivalry, she had now been drunk on love in which they had to retire. Immediately catching on from Marin's words and interpreting in a romantic way between her and Linitus, the Nordlings at the mead hall, as well as Peat himself who was heavily inebriated, cheered in a loud uproar. Though slightly embarrassed, Linitus in his display of modesty while blushing somewhat, knew this was about as good as a reason if not better than he could come up with in wanting to escape the loud and over-inebriated ambient clamor of the chieftain's mead hall. He and Marin, being discreet and quick, got out of their seats after receiving the chieftain's acknowledgment to be excused and depart. Wyatt, staying sober as much as Linitus, looked toward his comrades to teleport them back to the skyship when Linitus asked him to do so.

Linitus and Marin arrived back on board the skyship. Marin and Linitus retreated to the captain's cabin of the floating vessel. They would be alone to themselves. They would rest as comfortably as they had in some time while being more intimate.

Back on the surface, at the mead hall, celebrations continued until nearly all the Nordlings had their fill of mead, beer, and various foods. The dyr folk would retire along with Wyatt in one of the guest quarters of the chieftain's hold. The chieftain, meanwhile, rested on his wooden throne chair somewhat tired and inebriated. Peat and Arik, after exchanging several rounds of back and forth between compliments of admiration in the crafting of their weapons as well as tales of their great deeds with their own respective companions, eventually both passed out on the floor next to the dining tables. Their consumption had overtaken them more than their foes in combat, as they would realize and jest the next day after regaining consciousness and dealing with the aftereffects of their drunkenness.

Eventually, when morning arrived, aside from the loud crowing of the town's roosters, the sudden large ringing of bells as well as the blast of one of the town's palisade gate horns would be enough to awaken all the folks of the settlement, including the most inebriated, which seemed to be a tie between Peat, Arik, and the settlement's chieftain. Even from the skyship above, Linitus and Marin were awakened in bed next to each other in their captain's cabin while Wyatt in a separate compartment of the floating vessel, could also hear the sudden burst of alarming noise. The three of them onboard collected themselves before they teleported to the surface via Wyatt's magic. They arrived outside the chieftain's mead hall. The chieftain followed by his closest bodyguard emerged outside after hearing the unique noise of the teleportation flash to discuss more about the adventurers' quest.

Immediately, however, a full-grown bearded lone rider on horseback who wore a horned iron helmet of the Nordling fashion charged toward the chieftain. Linitus was prepared to raise his bow in defense of the chieftain until the chieftain motioned with his hand for the elf to yield and know that the charging rider was no threat. Linitus, still surprised and uncertain, did so slowly while being concerned if the horse rider would stop. He did so suddenly at a grinding halt only a few paces away from the chieftain. The chieftain, familiar with this rider, asked what news he brought from Frostburg. The rider announced himself as Halkir, a courier of Frostburg. The courier continued further to state that the jarl of Frostburg had sought information of a large raiding party belonging to the Winter Death Witch's forces making their way toward Lone Pass going west by southwest.

The Nebelheim chieftain was surprised and somewhat suspicious. His look became even more surprised when he asked the courier about the size of this raiding party. The courier responded that by his fellow scouts' estimates, they numbered in the thousands. After hearing this response, Arik could not muster amazement from holding back in asking aloud as much as what the chieftain was thinking. Why would they send so many of their forces so far away from any of the nearest Shimmerfrost settlements while making their way out toward one of the region's remote border passes?

Linitus and Marin, however, looked with utmost concern and became especially alarmed. They both took turns to interject that this had to be the transaction of Helskadi's forces being given to Decius's heir, Lucianus. The elf ranger and Princess Knight both knew these newly acquired forces would be used for the Imperial Remnant's future plans for domination in the south. The chieftain asked Marin with curiosity about this Lucianus, the supposed dark lord heir of the south under the influence of his father's ghost spirit, and what he had to give Helskadi in return. Marin responded in a cold, gloomy voice that the Imperial Remnant had what Helskadi's forces lacked. They had better and more powerful weapons including advanced siege weapons. They had enough to change the balance of who would rule over all of Shimmerfrost in Helskadi's favor once and for all.

Arik became amazed as much as the chieftain, not to mention all the immediate Nordlings within the vicinity. They all wondered how this was possible, especially considering that Helskadi was the most powerful evil being in the region they knew, and it was a surprise to them that Helskadi would seek to find the help of others who would normally be considered outsiders.

Marin and Linitus looked at each other and knew that these people clearly had not seen what they had, granted the elf ranger and Princess Knight were as unfamiliar with Shimmerfrost and its lore as these locals were most likely unaware of the dangers that inhabited the southwestern part of Hesperion. She and Linitus had only heard of Helskadi's horrors that plagued this land, but they knew these people had not heard enough about the horrors the two of them faced ten years ago in the south. For her and Linitus, Decius was far more the greater and more powerful evil. When he was alive, he thrived on death and destruction. Even in his mortal death, his spirit had been powerful enough to appear in the mortal world and spread his influence throughout Hesperion. Even now it had been enough, along with his surviving heir, to still seek common partners of darkness and evil to align with Decius's cause.

Recollecting herself while turning to respond to the Nebelheim chieftain in returning to his question, Marin said sharply that as powerful as Helskadi is in the region of Shimmerfrost, there are forces more powerful and just as dark if not more evil than her. She told the chieftain that it was imperative he let Linitus take control in mustering whatever forces and supplies the chieftain could spare to load into the skyship while she herself would explain to both him, Arik, Alani-Aki, and the dyr elder in greater detail about the less familiar ally of Helskadi, in which Marin and Linitus were all too familiar with.

Chapter Thirty-Five

Promising Developments and Unfortunate Tidings

A lone shadow hovered high above an open grassland dotted with the occasional series of trees along a narrow valley. The valley itself stood out majestically with a prominent small mountain range to the north that was snow-capped at the summit. Several kilometers away from the mountain range lay a small lake. It was just south of the valley pass that became known by the Nordlings of Shimmerfrost as Lone Pass. This valley and its small lake glistened from the daylight while an oncoming flow of migratory birds made their way north. The occasional animals passing by included deer and exotic white snow rabbits hurdling away as they heard the loud frightening noise of the source, which cast that shadow.

In the sky above, it was a lone skybeast vessel. The vessel was a large steel dark metal hulking beast that floated high above the air at a steady speed. This vessel had several large dark blue-grayish orcs along the canopy manning the siege weapon mounts while looking above for any targets or threats from the surface below. Inside the bridge of the floating warship, which was tightly cramped with many crates of armor and weaponry, stood several figures who looked at the view from the cockpit window. Among them include a goblin shaman along with two elite human Citadellan Black Wolf knights clad in heavy, dark steel plate armor. Agaroman, the lone dark-cowled bald human wizard in the vessel, was also present along with his young master, Lucianus.

Lucianus, still a young werewolf child, was also now considered one of the most powerful and youngest leaders in all of Hesperion. Now this werewolf youth and dark lord successor prepared a small altar table along with the goblin shaman and Agaroman. When ready they would conduct the incense and libation ritual while proclaiming incantations on behalf of Lucianus's late father and mother, Decius and Lucia.

Within moments, Decius's apparition appeared before them. Startled and uneased, Decius composed himself to realize his surroundings while assuming his ethereal spirit form in the mortal realm. He looked and noticed that before him were his son and his former wizard advisor. The latter two both kneeled before him along with their dark minion servants. Decius told them to rise while inquiring with his son about the status of what he was doing and in which he summoned his father.

Lucianus replied to Decius that he wanted to give his father an update. They were proceeding early, ahead of schedule to deliver the arranged shipment of weapons and armor to Helskadi. Decius, though occupied with Lucia's capture, still composed himself to focus on Lucianus and congratulate his son on the good news.

Lucianus went further to let his father know he had even more positive developments, including plotting revenge for his mother's passing. He told his father's spectral ghost that he had managed to devise a false flag plot in which they secured Helskadi's cooperation to use one of her client subjects to deliver their sworn mortal enemies to him in order to dispose of. Decius became more impressed. He commended his son while also warning him to tread cautiously in not underestimating the elf rogue ranger nor the Princess Knight as he once had during their last mortal encounter. Lucianus nodded while clenching his fist and vowing to ensure that he would do everything possible to prevail and get the better of them to be worthy as Decius's dark lord successor and heir.

Decius nodded again, though still he seemed preoccupied. Lucianus noticed and asked his father what was wrong as well as why his mother, Decius's wife, Lucia, was not present with him when summoned. Decius begrudgingly unleashed a mournful-like howl before explaining to his son that regretfully Lucia had been captured by his sworn rival in hell, Orcus, the Lord of Punishment, in which Decius was contending to usurp his place as the undisputed supreme dark lord of that infernal place. Lucianus howled back mournfully in mutual concern while demanding that his father do everything possible to ensure that his mother, Lucia, is rescued and avenged by this infernal rival.

Lucianus still pondered about this recent revelation. He could not help but ask why he had not heard about this Orcus before. Decius replied that few in the mortal realm believed in Orcus's existence. Even then, in all the times he was summoned, Decius preferred to be discreet in not revealing to mortals aside from his former trusted wizard advisor and Lucia during her mortal life about the infernal conflict that Decius waged against his revealed foe. Decius would wait to reveal more once he had secured his claim in prevailing over the latter as the undisputed dark lord of hell. Decius did not want to give any attention to any other mortals of Orcus's confirmed existence beyond the few dwindling rival cultists in the mortal realm who already knew about Orcus and worshiped him in seclusion. Decius knew all too well his existence both in the spectral form and as a powerful ranking contender for the lord of hell had spread much influence in gaining fanatic zealous followers. He did not want to give away Orcus's confirmed existence and contention in ruling over hell, lest Decius lose any followers that Orcus might sway to his cause in the mortal realm. It was enough for Lucianus, despite his young age, to be prudent to understand his father's concern in not risking to empower his adversary's standing and prestige among mortals by mentioning the rival hell lord's name.

Meanwhile, Decius became ready to return to the manner at hand. He knew that his son, along with his chief advisor, Agaroman, had summoned him for further advice on Lucianus's plans. Decius inquired for more details on how Lucianus using the skybeast and Helskadi's subservient clients would lure and strike efficiently against the elf rogue ranger and his companions, including any forces they might bring with them. Lucianus replied he had studied and became fairly well versed in their enemies' famous written adventure exploits in which he would take and use one of their own tactics against them. He would use the skybeast under magical spell cover of invisibility to strike at the Comradery and their allies when they did not expect them to be there while one of the Helskadi's clients would lure the Comradery to attack a small army force of Helskadi's at Lone Pass.

Decius, in his ghost werewolf-like form, could not help but grin at his son's clever ability to be cunning while further commending him. At the same token, Decius also explained to Lucianus how Lucia would be rescued while his father would rally as many of the disenfranchised denizens of hell to find common causes to put their lot in the condemned afterlife in favor of him over his adversary. Decius would gather as many forces from wherever he could find while marching his way through the bleak hellish lands of Hadao Infernum to besiege Orcus's stronghold fortress. Lucianus wished his father well while telling him to promise the younger dux that he would rescue his mother. Decius vowed to his son that he would and that it would not be before long when he was summoned in the future that Lucianus would see both him and his mother in their spectral form. After assuring his son, Decius bid farewell while fading away from the bridge to return back in his corporeal form in the realm of hell to make good on his word to his son in rescuing Lucia. Lucianus also returned to his own matter at hand in which he would lie in wait patiently ready to strike while having Agaroman prepare his magic to make the skybeast completely invisible. No foe of theirs would know they were here or be able to respond until it was too late and the skybeast was ready to strike first.

Chapter Thirty-Six

Ambush Reversal

Several days later, overlooking the same natural terroir of Lone Pass from below, a lone skyship hovered above. The valley of Lone Pass seemed serene as it had been since the start of spring. Ambient noises could be heard from the wildlife below.

On the starboard outboard side of the floating vessel's deck, Linitus held a spyglass and gazed at the surface below. He noticed a small convoy of wagons (four to be exact) with several protruding weapons secured at the back of these covered wagons. The design of the wagons themselves was crude. They were made of some sort of spruce or aspen wood for both the bed and frame of the wagons. Each wagon was approximately four feet in width but was as long as fifteen feet and had large, prominent wooden wheels, axles, and tongues. Each wagon seemed to have a pair of green goblins manning it. This convoy was making its way northwestward. It was going through the pass that demarcated the border between Shimmerfrost and the coastal woodland frontier lands that would wind its way southward. The wagons carried the banners of the Imperial Remnant that bore a black wolf and a red sword pointed upward. The symbolism represented the titular deities of this faction, Calu and Laran, respectively.

Apparently, the scout reports from the courier of Frostburg were also correct, as Linitus had found more than just a small convoy of armed wagons. He also found a large raiding party. It was armed with a large guard presence dispatched by Helskadi to escort what Linitus surmised was a weapons convoy making its way to Shimmerfrost. Linitus made sense out of what he saw from the deck of the skyship. The elf ranger quickly divulged his findings to the rest onboard. Marin, Alani-Aki, Peat, Wyatt, and Arik took turns to see for themselves this convoy from the distance below.

Marin and Linitus looked somewhat dumbfounded at Arik while asking if his people had ever considered posting an effective perimeter of watch towers to guard their territorial borders against outside invading forces, including those that sought to aid their enemies. Arik shrugged with blunt honesty in stating that his people had not even considered it being necessary since until this point outside visitors coming into their lands became a rare occurrence and when they did so it was usually in far smaller numbers in which they made their way through the coast by boat or ship. He was as much surprised to see the same thing that his newcomer friends had witnessed. It was an eventful rare moment for them to witness. It was the first and what they intended to be the last supply provision of weapons between two dark forces that were now in an alliance.

For whatever reason or so everyone thought onboard the skyship, the armed convoy did not seem to notice them. Linitus along with Marin, Peat, and Wyatt plotted how best to quickly engage in combat and take out the convoy. They had several options, including attacking high above or teleporting soldiers on the ground to ambush the convoy using the scattered thickets of white spruce and quaking aspen trees. Ultimately, with some persuasive pressure by Arik and the other Nordlings on board who were eager for combat and ascribed to what they considered a more honorable Nordling way to conduct warfare up close, Linitus and Marin agreed they would lead the attack on the surface against the convoy. Wyatt and Peat would lead the attack in a supportive manner from the air while onboard the skyship. The halfling wizard and dwarf along with some assistance from Alani-Aki and a few Nordlings would stay on board to deploy the skyship's weapons from above.

Within moments, Wyatt teleported one group of warriors after another to the surface. Each group was positioned behind several suitable places for cover. They were also within range to raid the convoy while being armed with various melee weapons, as well as using longbows and arrows. They would attack when Linitus gave the signal for them to do so. The elf would signal to them once he deployed a hail of fire arrows using one of his sabot canisters to unleash upon one of the convoy wagons. With luck and what they considered careful planning, they were sure to have the upper hand.

They would deliver a sudden overwhelming and demoralizing blow to the enemy before they had time to engage the Nordling warriors in melee combat.

With the sudden timing, things seemed to have fallen perfectly into place. Perhaps too perfect. Marin could not help to comment, stating that while waiting patiently along with Linitus to unleash the first attack. This ambush, in many respects, reminded her of the one they conducted over ten years ago during the early part of Decius's rebellion against the Kingdom of Swordbane. It was a counter-raid against a band of goblin raiders led by the infamous human bandit Dirty Dale. The Comradery had a single carriage that was packed full of explosives and baited the raiders to attack before delivering the deadly blow. She could not help but cherish those younger adult years of adventure despite the hardship they faced together. Now it seemed to come full circle ironically while she reminisced about it.

Linitus looked back reflectively and cherished those years as much as Marin did. Still, he wondered out of caution how similar this raid resembled the one they had staged during those years. He could not help but point that out to her in an unexpected feeling of anxiety that had set in for her as much as when he realized it. Was this a counter-ambush that Helskadi's forces and their Imperial Remnant allies planned to use by baiting them? If so, and if they resisted getting baited, it could be possible that the tactic would backfire on the enemy. Linitus pointed out that when he and the rest of the company attacked at least from range, a carriage, if armed with explosives, would set off as soon as the rogue elf ranger's arrows had struck the armed barrels in the wagon. Linitus knew this tactic could work since they would keep their range while exposing their enemies to the effects of their own devastating munitions if they carried any. The elf ranger smiled. He looked with confidence toward Marin while pulling back the sabot canister with his bowstring while aiming his bow at a certain elevated angle toward one of the wagons. He told Marin right before releasing his shot that there would be one way to find out.

Within moments, the fired canister hurled through the air. The canister unfolded and deployed at least two dozen arrows blazing in a hail of fire that darted toward one of the wagons. Many of the shots connected and struck either the enemy warriors of the convoy or the wagon itself. However, the wagon did not explode. Apparently, it was not armed with explosives or the volley of arrows Linitus fired using the sabot canister did not strike the explosives on the wagon, if there were any. The elf ranger shrugged while letting Marin know it was worth finding out.

Upon seeing the signal, the Nordling warriors on the ground positioned at various concealed parts of tree foliage, unleashed scattered volleys of arrows of their own upon the unsuspecting wagon convoy. The Nordlings were not renowned for being skilled archers and many of their unleashed arrows missed their targets. However, several more of the enemy fell, including goblins, cave orcs, and several of the Imperial Remnant's orcs from the south. Even one of the few snow trolls that were part of this guard escort succumbed to its death from the surprise attack.

Gaining the upper hand, or so it seemed, the Nordlings including those led by Arik unleashed another series of war cries. Then they charged forward to engage the enemy in melee combat. Observing this, Linitus and Marin could not help but look at each other with bewilderment. They could not believe what their allies were doing. They literally gave away the advantage they had from range in taking out the convoy and its escort while choosing to close in.

Now these Nordling warriors were barely in formation in a near-charging free-for-all position to find the nearest orc, goblin, or troll to engage in combat. Part of Marin already knew and understood it from reflecting on her own partial Nordling heritage. This was the way the people on her mother's side conducted fighting. It was with a direct and brute force approach, though not one that was as organized or as well calculated as that which Citadellans on her paternal side would conduct war. It was also not how elves would conduct war in which the elves and Citadellans were more methodical and strategic in their approach. Marin took a moment to explain that difference in reminding Linitus. The elf, though somewhat upset, still kept himself composed and collected. He stated to Marin that they both had to at least press the attack from their position and do what they could to ensure they still prevailed. Marin nodded while stating that at least there was an upside to this. It would be a heated battle that they had not seen in some time. Linitus nodded while the two charged forward to catch up with their Nordling allies.

Within moments of the fierce fighting, the ambush Linitus and Marin's forces had set prevailed in taking out the dark forces of the enemy. Only a few still stood in opposition. The battle was in their favor and the Nordlings had taken few losses. In a few more moments, the fighting would be over. They could secure hordes of Imperial Remnant forged weapons that were being sent to arm Helskadi's forces. Within one of the wagons, a trio of Nordlings tore apart one of the white canvas covers. The Nordlings looked in surprise to see that the wagon itself was empty save for a few armaments. Another moment while mourning in upset anger, Linitus and Marin turned to see from the distance another wagon that had scarce items onboard its bed also. The elf ranger turned again to his wife, the Princess Knight, and they both shared the same sudden feeling of distraught and concern. Something was not right. They were baited into thinking they had the upper hand in ambushing their enemy. Linitus and Marin wished they were wrong, but they were in fact right in narrowing down the possibilities. Even Wyatt and Peat looking from the skyship above to the surface below had concerned looks. They both thought the same as Linitus and Marin. Their concern soon manifested within moments.

High above the air from a distance magically appeared from hiding a lone hulking dark object. This object descended in a downward strafing run by. Its form as it came closer resembled a beast with the shape of a bat and the head of a wolf carved into a dark stone-like metal. This object projected a screeching-like echo as it hurled closer and closer at a downward diagonal angle toward the center of the battle site, which amassed the bulk of the surviving Nordling forces around the halted wagon convoy.

Suddenly, a large howl projected out from the flying dark contraption. The voice scared everyone on the surface and all onboard the lone skyship that floated in the sky above. This howl was unfamiliar to the Nordlings but just as terrifying as the wailing voice of their familiar nightmare legend of Wendigo. This voice or howl, however, was all too familiar to Marin and Linitus. It was Decius's son, Lucianus. This werewolf adolescent warlord was out for revenge and they knew it. He wanted to take out as many of the Nordlings, not to mention the Comradery's skyship as soon as possible. He was hell-bent on avenging the deaths of both his parents, and he laid the blame squarely on Linitus and Marin.

Onboard the skybeast bridge, the view was as terrifying and awe-inspiring as that which was seen from the surface. Lucianus, seated at the cockpit pilot seat, with Agaroman seated next to him at the co-pilot seat, looked intently. Agaroman advised his young protégé and dark lord to strike the targets on the ground first before they had time to scatter and retreat. Lucianus unleashed another howl as the signal to prepare to attack. Within moments of preparing the weapons to deploy from the first howl, the few crew members onboard the skybeast that manned the siege weapon mounts quickly fired their munitions from the various positioned ballista and scorpion mount launchers. Meanwhile, after Agaroman nodded as a cue, Lucianus unleashed a third howl. This was the cue for several heavy orcs and Southwestern Hesperion trolls near the cargo hold to unleash the large latch of the skybeast's cargo hold near the rear ventral (or underbelly) part of the vessel. Upon doing so, the cargo hold crew members secured with harness straps came near the edge of the floor ramp of the cargo hold and began hurling dozens of explosive oak barrel casks down toward the small army of Nordling warriors on the surface below near the vicinity of the empty wagons.

Upon impact at the surface, the barrel casks exploded at various interval paces from each other. This strafing attack from the air clearly had done its intended effect in wiping out many of the Nordlings who were caught off guard. Very few among the many who retreated actually escaped with their lives. Even Arik among them had fallen. Linitus and Marin, who were further away from the ensuing devastation, looked with utmost fear, frustration, and anger. The elf ranger and Princess Knight had realized that they had fallen for the enemy's counter ambush that was planned all along. They were on the receiving end of a tactic somewhat familiar yet different from the one they once used many years ago. They had underestimated Decius's heir. Now they realized that Lucianus was just as deadly and cunning if not more so than his father, and this dark lord heir werewolf was not even fully of age, at least by human standards.

Now, after making the first strafing attack pass, the skybeast pulled up and eventually ascended before turning about. Linitus, looking at Marin, told her they had to pull back and get back to the skyship to defend it as quickly as possible. Linitus quickly fired a flashing arrow in the air as his cue. Wyatt immediately teleported Linitus and Marin along with the few surviving Nordlings back to the skyship above. Meanwhile, Peat commanded the crew onboard to load another volley of munitions with the few-positioned siege weapon mounts aboard their vessel.

However, before there was time to react and engage the skybeast in combat, the hulking vessel had suddenly in a flash vanished from the sky. Linitus and Marin noticed along with Wyatt while onboard. They were all dumbfounded and amazed at what they had seen. One moment the vessel was still there, already turned about and facing the skyship. The next moment, the skybeast was nowhere within sight. Linitus pondered how this could be. Wyatt interjected while explaining through several hand gestures, which Marin understood along with Alani-Aki.

Somehow, the vessel had to have been magically teleported or through some sort of contraption, possibly magic, rendered it invisible. Invisible, however, did not mean it vanished from the vicinity to no longer cause harm. Linitus knew that and assuming the second possibility, the rogue elf ranger quickly withdrew from his traveling backpack a pair of special green goggles. These were ones that Wyatt had specially made for him to use many years ago that came in handy during the second battle and recapture of the Swordbane capital of Citadella Neapola. Now, he would use the goggles again while scanning the sky from the last known position he had sighted the skybeast before it vanished. His facial reaction was in awe as he saw through the special optics of the goggles a glowing shape that was the skybeast itself, which hurled closer toward the skyship. It was on a collision course ready to ram the skyship at full speed. His expression, still in shock and utter surprise, could be seen in which Marin and the others knew the enemy vessel had to be out there. The elf ranger quickly ordered everyone to gather around Wyatt and for the young halfling wizard to teleport everyone onboard out of the vessel using his magic. Linitus did not know if it would be enough to save everyone and doubted it would if there was not enough time. Still, he thought to himself it just might have been enough to save his companions.

Moments before the skybeast was about to collide head-on with the skyship, it suddenly appeared before the visible eye. No longer was it shrouded in invisibility as it was before. A large howl emanated—along with several goblin, orc, and troll war cries—as a prelude to their final destructive blow and foreseen imminent victory. Another moment the terrifying vessel struck a powerful blow to the broadside of the skyship. Immediately, the impact caused it to shatter and fall into large pieces of debris with a minor chain explosion as a few explosive barrels were still onboard by the time of impact. The fallen floating caravel was no more.

However, onboard the bridge of the skybeast near the cockpit viewing port, both Lucianus and Agaroman noticed a sudden flash emitted just before the skybeast collided hard with the demolished enemy vessel. They were unsure of what happened though they both suspected that it was possible that the crew on board, namely the heroes of Swordbane, including Linitus and Marin, might have escaped imminent death and teleported to the surface. Looking about the surface below, however, they could not see any sudden flash of energy from the teleportation if it occurred. They also considered the possibility that they may have missed where their enemies teleported.

Without leaving it to chance, Lucianus and Agaroman dispatched a group of several Uruk Kazaht orcs and trolls that they had on board to survey the nearby landscape. They, however, had only limited time to do so as they had intended to continue to take the skybeast to its intended destination to deliver the massive supply of armament stowed on the floating war vessel. As they waited for the scouting party to complete their initial search on the surface below, Lucianus on the bridge of his ship with his crew present and bearing witness, declared his victory to serve as proof of his legitimacy as the rightful successor of his father in being the next true dark lord to reign throughout Hesperion. His speech was ambitious, confident, and vengeful despite his youthful age. He would make it known that it would be foolish for anyone to underestimate his determination to prevail like his father had before him.

Agaroman interjected in providing further praise to Lucianus by calling forth before several witnesses onboard the bridge of the skybeast to attest to what they had seen including a Nordling scout from Frostburg, the same one who had initially delivered the fateful message of the war party's presence in Lone Pass and who hid among the trees upon teleporting to the surface from the skyship. This scout, Halkir, still waited behind the trees while the rest of the Nordlings from Nebelheim engaged in the earlier raid in which they met their demise. The traitorous Nordling courier, however, activated a magical rune stone pendant during the raid in which one of the goblin shamans onboard the skybeast was made aware and able to spot the scout to teleport right before the skybeast made its first pass to attack the coalition of Nebelheim Nordlings.

Now this traitorous Nordling became impressed and agreed that he would inform his respective superiors, the jarl of Frostburg as well as Helskadi herself, of what he had witnessed. Despite seeing Lucianus as merely a cocky werewolf kid who fancied himself as an all-powerful warlord, the Frostburg Nordling courier saw him as having the potential in backing up his faction's claim in being a worthy partner to still align his interests along with those of his dark lordess Helskadi. Lucianus had after all practically wiped out most if not all of the enemy forces that sought to attack their decoy convoy.

Among those who became most impressed onboard the skybeast was

Agaroman. This false flag operation tactic reminded him of Decius's tactic in which he deceived and misled Swordbane's forces outside the walls of Sanctum Novus over ten years prior. It would take time for Lucianus to still develop and be as powerful as his father Decius, but now his first true battle had utterly convinced not only Agaroman but everyone else on board especially those few that were alive to serve Lucianus's father, Decius, that Lucianus was worthy to claim the throne as dark lord and back it up with his own leadership and planning. This outright slaughter had invigorated all those present. They believed they had truly been on the worthy side in service to the cause of darkness.

Chapter Thirty-Seven

Surviving the Onslaught

Several hours had passed since the initial battle near Lone Pass had ended. The dispatched scouting party of orcs and trolls from Uruk Kazaht scoured the surrounding perimeter of the central site of the earlier battle near the now-wrecked wagons. They looked for any survivors, but there were none that they could find. Eventually, they ended their search and returned near the same spot from where they were first teleported. Another moment and they were teleported back on board the skybeast as it departed away from the battle site and charted its course westward toward Jotunheim just as nightfall had begun.

Linitus removed his magical camouflage cloak after he emerged under the cover of forest foliage. The garment shielded himself and Marin. Meanwhile, a few feet away, using their magic together, Wyatt and Alani-Aki relinquished their magical hold in casting a magical globe-like barrier that shrouded them to appear invisible along with Peat and several fortunate surviving Nordlings that teleported with them just prior to the skyship falling asunder. From the distance, several of the Nordlings in their native tongue cursed from the aftermath of surviving while seeing many of their fallen brethren. Linitus and his companions watched with bitterness, though also with visible relief that the skybeast had sailed away in the dark sky. It was faint but still visible from the distance with its loud emitting noise and the visible flames that could be seen from its aft exhaust ports.

Linitus assessed the situation and circumstances they were in. The elf ranger consulted with Marin, Peat, Wyatt, and Alani on what to do going forward. It was hard for them not to weep in mourning the deaths of many of their fallen Nordling allies. This was especially true with the few survivors among them who were also Nordlings and knew their fallen fellow warriors as close kin. They had to either burn the bodies to prevent Wendigo from using its unnatural powers to resurrect them as undead walking corpses, or they would have to make the other tough choice of allowing such risk while fleeing for safety. It was a hard choice. Ultimately, they decided it was necessary to cremate the corpses. If they made a strategic retreat and did not prevent the corpses from falling under the control of Wendigo, then they risked this raised undead army to be used against any potential victims, including any of the Nordling settlements in the region. They would have to find some way to do this while being under the cover of night when Wendigo was in its most comfortable and strongest state to emerge and use its powers to summon the fallen corpses. Linitus, devising a rash idea, while considering that most of the fallen corpses were close to the center of the battle near the now wrecked wagons, had Peat and the surviving Nordlings move the wrecked wagons closer together around the center of the fallen corpses.

Meanwhile, Linitus directed Wyatt to use his magic to cast several fireballs at the wrecked wagons to set a light to create a massive bonfire. Upon doing so, Linitus would concentrate and use his supernatural powers in commanding nature to summon a massive whirlwind, hoping to spread this wildfire to consume as many of the fallen corpses as possible. It was risky and dangerous, but the elf ranger would have himself and his companions as far enough away as possible to do this. As they proceeded with this plan, Wyatt pointed out, along with Alanni-Aki, that a dark cloud-like mist was forming from a distance. Wyatt had yet to cast any fireballs while this dark fog or mist continued to expand. Linitus, Marin, and Alanni-Aki, however, knew that this mist that formed was likely Wendigo making his presence known by coming closer to them.

With a greater sense of urgency, Linitus ordered Wyatt to proceed as planned and cast the fireballs at the wagons as soon as possible. Wyatt nodded and chanted a few words while motioning his hands. He used his magical silver wand pointing toward each of the wagons one at a time as fireballs emitted from his hands. The wagons soon caught fire after Wyatt released the fireballs from his hands. The flames from the burning wagons became intense.

By this point, the dark mist continued to expand along with a pitch-black skeletal anthropomorphic figure having the skull of a deer. Seeing this figure from a distance. Peat pointed out to the rest of his companions that they had company. Wendigo across the distance stared at the surviving Comradery and their surviving allies. The dark, morbid creature became enraged. It sounded off loud shrieks of agony. Alanni commented about Wendigo's anger being aroused in the Comradery attempting to deny the horrifying creature of its potential servants to be possessed and summoned. Peat replied back with his dwarven bearded grin that this creature would have more to regret if it stayed around longer when Linitus had used his divine-like powers on it and its would-be servants.

At this point, Linitus nodded in agreement though he was nervous, knowing that he had to hurry and concentrate on using his powers to summon a large and ferocious enough whirlwind to encapsulate as many of the fallen corpses as possible. Concentrating his mind with assurance and support from Marin, who placed her hand on his back, Linitus quickly said aloud several ancient elven words of incantations while focusing on the center mass of the engulfing inferno that had consumed the wagons and nearby corpses. Within moments, a steady but developing whirlwind formed that became increasingly stronger and more turbulent within moments.

Wendigo shrieked more loudly after he observed the whirlwind. The dark creature became more enraged by what it had seen. The dark creature knew the elf's intended purpose was to challenge Wendigo from claiming the bodies of the fallen corpses. The elf would prevail at least partially in denying Wendigo the opportunity it had sought in possessing the bodies of the fallen, but not all of them.

After another few moments, Wendigo channeled its powers through a series of smoke and mist in the shape of tentacles emitted out of his body. It was a dark form of energy that traveled like a snake looking for its nearest targets. Upon striking the nearest fallen corpses, the bodies in an animated undead state began to rise up. The undead corpses wielded the same weapons that they bore prior to their horrifying possession. The corpses looking at Linitus and the other mortals from across the distance began to notice that a turbulent wind that the elf ranger had summoned began to expand and suck them in. Wendigo called out to these undead corpses to walk toward their dark summoner and away from the emerging whirlwind. The undead, giving horrifying growls, nodded and walked more quickly to their new master. Many of these undead, however, did not make it. The whirlwind became powerful enough to suck many of them into the burning vortex. However, several dozens of the undead warriors walked far enough to overcome the powerful suction of the whirlwind to maintain a safe enough distance and approach Wendigo. They then turned and gnarled spitefully for their undead comrades who had not escaped and burned inside the hellish tornado.

Meanwhile, Alani-Aki noticed and pointed out to the other survivors of Linitus's company while observing on the other side of the narrow flat plain of Lone Pass. The dyr druidess cursed at what she saw as blasphemy and an abomination of Wendigo's powers in continuing to possess and resurrect the corpses of the fallen that were farther away from the whirlwind. Marin turned to acknowledge. However, she knew all they could do at this point was hope Linitus could sustain the whirlwind as long as possible while moving it slowly toward Wendigo and his summoned undead followers. Linitus still channeled the forces of nature and attempted to direct them toward his foes. It was enough to intimidate Wendigo and his summoned undead to fall back further away on the other side of the plain in Lone Pass. Wendigo, angry at how many of its undead creatures had fallen after being summoned, still remained content enough to know that it was not empty-handed. Wendigo would retreat while making its way toward its own supreme master, Helskadi, at her mountain pass fortress of Jotunheim that lies northwest of Lone Pass.

However, the morbid dark creature knew it would probably be followed. Wendigo planned to escape to the outer ring of the mountain range that surrounded Jotunheim. Once there, it would take a detour. It would change course through a mountain tunnel and cave network to the north end of the outer ring of mountains, which lay just outside the Nordling settlement of Frostburg.

If needed, Wendigo would use Helskadi's secret clientele in that settlement to get involved and engage in fighting off the remaining enemies that followed Linitus and his comradery. It had another plan, however. If it was denied an opportunity by the elf to raise the undead corpses of the fallen in battle at Lone Pass, then perhaps it could stage hostilities between the Nordlings of Frostburg and this strange coalition allied with the elf ranger. In doing so, the aftermath of such a slaughter might gain the creature more company than it currently possessed.

Somehow, this fueled the horrifying creature's desire to do so out of spite and to remove its throbbing feeling of solitude. Even now, despite the few dozen undead it had in its control, it felt strange to Wendigo. In one sense, the dark creature felt no longer in complete solitude as it had for some time. Yet Wendigo still had the same insatiable desire to possess more undead to join its summoning. The creature hoped in due time it would possess enough to no longer feel abandoned by the living as it had felt.

Upon recollecting itself, Wendigo, along with his summoned undead, retreated away northwestward. It knew its enemies likely would either retreat or choose to follow and hunt Wendigo down, along with his undead servants. If his enemies choose the latter, then the dark creature would make it hard for them to track it while it would use his small cohort to distract and try to slay as many of the pursuing enemies as they could.

A few moments later, the engulfed flaming whirlwind that Linitus had summoned had begun to fade gradually. As it disappeared, he rested himself on Marin's body while standing. He was fatigued and would need a moment to recover his stamina before deciding what to do next. Marin, his lover, knew more than anyone else of his limitations when he felt temporarily drained from using his powers to maximum effect. Some passage of time was needed before they and their surviving company decided on whether to fall back for Nebelheim or to pursue the fleeing enemy that began to hide in the forest thickets away from the plain of Lone Pass while Wendigo and his followers made their way again northwestward.

Another moment after regaining his stamina and strength, Linitus after being informed of their enemies' retreat opted that he and the few remaining companions and allies should pursue Wendigo carefully as the earlier battle had taken its toll on Marin and Linitus's allied coalition. They did so while staying close together, centering on Wyatt, who used his magic to cast a magical ball of illumination that hovered above him.

The Comradery and its present company of allies would not stop pursuing Wendigo this time until they had hacked to bits and torched every one of the dark summoner's undead followers while in pursuit of Wendigo. Marin reminded her surviving Nordling allies that if they were apprehensive to fight their fallen brethren to remember that these were no more than walking corpses taken under control by Wendigo's dark necrotic powers. Disposing of them once and for all, she reasoned, would be the best way they could still honor their fallen comrades despite the living survivors being few in number after the battle. All heads nodded in confirmation while having firm resolve to go at full pace and close in deep into the emerging forest. They would see that they rid Wendigo, as well as what he possessed once and for all.

Chapter Thirty-Eight

To Raise and March an Army Through Hell

The plains and plateaus of hell were vast and dark, though it was bright enough from the many surrounding lava fires for one condemned in this hellish realm to still navigate. Among its vast reaches dotted many settlements of the condemned that banded together to increase their odds of staying alive from the many dangers that lurked everywhere. Like a flaming dust bowl of blood, swarms of red demonic flying imps flew across the vast wastes of this desolate infernal landscape. Decius led them from the surface below. The dux continued to charge at full hurdle, using all four of his canine limbs to traverse across hell.

Their first major destination would be the major condemned settlement of Civitas Tormentorum, also known as the "Community of the Tormented." It was perhaps the largest known settlement made up of condemned former human souls. They, like all others in their condemned form, looked like charred shadows of their former selves and very much the same as those among the condemned from Caverna Necropolis.

Decius approached the city and stopped outside the settlement's walls. He could see that it was well-guarded and fortified. The condemned walled the outer perimeter of the settlement itself with jagged, charred bricks and stone. It had an inner and outer series of walls connected by overhead causeways. Within the inner walls, various narrow, jagged, and crudely constructed buildings of the same material stood erected.

Within moments, a loud horn blow emitted from one of the settlement's guards. More of the local denizens formed up with haste to man the wall ramparts facing Decius and his imp swarm army from across the blackened hell plains. Only a few hundred feet separated them. Decius raised his hand while ordering his imps to lower their aggressive stance. Upon doing so, the werewolf dark lord next stepped several paces forward with his hands up to show he had no intention of harming them. He halted and called out the settlement's leader in which the dux sought to have a parlay and declare his intentions. The leader—a large, charred, bulky man—stood with some prominence. He wore some minor, prominent regalia to make him stand out from the rest of his fellow occupants. This condemned leader's attire included a makeshift crown made from the metal ores of Hadao Infernum. He called out to Decius, inquiring why he should trust his intentions and what would make him any different from hell's current reigning occupant, Orcus.

Within moments, Decius concentrated his mind. In one moment, still standing with his hands in the air, the dux vanished with no warning from the surface. He then appeared on top along the ramparts behind the back of this surprised and unsuspecting local leader. Decius, with a calm yet confident voice, responded he could slay him if he wanted to, but unlike Orcus, he held back. He was not the leader who sought to torture and punish others in the condemned afterlife for the sake of vile enjoyment. Decius sought to create an empire of his own in hell, much as he tried on Terrunaemara during his mortal life. He sought to wage war only against those who courted such aggression.

This condemned leader became lost in awe of Decius's powerful and daring display of wits. It was enough to sway this strongman local ruler and his fellow local condemned inhabitants to acknowledge that Decius's reasoning appealed to them. He was right after all, they thought. They were aware of his presence in hell and observed him on occasion from a distance. This was during Decius's arrival to hell when the dux explored and became familiarized to adapt over time in his once new surroundings. The local settlement's denizens were also aware of Decius's close but unsuccessful attempt to overthrow Orcus and take his position as undisputed lord of hell. Now, they had engaged in contact with this ambitious werewolf who was renowned for being a chosen vessel, both in the previous mortal life and still in the afterlife. They had seen both a rare and so far peaceful token display of his powers. He was not as cruel as the forces led by Orcus. Now they realized, including with their condemned local ruler, that their lot in life would be better by allying themselves with him. It was enough for the local condemned ruler to ask Decius what he wanted in return. The condemned local ruler also acknowledged Decius's reputation as being the only one who challenged Orcus and still lived in contesting the rulership of hell.

Decius accepted the mild praise. He responded with gratitude while understanding the ruling strongman's bluntness in expecting a transactional or patronage relationship that he posed to inquire. Decius would command them as he pleased in return for the condemned's well-being and presumed safety while submitting under Decius's rule. The dux told him he would send at least half of all able fighting denizens of the settlement's condemned to march with him against the forces of Orcus. The condemned of Tormentorum ultimately would aid Decius in installing the dux as the new lord of hell after overthrowing Orcus.

The condemned leader took a moment to process what the dux had said. The local strongman ruler grunted with reluctance but nodded. He admitted that doing this was risky and may invite the courtship of revenge if Decius failed, as he was rumored to have from before in his earlier attempt to overthrow Orcus. Decius nodded also but at once replied that he would make sure he became fully prepared, unlike the last time. He was more determined than before to see it through that he would prevail. He would go to as many of the condemned settlements that separated his stronghold fortress from Orcus's stronghold. Along the way, the condemned leader would help Decius raise more forces and march alongside the dux's army through hell against Orcus. They would end the torment that Orcus revels in once and for all. Afterward, there would be no more unnecessary second deaths in Hadao Infernum, at least not as long as those under the dux's authority submitted fealty to him with unwavering loyalty.

Upon what he heard after Decius had spoken, the strongman ruler gave a slight chuckle of sarcasm and disbelief. He asked Decius how sure the dux could believe himself to mean that. The condemned leader especially thought it was hard to imagine that slight hope of a future in a bleak place where they were sent to suffer as much as possible before enduring the second and final deaths of their spirit. Decius responded that it could change. The dux stated, however, that in order to do so they had to remove all belief in the fatalism that they ascribed to. They had to accept that they were the ones to make this change happen if they wanted it to happen by banding together.

Hearing those words was enough to stir conviction in the local strongman ruler to grunt again while nodding that it seemed as if he agreed with the dux. He told him that agreed with what Decius had to say and that he would declare on behalf of the settlement in his fellow denizens' loyalty to Decius. Decius nodded while praising him in return for making a wise choice from which his fellow denizens would benefit once they had rallied their forces along with the other condemned settlements to march against Orcus.

Moments later, a gate opened while a drawbridge lowered from outside the gatepost to connect to the other side of the land that separated the settlement's perimeter from the rest of the plains of hell. This area was also separated by a small river of continuous running lava. Emerging through the gatehouse numbered thousands of charred, condemned denizens of Civitas Tormentorum. As the numbers continued to swell in formation next to Decius's swarm army of imps, Decius looked in amazement. He only had two more condemned settlements that separated him from reaching his destination of Orcus's fortress lair. If he could sway them to join his cause and follow under his banner, he knew that combined with Civitas Tormentorum and the forces of Caverna Necropolis that followed behind it would be enough to overwhelm Orcus's forces and at least give Decius an even playing field to challenge Orcus for a single combat duel without having to contemplate Orcus's minions to come to his aid and have the upper hand when Decius would best the former in a duel for the throne of hell. More than that, he would also see to it first to rescue his soulmate. His thoughts and worries still centered on Lucia and seeing her captured by his hell lord adversary's forces. Decius would rescue her first before he would challenge Orcus if he could orchestrate this to happen somehow.

As his mind stirred in contemplation, it became obvious enough for the newly sworn vassal and strongman ruler of the settlement to read his face to know his new lord was preoccupied and the vassal could not help but ask what was on his mind. What else did he intend to do? He surmised Decius was in pursuit of something or someone beyond just wanting to overthrow Orcus. Decius, being candid, nodded and divulged that he sought to liberate his soulmate imprisoned by Orcus. The charred vassal grinned and nodded while laughing modestly. He responded about the irony of what love, if any, exists in this hell and could not blame Decius for going after the fortunate love he found. Decius nodded while telling him that had it not been for his love and recognizing her wisdom in forming alliances with the condemned that she initiated on his behalf, he may have never bothered to come to Tormentorum to offer to end the greater suffering Orcus had caused his vassals and condemned subjects. He would have secluded himself from his fortress on the higher plains of hell indefinitely.

The charred vassal, impressed by what he heard so far, was also moved by this realization that someone as powerful as Decius had cared about the wellbeing of hell's denizens. It was something no one would expect. The condemned denizens of hell only cared about looking after each other for the sake of self-preservation in banding together to have a greater chance with strength in numbers. They did so in order to withstand Orcus's forces perpetually raiding them every so often. It was Orcus's raids in which several unfortunate local condemned denizens would be snatched against their will to be delivered to Orcus for his own personal enjoyment in torturing and ultimately killing gruesomely. Decius nodded again to affirm what his new vassal had stated. As he did so, the vassal, however, pointed out to the dux the irony of them working together in hell when they were previously enemies.

Hearing that caught Decius by surprise and left the dux dumbfounded. He asked the vassal what he meant. The vassal, looking straight to his face, was surprised his new lord of patronage had not yet realized. He had not realized they knew each other, albeit briefly, during their time in the mortal world. Decius, even more perplexed, asked him to explain. The vassal laughed while asking Decius if he had not realized by his accent who he might have been. Decius pondered while thinking back to his mortal years. He thought about what his vassal had meant and agreed that his accent was different. Almost guttural and coarse. He asked the vassal if he was a Nordling. The vassal nodded while looking straight at Decius's jagged werewolf face that he was in fact once an enemy of his. He was the Nordling chieftain whom Decius had slain over ten years ago during his raid outside the Nordling settlement of Barbarum Aries.

Decius could not believe what he had heard. If they were both alive again in the mortal world of Terrunaemara, he likely would have slain the former Nordling chieftain again as he had before. Alas, he realized circumstances were different and now even this former Nordling chieftain had removed all past grievances to focus on their present place and circumstance of infernal misfortune. He told Decius since being in hell he had time to reflect on his past misdeeds for being harsh toward his Nordling subjects prior to dying from Decius's blade. This condemned creature had come a long way in learning from his mistakes to not be as cruel or harsh as he once was, not even in Tormentorum in which he found himself in the position of leading the settlement only after its former appointed ruler had been captured and presumably tortured to death at the hands of Orcus.

Decius now became equally impressed by what he had heard. He swore again to his now newly sworn vassal that if the latter could move on from the past and recognize the dux's authority, Decius in turn would do the same and be more determined to make sure that he was a worthy leader for all his subjects. The vassal nodded in agreement. The two marched outside the gates of Tormentorum to join Decius's ever-growing army. They would this time find understanding in talking about their past from what they could recall of it, as well as Decius telling him about the events that transpired after his death, and when Decius eventually entered the same hell they were in. The vassal and former Nordling chieftain admitted with a sense of irony that he was pleased Decius at least incorporated the survivors among the former Nordling chieftain's people into the Imperial Remnant's army to fight and seek greater glory, even if it was under Decius's command. The former Nordling chieftain saw it as being fitting for someone who had bested him in combat to lead the survivors in his tribal settlement. Decius replied in agreement while telling him that this tribe was loyal and fought honorably for the dux's cause once they were annexed into the Imperial Remnant's domain. Their ferocity was comparable in matching up with the most intimidating of the orcs in his army. The vassal told Decius he would see to it that he and his fellow condemned would fight as honorably as his tribe did for the dux during his previous mortal life.

Within several moments, after thousands of the settlement's newly conscripted populace mustered outside the fortified walls, they formed several columns and marched at a quick and steady pace northwest toward a large volcano crater with a series of volcanic magma fissures known as Crater Ignis. From there, they would find passage to an underground cavern known as Caverna Desperatio, from which Decius would recruit the supposed condemned underground settlement to join his cause as the other condemned have so far. Ultimately, from there, the dux would emerge from the cavern network as close as possible to Orcus's stronghold to launch a full-scale surprise assault, but not before recruiting more forces from one more condemned settlement. The plan seemed simple but still dangerous and bold. However, Decius knew he was off to a good start. He also knew he had to finish enacting his plan as quickly as possible while there was still time to rescue his beloved Lucia.

Chapter Thirty-Nine

Young Dark Lord's Deliverance

A lone black object soared high above the high jotunn mountain range that lay north of Dyr Valley and farther north of Nebelheim. This flying object hummed loudly in a blaze of terrifying velocity that none throughout the lands of Shimmerfrost had seen or heard before. From the naked eye, it looked like a large flying beast—and it was, though one of manmade construction. From the distance, as it flew past the inner ring of the Jotunn Mountains, the ferocious skybeast soared and pressed onward to its intended destination.

Meanwhile, various beast creatures that inhabited the mountains looked at the skybeast with a mixture of curiosity and astonishment. They were terrified, yet they saw this behemoth flying contraption as an omen of good meaning. It carried strong vibes of intimidation from its appearance, from what they could make of it in the sky. Its loud engine-like noise terrified the inhabitants into submission, knowing that a great powerful force was on its way. It would beckon to see the greatest known darkness in the lands of Shimmerfrost, Helskadi. Only the intermittent howl had assured them that this visitor, this force of power, was one of darkness like them. Had they not sworn fealty to the Winter Death Witch, all of them— cave orcs, goblins, snow trolls, ogres, and possibly even some jotunn giants themselves—would follow this omen to the ends of the world. They would pledge their undying loyalty to it. They knew this leader had commanded with the voice of his howl an edict full of anger and wrath, which they liked and wanted.

Lucianus howled more frequently. It was enough to cause some of the snow on the mountains to collapse and tremble before him, and he had no problem doing so. Lucianus wanted to make known before all, even the forces of nature, about his indomitable presence. He felt worthy enough to assert his legitimacy and birthright of his father's ascribed title as dark lord. He would covet it at all costs while commanding the respect he felt it deserved. Lucianus would see to it that Helskadi would receive what he promised of the many hundreds of armaments and armor to his northern ally. He would also see that in return as promised and expected from the exchange, she would give him hundreds of warriors. These warriors included goblins, cave orcs, and snow trolls to pack up on his flying warship to take south back to his Imperial Remnant to use at his bidding to conquer more lands outside of the borders that his Imperial Remnant shared with the Kingdom of Swordbane. In a time of his own choosing, he would plot and pick the right moment to attack and conquer Swordbane. He would resume and finish the war that his father had started. Lucianus would honor and fulfill his parents' legacy in establishing a new empire based on the Lupercalian model. He was certain of that.

But now, the young werewolf warlord returned to the cockpit from the canopy deck. Even inside the bridge as he looked on from the cockpit window, Lucianus enjoyed the impressive view of the massive mountains that encapsulated along a narrow cliff path. He even took notice of the jewel of this geographical feature, the central stronghold settlement of Jotunheim. It was Helskadi's capital. Lucianus became further entranced by the sight of this stronghold. It was a marvelous multilayered terraced structure with a tall tower mounted onto it, as well as several additional large towers surrounding the base of the massive structure. The central prominent tower had a flat roof large enough for Lucianus to vertically land the skyship and with enough space to unload the shipment of arms.

Lucianus landed the craft after engaging the landing gears that resembled jagged claws. It was a smooth landing. Within moments, the young werewolf dark lord stepped outside. He was followed by Agaroman along with the same Nordling scout from Frostburg who, with treachery, misled Linitus and his assembled forces into a false ambush attack. Behind them followed in procession a goblin shaman along with several Uruk Kazaht orcs, Shimmerfrost cave orcs, snow trolls, and goblins. Only a small piecemeal size of the remaining crew, composed of goblins, stayed onboard to man the bridge of the warship. They would remain ready when ordered to take off after unloading.

Lucianus walked down the cargo hold ramp of the skybeast. He was impressed even more upfront in seeing the awe-inspiring view of Helskadi's stronghold surrounded by the narrow cone-like jotunn mountain range. Vast stretches of bottomless depths surrounded the mountains and rising narrow land mass causeway that connected the stronghold to the southern pass that bordered the mountains and Dyr Valley. Noticing on both sides to his left and right, a steady stream of several jotunn warriors filed out from the stairway to line up and greet their expected guests. Following behind them came a large muscular jotunn female with blond hair and pale fair skin who wore ornate regalia while wielding an ornate sharp-pointed staff (also known as a spear staff). Standing behind her was her chief bodyguard and supposed secret love interest, Chief Fornjotr of the jotunn Deathspike Tribe. He was gigantic as they came for jotunn who were already monstrous to begin with. He had and carried a large stone war hammer with a long wooden handle or shaft. Fornjotr wore a large protective loincloth along with leather boots, gauntlets, and gigantic chainmail upper armor. He also wore a horned helmet with two horns rising on either side of the helmet and several rising from the front. His presence and size were intimidating to strike fear in the hearts of everyone and reveled in doing so when the opportunity became known and presented itself.

Lucianus paused after taking a few steps off the ramp. He and Agaroman stared straight into the face of their newfound ally whom they finally met after conversing and plotting many miles away. Helskadi and Fornjotr did the same while curious to see Decius's heir in person. She wondered if this young werewolf adolescent was any good or worthy enough to claim as heir to the title of dark lord. It would not take her long to confirm that he was indeed. Lucianus, when asked by her about the shipment, gave a noticeable canine-like grin. He told her the news that indeed they had brought all the armor and weapons forged from his people's armories as promised.

Helskadi gave a deviant smile while congratulating her newfound ally. Lucianus nodded while inquiring with her if she had enough minions to transfer to his command. Helskadi nodded while grinning and saying he could have as many of her non-jotunn followers as would fit the cargo hold of the skybeast after unloading. It was enough for Lucianus to give a delighted howl as he stared at her.

Within the next two hours, Lucianus's forces, combined with Helskadi's warriors, unloaded the weapons shipment. Meanwhile, Lucianus, Agaroman, and Helskadi observed the transportation of weapons while discussing the current geopolitical affairs between the Imperial Remnant and the territories that were under the direct control or influence of the Winter Death Witch. Helskadi informed Lucianus and Agaroman that the next time they delivered again, she would allow them to load more of her beast race servants into his flying contraption. Lucianus nodded again, but still could not hold back the random thought in his head. Where did these creatures come from? He became curious to know more about the beast races so that he might consider recruiting them himself and outright relocate them to serve in the Imperial Remnant's forces.

Of course, Lucianus knew he could not expect to reveal his intentions outright and receive the desired response from Helskadi telling him. That would leave Helskadi no longer having a mutual advantage of being a middleman or proxy conduit to supply Lucianus with more beastly warriors in exchange for more of the advanced Imperial Remnant armor and weapons. Still, Lucianus became discreet to ask away while he noticed from the distance various remote huts and caves dotted along the side of several mountains with rising smoke. He wondered if those were more of the beastly races related to the ones that he had acquired earlier from Helskadi. He asked Helskadi about the faraway small plumes of smoke if those were indeed snow trolls, cave orcs, and goblins. Helskadi did not detect or notice his intentions to assume anything other than this young werewolf adolescent being curious. The Winter Death Witch responded in the affirmative about his question while nodding. His next immediate response along with his reaction showed her suspicion becoming elevated. Lucianus concluded with a realization of excitement, stating with wonder that more of them must also live in similar conditions along the other mountains surrounding Shimmerfrost. Helskadi said nothing while having a visible facial display of resentment of his realization and responding in a cold tone of confirmation. However, the Winter Death Witch also warned the young werewolf warlord in a sharp response that her beast servants' dwellings were of no concern for him.

Agaroman noticed the delicate situation in which Lucianus drew his ally's displeasure. Agaroman diverted Helskadi's attention with another matter at hand. The wizard mentor to Lucianus asked the Winter Death Witch if she would need any future orders of armaments in which they could coordinate the next delivery for another cargo hold full of the exotic beast creatures of Shimmerfrost to be at the Imperial Remnant's service. Helskadi nodded and told the black-hooded wizard that she had many warriors to arm. She went on to say that Lucianus and his Imperial Remnant were welcome to make the same exchange as they would this day. Lucianus nodded though he still had his thoughts about the dwellings of the beast races in Shimmerfrost. If he could go to them directly to convince and recruit them to his cause, then he would not have to supply as many arms if any to Helskadi. Lucianus knew as soon as he encountered them on their own turf outside of Helskadi's immediate domain of Jotunheim and the surrounding Jotunn Mountains, they would join his cause without demanding any substantial supplies in return, as long as they got to shed blood and raid on his behalf for spoils in the warmer lands further south.

For now, Lucianus conceded to himself that he had to go along with Helskadi's terms and conditions. The young werewolf warlord would do so in order to gain as many new powerful recruitments for his Imperial Remnant army if he was ever to expand the power of his empire and plot revenge against Swordbane for the death of his parents.

After spending the next two hours boarding inside the skybeast cargo hold of the beastly servant warriors that Helskadi had transferred to serve under Lucianus, the skybeast warship prepared to launch back into the sky. Lucianus was pleased with the new forces he had under his command as much as they were pleased to serve under one whom they not only felt they could identify with in having him as their leader but also counted him as a fellow beastly creature given his werewolf appearance. Their fervor would increase as time passed while the newly joined crew would hear from the veteran soldiers of Lucianus about his worthiness in fighting off Swordbane's best warriors including in beating them in their last encounter while leaving them for dead against Wendigo and his summoned undead warriors after Lucianus smashed the Comradery's skyship to pieces with the skybeast.

Meanwhile, in the bridge and cockpit of the ship, Agaroman congratulated Lucianus for building his reputation as being as worthy as his father as the next dark lord. Lucianus nodded while asking if Agaroman had a tally of how many forces they had gained with Helskadi. Agaroman responded that in sum they had packed the skybeast with more than three hundred warriors including two dozen snow trolls, one hundred cave orcs, and two hundred goblins that were native to the Shimmerfrost region.

The floating vessel was packed but still able to traverse across the snowy mountainous landscape surrounding Jotunheim and to sail southeastward along the forested jagged fjord coastline that made up much of Shimmerfrost. In due time, Lucianus with his newly raised army would reach their destination. They would reach the borders of the Imperial Remnant and Swordbane. Once there, the new young dux would eventually have these beastly servants set up raiding camps along those borders to raid and plunder any valuable goods they could get from any raiding across the border without officially being identified from wielding Imperial Remnant armament nor wearing anything that would give away their clandestine operation in seeming to be a migratory nuisance of their making. In doing so, Lucianus would hope that the raids would weaken Swordbane in protecting their borders, which the Remnant would later exploit to its advantage.

Chapter Forty

In Pursuit of Darkness

Hours had passed deep into pursuit during the night. Linitus led the pursuit along with Marin, Alani-Aki, Peat, Wyatt, and the remaining few surviving members of the allied Nordling warband. They clustered together being spaced only a few feet apart. They were tired and exhausted. However, they were also determined this time to search and find Wendigo who had fled still westward through the narrow valleys and high gorges that were separated only by a few miles. Eventually, they found the Jokull-Flod. It was a large river that ran from north to south. The river bled into the ocean surrounded by many fjords just like much of the rest of the coastlands of Shimmerfrost.

The Comradery kept up with the pace of Wendigo. Linitus paid attention to the noticeable tracks the dark dyr beastlike creature left behind. However, he noticed other tracks that followed. They were the footprints of humans, as well as some goblins and orcs. The tracks had dispersed in different directions. Linitus motioned with his hand raised to signal for the present company to come to a halt. The rest of his companions followed his direction. Marin, curious, however, asked what had prompted Linitus to give the order. Linitus told her the undead had scattered. Marin shrugged and suggested they split up in groups to hunt each of them down but Linitus cautioned not to. He had a feeling that this was exactly what Wendigo would want them to do if it would make it easier to escape and kill some of them off. Linitus, however, presumed that perhaps a darker deception was afoot.

Alani-Aki interjected and confirmed that Wendigo was known to deceive and bait his enemies before taking their lives and claiming their physical corpses. She said that knowing what she does to him, he would try to entrap them. As soon as she said that, Linitus instructed their group to form a perimeter and be ready to be ambushed from all directions. Everyone nodded while forming an outboard circle formation.

Another moment went by. The elf rogue ranger's presumption was indeed correct. He and the rest of the present company could hear loud moaning and grunting noises from various directions. Linitus readied his bow while paying closer attention to the direction the noises came from. Despite being deep in a forest thicket at the center of the valley, the trees had looked dead while undergoing the previous winter dormancy and still had not grown their spring leaves. This made it somewhat easier to see the enemy from a distance even at night along with Wyatt's magic in using an illuminating ball of light to hover over them. Still having his bow at the ready, Linitus with his drawn bow let loose an arrow after Marin set it aflame with her flaming sword. The impact had made a large thud that could be heard along with an awkward moaning noise of pain that intensified. The undead creature, the corpse of a Nordling, dropped his war ax and shield while moving aimlessly as the fire consumed him.

Wyatt followed suit with his wand and cast a series of magical spells, including several explosive fire burst markers on the floor a few meters outside the circle of his companions. With haste, he motioned his wand to cast multiple fireballs in various directions in a 180-degree arc before him. Meanwhile, Linitus repeated the same process as before in locating the source of the sound of the groaning voices and letting loose more arrows that Marin would set aflame with her flaming sword.

The rest of the group waited patiently to engage in melee combat if it would come to it. Peat relied on his experience from fighting the undead warriors at Jokull-Hellir. The dwarf guardian advised the rest of the group to fight for their lives and to smash and break apart these undead warriors in order to set their bodies free from the control of Wendigo. The rest of the group nodded while reading their weapons. They were outnumbered at least six to one. However, Alani-Aki, thinking of what to do, used her knowledge of magic and nature while enchanting several words. Various pieces of fallen wood began to swirl and assemble into small, jagged creatures about the same size as Wyatt. These tree creatures were a rare sight that nobody had seen before and only the Nordlings of Shimmerfrost had heard of as being the fabled tree barkling creatures. Now half a dozen of these tree barklings had formed and stood a few paces away, forming a perimeter around the Comradery's circle.

Within moments, more of the enemy undead charged closer toward the Comradery from various directions. Though somewhat sluggish, the enemy undead were still persistent because of the constant magical effect Wendigo had on them. From various directions, the undead warriors triggered Wyatt's magical flaming spell traps after walking on them. Large bursts of flame exploded from the surface and engulfed the creatures. They fell in agony while succumbing to the burning fire that consumed their bodies. At least three dozen of the undead creatures remained. Linitus continued to fire three more flaming arrows, but alas he had to stop as he ran out.

Marin, meanwhile concentrated her powers to emanate a shining searing spear from one of her hands that she would take aim and hurl toward the undead creatures. It made contact and took out two of them while piercing through the first undead warrior she initially aimed at.

Linitus noted Marin using her powers while remembering that he had also learned before that he could do the same to emulate. He concentrated his mind while enchanting in a prayer-like form. Then he drew his bow back to emanate a shining, searing arrow of light. He let loose the bowstring to shoot off the arrow. The enchanted arrow flung in the air and pierced the skull of one undead warrior who fell instantly.

The summoned undead still outnumbered Linitus, Marin, and the surviving allied company by two to one. Wendigo's remaining summoned undead warriors that had not yet fallen continued to close in and engage in fierce melee combat with Linitus's company and Alani's summoned tree barklings. The Comradery and their surviving allies held their ground and disposed of the remaining undead. Linitus looked about to survey the immediate aftermath of Wendigo's failed counterattack. The elf ranger and Marin then took an impromptu muster to account for who was still alive in their present company before they resumed pursuing Wendigo again. The Comradery and present company took no further casualties except only three of Alani's summoned tree-barkling creatures.

Peat could not help but ask while taking his smoke pipe and lighting it to surmise if that was the last of the undead. Though no one kept count, Marin said if there was any more it would not be as much of a workout for the dwarf to keep in shape. Peat then found himself choking up and coughing while laughing at the same time in amusement at Marin's sense of witty humor. The dwarf stated that despite being human, she was just as much dwarven in heart and spirit as him to conceive of her having a sense of dwarven humor. The few other Nordlings that were present also seemed to enjoy the remark and laugh as well, while one of them stated that perhaps there was a common ancestor between their two peoples, Nordling and dwarf, to share such laughter.

Linitus and Wyatt did not laugh though and looked somewhat surprised by the humor while Alani looked at them both and asked the meaning of what would cause such laughter as she failed to understand as well. Linitus, however, knew Marin well enough to explain to the female dyr druidess that it was a sarcastic response in commenting on the physique and martial prowess, which he admitted the dwarves and Nordlings seemed to share high value in. Alani understood while nodding and stating that while she still did not fully understand what was said, she understood those qualities that the Nordlings exhibited, and she presumed the dwarves would also share in common whether they were the hostile pale dwarves from Shimmerfrost or the ones like Peat who were from the southern regions.

As the group of companions continued to be at ease, a ghastly figure from behind slowly crawled while moaning in pain. It was an undead warrior that Marin had pierced with a magically summoned spear of light. This creature's voice was audible for the company to take notice and withdraw their weapons to prepare for the next surprise. Marin spotted the figure. She walked slowly toward it, intending to finish where she left off and put the corpse to rest once and for all.

As Marin prepared to raise her flaming blade above her shoulders while being one stroke away from severing this possessed corpse, she suddenly froze and came to a halt. She was terrified at recognizing who it was, or at least the corpse of who it once was. It was the possessed body of Arik, the first Nordling who had befriended her and Linitus in this harsh and remote far-away region. She knew the corpse was only a possessed form of being animated to move, and that it was not the soul of Arik himself, but still, she struggled to bring herself to deliver the final blow. It became ingrained in her mind that even though she knew it was not him, it was still unbearable to strike him thinking as if it was still a mortal part of him she would inflict pain upon.

Suddenly, as the creature crawled and was within reach in grasping onto her, a sudden hissed sound passed by her along with a bright elongated bolt of lightning in the shape of an arrow. The sudden impact made a large crackling thud sound that struck and shattered the skull of the undead creature. Instantly, a dark fume of mist rose and receded westward toward the Jokull-Flod and eventually beyond toward the Jotunn Mountains. Marin however turned as she saw behind her that Linitus had struck the final blow in freeing Arik's bodily corpse from Wendigo's possession. Still, she froze before turning again to the corpse itself. She had seen a lot in the course of her life span, but this was one of the few moments where she fell on her knees and wept. It was a painful reminder to her of those she would consider and could call friends. Now she finally came to terms and took more time to process how much loss they had endured. Marin considered the fate that would be in store for the later-slain Nordlings and other beings that would fall in combat if she, Linitus, and the rest of their companions did not vanquish Wendigo before it became too late and the dark creature could unleash a horde of undead upon Shimmerfrost.

The Princess Knight gently felt a soft calm hand placed on her shoulders as she wept. Marin knew it was her lover in which she returned the gesture of him providing solace by placing her hand on top of his. She took another moment while collecting herself before getting herself up and grabbing onto Linitus's hand. Linitus told her when she and the other companions were ready they would continue their pursuit of Wendigo. She gazed at him after hearing his words and told him to promise her that even if they had to chase this dark summoner to the furthest northern end of the world or to the highest mountain, they would not stop to do so. Linitus looked straight into her face and nodded vowing he would do so.

Relieved, Marin embraced Linitus for a quick moment as lovers before planning on what to do next. Linitus instructed the rest of the Comradery to pick up the fallen corpses with care and to build a makeshift funeral pyre in which they would honor their fallen comrades as well as some of the fallen enemies that had their corpses previously summoned. As soon as they had completed their task, they would take a brief rest while rotating to stand guard in case of ambush before departing early the next morning to continue their pursuit of Wendigo.

Chapter Forty-One

Prize of Torment

Tortured and humiliated for several days, Lucia had only a few moments in between to rest while still being secured to the pillory Orcus had set up at the top of his tower. Between each interval, the same process would happen repeatedly where each of the hell lord's succubi would take turns to inflict pain upon her. They would do so in various humiliating ways including whipping her with pain-stinging weapons. They jeered with enjoyment as their prize of torment screeched and wailed in pain. If they could they would have easily dissected her body. However, they held back. They did so out of fear of retribution by Orcus. He had given them strict orders to only inflict minor pain upon Lucia's body. Still, one succubus wanted to further humiliate her while contemplating how. Lucia had nowhere to go while quenching her fists as a crossbar from the pillory tightly secured her neck and her hands. It limited her visibility from seeing only what was more or less in front and below her.

Still defiant as ever, Lucia cursed at her tormentors. She warned them that when it was over, she would exact her revenge on them. The succubi laughed while further mocking her for how she would do that while being tightly secured and restrained in lifting even one finger upon them. Internally, however, Lucia paid little attention while reminding herself this period of humiliation would pass. Lucia swore in time she would be true to her word and have revenge against every one of Orcus's demonic handmaidens. She would see that she tortured them to the point of wanting death before she would deliver it to them slowly and painfully.

While her mind concentrated on such thoughts, only heavy footsteps from behind and coming around caught her attention. She looked up and then looked down after knowing who it was. This figure, however, would not relent. Instead, he grabbed her by her hair to lift her head up with a noticeable amount of force. She looked at his face with utter disgust and hate, only to receive a laughing response. Orcus told her that soon in a matter of a few days, the moment would come that he would vanquish her lord, her dux, her soulmate right before her eyes. He threatened to make her watch every agonizing moment in pain while letting her know no matter how hard she would plead for mercy, he would show none before brutally killing Decius in front of her and then deciding how else he would torment her as his captured prize.

Lucia heard enough. Filled with disgust, she spat once again at Orcus's face, only to receive in response by Orcus a hard slap that stunned her for a moment. He laughed, telling her how helpless she was to do anything else. Lucia waited a moment before laughing back and surprising her capturer. When he wanted to know what prompted her, she stated he should enjoy his last few days, including with laughter, for she would see that Decius would make him wish he was dead. Orcus furiously grabbed Lucia's neck, which was partially exposed outside of the pillory crossbar near her head. The red demonic overlord choked her for a short duration. He let go while seeing her gasp for air and after being on the verge of suffocating to death. As she recomposed herself, Orcus laughed again while telling her she was foolish to test his patience while insulting him. He cautioned her to not be surprised that he would torture her as brutally as he wished at any moment.

Lucia this time had nothing else to say and remained quiet, though still showing a visible disgust for her tormentor. She wished it was now that would be the moment in which the roles were reversed and that Orcus would beg to be killed after she had her way of torturing and humiliating him. Still again she reminded herself that the day would come soon when he would find out and confess before her, before her husband, before his minions, and before her husband's minions that instead of him, it would be Decius who would prevail in the battle of wills against Orcus. It would be Decius and her in which he would acknowledge them as the lord and lordess (or lady) of Hadao Infernum, rulers of the infernal realm of hell. And when Orcus confessed their undisputed rule and claim to the throne of hell, only then would she let him beg for being disposed of once and for all. It would be then that she, along with her husband, would decide his fate. She would weigh in and encourage Decius when it became more known to her what would be the best way to make Orcus suffer slowly and painfully along with his succubi followers. She would humiliate him far worse than what he had made her endure.

Lucia would have time to contemplate while resting from the pain she endured as a lone flying imp came to Orcus's attention. The imp, speaking in its own demonic tongue while Lucia feigned slipping into unconsciousness, had made out what the small demonic creature said to Orcus. She could tell that it was concerning that the imp had disclosed that the contender (whom Lucia presumed was what Decius was being referred to as) was on his way with a large sizeable force. Orcus replied in a stern and calculating tone to inquire how many days this contender's forces would arrive at the hell lord's stronghold. The imp replied it would be in a matter of two or three days if this contender continued to do as he had so far in stopping by the various condemned settlements to recruit in his army.

The news Orcus received was enough for his face to become stiff and both his hands and feet to harden and quench with a subdued expression of anger. The red demonic overlord knew Decius was serious in his bid to unseat him and claim the title of being the undisputed lord of hell while recruiting any potential allies he could find that would have sufficient cause to lend their support to him. Still, Orcus would be ready for Decius as the former still had his own devices, which he intended to use in order to assert his unquestioned infernal reign and end any signs of rebellion once and for all.

After taking a moment of silence in pondering while smiling with malice, Orcus looked about calling forth for his minions outside including both the succubi and the many demonic imps. He briefed them inside his throne room deep in the lair of his tall jagged fortress. As the passing time went by, however, Lucia meditated while resting and gathering strength. She could channel and feel her thoughts connect with Decius, which Orcus had not been aware of.

Decius, though separated by over several dozen miles from her location, could feel and share her thoughts with her. He knew and sensed that she was in pain and that while she was fatigued and humiliated, she would not give in to despair. She still had the same hope and unquestioned faith in her eternal lover that he would find her, set her free, and together exact vengeance to secure his reign, and by extension her reign in union with his, to rule over their current domain. For now, she had to be strong, to conserve her strength, and to be patient until that moment would come.

Chapter Forty-Two

A Titan's Path to Chosen Vesselhood

Only after two days had passed since Lucianus arrived with his terrifying skybeast and delivered the promised weapons and armor that Helskadi had sought did she finally outfit the armament with a chosen select batch of the most elite cave orcs and snow trolls. These beastly creatures were summoned from their dwellings in the closest vicinity along the inner ring of the Jotunn Mountains. More of the beastly creatures would arrive at Helskadi's fortress complex and she was pleased watching from the top wall walk tower mounted on top of her stronghold. She could see and envision a future she desired while she watched the steady streams of orc and troll columns march into one of the two entry gates of her fortress complex. These stone gates including the main gatehouse and the rear postern gate were the only accessible paths of entry into this settlement, which was fortified heavily with jagged stone palisades or vertical slates that shielded the fortifications and stronghold from both invading forces and the harsh cold freezing wind that was quite normal inside the inner ring circle of the Jotunn Mountains.

As more of the orcs and cave trolls marched into the fortified settlement of Jotunheim, they quickly stood in formation outside the stronghold courtyard. They looked above to see their jotunn female warlord while giving gestures of salutations in a manner of sporadic beastly war cries and grunts. Helskadi grinned and acknowledged their salutations while giving a stern nod. Within moments, these elite cave orcs and snow trolls looked about and saw their comrades covered in exotic dark forged plate and chainmail metal armor. It was the likes that they had never seen before. Still, they were in awe as their comrades communicated to them to be at ease while helping them don the same armor and receive the same weaponry, which varied ranging from spears and swords and shields made from the same material. Though heavy, they could withstand the weight and they noticed these weapons were far more durable than the ones, which they dropped, including large wooden clubs and wood spears made of wood and either flint or obsidian.

After a few more moments of her forces being outfitted, the female giant monarch, considered a living titan goddess among the dark denizens of Shimmerfrost, raised her hand to command their attention. The outfitted trolls and cave orcs, along with other present companies, including several goblins and the local giant jotunns, observed quietly what their titan monarch had to say. Helskadi then raised her exotic spear-like staff. She declared loudly that today would mark a new beginning for the forces of darkness in Shimmerfrost. She announced that these warriors who were outfitted would be the shock troops of her army that would lead the rest of the beastly creatures to attack and either force them into submission or outright destroy the remaining Nordling and dyr folk settlements that resisted in submitting before her authority. Helskadi told them it would be them as well as her fellow male jotunn warriors and herself who would find plenty of blood and death to spill. Whether the Nordlings in Shimmerfrost resisted or submitted, her forces would continue southward to attack more Nordling tribes along the southern forest coastline. They would shed enough blood to quench her war lust in order for her to attain the same status, which she envied and thought she deserved as much as Decius before her to be deemed worthy as a chosen vessel among one of the various deity spirits.

However, when Helskadi had attained chosen vesselhood, she would not stop. No, instead, as she continued to declare before her dark followers, she would use her status as the chosen vessel and as a titan with near deity status to ascend to the place of godhood or full deification, which she thought was rightfully hers. There would be no stopping her, nor by extension her followers before her. Right after she finished her speech, all those present erupted into a wave of jubilant war cries. They had waited, especially the jotunn giants living hundreds of years, for the moment to come in which their giantess titan would unleash her fury toward those in the region that resisted her influence. Helskadi would spare only the major settlements of Frostburg and Shimmerheim since both had already recognized her suzerainty over them.

Once her army finished outfitting themselves, she would have to decide who to attack first. There were several ideal places that she considered striking. Nebelheim was perhaps the most accessible, as she could march her forces due south through a pass that led outside the Jotunn Mountains. The Nordling settlement, formidable as it was, would make an ideal to start her path in satisfying the lust of war and death of the deity spirits of Laran and Calu. In doing so, Helskadi hoped by that point in time they would bestow upon her to one day attain chosen vesselhood just as they had done to Decius.

Another target the Winter Death Witch considered while having her army venture south out of the Jotunn Mountains would be to turn westward to raid the dyr folk's settlements. One of her lieutenant minions, Wendigo, would want nothing more than to have what it considered revenge for how he felt discarded by his dyr kinsfolk. To control their corpses after death would give Wendigo the satisfaction to continue to do Helskadi's bidding. However, she also considered the other possibility, which might give a reason for him to feel content in possessing the corpses of so many and no longer seek to serve her. She was not sure of the dark creature's loyalty and how far it would extend once it was appeased by having the revenge and awkward sense of unity it desired in possessing the corpses of the same creatures that had treated him as an unwanted outcast.

For now, Helskadi became content to know there were several options of where to attack first to start her campaign to dominate the entire region of Shimmerfrost. She would spend some more time pondering and deciding by the next day when she would deploy her army, which was now better equipped. She would consult with her chief of guard, Fornjotr, a fellow jotunn, for his thoughts on the matter. Perhaps he would have a better sense of where to strike their first target.

Helskadi dismissed her mustered forces to return to the barracks of the fortified complex while she herself would do the same as she descended the flight of stairs from the top of the main fortress tower. She would sit upon her ice-cold stone throne in her royal chamber to continue to ponder her plans. These were dark and cold days for Shimmerfrost even during the spring season. Helskadi would set her mind to making those days even darker and colder as she would assert the full power that she yielded while no longer holding back. In her mind, it was her time. It was her time to rule the northern remote lands uncontested. It was her time to end this perpetual warfare and no longer face any more resistance, whether it be from the dyr folk or from the various Nordlings settlements that were still stubborn and defiant in recognizing her as their undisputed sovereign.

Chapter Forty-Three

Discovery From the Vast Blue Yonder

Another day and another sunrise, footsteps moving rapidly like thunder upon the ground could be heard. The trees would tremble if they had the same feeling of fear of being pursued. Passing by, however, only the shadows would touch the trees as the pursuing figures followed in a dauntless pursuit of something else. It was something that they considered far more sinister and worthy of pursuit. These figures, which were made up of Linitus's Comradery, followed behind the elf rogue ranger as he led from the front while using his senses to track Wendigo. The dark, dreadful creature by the elf's estimate was only a day at most away from them. With patience and luck, Linitus believed they could intercept Wendigo. They could corner the creature as they continued to close in, provided the rest of the group could still keep up and give chase.

However, as they followed the foul creature's foot tracks, they realized Wendigo was still a step ahead of them. The remaining small tree-barkling creatures that Alani-Aki had summoned followed ahead of their party. However, the barklings had lost their mystical connection and presence to Alani. She felt a flow of coldness and emptiness in channeling her thoughts to them in which it had ceased. Alani could not hide her reaction of shock and slight horror. She knew somehow these creatures had fallen. What was more terrifying was that her suspicion of the situation was affirmed. These creatures had been consumed by Wendigo's dark aura, in which he now controlled them to do his bidding.

Marin saw Alani's shocked face. The Princess Knight placed her arm upon the dyr druidess's shoulder with modest concern about asking what she sensed. Alani struggled to recollect herself but did so in a moment, staring coldly that they were coming for them. Marin, still curious, asked who. Alani replied that it would be her summoned creatures, though they were no longer under her command. She had lost her connection to them.

Meanwhile, Linitus wasted no time. The elf ranger in an instant aimed his bow while concentrating on his supernatural powers to generate an arrow from his hands in the shape of bright, visible, searing light. Marin did the same while emanating a searing bright, throwing spear of light. Wyatt, with haste, placed a large fire magic trap enchantment marking on the ground. It was ready to explode at the first step of any foes that would close in on them in being at least a dozen yards away. The rest of the present company readied their weapons while forming an outboard circular wall around themselves. They would cover their flanks while being surrounded by a forest of melting and receding snow at an elevation of well over a thousand feet.

In another tense moment, the various members of Linitus's company were eager to engage against any would-be foes. They still composed themselves and waited. Marin confided in a quiet voice to Linitus. She admitted to being surprised that the surviving Nordlings in their group had not lost their discipline to rush out to seek the enemy head-on. Linitus nodded while replying that perhaps they had learned from their previous engagements that a more concerted approach in fighting in unison was their best option for survival. Marin nodded, admitting that this could be the case. Linitus reflected and noted that, in a certain way, the surviving Nordlings were learning and maturing to be an effective fighting force. It reminded the elf ranger in times past how he and Marin, along with Peat and Wyatt, had learned to fight together and overcome insurmountable obstacles. In that regard, the elf rogue ranger saw this as a promising sign of the Nordlings. They had the potential in Shimmerfrost to be sufficient and strong enough to resist the forces of darkness. The elf believed that was true not only against Helskadi but in the foreseeable days to come after the Winter Death Witch was dealt with.

Marin nodded again while agreeing with some caution in stating that would be true, provided that these Nordlings would stay united and not fight among themselves. Linitus turned again, surprised at considering such a possibility. Without even saying a word, Marin had known him and his reactions well enough to dispel his concerns for the time being. She reminded her elf lover that for now they had to focus on getting as many of the Nordlings and dyr folk united as possible. They had to do so at least to stand against Helskadi's forces. Linitus agreed, but as soon as he did so he heard a sudden series of rapid footsteps.

Meanwhile, from a hundred yards away, the possessed corpses of the tree barklings dashed toward them. As they ran while closing in, Linitus let loose his enchanted summoned arrow while Marin did the same in throwing her enchanted magical spear. Both of their attacks had delivered strong enough blows to crush and shatter two of the barklings while the third still ran too close in. Peat instructed the Nordlings to take cover. The rest of the group waited until the last possessed barkling had stepped on the enchanted imprint marking that Wyatt cast on the ground. Once it did so, it triggered a large, flaming explosive burst that had set the creature on fire. After wandering aimlessly, the creature succumbed to its wounds and fell apart into broken pieces of burnt wood.

Another moment went by. The Comradery could only hear the ambient noise of the winter forest with trees that looked dead while a small breeze of wind gusts blew toward them from the southwest. Linitus along with the others held their stance while somewhat anxious at not being sure what to expect next. Waiting another moment, while looking about, the elf ranger signaled with his hand motioning downward that his comrades could lower their weapons. They did so. Another wind gust blew by and one of the Nordlings spoke to another Nordling. Marin could make out the meaning in their native tongue. The Nordlings pointed at the direction that the wind came from as being an omen in which they should investigate. The Princess Knight informed the rest of the company, despite her hesitation in sounding superstitious. She knew it was possible that the direction in which the wind came from might lead them along the coast to better navigate in knowing their sense of direction while still being on track to pursue Wendigo.

Linitus, meanwhile, looked closely for Wendigo's tracks. He confirmed the creature had indeed traveled in the same direction. The elf ranger continued to make haste to follow Wendigo's trail. The Comradery and immediate company followed behind him as he continued to follow the tracks that were left behind in the snow. Eventually, this thin snow-covered floor along with more forest trees gave way from which they could see more clearly from a distance. They were on a higher elevation, either a small mountain or even a large hill. Regardless, they saw below and afar. They could see the gradual descent along with spruce evergreen trees dotting the landscape. Along the lower plain, they also saw a small river that bled out into a large delta network that stood out with various outlying fjords across the distance. The sight of it was mesmerizing and beautiful to look at from their vantage point. They could also see several forms of animal life from afar. This included migrating caribou and two bears near the river looking for fish to catch and consume. There was also a lone bald eagle that flew with majestic grace high above the sky. Surrounding the lower plain and still further across the distance from the other side of the river were a multitude of snow-capped mountains and gorges, including the one they were standing on.

Linitus pondered if he could catch the eagle's attention and use his chosen vesselhood powers of nature to command the creature to help them find Wendigo. Alani sensed and noticed the elf's speculation. Thy dyr druidess encouraged him to not hold back but focus his thoughts on using the powers of nature to command and summon the flying bird. Linitus nodded and took a moment to concentrate his mind while unleashing a strange eerie whistle that in moments caught the eagle's attention.

Within a moment, the swooping eagle descended from the sky. It came to a halt while perching its talons on Linitus's outstretched right arm that was protected by one of his pair of leather bracers. The elf rogue ranger focused his thoughts. He had his mind attuned to the creature's mind; Linitus conveyed and exchanged thoughts with the creature. He was stunned by what he found out. Even more so, everyone else in his company became amazed at seeing how deeply connected the elf ranger had been in reading the mind of the creature and vice versa.

Linitus mentioned aloud while still concentrating his mind and thoughts on the creature that they were not alone. In fact, the creature had come scouting ahead in service to its owner, who had trained this animal as a pet. The owner himself traveled high in the sky with a partner of his. Upon hearing this, everyone became more astonished. Marin and Peat both interjected, asking who it was. Linitus said that he would find out soon while commanding with his thoughts to the bird to take flight and soar back to its owner. The bird shared its vision in which the elf ranger engaged in a trancelike meditation state. He had stood motionless and his eyes, though seeing straight across, were sharing the same sight as the flying eagle. He let the bird (since it knew its owner's whereabouts) fly by its own control. The eagle still allowed the elf to share its sight vision to observe the direction and location it traveled to reunite with its master.

After several minutes, the rest of Linitus's company stood by waiting patiently. Then a small lone object in the sky emerged. As it approached their direction, Wyatt caught notice and signaled everyone else's attention. All present companies speculated what it could be. Marin discerned along with Wyatt to point out that the approaching object was in fact a small flying sailboat, or rather a skyboat. This vessel was supported by a gas bag balloon with a propeller blade behind the frame assembly that secured the small boat's hull to the hull of the balloon. As they looked with further astonishment and excitement. Wyatt used his wand to cast a bright, small, harmless flare of dispersed light sparks to show their position for the flying vessel to spot them.

Within moments, the eagle looking down toward Linitus had signaled to the elf that the bird's master had come to his location from above. Linitus broke his telepathy meditation and shook his head in adjusting himself back to his own vision of seeing. Marin and Alani had noticed this. Marin became concerned. She put her arm on his shoulder gently and asked her lover if he was okay. Linitus nodded. Alani asked him how it felt to share such an attachment with a majestic creature of nature, such as that eagle. The elf replied it was surreal. He felt as if he was in his place, flying in absolute freedom.

Linitus took another moment to assess the situation while realizing the skyboat lay above them. The floating craft slowly descended to the surface. The elf instructed his company to leave space for it to land while waiting patiently until it had done so. Except for Linitus who saw the occupants from the eagle's shared vision of sight, the rest of the company were eager to see who piloted the skyboat for the first time. To their surprise, they saw that it was two small dwarves that emerged from the small flying contraption after dropping tied weighted bags onto the surface while adjusting the controls of the craft in making its gradual landings. These dwarf occupants were nearly Peat's age and size by the looks of it. One of them was a male who had a long, flowing blond beard and mustache. The bottom of the newcomer dwarf's beard flowed down to just above his waistline and secured by a gold clasp. He wore a mix of scale mail armor that was in alternating colors of gold and blue while his cuirass was of plate mail and a bronze-looking color. Most notably, what stood out was his helm. It was a gold and blue helmet that had a set of side rear protruding wings that were blue laced with gold. The same eagle Linitus had seen earlier was now perched onto the dwarf's gauntlet on one hand. The dwarf wielded in his other hand a moderately sized one-handed double-bladed war ax that appeared to be made in the dwarven fashion along with dwarven forged steel. Beside the male dwarf and next to the operating controls of the flying contraption was a female dwarf. She wielded a bright blue stone-encrusted one-handed war hammer secured by a wooden shaft. This female dwarf had fair skin like her counterpart, though no beard, and she had black flowing hair going down to her shoulder line. She wore a set of similar armor. Her helmet was made of leather with a blue encrusted stone that matched the color of her war hammer.

Linitus looked curiously at the strangers who shared the same look toward him and his present company. The elf broke the shock of staring by motioning with his hands while raising one of them to give a salutation gesture while introducing himself. The two newcomer dwarves stood at first nearly dumbfounded and made the company question if they had encountered someone who could not understand them. Another passing moment, however, the two dwarves laughed unsuspectedly at Linitus. They then proceeded to speak in the common Citadellan tongue that this was not their first time encountering an elf, much less any Nordlings. However, they paid special attention to acknowledge Peat being the only dwarf they pointed out whom they had not seen of their kind in over a month. Peat being surprised, identified himself by name and his known dwarven ascribed title of being a chief guardian at one time of the Sacred Stone Clan in the Kingdom of Swordbane's dwarven fortified settlement of Karaz-Barazbad. The two dwarves reacted warmly. They told Peat they were familiar with that site by taking a pilgrimage there to see the dwarven temple dedicated to the Sacred Stone of the dwarf deity of Baraz. They informed Peat and the rest of the company that they originally hailed from an isolated fortified dwarven settlement along one of the northern ridge chains of the Great Eastern Mountains. These mountains were also known as the Wall Stone Mountains. This massive mountain range from far away ran north-south. It separated the continent of Hesperion to the west from the other half of the landmass to the east known as Yaxia-Dalu by the Far Eastern indigenous elven peoples of that continent who called themselves Xiao Jing Ling.

All present company took some time to get acquainted with the two newcomer dwarves. Marin, Linitus, and Alani alternated in taking turns to fill in the two dwarves about the latest important developments that had been happening in the region with the threat that Helskadi's forces posed in taking over. They also mentioned the present company being fortunate to survive a baited counter-ambush attack unleashed by Helskadi's allies, the Imperial Remnant. As Andarin and Alvissan listened with genuine intent, their reaction did not seem too surprising. Both of them actually sounded as if they knew about the backdrop of these aforementioned conspiring factions of darkness. Andarin and Alvissan let everyone else know that they were familiar with hearing folktales of Helskadi and Wendigo by the local Nordlings in Shimmerfrost when the traveling dwarven couple made their routine visits of trade in the springtime.

Meanwhile, Andarin and Alvissan also confided that like many other peoples of Hesperion, including from the western side of the Wall Stone Mountains, word-of-mouth had already spread like wildfire from time to time about the Imperial Remnant. Everyone seemed to know that this faction founded over ten years ago sought to expand its territorial control and sphere of influence beyond its mostly desert and high basin borders. The only surprise to Andarin and Alvissan was that the Imperial Remnant had spread its influence as far north as the remote frontier of Shimmerfrost.

As they finished their conversation, both dwarves of the flying vessel offered their hospitality and help to Linitus and his company. Linitus knew it was perilous, even for these two new acquaintances. The elf warned Andarin and Alvissan of the danger that Wendigo posed. Linitus suggested to the two respective dwarves that they could fly within the vicinity of Wendigo in which Wyatt would use his spell casting to teleport the company to the surface to engage in defeating the vile monster once and for all while allowing the two dwarven couples the flying boat to speed away for safety. Andarin and Alvissan, however, laughed, causing a somewhat surprised look by Linitus, Wyatt, and Alani. However, Marin, Peat, and some of the surviving Nordlings understood. Marin reminded Linitus that Andarin and Alvissan were still dwarves, and this went against their code of honor to consider retreating. From the many dwarves Marin knew growing up even as a child, they were not known to take kindly in the offer to retreat from an ensuing battle.

Linitus nodded and chuckled. He admitted he should have presumed so granted these dwarves stood out from the many he had known before. Rarely had he seen dwarves in the merchant profession, not to mention traveling in a small flying craft to carry goods. Andarin and Alvissan sought a conciliatory way by hugging Linitus tightly with his arms in a warming embrace to show that the elf had caused no offense in his presumptions of the two dwarven merchants.

Upon everyone being loaded onto the deck of the flying boat, Andarin undocked the weighted objects that secured the flying contraption to the ground. Meanwhile, Alvissan operated a series of lever controls next to the steering helm. The flying boat was soon enough several hundred feet in the sky while still gradually ascending. Its destination continued to go westward due north in the hopes of Linitus and his comradery to track down and vanquish Wendigo once and for all. The sky, though partially cloudy, was still beating brightly, with the sun looking down. Its majestic rays of light touched down with elegance upon the coastal fjords, as some glaciers near the shore would eventually melt. With luck, Wendigo would have nowhere to run. The dark creature would be intercepted by the Comradery within the next day or two at the most.

Chapter Forty-Four

Unleashing the Primal Beast

Gusts of wind carrying lightly burning ash swirled in the air among the hellscape ruins in the near distance. The site was known as Templum Tormentum. It was also known as the Temple of Torture, a site with many dilapidated ancient buildings, or ruins. It attained that name for not so much the physical torture that would exist there alone, but also a symbolic mental and emotional state of torture. It was this place that was shared among some of the condemned inhabitants who hid among the jagged constructed ruins. They did so out of fear of exposing themselves in being out in the open plain between the ruins. Had they not stayed hidden, they risked being noticed and captured by Orcus's minions. From that point, the hell lord's minions would take the unfortunate abductee to Orcus's fortress lair to meet his or her ultimate torture and likely demise.

The ruins were also frequented by Orcus himself periodically. He would scour for any potential victims to torture. Sometimes, however, the hell lord would send in his stead one of his succubi representatives along with a swarm of imps to exact tribute of human sacrifices. Upon arrival on a typical occasion, the demonic hell lord's forces would announce their presence. It was expected that the inhabitants would send one of their own outside among the scattered ruins to be taken as sacrificial lambs for torment to avoid Orcus's forces taking more of the condemned by outright force. Ultimately, their pain and suffering would be offered for the sadistic pleasure that the reigning lord of hell sought to quench. If his quench was not satisfied by a refusal from the settlement's inhabitants to give up a small offering of their own, it would cause Orcus and his minions to exact the human sacrifices through force. Orcus and his minions in such a case would take it upon themselves to satisfy their bloodlust even if it meant slaughtering larger numbers of the settlement's inhabitants as retribution.

Now, however, as always, the condemned still hid among large debilitated and partially crumbled ruins, watching frantically while hearing a growing loud and steady march. From the distance, beyond the obscured sight of the small swirling wind of ash, they could see a small but growing series of figures. This was not the army of Orcus being dispatched to compel them to offer another periodical tribute of the condemned, but they were a large marching army of condemned themselves. The locals of the settlement could not believe what they saw. They talked in whispers among themselves, speculating about what had caused such a large mass exodus to make their way to their settlement. It was surprising to them knowing that they were usually the first to be preyed upon by Orcus's minions from being so close to the hell lord's lair compared to the other condemned. Or at least so they thought.

Soon, however, their anxiety and suspicions became more heightened when they saw something even more startling emerging from the distance in the dark cloudy orange sky above. Several large columns of swarms of imps hovered above. Their screeches drowned the sky from any other ambient noise that could be heard, while the swarms stopped and circulated around the ruins in a tall vertical column above the center plain that separated several of the large building ruins from each other.

Eventually, a dark werewolf figure emerged through teleportation at the very center between the ruins. He gave a large howl as if to announce his presence and command respect. The figure announced himself as Decius while claiming the title of the rightful sovereign of Hadao Infernum. The various eyes peering out became enlarged in awe while hiding among the buildings. Enough audible gasps could be heard among them, which Decius acknowledged and called them out while assuring them that they would have nothing to worry about. He would not torture and sacrifice them for a crazed bloodlust in the way Orcus would. However, no one believed him, while a lone voice of defiance, presumed to be the leader of this condemned settlement, called out and challenged the dux over his legitimacy and demanded that he prove his right in claiming the sovereignty of hell over them.

Decius heard the challenge. He nodded with a horrid stare that locked his sharp canine eyes toward the challenger. The dux responded loud enough for all to hear that he would show them soon. The local denizens became shocked at hearing his loud voice, the unleashed screeching by the flying imps, and the howling moans of the condemned army that followed behind him. The same lone voice hiding among the ruins that had challenged the dux's authority was nervous while questioning the contestant hell lord of his course of action. He let Decius know he was crazy to be that loud and risk alerting his presence for any of Orcus's minions to detect.

Decius, in his jeering werewolf manner, laughed and howled several times while replying inquisitively if that was what the speaker of the condemned hiding in the ruins wanted—a challenge for those watching hidden among the ruins to determine who would be worthy for them to follow. The dux followed up and stated he wanted to attract the attention of Orcus's forces as much as possible. He would do so in order to display his power and legitimacy for the claim as the true lord of hell. Decius would also use this display to make an example of Orcus's minions.

Within moments, the orange hellscape sky became darkened with blots of red. Many of Orcus's imps and several of his succubi lieutenants heeded Decius's call to alert them and investigate their soon-to-be enemy in battle. As the swarm of flying imps and succubi flew closer to the ruins of Templum Tormentum, Decius channeled his thoughts and concentrated in his mind. He challenged himself to do what he had not done in many years. He struggled several times to unleash the same full display of destructive powers in hell as he once did on the mortal surface realm of Terrunaemara. Still, he concentrated and closed his eyes. He thought about how he did it once before, only that he could not. This time, however, it was different. He had a reason to find his same powers again as the chosen vessel to tap into and deploy its full effect. He thought of Lucia. His mind would not accept the fact of wanting to wait any further for those among his enemy, sworn in fealty to Orcus, to cause further harm to his beloved Lucia. She was his soulmate, and if there was any thought or reason in which he would transcend and defy the conditions of hell, this time he would do it.

Decius concentrated again while saying several enchanted words in the ancient Lupercalian tongue. Within moments, what had not happened since his mortal life (except for one particular rare occasion) had finally happened again. A large combination of blood-red and pitch-black mists swirled around his body while he opened his mouth and unleashed one large deafening howl that all could hear as far away as Orcus's fortified stronghold itself.

After another moment of quietness, the approaching enemy swarm army numbered in the thousands came to a halt. They observed and then laughed at the mockery they thought Decius had shown in trying to scare them. The enemy swarm army was ready to engage with Decius or so they thought until the ground suddenly shook loud enough and erupted in a loud explosion leaving behind a large crater.

Appearing before the crater epicenter of the debris-like explosion, emerged something that the denizens in all walks of hell had not seen before at least in this fiery realm. Not the succubi, the imps, nor any of the condemned (save a few warriors that fell in battle and served alongside Decius during their mortal lives) could tell what it was. This emerging creature was gigantic and easily stood over a hundred feet tall. It unleashed a large and even more terrifying howl than Decius had before. This was the returning and resurrected summoned avatar bearing the same werewolf anatomy as its summoner only that this avatar was much larger. It was a colossus beast-size werewolf.

Startled and trembling from the sight of what they saw, the various servants of Orcus were stunned. Some reacted by resuming their charge in swarming to overwhelm the behemoth werewolf while others held back to observe the summoned creature. Still, a few cowardly enemy imps became consumed with enough fear to want to retreat to safety. They flew back to seek their hell lord master, Orcus, to warn him of what they saw.

For the many imps and succubi that choose to attack the colossal summoned werewolf avatar, they did so with an aggressive stance while executing a flying charge. Some others tried to outflank the gargantuan creature more cautiously. Regardless, this would be a battle in which Orcus's army had never endured of the like before. For Decius, however, this was one in which it would be critical for him to secure victory in order to attain the fealty of this condemned settlement to join his forces in making his final push toward his opponent's stronghold and rescue his beloved Lucia.

Decius wasted no time while going on the offensive. He and his gigantic avatar of himself both howled one last time before the gargantuan of the dux ferociously charged, leaped, and crashed down with its full force above upon the many imps and at least two of the succubi who were caught off guard and flew low enough to be trampled on. The results were sudden and terrifying as the impact amounted to the instant death of the enemy corpses being splattered. For the temporary fortunate among those who either evaded the gargantuan werewolf's attack or who still stayed back while moving around to find an open flank from which to attack either Decius or his avatar, they would find less relief as the dux's forces from the other side of the ruins rushed in after initiating their own form of war cries and screeches. Decius's imps quickly flew and pounced upon their rival demonic brethren still loyal to Orcus. Meanwhile, the army of the condemned used great caution and discernment to attack only those imps who swirled and swooped toward them.

The condemned loyal to Decius also used their own makeshift slings, hurling various hardened pieces of volcanic rock toward the succubi that still survived and stayed behind. The battle was fierce, but the tide eventually turned in the favor of Decius. The condemned from the ruins of Templum Tormentum waited long enough to reach a feeling of strong mutual consensus that their lot in surviving and having better conditions would be best suited in aligning themselves to support Decius. Emerging from the ruins these local condemned had their own makeshift weapons very much similar to their other condemned counterparts including makeshift spears, crude blunt objects, small sharp objects, and volcanic rocks that they hurled toward the succubi and the enemy imps that could be discerned as belonging to Orcus's side based on their behavior toward attacking Decius and his colossus avatar.

As the battle continued to rage on for nearly an hour, it became a war of attrition. Despite the toll it took on both sides with heavy casualties, the outcome was in favor of Decius and his overwhelming larger number of forces prevailing decisively against those that were dispatched and belonging to Orcus. Decius instructed the remaining survivors on his side to bury the remains of their fallen comrades, both condemned and imps alike. He instructed his forces to slay any of the wounded and leave no survivors. He wanted to make an example of what became of those that opposed him and he wanted his forces to do it swiftly and mercilessly. Regardless, he knew, however, there would be survivors as a portion of his nemesis's army had fled in the ensuing battle when he first summoned his gargantuan werewolf avatar. These fiends would let their master know of what they saw. Perhaps it was better that way or at least Decius considered that possibility.

While assessing the aftermath of the battle on the burning hot plains of hell, Decius turned and noticed a large number of his remaining condemned followers chanting his name. In an expedient and exponential manner, the chants of the condemned along with ones that sound like screeches by the imps continued to chant. Their hands moved up as quenched fists while beating their chests. Several of the large condemned who were orcs in the mortal world (but now shadowed and charred imitations of their former bodily selves), walked forward and picked up the dux over their shoulder while presenting him in front of his army. It became more epic as Decius saw all those before him submit themselves kneeling on both their knees while still raising their clenched fists and beating their chests. He heard them call him not only by his name but by his title while giving salutations of hailing him. They called him the one true, rightful dark lord and sovereign of the hell they lived in.

This proclaimed hell lord took it in before howling in his large werewolf voice to signal for silence and attention to him. He received it and then he told them of a new covenant in which he would establish with them and all the denizens that he would reign over in Hadao Infernum. As long as they followed Decius with genuine devotion, he would see that no harm would come to them and if it did, he would address it in order for it to cease.

Loud cheers erupted again only to follow for another howl by Decius. His next edict was for all the condemned that sided with him to join the rest of their counterparts and his swarms of imps to march to their final destination, Orcus's stronghold. He told them they not only would help in toppling their tormentor and oppressor but they would also benefit themselves by helping their proclaimed leader to set his wife and eternal soulmate free from the clutches of his infernal rival. In doing so, they would not only have their lord of hell to reign and watch over them, but they would have a lady counterpart of their lord in providing for their needs. Lucia, as Decius proclaimed her name before his army of followers, would be their anointed infernal mother.

As Decius finished his proclamation, another series of celebratory chants erupted from the crowd of followers. The dux's thoughts turned to thinking more deeply about his infernal lover. His face turned toward the direction of Orcus's lair. She was there and still bound in torment. He hoped she would hold on and not give in at least long enough for him to be there and set her free. In doing so, they would exact their revenge by slaying as many of Orcus's followers as possible and tormenting some of the remaining enemies as revenge. Decius would also deal with Orcus himself once he encountered the incumbent reigning hell lord. Decius was only two, maybe three days at most, away by a standard march to meeting his rival once again. This time when they meet it would be the last time as Decius vowed to himself that he would prevail once and for all.

Chapter Forty-Five

Sacrificing Light to Purge Darkness

The sun was setting down with the light still shining in a weakened form toward the cold Shimmerfrost landscape below. A trail of black mist streaked across the snow-covered mountainous slopes and mélange forest of quaking aspen, weeping birch, white spruce, and maple trees that dot the landscape. The Comradery looked below. The sight was impressive but also frantic. It was a race against time for Linitus, Marin, and their companions. Their newfound sky-faring hosts provided them a new means of traversing the landscape once again from floating in the beautiful blue sky above separated by various clouds from various directions. If Linitus could spend the rest of his days holding his arms alongside Marin's as they did during their younger years, he would have wished for it. Now, however, they both have learned over time, including at this point that the innocence of such dreams had to wait with the important matter at hand. They were tracking the deadliest creature throughout all of Shimmerfrost. They knew they had to intercept it before it would escape them and retreat to the lair of its master within the bowels of the Jotunheim Mountain range.

However, such a task as they knew was not as simple as it seemed. Linitus could tell the trail was slowly fading, and that Wendigo was a fleet of foot starting to outpace the small skyboat. The creature was close to reaching the mountains in which the snow-capped peaks could be seen from over the horizon. Linitus pointed his observation out, knowing that the dark creature was close to reaching his destination. Once Wendigo had done so, there would be no chance for the elf ranger and his comrades to stop him when he stayed hidden within the mountains and its many caves. Marin, however, thought back to her earlier exploits at Jokull-Hellir. She recalled how she and the other members of the comradery escaped with Wyatt's use of magic being tested in teleporting rapidly. Marin remembered they had traversed great distances in which the halfling wizard had been tested in his own capabilities. If Wyatt could do this much, perhaps he could teleport them from such a far distance to just outside the footsteps of the southeast mountain range.

Before Linitus said anything, he could tell from Marin's thought process and told her he thought the same thing as well. They had to try to. It was worth the risk of knowing Wyatt was perhaps the most formidable wizard to pull off such a feat. Marin nodded. Both of them turned to Wyatt. She tapped his shoulder and caught his attention while Linitus explained it was time for him to be tested with his use of magic. Wyatt looked surprised at first. Then the halfling wizard nodded when the elf rogue ranger explained the plan he and Marin devised. Marin also explained it to the rest of the crew onboard, instructing them to brace for the unknown upon teleporting. Everyone would go except for Andarin and Alvissan. The two dwarves would remain to pilot the floating skyboat. They would be ready to assist from above once they sailed closer to the mountains.

Peat looked at Wyatt after taking a deep breath. The dwarf warned the halfling sarcastically. If Wyatt transported Peat inside the mountain, there would be a great deal of punishment for the halfling to pay when the dwarf got out with his hammer. Wyatt blinked and gulped with somewhat of a sense of being intimidated. Marin overheard and scolded her former mentor and comrade for scaring their wizard companion into questioning his own confidence in using magic. The dwarf laughed while padding the halfling wizard hard on the back, saying he was only kidding. However, as soon as he did it, Wyatt motioned his wand, and suddenly Peat disappeared. Marin gave a slight grin while Linitus visibly disapproved. The Princess Knight retorted back saying that it was not as if anyone could say the dwarf did not deserve a little surprise mischief in what he put Wyatt through. Linitus nodded while admitting Marin had a point, perhaps. Taking another exhale, he held hands with Marin before looking and nodding to Wyatt to teleport them next. The wizard nodded while motioning his silver wand. Suddenly, his other two close comrades vanished from thin air. Wyatt began to teleport Alani alongside the few surviving Nordlings in their company. The wizard himself took a bow while looking at Andarin and Alvissan before self-teleporting.

The two dwarven pilots were still stunned and dumbfounded at what they had seen. They both became impressed by what the wizard had done including making himself disappear. Andarin could not help but turn to his dwarven counterpart's wife and ask her to remind him next to hire a wizard in their later travels. When Alvissan asked why, Andarin had replied that it would make the heavy lifting much easier by utilizing Wyatt's teleportation spell-casting so he could have more time to enjoy a good smoke from his pipe and drink a pint of dwarven ale. Alvissan pushed Andarin's shoulder, telling him that if anyone should have the ale, it should be her for putting up with him as long as she did in their travels. Both dwarves laughed before returning to the matter at hand while keeping their course and heading toward the Jotunn Mountains that lie straight before them.

As the lone skyboat continued to float, inching closer toward the Jotunn Mountains, Wendigo, in his dark, near shadowy form, could not help but look back. He then turned toward the base of the mountain and proceeded toward a cave opening that went under the mountains. He was only a dozen yards away before noticing a large shimmer of light streak across the distance. Then it stopped while the dark creature felt the impact of what was a bright glowing arrow that had struck it. Wendigo gnarled in pain. The blow was powerful enough to cause the creature to stagger while turning about to see the direction from which the assailant had struck.

Wendigo noticed after turning that his attacker was a slender elf wearing ornate leather armor from a distance. It was the same elf it had encountered before. This elf held a bow while using his supernatural powers to call forth another bursting projectile of light to pull back with his bow and bowstring. As the creature struggled to pick up momentum to attack, Linitus let loose another arrow striking it again. Still, the creature, though coming to a slow pace, would not relent in approaching its attacker to exact retribution.

However, Wendigo would find out soon enough that this elf was not alone. He had his companions, including a tall slender Nordling woman wearing ornate mythic armor of the Golden Valkyrie. This woman wielded and aimed a bright, shining spear of light. She hurled it while unleashing a war cry of sorts toward the creature. The enchanted spear connected and pierced through the abdomen of Wendigo. The dark creature unleashed a harrowing shriek that could be heard in every direction going toward the horizon.

Wendigo, filled with absolute hate and anger, looked intensely at its targets but did not realize that another had skillfully outflanked it from behind. Wendigo unexpectedly felt the full force of a jab as it turned to realize one of its former kind, a dyr folk, had stabbed him. This one was the same one it had encountered on several prior occasions, but never had the two been so close to each other, even in battle. Now, however, this creature with a downward-turned head gave a look of sadness and pity as Wendigo winced in pain while dropping to its knees. The beautiful dyr creature known as Alani again looked with remorse while she dislodged the special enchanted spear she had used to impale her dark nemesis.

The dyr druidess took another moment. She concentrated using her mind as she put both her hands on Wendigo's head. The creature felt alone, and she knew it. She knew its history well enough to know that it was full of loathing, disdain, and an insatiable appetite to never feel alone again. It had no one to care for him genuinely. Even Helskadi harbored no genuine feelings of care and remorse for the creature despite feigning on past occasions as if she did. The Winter Death Witch only cared if whatever troubled her chief lieutenant minion would later pose a challenge to her own rule.

However, Alani did care about Wendigo. She pitied the creature and used her supernatural powers to establish a mental bond between the two while having physical contact with Wendigo. She sensed deeply the pain the creature had felt. She knew at that moment it could be redeemed and freed, but in doing so, it would have to be purged from the darkness that filled the creature's heart. She would have to be the one to use her mystical powers as a druidess to purge it. In doing so, she knew it would require a great sacrifice on her part. In fact, it would be the ultimate sacrifice. Alani would give her life to purge the darkness and to end the life of terror and loneliness that consumed this creature. She told the creature to accept her help and that it would no longer be surrounded by the darkness alone. She would sacrifice her light to purge its darkness, and she would use as much of it as possible to ensure the cycle of its pain was over.

As the two creatures stood still, almost like statues, an ever-growing set of auras began to expand and surround them. One was of a pitch-dark shadow while the other became a series of flashing bright colorful lights. The two auras coalesced and fought for dominance. The impact caused an uneasy shaking vibration that could be felt throughout the nearby proximity of the ground and the base of the mountains. It was enough to startle Linitus, Marin, and the rest of the Comradery to stare in awe before recomposing themselves to take cover. Linitus ordered everyone to fall back while he himself, along with Marin next to his side, stood still, mesmerized by what they had seen. It was enough, however, for Alani to turn and glance at them. She told them in a cryptic manner that her time had come when it would be up to them to finish what they started. Marin and Linitus would continue the quest to finish setting Shimmerfrost free from the growing power and threat of Helskadi.

As the two heroes looked onward, Linitus nodded while grabbing Marin gently by her arm and signaling that it was time for them to leave. Within moments, the two adventuring lovers retreated away from the base of the Jotunn Mountains. Meanwhile, the competing auras between Alani and Wendigo became powerful and unstable enough until the competing auras combined and absorbed each other. A beam of light then emanated from with substantial force before the force of the merged auras. This released a loud shockwave boom that echoed across the distance several dozen yards. The force of it was large enough to shake the foundations of the mountain base in which it trembled.

Marin and Linitus, meanwhile, found themselves teleported several dozen yards away where they lay prone after leaping head-first away from the exploding shock wave only to find out that their comrade, Wyatt was the one who had delivered them out of harm's way. The Princess Knight and the rogue elf ranger both sighed and nodded while thanking their halfling wizard friend. Wyatt nodded while Peat and the present company of Nordlings ran a few yards away to look and comment at the site of where the explosion occurred.

Linitus and Marin turned back toward the direction of the blast from which they had fled. The two companion lovers saw only a large smoldering black ash with flickers of embers and static shocks that remained. Whatever had happened, they knew Alani had disappeared, and likely forever, along with Wendigo. The elf ranger and Princess Knight realized they had lost another person whom they became close enough to call a friend, much like Arik. It was enough for Marin to shout in a loud moan before she cried. Linitus, with a saddened face, put his arm around her to comfort her. He wiped her tears from her face as she turned to him. She asked how many more lives they had to lose, especially those they would become close to as companions. The elf nodded. He replied in a soft and compassionate manner that they both knew the answer. It would be necessary to make these sacrifices in order to give Shimmerfrost a chance to be at peace from darkness.

Marin nodded also but wondered why. She hesitated at first but still decided to ask if that would be enough. What if after they removed the ultimate darkness from being a threat it would not be enough for their sacrifices to still have meaning in this region to find peace? Linitus placed his hand on her shoulder. He told her it would be up to the people of this region. They would decide and make of it as they wanted to once she and Linitus had done their part to help them. It was not the answer Marin would want to hear, but it was the one from a place of honesty and wisdom, which she needed to hear. It was an answer in which it made their efforts still worth pursuing and finding out.

As the two of them stared while valuing that rare moment together even in the presence of their companions, they both embraced each other and shared one brief intimate kiss. They were still alive and knew it was moments like this in which they had to cherish the presence that they shared while not knowing if it would be their last in this cold region that they still considered harsh and unforgiving.

Only the loud blow of a horn followed by a series of war cries however disrupted that moment. Both Linitus and Marin recomposed themselves and turned while preparing their weapons at the ready with sword, shield, and bow and arrow in hand. Emerging from a large hole opening near the base of the mountains, poured out a small but steady stream of multiple groups of small burly dwarves with pale white skin and adorned in various crude forms of animal bone armor. One of the Nordlings in the Comradery shouted out in identifying that these were the snow dwarves who served under the Winter Death Witch.

The snow dwarves charged forward. They raised their makeshift wooden, stone, and animal bone war clubs and other crude melee weapons. They hurled loud curses as they closed in for melee combat. The Comradery could tell that these pale dwarves had no intention other than to strike them down from where they stood. Linitus called the rest of the Comradery to arms. Marin, without hesitation, quickly emanated from her hands a lightning bolt in the shape of a spear. She hurled it at the nearest snow dwarf that was closing in just less than a dozen yards away. Wyatt also used his magic from his hands and silver wand to cast several bolts of lightning and small fireballs at the approaching enemy snow dwarf war party. Peat and the other companions who were all Nordlings at this point formed a close shield wall behind Linitus, Marin, and Wyatt while Linitus quickly unleashed one arrow after another at the enemy. The steady stream of discharged arrows took out one charging snow dwarf at a time as they began to fall in droves.

The battle between the Comradery and the snow dwarves continued to ensue by unfolding into fierce melee hand-to-hand combat. Linitus spotted above his companions the skyboat. The vessel continued to float and close in from above while being piloted by Andarin and Alvissan. The rogue elf ranger signaled for Wyatt to use his magic to teleport their company back to the flying vessel. As the halfling wizard did so, the elf quickly devised another idea while noticing the continuous steady stream of enemy snow dwarves still coming out from the cave opening at the base of the mountain. It was clearly a threat if left unchecked and if the snow dwarves or any of Helskadi's other minions were to use it to raid any of the Nordlings' trade caravans and any remote Nordling settlements that may be defenseless in resisting their attacks.

Linitus quickly told Wyatt to teleport the two of them as well as Marin to be as close as possible to the base of the mountain near the mouth of the cave. Marin stared with a face of confusion at first. She wondered if her lover had lost his mind in doing something that seemed both reckless and suicidal, the likes of which she would be more apt to do when they were ten years younger. Linitus grinned while telling her it was exactly what he was planning for them to do except he still planned for them to make it out alive.

Before they teleported, Linitus looked at Marin's surprised and somewhat angered face in not knowing what her elven lover was up to. Linitus quickly clued her in while asking how strong was her voice to shout and wail at the mountains above the snow dwarf cave entrance. Marin shrugged, saying good as ever while suddenly realizing his plan. Her face turned to more shock at seeing how daring he was to actually expect her to use her newfound powers. Before she had time to say anything else Wyatt had quickly teleported the three of them right to the side and next to the mouth of the mountain cave. Linitus and Marin turned to assess their surroundings after teleporting. They wanted to make sense of quickly understanding their positional frame of reference and surroundings.

Then with a quick reaction, Linitus pointed to Marin and told her to use her powers now. As Marin turned to face the rocky base of the mountains, she quickly raised her head up while inhaling a deep breath before unleashing a loud growing wail that sent shockwaves toward the snow-capped mountains. As she did so Linitus and Wyatt respectively unleashed more arrows and projectile spell magic at the snow dwarves that had realized where their remaining adversaries had disappeared. Within moments, however, it was enough time for enough damage to be done in which part of the exterior range of the Jotunn Mountains quaked before the powerful wailing voice coming from Marin. From the foundation to the summit of the mountains, it all shook furiously. Large chunks of ice and rock began to fall down from the immediate part of the mountain range. Wasting no more time, Linitus quickly signaled for Wyatt to teleport the three of them back to the safety of the skyboat.

Just within time, the three of them in a quick flash teleported right when several large boulders of ice and rock shattered down against the very ground in which they were standing only a moment before. Meanwhile, many large pieces of ice and rock debris pummeled down and crushed the many less fortunate snow dwarves that tried to disperse upon realizing the impending danger that they were now in. Within moments an avalanche began to form and crumble down upon the surface base. This calamity effectively wiped out the last of the snow dwarves that stayed outside the mountain cave entrance while the entrance itself was effectively sealed. While not the most ideal, it was sufficient for Linitus and the other members of the Comradery to look down and know they had averted two disasters: the escape of Wendigo and the prevention (even temporarily) of a launching point for the dark forces to use in mounting a raid or possibly an assault against Shimmerfrost.

Still, it was not enough. Not for Marin and Linitus, anyway. As the rest of the occupants onboard celebrated their notable victory with the demise of Wendigo and several fallen snow dwarves, the Princess Knight and elf rogue ranger turned and looked inward at each other. It was indeed a victory but at a high personal cost. They had lost one of the most kind-hearted persons they had ever known not only in Shimmerfrost but even in the greater world of Terrunaemara. They both had time to take a moment to pause and process what they had gone through and seen. Marin could not hold herself together. She unleashed several tears and expletives to express her remorse for one who she could have easily felt was almost like a sister to her. In fact, Alani was the closest that Marin had ever come to feeling as if she could call the dyr druidess a sister.

Linitus embraced Marin and hugged her tightly. The elf ranger told her calmly he too missed Alani. He reminded her it was important for them both to finish the path that they had started with her in freeing both her dyr folk people and the Nordlings of this region from the same evil and terror that sought to diminish them. Marin nodded while wiping her own tears. She told her elf lover she knew and that together with the Nordlings and dyr folk of this land they would make every sacrifice count. They would purge this region of Helskadi and any other evil they came across.

Taking another look toward the Jotunn Mountains with much of the snow falling down, Marin asked Linitus to seek consultation on what they should do next. The elf ranger pondered for a moment. He thought of only doing what they had started, to go to more of the major Nordling settlements and have them join this new coalition. Though Andarin and Alvissan were the captains and owners of their skyship, they sensed as the others in their present company that Linitus was guided with an instinctive natural ability to lead and be guided in making wise decisions through his own perceptive abilities. He also possessed a great sense of morality. The two dwarves resigned themselves to follow his orders while putting off their plans to go to Nebelheim for a trade of their merchandise inventory. They both knew their business affairs could wait. There likely would be another opportunity to trade in whatever other Nordling settlement Linitus would choose for them to set sail.

Alvissan looked to the elf and told him plainly that both she and her dwarven husband were at his command with Andarin nodding in agreement. The elf ranger nodded and inquired to the two skyboat dwarf owners of the nearest notable Nordling settlement from their current heading after Nebelheim. Andarin replied it would be Frostburg due north that lay just a few miles outside the exterior northeast ring of the Jotunn Mountains. Linitus nodded while pointing his hand north for the dwarven pilots to set course.

As the skyboat traveled in the coming hours, Linitus and Marin both reminded the rest of their surviving companions of the same thing that they had reminded themselves of. They had undertaken this quest to purge the forces of darkness from taking hold of the region, which would not only require them to seek an alliance among Nordling and dyr folk settlements including ones that had past rivalries with each other but also to make sure every sacrifice they made, if needed, would not go in vain from achieving their goal. All present on the skyboat nodded solemnly. One of the Nordlings who knew enough of the basic Citadellan tongue from conversing with Marin and Linitus spoke on behalf of the other few surviving Nordlings. He stated that the elf ranger and his Comradery had their full loyalty to go to the ends of the earth, to the furthest north of Shimmerfrost and beyond to the cold frozen wastes and frozen sea of ice. Linitus nodded while thanking them. The elf told them with Marin nodding and translating that both of them along with Peat and Wyatt would do everything possible to help before returning to their home in the warmer lands of the south.

As the night went on, before they rested in cramped but tolerable conditions on the small skyboat, Marin and Linitus took this moment to share together while still reflecting on the losses of their befriended allies, especially Arik and Alani. To both of them, it was a mournful partial victory at best now that Wendigo no longer existed as a threat to the region. They both held hands while being in one another's embrace. They confided to each other in struggling with how to make sense of the quest they had undertaken so far and what was still to come. It was still an uncharted journey of uncertainty.

The one silver lining that the two lovers took as a sign in trying to imagine what the future might hold was when they both looked to marvel at the awe-inspiring view of the limitless sky above and the natural landscape below. To them, it represented a bright place of hope in an otherwise dark, perilous path that they would still traverse to overthrow and rid this region of the Winter Death Witch's presence. This moment however that Linitus and Marin shared was also different from ten years ago. They cherished the days that they would spend together to enjoy the sunsets and sunrises aboard a flying vessel, but nothing before had compared to the beauty of the nighttime auroras. They would absorb whatever beauty they could to remember from seeing this natural atmospheric phenomenon.

Linitus and Marin continued to stay awake throughout the evening a little longer before coming to rest onboard the skyboat. They still became mesmerized by the feeling of serenity and solace they found in the sun's absence by the colorful blue, violet, and green array of the northern light aurora. This phenomenon showered the darkness of the nighttime sky that was otherwise glittered by a sea of many bright, white-looking stars. Only one other place had reminded them of such an impressive sight to compare during their adventures from over ten years ago. It was when they traveled together along with Marin's father, King Ascentius, to the abode of the deity spirits known as Caelum Presidium.

Chapter Forty-Six

To Court and Find Deception

The distance to travel from Nebelheim to Frostburg on foot if one was fortunate to make it alive by his or her own resolve, would take up to two weeks. It would take up to a week to travel by domesticated animal means of transportation, including sled or wagon—again, if one was fortunate to not be ambushed. By sailing the sky above, which was far safer though far less common, it would take a mere two to three days at most if the winds were kind. From the skyboat, with the Comradery onboard, they traversed the skies outside the southeastern ring of the Jotunn Mountains, which was northeast of both Dyr Valley and Nebelheim. It took the floating vessel two more sunrises and one more nightfall to arrive at its destination, Frostburg.

By the second sunrise, the skyboat had arrived floating around the periphery of the Nordling settlement. The view from looking down was majestic and picturesque, as one could dream that had never seen Frostburg. Frostburg itself was a mostly rocky-cliffed island surrounded by a semi-frozen river, called the Shimmerfrost-Flod (or more commonly known by foreign visitors as the Shimmerfrost River), with large, thick patches of ice in spring, though it was thawing and breaking apart. The river itself was famous for being ascribed to that namesake. It stood in full elegance at night with the reflection of the auroras being vibrant and in full array from the river's ice.

Within the island itself stood an enormous stone wall that went about the circumference of the island. Many of the buildings were made of either stone, timber wood, or a combination of both. The buildings were clustered together along with many of the dwellings that housed the locals, save for a wide enough pathway for wagons to pass through the central market. Perched on the highest slope of the island was the chieftain's stronghold. The building was styled with Nordling architecture somewhat similar to the chieftain's hall in Nebelheim. This stronghold in Frostburg was also unique in being made entirely of stone. The stone was quarried from the surrounding lands outside the banks of the river and against the surrounding mountains. The chieftain's stronghold (commonly considered a meeting hall among the Nordlings) in Frostburg was also distinct in being the largest of the chieftain strongholds in Shimmerfrost. The settlement of Frostburg itself matched the reputation of its stronghold as also being the largest among the Nordling settlements in Shimmerfrost.

Two other noticeable structures stood out besides the chieftain's stronghold in Frostburg. One was a lone large docking pier that jutted out from the northwest end of the settlement. The pier was sparsely populated since many of the local fishermen and merchants were not able during this time of the year to fully venture out into the waters. It was not safe enough for the ice in the river to fully melt. Next to the pier stood a large promontory lighthouse at the end that guided a large incoming Nordling water vessel known as a longboat.

Still amazed at the view, only the interruption by Andarin's loud shout declaring their arrival had disrupted the long stare that Linitus and Marin had shared. The two of them held each other while looking at the view from the starboard side. They got themselves up to assess the settlement's layout in further detail while standing. Marin inquired with both Andarin and Alvissan which part of the settlement they would recommend for Wyatt to teleport them to. Both dwarves cautioned Marin to let them take the lead. They had experience in interacting with the local governance and population of the settlement. The two dwarves reasoned this would better ensure a peaceful dialogue established between the Comradery and the settlement's jarl to join the coalition against Helskadi. Marin nodded along with Linitus in deferring to Andarin and Alvissan's approach to entering the settlement.

Before they departed the skyboat Marin, Linitus, Peat, and Wyatt donned hooded capes at the suggestion of Andarin and Alvissan. The Nordlings from Nebelheim however, still wore their regular attire. The skyboat then descended near an open spot within walking distance from the settlement's market and a few stones' throw distance from the chieftain's stronghold fortress. As the company proceeded, Andarin and Alvissan were familiar with the layout from being in Frostburg before. The two of them greeted various local Nordling civilians and several members of the local town guard.

Meanwhile, as they proceeded the two traveling dwarves tried to keep their hooded friends' presence as conspicuous as possible. So far they had succeeded while they requested the chief town guard in front of the jarl's stronghold to gain entry. Andarin and Alvissan, followed by their acquaintances, stated their business before the town guard. According to them, they were here to inform the chieftain about an important development of Wendigo's downfall and a proposal to unite all of the Nordlings against Helskadi. The dwarven couple also inquired if the chieftain had new terms to renegotiate since the last time they were at Frostburg, at least a year ago. They waited eagerly while trying to be calm. After a few moments, the chief town guard signaled the jarl of Frostburg's approval for having an audience with him. The dwarves with their present entourage made their way as quickly as possible inside the great feasting hall of the chieftain's stronghold. Once inside, Linitus and Marin both marveled in observation at the impressive large vaulted architecture while still trying to keep a discreet profile.

A nice series of interwoven and overlapping blue with white lace runner rugs followed from one end of the feasting hall all the way to the other. An ornate stone throne stood out at the end of the hall. The Nordling chieftain was seated on the throne. He wore a gray stone crown while sporting a long, prominent blonde beard and called forth to Andarin and Alvissan to come forward along with their guests. The two dwarves nodded and approached, followed by their company behind them.

Curious and intrigued, the Nordling chieftain asked who these guests were that came with the two dwarves, including most notably the ones covered in hoods. Andarin struggled to say a coherent response. He tried to find the words to explain this situational predicament that he and his wife found themselves in less than a week. Alvissan interrupted her spouse impatiently while letting the chieftain know these guests were adventurers with whom they had witnessed defeating the legendary and infamous Wendigo.

Shocked and in full awe of what he heard, the chieftain erupted in a loud laugh of doubt. He believed the dwarves were being sarcastic to see how gullible he was. The chieftain also considered that they might have been swayed by hearsay from the townsfolk cloaked in hoods and pretending to be their acquaintances.

Marin interjected while removing her hood. She revealed herself as the recognized Golden Valkyrie and stated in a plain voice to the chieftain that this was no form of jest or hearsay on their part. They had indeed defeated Wendigo. The chieftain looked shocked while being intimidated at the realization of who he now let into his fortress stronghold. At once, he called for his household bodyguards, also known as housecarls. As soon as he called for them, over three dozen of them entered the stronghold chamber hall, forming a perimeter around the chieftain.

Linitus and Marin observed these housecarls had maintained a shield wall formation, with the housecarls holding their shields and melee weapons at the ready. As the Comradery looked about while maintaining a defensive posture, Linitus noticed one of several figures next to the chieftain. This stranger looked familiar. The elf ranger took a moment to reflect. He realized and said aloud that it was him. It was the scout, the one called Halkir, from this very settlement of Frostburg who encountered the Comradery at Nebelheim to the south several days before their fateful reverse ambush at Lone Pass.

The courier grinned and laughed alongside the chieftain while various members of the Comradery realized the same revelation Linitus had pointed out. As their laugh ended, the courier confessed it was him indeed. He disclosed he regretted that his services to his chieftain and their overlord jotunn matriarch's newfound ally, the Imperial Remnant, did not ensure the utter destruction of the Comradery. The chieftain then interrupted. He claimed it would not matter that the Comradery survived up to this point. According to the chieftain, it would come to pass that the Comradery would be slaughtered by his forces in his hall. He then motioned to his housecarls to be ready to attack.

However, Marin interjected. She spoke with a sense of authority and command in Nordling, demanding a duel. This chieftain, if he was worthy to be called a konung, or king, would have to accept her challenge of a trial by duel in contesting his claim. The chieftain growled while cursing in the local Nordling dialect. He acknowledged that by tradition and rite, he would accept her challenge. However, he would also raise the stakes by issuing a counter-challenge. The Frostburg jarl would also summon forth his counterpart from Shimmerheim to challenge the elf ranger he had heard of being worthy in combat. For the jarl, it would allow the opportunity for both Nordling chieftains to dispose of the two contestants that threatened their power hold and the informal alliance they had with Helskadi.

Linitus, with a calm yet loud and commanding voice, replied that he would accept this double trial by duel. He would fight alongside Marin to put down both this chieftain and his counterpart if necessary. The Princess Knight and the elf ranger knew it would make Shimmerfrost one step closer to being free under the yoke of the Winter Death Witch.

With anxious eyes between the other members of the Comradery, Andarin, Alvissan, and the housecarls, the moment of tense unease suddenly ended. The chieftain lifted his hand and told the housecarls to escort the visiting guests outside his stronghold. The chieftain rose from this throne chair. He proclaimed in a loud voice to both Linitus and Marin that they would meet him and his counterpart chieftain of Shimmerheim outside the gates of Shimmerheim. Once there they would fight in a duel on the fourth sunrise from this current day. The prevailing victors would be just and righteous by the deity spirits of who should guide the various inhabitants and settlements of Shimmerfrost according to the jarl.

Within a moment, Linitus motioned to the rest of the Comradery to back away while exiting the feast hall. As they did so, the chieftain's housecarls adjusted their formation. They formed a wall that blocked the distance between the Comradery and the chieftain until the former had exited outside the chieftain's stronghold. A few moments later, the Comradery returned to the skyboat which Andarin and Alvissan had readied to make haste preparations to take off. The two dwarves mildly lamented with a sarcastic tone of humor of not being able to have time to trade their wares and goods. Still, they both understood with a deeper inner sense of conviction that they had made the right choice in supporting their still relatively new welcomed passengers and makeshift crew onboard. To the dwarven couple, the Comradery seemed to know that they were fighting for a more rightfully guided and just cause. By contrast, the jarl of Frostburg had made the dwarven aviators feel unsettled. Andarin and Alvissan had now realized the jarl compromised his honor by throwing his lot to support those with dark, evil intentions in exchange for retaining and furthering his power. This was a betrayal of the character of a mild and neutral Nordling chieftain that the two dwarven couples thought they knew from before. If their newly acquainted elf and half-Nordling friends were to be victorious in dueling the Nordling chieftains of the two most historic and prestigious Nordling settlements in Shimmerfrost, the two dwarves knew they could resume their trade later while feeling more content with making the region a better place than when they first came upon it in their various travels.

By midmorning, the skyboat was far enough across the distance to still see Frostburg from the horizon. It stood out as a beacon of noticeable large-scale human settlement in a land that was otherwise cold and lonely, partially surrounded by mountains with the same semi-frozen river running across an open valley filled with various trees though the most common included quaking aspen, birch wood, white spruce, and even some black spruce and larch trees. Linitus and Marin looked toward the settlement, wondering and contemplating how they would get the Nordlings to follow them if it would be that easy once they had bested the chieftains of the two nearby settlements.

Peat, sensing the two having some anxiety in feeling what he considered the weight of rulership, told them they should not worry, for they had it in them to let things sort themselves out once the deed was done in falling the enemy chieftains. The dwarf tugged sarcastic and gentle manner on both the Princess Knight and rogue ranger elf's cheeks. Peat stated that after all, they were both born and honed to be rulers. He also reminded Marin that it was perhaps past due for her calling to follow the path of her father in being a ruler for once alongside Linitus.

The elf gulped. He became apprehensive about wanting to undertake such responsibility. He told his dwarven counterpart that being a leader and leading on heroic adventures for worthy pursuits in defending others against evil was one thing. However, it was an entirely distinct skill set in which he did not feel he was equipped and able to rule over such a large and unfamiliar land. Marin nodded but told her lover that Peat was right in letting things play out according to their own actions, one step at a time. They would know what to do when the time came. They would find a way for their new found coalition to rule among themselves once they remove the forces of darkness and evil from still posing as a formidable threat to the region. Linitus nodded while changing topics in inquiring if anyone knew where Shimmerheim was and how far it was from Frostburg. Marin did not know firsthand. However, the Princess Knight recalled from her knowledge of the tales she remembered being told as part of her mother's Nordling culture. She pointed to the direction they were heading, west toward the Shimmerfrost River as it flowed in that same direction before turning and flowing southward toward the dyr settlements that lie west of the Dyr Valley and southwest of their current bearing. Andarin and Alvissan both nodded and confirmed that Marin was correct.

They were on a trajectory to circumvent the ring of the Jotunn Mountain range to the south of the Shimmerfrost River. Though unsure how long it would take them to arrive at their next destination, Marin told her elven lover that more than likely they would see another spectacular view of the auroras at night. Once again, they would gaze at the magnificent reflections or shimmers it would cast when looking down upon the semi-frozen river. It was a sight they would behold once more, perhaps twice before they would arrive due west of Frostburg at the high cliff settlement of Shimmerheim.

Chapter Forty-Seven

Settling a Final Infernal Old Score

Hadao Infernum's sky was a unique phenomenon with the intermittent spewing of molten lava and ash that both illuminated and darkened the sky, which still bled red in various shades contrasted with dark black and grey clouds. Below the murky sky, perched on top of Orcus's highest inner stronghold tower, stood two fair-skinned, red-haired succubi. They paced about the tower wall walk while at the center stood a red-skin-tinted black-haired succubus, Lucia, secured as she had been for many days in a pillory. The two succubi jeered and laughed at their red-skinned counterpart prisoner. They pointed out in the distance that her lover, Decius, had apparently summoned a gigantic avatar form of himself. His colossal avatar could be seen, however, maintaining distance from far away where Orcus's fortress stood. The succubi mocked Lucia about her lover Decius lacking the courage to dare rescue her while he and his army stood still for three days besieging Orcus's stronghold.

As they continued to mock Lucia, the two succubi alternated with using a spider silk leash to whip her from behind. Lucia, in her mind, swore her torturers and their other succubi sisters would face her wrath and her husband's wrath when she was set free. For now, she still held back in giving any satisfaction to her torturers in acknowledging them. Still, the pain she felt from each lash became more intense. She could not hold back much longer from shouting in agony. Only after a few dozen lashes did the succubi torturers stop. Again, they mocked her, asking her where her lover was to save her.

Lucia, though tired and in pain, collected herself. She could feel that something was different. Decius's presence was no longer across the staging point of the soon-to-be battlefield. Instead, she felt him being much closer. With her eyes burning like fire, Lucia shouted with a sense of condemnation and fatalism toward her torturers. At the same time, a dark mist-like shadow of energy emanated behind the succubi torturers. Decius was now right behind them.

The two succubi torturers froze in both shock and fear after they heard both Lucia and Decius's voices. Before the respective succubi could turn, a large quick slash ran across them, severing both their heads. Before the heads even fell to the ground, a strong muscular black hairy arm had caught them by the hair. Decius's other hand still held the dark spectral long blade that he had emanated. He now used the enchanted blade to hack at the protruding arms of the pillory assembly. With a stern, confident voice of compassion, he called out to Lucia. He told his love to hold on still. As she did, the pillory after several strikes broke apart. The shackle-like restraints holding Lucia's hands had also broken apart. Lucia was now free of her restrained bindings. She struggled to stand up straight and still. Her lover Decius, held her up by one of his arms. He told her not to worry. He explained with haste that he had come to rescue her. Lucia, weakened, nodded, though told her lover after giving him a brief, subtle kiss that she knew he would come for her. She knew that he would come to avenge her capture and torture. She knew he would lead all the forces that he could muster from this infernal domain to use against this cruel, demonic hell lord to depose. Decius held Lucia more tightly. He told her it was time that they would both have their revenge. They would claim this domain of hell as theirs by the taking.

As Decius prepared to teleport the both of them back to his forces' besiegement camp, a loud vile laugh emerged out of the fortress dungeon below. It was a recognizable one that became louder. Decius turned, looking all about, and noticed that though it was Orcus's voice, he was not there. The voice called out for him to enter his lair and fight him there where he awaited him. However, Lucia, though still sighing from the soreness of the torture she endured, put her red, elegant hand on her lover's black chest and cautioned him not to. She warned him that Orcus likely planned to lure him there and overwhelm him with whatever minions Orcus could muster to ensure Decius would not triumph against him. Though Decius was angered by Orcus and the torment the latter inflicted upon Lucia,

Decius saw through the devices of his nemesis. Decius recognized that Lucia had spoken with a voice of both wisdom and prudence to not be tempted to be drawn in by his adversary's terms of fighting. Decius knew if he was to be the supreme infernal lord of Hadao Infernum, he needed to command the tempo of the battle. It had to be on his terms and not by his incumbent rival.

Decius paused a moment while holding onto Lucia. He told her to wait as he also happened to still hear the hellacious voice of Orcus. The demonic hell lord continued to laugh and mock the dux in holding back from pursuing and fighting Orcus inside his own lair. A large, black, shadowy mist followed by a burning ring that looked like a portal emerged. Decius, carrying Lucia in his arms, walked toward the portal. Before he entered the portal, however, the dux, with his pronounced black canine snout, turned back and howled. He swore to any who could hear that he would exact his revenge upon Orcus and all the remaining succubi. Hadao Infernum, in his words, would see the extinguishment of an unworthy lord of hell to lead the forces of darkness. Then, taking several steps forward, Decius walked through the infernal portal while still carrying Lucia. The both of them teleported just within the horizon to Decius's besiegement camp. It numbered with countless thousands of imps and the army of the condemned. As he arrived at his besiegement camp, various figures, including prominent leaders of the various condemned settlements and Decius's most high-ranking imp lieutenants, were all present.

Various voices, especially among the condemned, however, gasped upon seeing who Decius came back with. Some knew the figure of the alluring red-skinned succubus with dark hair he had carried was his beloved Lucia. She was, after all, the catalyst that had brought together her lover to ally with the condemned settlement of Caverna Necropolis. Still, others from many different condemned settlements were unfamiliar with her and chattered about in whispers speculating who this person was that their recognized infernal sovereign was carrying.

The quiet but noticeable rumors were enough for Lucia and Decius to both hear. Lucia gave a slight moan, still fatigued from the inflicted pain and torture she endured earlier. She turned to her lover and savior to tell him in a low voice that perhaps it was time he explained who she was to the other condemned followers who recently joined his cause and were unfamiliar with her. Lucia expressed her belief that they needed to know he came for her as much as to liberate them from the reign of Orcus. She knew they needed to know before the two of them further instructed their army to go forward with the confidence of their followers against Orcus's forces.

Decius looked down while holding her in his arms. He nodded and told her to rest while acknowledging that he would do as his lover suggested. As he continued to hold his soulmate, the dux using his mental will commanded his large gigantic werewolf avatar to pick them both up with careful ease. The gigantic canine beast nodded while complying and held them up from the palm of its large, sharp canine-like paw. The dux stared at his forces from below with many of them looking back at him also. Decius paused for a moment. With a sense of command and conviction, he declared before his forces that the person he had come for before facing off against Orcus was important. She was known in her previous mortal life as Lady Lucia Diem of Imperium Sanctum Novus. She was the reason, according to Decius, that he chose to listen to her and help lead those less fortunate in Hadao Infernum. It was Lucia, Decius continued to say, that had illuminated a new light in an otherwise dark and despairing hell hole. She made him realize, along with the condemned, that together they could end the suffering, which Orcus had caused by getting rid of Orcus's reign altogether. Decius declared before his army that if there was any maiden worthy to rule alongside him, it would be Lucia. She had chosen to be with him when she was meant to be assigned to the realm of paradise, which the dux emphasized the most to his army. It was his eternal soulmate, Lucia, in which Decius stretched out his arms while revealing his succubus lover more openly before the crowd.

Lucia looked about. Still somewhat frail, she turned to her lover and asked him to put her down. Decius became apprehensive about not wanting her to struggle in pain while standing after what she endured from being tortured earlier. However, Lucia noticed his hesitation. She responded that if she was to rule alongside him, she needed to stand before their subjects and assure them she could lead and advocate on their behalf. Decius nodded while gently positioning his lover upright. She struggled but forced herself to stand upright while Decius held one of her hands for support. As the multitude of the condemned looked on, they became mesmerized by what they had seen. Lucia was not only alluring, but she also had a disposition of determination and defiance. She demonstrated this ever since her arrival in this burning hell. She assured the large army of followers that Decius had never gone astray for the cause he believed in nor for those he fought for and alongside. She told the crowd that he was not only a dark lord in his last life but always would be for eternity. He was, in her words, also worthy to be proclaimed sovereign lord of Hadao Infernum. As grim as this infernal realm was, he would make it better as he had done with the Imperial Remnant in the mortal world of Terrunaemara.

After her proclamation, there was utter dead silence. Within another moment of passing, a steady, loud stream of chants and cheers erupted louder than any volcanic mountain that could be heard in the infernal realm. All the condemned in unison stood up and raised their fists in solidarity to recognize Lucia as their infernal matron mother. Until now, they had not known what source of inspiration had caused Decius to go on this far-reaching crusade throughout the various domains of hell. Now they had known and without dispute, they could see from their hell lord's own sense of genuine admission. They were also just as convinced by Lucia's own arousing speech that she indeed was worthy to be ascribed to the rendered title in which they revered her almost as much as Decius.

Lucia turned to Decius, the latter of whom became speechless and in awe of his lover's words. The galvanization, which she had stirred his army of loyal followers and minions became unmatched. Lucia said in a stern tone toward her lover that now his army was ready as she was also ready to be at his command. Lucia explained now was the time to strike, for they had the very one variable in which Orcus's army was lacking. When Decius asked what it was, Lucia replied by surprising her lover with a brief, deep kiss. She stated to him it was devotion and faith in his leadership that he attained from her and their followers. He was the rightful lord of hell. If he could not have Terrunaemara other than to pass down to his heir, it would be fitting that he would be the only true one to lead this infernal domain while he attained his revenge against Orcus. All of Decius's followers in hell believed this was the new day of reckoning and that Hadao Infernum would now be his for the taking.

Decius nodded while unleashing a loud howl. His gargantuan avatar followed in the same manner unleashing an equally loud, deafening howl. The dux at once commanded his forces to deploy the siege weapons that they had positioned facing across the plain toward Orcus's large fortress lair. The fortress itself stood perched on top of a jagged plateau gorge with only a narrow path of ascent that connected the plateau to the rest of the infernal plain. Within moments, the condemned of various races stood in formation behind the siege equipment of makeshift ballistas, catapults, and scorpion launchers. They began a long series of multiple salvos, hurling various heavy, burning ash-like brimstone projectiles. These projectiles pelted and battered down at the walls and towers of Orcus's stronghold.

Only after the first salvo did a loud haunting mixture of laughter and a loud demonic shout echo from the stronghold toward the siege encampment. It was Orcus, and he was aware of Decius's plan. Orcus was unsuccessful in luring his rival to his subterranean lair that lay deep within the bowels of his fortress. Now the red-skinned demonic hell lord was forced to come out and fight Decius on the latter's terms. However, the loud eruption from Orcus's voice was as much of a call of anger and intimidation toward his foes as it was a summons. His various minions heard his call across the plains of Hadao Infernum. Within moments, various swarms of imps loyal to Orcus led by a few dozen succubi began to form and attack in an overwhelming rush-like manner toward Decius's main encampment.

Decius looked somewhat shaken but recollected himself, knowing this was his moment as Lucia had reaffirmed to him also that it was time to command. The dux nodded. He asked his lover if she was able to fight. Lucia nodded with affirmation. He then told his lover to take a large swarm of imps to command and use them to bait and lure the enemy's flying force between the siege weapons and Orcus's fortress. Lucia grinned while pointing out her admiration and acknowledgment of her lover's tactic. It was a feigned attack that Decius devised. However, he cautioned Lucia to be careful in having enough distance away from the enemy's imps and succubi so as not to be caught in the siege weapons' crossfire. Decius told his lover that after firing the first salvo of siege weapons, he would send forth the rest of the imps to attack the flank of what he hoped would be a demoralized or shocked enemy force. Nodding again, Lucia gave her werewolf lover a brief kiss before mustering her strength and signaling while screeching for one of Decius's formed imp battalions to follow her toward Orcus's stronghold. The chief lieutenant imp of the battalion acknowledged her command and motioned while screeching also for his imp subordinates to follow Lucia's lead.

The imp battalion clustered behind Lucia numbering in the thousands. They flew in the air with immense speed and caught sight of three different swarms of imps approaching them though several kilometers away. One enemy swarm came from Orcus's fortress while the other two approached from various caves and underground dwellings in opposite diagonal directions from the fortress. Closing in about three kilometers away, Lucia quickly led her imp swarm while flying to ascend vertically. Another moment in unison, Lucia's imp swarm prepared to dive forward in a sharp descent as low as possible to the surface without hitting the ground. As they descended, they fell back toward the siege encampment. Lucia concentrated her mind and used her attuned thoughts to channel her mind connection with Decius. She would let him know when to give the order for his army to let loose the siege munitions. With the enemy following right behind them and trailing a mere kilometer away, Lucia quickly motioned to the imp lieutenant in midair to take half of their swarm battalion to fork sharply to the port side facing the siege encampment while she would take the other half along the starboard side. It was an erratic and unexpected flying maneuver that had caused confusion among Orcus's forces while pursuing Lucia's now divided imp battalion. Orcus's imp swarms hovered in the air undecided of which part of the divided enemy battalion to engage. However, this maneuver was deployed in time for Lucia to unleash another screech to motion with her mental thoughts directed toward Decius to fire the munitions quickly at will.

 The screech became loud enough for Decius to hear. He acknowledged and motioned with his arm that was imitated by his gargantuan avatar for his forces to commence the attack, starting with the siege munitions teams. The condemned that operated the various infernal siege weapons let loose quickly a salvo of projectiles. The flying munitions struck the enemy forces at various locations. Decius's war plans had achieved the intended effect of demoralizing the surviving enemy imps and succubi loyal to Orcus.

 Decius wasted no time in seizing the advantage. He quickly motioned for the rest of his forces to charge and engage the enemy. Though some of Orcus's minions tried to retreat, it was not enough for Orcus's forces could escape the brunt of the impact, especially with the large bulk of imp battalions that Decius had under his banner. These imps, sworn to the dux, deployed at rapid speed while Lucia and the lieutenant imp of their split battalion made a pass to attack the flanks of the enemy force. It became a sight of impressive strategic and tactical warfare, which had not been seen before in the infernal realm.

 Even Decius's own avatar charged forward, hurling a large volcanic rock toward a group of imps and two succubi that crushed them before the gargantuan continued its onslaught in swatting various remaining surviving forces of Orcus. The condemned soldiers themselves hurled with makeshift slings, their stone projectiles, and throwing spears. The numbers of Orcus's forces dwindled quickly enough that even the lord of hell peering out from the distance within the cover of his own tower walls became enraged at seeing his forces diminishing so quickly without putting much of a challenge against his rival.

Indeed, the overwhelming tide of the battle was enough for Orcus to shout out in anger and resentment. He stormed out of his own fortress in a fit of uncontrolled rage. From the distance, he shouted loud enough toward the focal point of the ensuing combat, waiting for those within his presence to have his attention. The belligerents on both sides took notice and suddenly stopped. Orcus, after pausing, then called out Decius to settle their dispute permanently with the two of them fighting in a one-on-one duel. The declared winner would be recognized once and for all as the worthy sovereign over this infernal realm.

Decius howled loudly. He suddenly focused his concentration on teleporting before Orcus across the open black ash plains of Hadao Infernum. Before the surviving armies on both sides, they would see the most epic battle that would unfold in this infernal realm. Decius and Orcus both paced about in circles while sizing each other to decide how each would attack and predict the other's next move for evading and counter-attacking. Eventually, Decius jeered back at Orcus while mocking him for his failed leadership to galvanize his forces to crush the opposition, which the dux pointed out he had done overwhelmingly against the reigning hell lord. Orcus swore confidently that he could incur such losses as he saw fit. The incumbent sovereign of hell claimed that ultimately he did not need his forces to defeat Decius or his army and that he would make an example against his upstart condemned werewolf adversary before torturing and punishing the rest of his followers.

Decius jeered again, reminding Orcus that the last time they fought he barely could match him and that if only his succubi had not intervened, the dux would have already been the undisputed lord of hell then instead of now. Orcus laughed again while asking his rival what had made him think anything would be any different to which Decius replied that this time there would be nobody to save Orcus, not even his succubi whom the dux had assured the incumbent infernal sovereign that he would bear witness of his demonic seductress followers enduring a most agonizing torture and death before Orcus would also meet his final tormented demise. Orcus rebuked his werewolf rival, telling him it would never happen while somewhat charging toward Decius in making the first move to strike at him. Decius, however, quickly used his concentration to teleport several meters away behind Orcus. The werewolf warlord's appearance startled and impressed all those spectating while stunning Orcus in wondering where he went before realizing too late that Decius was behind him. The latter charged and kicked his feet in the air against the back of his large hell-lord rival.

Orcus lost his footing and plunged forward. Decius wielded his dark ebony spectral long blade, which he lashed toward his foe to carry out his next follow-up attack. The dux swung the blade down with both hands in a long vertical arc. The swoosh-like noise made a sudden cling as Orcus parried back while making a last-second horizontal arc swing with his large two-handed cleaver-like blade. The competing infernal warlords parried each other's attacks and became locked in a bind with their weapons. The two competing armies that had ceased fighting for the moment and stayed at a standstill became captivated as they watched the epic fight unfold before them. Lucia had also commanded her flying battalion of imps to stay at ease in the air while being vigilant in looking above to ensure that none of Orcus's succubi would make a move to intervene on their hell lord's behalf while the duel ensued. None of the succubi however chose to intervene this time but rather watch the ensuing fight as everyone else had done.

Meanwhile, Orcus, perceivably being the physically stronger of the two, used his weight to push forward against the ground while breaking the weapons' binding he had with Decius. In doing so, Decius evaded while leaping several steps back before unleashing another attack forward in a diagonal slash that Orcus countered parry again. The red-tinted swine-looking hell lord then lunged with his foot kicking back against Decius's abdomen. The black werewolf dark lord groaned in pain and fell back against the ground while his enchanted black blade temporarily disappeared. Orcus seized the advantage. He next tried to press his own follow-up attack in near exact imitation of Decius's earlier attack with the former leaping forward swinging downward in a vertical motion with his large cleaver blade. Orcus expected to act quickly to leave his foe bleeding horribly or possibly that Decius would parry the same way Orcus had earlier. Much to Orcus's surprise at the last moment while Decius was on the ground the black werewolf's eyes glared a burning red color that stared straight into Orcus's eyes. Orcus looked surprised, almost puzzled, and fearful of what his foe was up to, which he could not avoid. Still, only inches away from hacking and slashing the chest of his foe, Orcus did not hold back in committing his attack.

However, at the point of near contact, Decius suddenly disappeared with Orcus's crude massive cleaver blade striking the ground. The hell lord, as well as everyone else spectating, was stunned. Orcus looked about while swinging his weapon wildly across the air, expecting Decius to teleport behind him. However, Decius did not. Not yet. Not until Orcus called Decius out as a coward, did the former turn again and saw suddenly before him his werewolf adversary emerging from a burning infernal teleportation field. Decius suddenly plunged his long black spectral blade through the abdomen of Orcus. Orcus moaned in pain while Decius, staring straight at his foe's eyes, followed up his attack by quickly taking his ebony blade out from Orcus's impaled abdomen and suddenly making the blade disappear. Decius moved his other non-wielding hand in a swiping motion and used his powers to cause the same long blade to reappear. At that instant, the dux slashed with the blade viciously across the neck of Orcus with enough intensity and force to sever Orcus's large pig-looking head from the rest of his body. The red-skinned demonic hell lord's body fell motionless to the ground while Decius caught Orcus's severed head by holding on to one of Orcus's horns.

Orcus's body remained motionless on the ground. Yet, somehow he could still move his severed head, at least when it came to his eyes and mouth despite being in immense pain. He was in utter disbelief at what had happened. His adversary had now defeated him, yet the now apparent former lord of hell was a living trophy of humiliation by his challenger. It was a fate truly worse than death in which Decius would make good on his vow against his defeated rival.

Decius turned about while looking at the two armies that had spectated and stood in the same disposition of disbelief and awe as the vanquished former incumbent lord of hell. The imps on both sides of the army lowered themselves down to the ground while bowing down on the ground toward Decius. The condemned that had followed their newly chosen leader followed suit and did the same. Lucia still flew in the air and was prepared to do the same, only that she noticed the demoralized succubi that had fought on Orcus's side attempted to flee. The duchess would not allow such a chance to happen. This was especially true now that Decius's forces became overwhelmingly stronger after Orcus's imps had submitted themselves before Decius. Lucia called out to all the remaining allied forces to capture and, if needed, slaughter any of the succubi that tried to escape. The imps, including the ones formerly fighting on behalf of Orcus, nodded and obeyed while screeching and darting out across the air to overwhelm about a dozen or so remaining succubi that tried to escape. Within moments, all the remaining succubi were subdued and brought down by the swarms of imps. Lucia would make sure that each and every one of these demonic seductresses would answer for their atrocities as much as Orcus.

As soon as there was no remaining force of visible opposition, Decius took several steps forward while facing his army of imps and the condemned who had resumed their posture in kneeling before him, save only the imps that had restrained the defiant succubi. Lucia, in her alluring red-tinted demonic seductress appearance, slowly flew down toward Decius while prostrating herself before him. The dark lord werewolf with his snout glared at her. He softly and gently placed his right jagged hand on her shoulder. He commanded his soulmate to rise. Lucia obeyed while keeping her head still lowered as a sign of respect and submission before her lover. Decius understood the gesture of piety and submissiveness by his lover, but he still felt guilty for her in doing so. He told his lover to raise her head and look at him to which she further nodded and did so. As Lucia gazed at him, she told him it was over and that he had won. He was the undisputed dark lord to which everyone, including herself, would submit before his infernal reign.

Decius nodded while giving his lover a soft and brief kiss. He looked and told his lover that she, out of all those in this hellish realm, would not have to prostrate or kneel before him. She would rule alongside him as his coruler. Lucia nodded while telling him she knew he would allow her to do that. She explained to her lover, however, that she would still elect to submit herself in such a way before him. She would do so because she loved him dearly and wanted to present herself in submission before him. She believed a genuine and proper wife should do so in following the customs of their former Citadellan culture.

Decius nodded again solemnly while placing his jagged hand softly against Lucia's red-tinted chin and told her truly in both this life and the previous mortal life there was no better person that he could have found to share his life with. She was the ultimate soulmate and epitome of a devoted wife. He only wished he could give her more, both in the present and previous lives. He believed while indicating that she deserved so much more.

Lucia nodded. She told her infernal lover that she got exactly what she wanted in sharing her life eternally together with Decius. Regardless of what place in the afterlife, they would be together. Whether in the abode of paradise or the abode of condemnation, she was with him at his side. She knew her shared support for his ambition was only rivaled by his true devotion to being a husband who respected her and the ambition she had as well. As she told him that, the two stared intimately at each other before mutually bracing with a deep kiss.

Looking on, the various condemned subjects and imps cheered in what they considered one of the few most endearing and cherishable moments that they thought would be incomprehensible to see in this infernal setting. It was a true genuine love between two souls.

The dux and duchess (or ducissa in the Citadellan tongue) turned to the masses of their army while holding hands. Decius broke the quietness, announcing that the infernal war was over. There was now one victorious and undisputed lord of hell. Decius would see to it from that point forward in which the needless torture imposed by the previous reigning occupant had ended for the condemned. He followed up by stating that this would be so after retribution was made in exacting justice and punishment toward Orcus and his succubi to face the same torture more or less that they had imposed on others. He looked toward Lucia while proclaiming before his loyal denizens that if he was their new lord of hell, she would rule alongside him and he would let her dispense justice as she saw fit among the succubi while he would have his way with what was left of Orcus.

After another moment of silence, sporadic cheers among the masses of the condemned erupted and spread out in waves. The imps screeched in elation at their new uncontested dark lord's edict. This became a transformational moment in Hadao Infernum that nothing could compare to being more epic than what had been achieved in which they had witnessed. Decius and Lucia allowed their denizens to savor the moment. The dux and duchess, meanwhile, were carried by the palm of the jagged hand of Decius's gargantuan avatar. They marched forward with his army of followers trailing close behind. They set out to traverse back in the other direction across the hellish plains of Hadao Infernum. They would go back toward Decius's ornate jagged fortress palace that stood prominently above the highest plain mesas in this realm of fire and ash.

Chapter Forty-Eight

Delayed Showdown

Snow fell across the surrounding landscape and settlement of Shimmerheim. Despite it being the spring season and daylight becoming longer than night time, it was not unusual for this part of the region to experience such weather, especially being at a higher elevation than the coastal part of Shimmerfrost and in terms of latitude being further north, closer to the arctic circle of Terrunaemara. The town itself was surrounded by a large, thick wooden palisade ring wall having only one wooden gateway entrance and several wooden sentry towers inside the perimeter. Within the wall ring stood dozens of enclosed wooden huts. At the center of the settlement was the massive chieftain's longhouse. It stood four stories tall and became narrow along its vertical slope when transitioning between each floor level. A small, open courtyard gap with several wooden trade stalls separated the chieftain's longhouse stronghold from the rest of the dwellings. Though the site of the settlement itself was less impressive compared to Frostburg and even Nebelheim, its location seemed to be quite ideal. Shimmerheim stood on a hilltop gorge with half of it looking over the Shimmerfrost River below. The Shimmerfrost River itself was bordered between the settlement's hilltop gorge and another tall hill gorge. Any occupants that wished to enter the settlement would have to do so by approaching it from the southwestern side slope, which, though slightly steep, was still accessible on foot.

Linitus and Marin looked below with fascination while onboard the skyboat floating high above the sky. The sight of both the natural scenery and the settlement still invoked feelings of excitement and discovery for both of them. Marin admitted to Linitus that she still remembered these various tales of Nordling lore about this part of Shimmerfrost that her late mother had once told her when she was a young child. Still, it had amazed Marin as an adult to actually come to face the reality that those tales were all true. Of all the unique places she had seen, she wondered if anyone back home would believe her accounts of her own exploits with her companions in this faraway land.

Linitus turned to Marin while holding her hand and he could understand, as he had felt the same sensation of awe. He told her subtly and quietly for just the two to hear about his own validation of acknowledgment. Even Linitus became amazed at how much Marin's secondhand telling of her mother's tales was accurate about this far away harsh yet beautiful land. Marin nodded while thinking better about her memories of her late mother. Though it was only a few short years she had known her late mother, Gretchen, they were cherishable.

As the two of them stood looking downward about at the settlement, Linitus, with a keen eye, noticed from the distance a small convoy of mounted horse riders. They were several kilometers away from the settlement, approaching their direction. He motioned to Marin and the rest onboard while Andarin used his spyglass to observe and acknowledge that this was the Frostburg jarl's company.

Peat nearly choked on the content of his smoke pipe. He was surprised, while not withholding how quickly the Frostburg ruler had traveled. Andarin nodded, though pointed out that the Nordlings familiar with this part of the region did well in traveling fast between the two settlements when commuting.

Linitus and Marin looked again back to the settlement. They both surmised since they arrived first that it was conceivable the chieftain of Shimmerheim likely did not know what was about to happen. He likely had no clue at all that his neighboring chieftain from Frostburg had volunteered him to co-fight in a duel against the elf ranger and Princess Knight. Marin wondered what the odds were if the Shimmerheim chieftain would back out. She pondered how the Frostburg chieftain would react if left to fend for himself in a duel against her and Linitus. Linitus nodded. He could only imagine how perplexed the Shimmerheim chieftain would react in finding out. This was especially true when Linitus mentioned that the

Frostburg chieftain had issued the location of the duel to be outside the palisade walls of the settlement. Ironically, nobody was there yet.

However, Linitus cautioned Marin that they would wait until the Frostburg chieftain entered the settlement. They would let him be the first to notify the fellow chieftain counterpart of the planned duel. Only then would Linitus offer the Shimmerheim jarl an opportunity to withdraw from the duel since he did not initiate the challenge. The elf ranger felt it was unfair for the Shimmerheim chieftain to be caught in a crossfire dispute that he did not initiate, unlike the Frostburg chieftain.

Peat overheard and laughed. He stated that knowing as many Nordlings as he had over the years, the Shimmerheim jarl would be persuaded if not outright coerced into accepting the duel. He would do so at least out of a sense of Nordling honor and manliness by the other chieftain to not back down from the intended duel. Linitus and Marin both nodded. They agreed with the likely conclusion their dwarf comrade came to. However, Linitus responded also by indicating that time would tell ultimately how this matter was to be decided by the local ruler. The elf ranger recalled the Nebelheim chieftain's warnings about Frostburg being as much compromised as Shimmerheim was in being clients to Helskadi to do her bidding, whatever that might entail.

Meanwhile, Linitus and the rest of the crew onboard still looked about toward Frostburg's chieftain. The Comradery noticed that this chieftain and his company were several hundred yards away from entering the settlement through the now-open wooden palisade gate to the Nordling settlement. As this chieftain proceeded with his horse rider company of bodyguards, a lone menacing sled being pulled by a pack of dire wolves shadowed their movement from further behind. This sled traversed through the snow under the cover of a minor winter wind that blew snow to obscure part of its cover. This sled also had left from traveling with the Shimmerheim chieftain's company outside the gates of Shimmerheim. The sled and its occupants then departed and changed their next destination, heading west toward the western range of the Har-Fjell Mountains. These mountains formed a curved shield that insulated the core interior of the more heavily populated part of Shimmerfrost from the outer frontier lands that lie further north and west. Those frontier lands were even more harsh during the winter. It was so much so that very few Nordlings had settled further north, beyond the Har-Fjell Mountains. The mountains themselves were treacherous in being susceptible to natural avalanches that occurred to wreak havoc on the immediate foothills below, which few Nordlings would settle upon also. Within these mountains dotted many caves. Rumors circulated of these caves being rich in deposits of various valuable metals and rare minerals deep within. However, they were also inhabited within and near the entrances by many beastly creatures, including cave orcs, goblins, dire wolves, snow trolls, and a few snow dwarves. None of these creatures would be so welcoming to allow a human Nordling to have permission to enter their dwellings for the latter's own gain, though some exceptions were made if it benefitted the respective beastly creatures.

At the helm of this sled, interesting enough, were two uncommon figures to stand alongside next to each other. These two sled riders comprised a goblin shaman wearing a small fur cloak hood along with an ornate bone headdress and a full-bearded Nordling wearing various articles of fur along with a thick brown rectangular cloak made of wool. The goblin shaman was known as Knower of Many Tongues (or simply Many Tongues) for possessing the knowledge to communicate in various languages. Many Tongues's Nordling companion interesting enough was the same deceptive one, the courier known as Halkir, who had betrayed Linitus's Comradery at the reversed ambush at Lone Pass and who had a less warming re-encounter with the survivors at the Frostburg chieftain's mead hall. Now once again Halkir would be dispatched to serve his Frostburg chieftain's bidding once again.

Meanwhile, the Frostburg chieftain himself would court his Shimmerheim counterpart to convince him of his plan. They would delay Linitus and Marin from having the duel outside the gates of Shimmerheim and instead convince the two heroic outsiders to agree to have the time and location of the duel under more fair conditions in which it would take place in seven days further south at a place in which the Shimmerfrost River spread itself out in a wide area in which many sandbanks and river islands form with a low tide being present. The river itself continues flowing south to the various dyr villages near the coast and west of Dyr Valley. The dyr folk and their language knew this place of the impending duel as Abhain Gainmich Mawr.

Chapter Forty-Nine

A Cunning and Deadly Proposition

    Only about five days later, the lone dire wolf sled had finally reached its destination. It had reached the base of the Har-Fjell Mountains. The conditions were no longer suitable for the two occupants, Many Tongues and Halkir, to travel on sled. The goblin shaman and the Nordling courier from Frostburg discarded the sled and opted to ride on top of two of the eight dire wolves. The rest of the wolf pack followed behind. As the two travelers and their pack of dire wolves ascended to the higher elevations, the view from below was breathtaking. These mountains, though filled with snow, were brightly lit with the spring sun still piercing its rays downward. The goblin and Nordling courier could see the lower green and brown foothills with a breathtaking view from high above. The two travelers saw and noted, looking at those lower elevations, that the snow was not present but had already melted. They also saw the lower valley and escarpment being covered by various birch, spruce, black cottonwood, and quaking aspen trees. Many of the perennial trees sprouted with various new vivid green color leaves.

    At the higher elevations of the Har-Fjell mountains, the conditions were cold and windy compared to the lower elevations. Still, it was tolerable enough for the Frostburg courier and his goblin shaman companion to traverse to the nearest occupied cave. The cave in particular would be one in which the goblin shaman was familiar and took the lead, guiding his Nordling courier companion. The mouth of the cave appeared damp, dark, and bleak. Somehow it was clear enough from the outside entrance for the

Nordling and goblin shaman to see dozens of glaring catlike eyes looking at them from the shadows. The goblin shaman spoke in his native goblin tongue. He uttered several words while raising his hands with his palms facing the staring eyes in a peaceful and submissive manner. The human Nordling followed his counterpart's lead and imitated the same gesture. A moment later, several goblin figures emerged from the mouth of the cave and spoke in the same goblin tongue while uttering several words to the shaman. The courier observed and could tell that these goblins from the cave became suspicious of his presence. The shaman, meanwhile, replied in the same goblinoid tongue to his goblin brethren to ease their suspicion of this human Nordling visitor. The Nordling courier observed. While uncertain of what was being spoken, he could still tell his presence as a human became somewhat startling and unwelcomed by the goblins.

The courier sweated and was fearful that the goblin sentries who stood guard near the cave would at some point attack him. He wondered also if this had been a fool's errand as a messenger to accompany the goblin shaman as his chieftain wished. Halkir also wondered what use he would have been to accompany Many Tongues aside from being a witness representative on behalf of the Frostburg jarl. The goblin shaman after all was well-spoken in being able to communicate not only in his goblin tongue and the Shimmerfrost Nordling dialect but also in other languages. Among those languages included the Southern Nordling language of the western woodlands and even the more common Citadellan tongue of the southwest lands of Hesperion. It was this goblin whom Helskadi had assigned as an ambassador and translator between her beast race minion servants and her Nordling client of Frostburg. The goblin would, in effect, act as an intermediary in coordinating their efforts to serve her. In this circumstance, the chieftain of Frostburg took even more liberty to use this shaman to his advantage in engaging in diplomacy with the beast races of Har-Fjell.

Only now did the courier see this rare and unexpected move by his lord jarl come to fruition. It became clear to Halkir after the goblin sentries conversed for a brief period with the goblin shaman that the mood became more amicable. With no further qualms, the sentries motioned their hands to wave off in granting permission for the shaman to enter with the Nordling courier following behind. Upon gaining permission, the two of them followed behind one of the goblin sentry guards who escorted them deeper within the bowels of this dark, damp, and somewhat cold cave. The only reprieve of warmth that the courier and goblin shaman had was from the lit torch that the goblin sentry carried while proceeding through a gradual descending pathway. The cave itself was like many others in Shimmerfrost. It had a mixture of ice stalagmites and natural rock stalagmites. The cave tunnel also had several bats fly in scattered directions upon being awakened from the lit torch that the goblin sentry held. The descending cave pathway led to a more open cavern complex with several tunnels going in other directions in the cave network. This cavern was curve-shaped with a looming underwater lake below. On the ground surface above, many dozens of primitive fur, wooden, and animal bone huts were lit with blazing fire pits. These pits were outside the huts that were erected and occupied by various goblins and cave orcs. The two species lived together cooperatively for the sake of mutual interest and benefit. They supported each other while teaming up to prey upon any targets they considered worth raiding and hunting.

Now with the goblin sentry leading the way, he gave a loud screech-like war cry in his native goblin tongue, which caught the attention of many in this cave settlement. The local denizens emerged outside their primitive dwellings and found out the cause of the disturbance. The sight of so many had internally bewildered the Nordling courier. Regardless, he still composed himself in being stern while not displaying any visible signs that he was shaken and afraid of their presence even ever so slightly.

Soon a large muscular cave orc wearing a bone and feather headdress approached the goblin shaman. The cave orc spoke back to him in orcish in which the goblin shaman also understood that language. This came not as a surprise to the courier. It was common knowledge that many of the goblins and orcs coexisted side-by-side long enough to understand each other's social behaviors and their languages. This cave orc, however, also stood out in donning exquisite black ebony-looking armor. He also wielded a long broad-bladed sword in the same color metal material as his armor cuirass, gauntlets, and leg greaves. It was unlike any other armor that the Nordling had seen in all of Shimmerfrost. However, Halkir recalled that this armor resembled in many respects the armor worn by some of Lucianus's warriors onboard the skybeast. With the courier's attention still being focused on the orc chieftain, the latter eventually noticed and turned while grunting and speaking in orcish to ask why he was staring at him.

The goblin-speaking Nordling interpreted the question to the courier. The courier recomposing himself asked the orc to pardon his offense. He explained in a complimentary way that he found the orc chieftain's armor to be impressive and suitable for one of such impressive stature. When the goblin shaman translated into orcish, the orc chieftain laughed. He explained with his words being translated that this armor was gifted to him from a powerful new ally of their overlord, Helskadi. The orc chieftain, in exchange, pledged a retinue of their orc and goblin soldiers from various clans to be transferred from this settlement in service to this new, dark ally.

The Nordling, impressed and curious, asked about this ally, including who he was and his whereabouts. The orc chieftain in translation replied that they knew very little. Helskadi knew barely more than them, perhaps other than that this ally was a werewolf adolescent. He was also an heir to a powerful dark lord in the southwestern lands of Hesperion. This powerful heir and his nation-state possessed the means to produce impressive weapons of war and the means to transport them, according to the orc chieftain.

Impressed again after having the orc's accounts reaffirm his suspicions of Lucianus being the source provider of the armor, the courier thanked the orcish chieftain for what he divulged while suggesting that perhaps in the future his clan will have many more promising opportunities in collaborating with this dark lord from the south on behalf of the service to their female jotunn overlord. The orcish chieftain nodded and agreed.

After briefly conversing, the goblin shaman informed the Nordling courier that the orcish chieftain agreed to the courier's request to supply a large war party of cave orcs and goblins to launch a surprise raid against a dyr village near Abhainn Gainmhich Mawr in order to draw these new heroic strangers into the battle and overwhelm them by using the large numbers of the cave orc chieftain's war party. It was this raid that the chieftains of Frostburg and Shimmerheim intended to use in luring their newfound outsider adversaries to their deaths in trying to save the dyr village before the duel would begin so as not for Nordling chieftains to risk their lives against the strange elf and half-Nordling newcomers that challenged their authority and their allegiance to Helskadi.

The courier pleased by the orc chieftain's decision, heaped praises upon him, which the goblin translated. The chieftain nodded again, stating that he did this for what he believed was the ultimate cause of serving his overlord, Helskadi, and by extension the forces of darkness.

Upon turning and preparing to leave with the goblin shaman to relay the granted request to his Frostburg chieftain, a loud shout of anguish deep within the bowels of the cave emerged. It presumably came from the lower elevation of the surface near the large underwater lake. This audible disturbance had a particular voice, which the courier could identify by species, though barely. It was the voice of a jotunn.

The orc chieftain, along with the various cave settlement denizens of goblins, cave orcs, and a few snow trolls, looked at the courier's curiosity. They knew that his perceptiveness was astute and perhaps required for them to address. The courier turned to recognize their stares at him. He decided the best route to react to not getting savagely and unceremoniously executed was to ask sarcastically. He inquired who the lucky prisoner was and offered his help to them to quiet down their jotunn victim as an act of friendship. Eventually, the stares turned to clamored laughter. The orc chieftain told the courier that it would not be needed, for this was a special jotunn prisoner who had periodically shouted in anguish and lament from his indefinite torture and captivity.

The courier asked, still out of curiosity what his crime was to merit a jotunn, being one of their overlord's fellow species to be imprisoned. The orc chieftain stated that while he should not divulge, he admitted to liking this courier for a human Nordling so much that the chieftain felt it would not hurt to disclose that information since they were ultimately both fellow servants of the same master, the Winter Death Witch. The courier nodded and the orc chieftain explained that this was a special male jotunn. This jotunn was nearly as powerful, if not just as powerful as Helskadi. Helskadi had challenged his authority since they were both near divine titans for who should rule undisputedly over the jotunn folk and the rest of the domain in Shimmerfrost. He and Helskadi fought an epic battle in which the female jotunn overlord prevailed over him. In the aftermath, Helskadi thought it more fitting instead of slaying her defeated rival to have him imprisoned and tortured by the lowliest of her subject minions deep within the caves of Har-Fjell.

The courier now realizing the folktale gasped in shock while stating the name of this once legendary figure was none other than the legendary Wothunak. The orc chieftain nodded while affirming that it was indeed the jotunn male titan and once a former rival to Helskadi. Wothunak, like Helskadi, was a powerful jotunn titan who claimed divinity like the female jotunn titan. The male titan was also known for being both a trickster and deceiver and being associated with strength and lightning. Regional lore also considered him the older sibling of Helskadi. Ironically, when

Helskadi bested him, it was not by her own prowess itself. Rather, she bested Wothunak by convincing the other jotunns to side with her and overpower Wothunak in exchange for Helskadi promising the jotunns to one day expand their range of control beyond their home in Jotunheim and the Jotunn Mountains. Now, however, even to this day, the courier marveled at what was revealed. As he heard the cry of suffering being lashed out from a being older than perhaps thirty generations of the courier's own Nordling family line, Halkir still almost could not believe that it was the same titan he grew up hearing stories about.

After pondering what was revealed, the Nordling courier, however, recomposed himself and shrugged his arms while nodding. He looked at his goblin shaman counterpart to indicate that they were ready to exit the mountain cave and return to the surface. Behind them, a long line of cave orcs, goblins, several packs of dire wolves, and a few snow trolls assembled and followed the shaman and courier. They would lead this war party alongside the cave orc chieftain that followed them. This war party, or rather raiding party, would make their way within two to three days to their intended destination. They planned to arrive with bad intentions at a dyr village that lay just south of Abhainn Gainmhich Mawr.

Chapter Fifty

Battle of Abhainn Gainmhich Mawr

A week after arriving outside the settlement of Shimmerheim, the floating skyboat carrying Linitus and the Comradery now found themselves above another majestic sight to behold. All aboard the skyboat looked down from the sky above. They saw the Shimmerfrost River still flowing, though obstructed by multiple sandbars and river islands. There was also a small looming hill to the north with the surreal massive Har-Fjell mountains lying further away in the background. Throughout the immediate surrounding terrain including on the river islands, numbered thousands of green and yellow-leafed birch trees as well as several spruce trees. From the distance further south, Linitus pointed and spotted a dyr village with dozens of wooden longhouses and a ceremonial religious site. The ceremonial site itself had a circular ring mound surrounded by several menhirs (or megalithic standing stones). There was also a large dolmen (or two standing stones supported by a flat horizontal stone slab) at the center of the circular ring mound.

As Linitus and the rest of the Comradery looked about, they noticed that the two chieftains from Frostburg and Shimmerheim. The chieftains stood near the top of the hill bluff that loomed over the forest tree line close to the river. However, even more alarming several kilometers away was a fast-approaching formation of goblins, cave orcs, and a few snow trolls that in sum numbered at least two hundred. At the forefront of this beastly horde were packs of dire wolves mounted by goblins. This horde did not converge, however, with the Nordling chieftains. Rather, the beastly horde pressed onward and descended downward from the hill and traversed across the shallow river while crossing over between the various river islands and sandbars. Both Linitus and Marin could tell where they were likely headed.

Marin said abruptly aloud with a sense of alarm and startlement that this beastly horde was likely going to raid upon the dyr village. The village itself lay several kilometers to the south along the river bank. Linitus nodded after hearing the sense of urgency that Marin conveyed of a likely attack on the village. The elf ranger inquired with Wyatt if he could transport several of the Comradery onboard to the village in order to warn the locals of the impending attack. Wyatt nodded but Marin had an additional idea. She, Peat, and the others onboard would fight to hold off the raiding party. Meanwhile, Wyatt would send Linitus to the village to warn them in time about the oncoming enemy raiding party. However, Linitus was not fond of the proposed plan. He did not want to leave his companions to fend for themselves in saving the village without him contributing to the impending standoff. Still, he recognized Marin's point and nodded reluctantly, seeing that he perhaps knew how to communicate with the dyr folk better than anyone else onboard.

However, out of nowhere, Andarin interrupted. He stated he could be in place of Linitus since Andarin knew the dyr folk and the language well enough to communicate to them about the beastly invaders. Linitus, surprised, inquired with Andarin if he was comfortable enough to go alone to warn the dyr folk. If so, the elf ranger would plan to lead his companions in holding back the onslaught. Andarin nodded while stating the locals knew him well enough and vice versa from conducting past trade transactions. They would trust him at his word about what was going on in which the elf's presence would not be needed to go with him. Linitus nodded and gave a slight smile. The elf turned to Wyatt and instructed the halfling wizard to transport Andarin to the village. Once Wyatt did so, Linitus directed him to transport the rest of the company to confront the beastly horde from a distance behind one of the thickets. Wyatt nodded and within moments, the halfling wizard waving his sparkling silver wand teleported Andarin to the dyr village several kilometers away.

Before Linitus teleported next along with Wyatt, the elf ranger instructed Alvissan to change the course heading of the skyboat to sail in the sky toward the dyr village. Linitus told Alvissan to request from the village to have as many of the dyr folk board and evacuate as the floating vessel could hold. Linitus knew it was important to do so in case he and his companions could not stop the remaining beastly horde from their advance to raid the dyr village. Alvissan nodded after understanding Linitus's instructions. She assured the elf she would do everything in her power to save as many of them as possible. Linitus appreciated and felt assured by his new friend's vow. The elf ranger directed Wyatt for the two of them to depart and teleport along with Marin, Peat, and the few Nordling warriors that survived this far into their journey.

In an instant, Wyatt waved his wand and a bright flash appeared and disappeared before the Comradery and its present company. All of them save for Alvissan had now teleported to the surface of Abhainn Gainmhich Mawr. The teleported company made sense of their surroundings while looking about. They found themselves at the top of a small bluff. It was obscured by the cover of several birch trees on one of the larger river islands positioned halfway between the advancing enemy horde and the dyr village south along the downstream river. The low tide and sandbars along the river made it easy for the enemy horde to traverse directly southward. However, it still slowed them down from moving as quickly as they had near the larger hill that stood on the north side of the Shimmerfrost River.

From the distance on top of the north-facing hill, the Frostburg and Shimmerheim jarls both keenly noticed and observed with wide bearded grins and devious intrigue. Their plan to divert their challengers' attention to be in harm's way against a more imposing force out of a sense to save those in danger seemed to pay off. One jarl laughed alongside the other. The Frostburg jarl speculated with his peer that their challengers would foreseeably fall from that battle against the beastly horde before the duel with them could begin.

Meanwhile, Linitus spotted the horde from the north. He pointed their location to the rest of his companions and directed them to take position. They formed a facing front to brace for battle against the enemy horde once they closed in for close-quarter combat. The few surviving Nordlings along with Peat formed a shield wall in front of Linitus. The elf ranger quickly readied his bow. He used one of his makeshift arrow canisters filled with arrows in a honeycomb arrangement that he made after the ambush at Lone Pass. Linitus waited with patience while pulling back on his bow until the main bulk of the horde army was within range of just over three hundred yards. Once they were, the elf ranger released the bowstring, sending to fight the honeycomb canister holding nearly two dozen arrows that dispersed from the canister in a small hail. Less than a few seconds passed, in which most of the dark hail of arrows struck multiple targets within the core body of the charging horde. The attack caught the surviving orcs, goblins, and a few snow trolls by surprise. They looked about to locate the source of the attack while still being out in the open on top of the sandbars and low tide riverbed. It was long enough for Linitus to prepare to launch another arrow sabot canister full of arrows. Marin meanwhile, used her supernatural abilities. She concentrated and uttered several incantations in forming a spear of bright flashing light before hurling across the distance toward the enemy horde. The enemy war party lost at least several of their warriors from Marin's attack.

Wyatt also prepared to cast multiple spells. This included enchanted explosive fiery markers that would trigger off upon contact. The wizard placed these markers several yards away in a semicircular pattern in front of his companions' formation. Upon finishing his magical snare traps, the halfling wizard next turned his attention to casting as quickly as possible large fireballs and bolts of lightning toward the beastly horde. By this point, the enemy horde army had already located their attackers' position. The enemy horde, however, lost already a quarter of their original numbers. They would lose another quarter of their army as the barrage of attacks alternating between Linitus, Marin, and Wyatt continued.

As the enemy horde closed in toward the Comradery, the goblin-mounted dire wolves were the first to fall. They charged at full pace while triggering off the magical explosive fire markers that Wyatt had deployed around his comrades' vicinity. Only a few of the horde cavalry made it through. By this point, the Nordlings along with Peat slowed the remaining enemy advance. The Nordling and the dwarf braced the impact of the enemy charge by holding steadfast with shields and delivering deadly blows from their axes and spears. Peat, however, used his enchanted war hammer during the ensuing melee. The mounted dire wolves fell one by one along with their goblin riders. Several non-mounted dire wolves penetrated through the shield wall while taking down one Nordling, who became severely injured. Another dire wolf delivered a nasty bite toward Peat's leg. The dwarf guardian shouted in pain and anger. Peat then reacted by punching the wolf while following up with a second mortal blow with his war hammer to the beast's skull. Peat continued to curse while stating his adversity toward dire wolves and wishing he could smite them all in one blow of his war hammer.

Marin took notice of her old dwarven mentor's reaction to being in pain. She came to his aid while uttering several words of prayer incantations. She concentrated her thoughts on using her divine-like supernatural powers in order to emanate a turquoise-like globe that expanded outward from her hands that were in contact with Peat's wounded foot. Within moments, the healing aura of the sphere had healed the dwarf. Peat replied, expressing his gratitude toward his comrade. He also informed Marin to check on the Nordling who was also wounded by the dire wolves. Marin nodded and repeated the same process in healing the downed Nordling warrior. The Nordling also thanked her after being healed back to his full health, much to his surprise and the surprise of his fellow surviving Nordling comrades.

The Comradery, led by Linitus, continued to stave off the initial wave of the charging cavalry of mounted dire wolves. Only less than a minute after they fended off the last dire wolf, the main body of the horde infantry still pressed on and were closing the gap that separated them from the Comradery. Linitus still continued to let loose one arrow after the other while Wyatt continued to alternate in spell casting between fireballs and bolts of lightning. It weakened the numbers of the attacking horde, with only a few dozen of the beast horde attackers still alive. Peat had one trick up his sleeve and removed a cloak behind his back, revealing a round barrel keg with a fuse. He grinned wildly while looking at the rest of the companions and told them to stand back. The dwarf took a few paces back while holding the barrel after he unfurled it from the back strap assembly. He motioned and told Wyatt to get ready to cast a fireball on the barrel. Wyatt nodded, while Peat sprinted and heaved the large wooden barrel across the air. The dwarf watched the barrel still travel through the air close to the main body of the enemy unit. He quickly told his halfling wizard companion to unleash his magical attack. Wyatt nodded again. With haste, he cast a fireball with the wave of his wand.

Within moments, a large, searing ball of flame emitted from Wyatt's hands and wand. This fireball soared forward and struck the barrel in midair, only a few yards away from the front ranks of the enemy formation. Immediately, the barrel burst into a gigantic explosion that took out more than half of the remaining dark minions. With the dust clearing, Peat, Linitus, and the other companions watched the damaging effect this explosion had. Only a few figures emerged from the smoke of the explosion that would dissipate. Peat turned to his elf companion and told him not to tell Andarin. Linitus appeared surprised and dumbfounded. The elf ranger asked Peat about what he meant and what he was referring to. The dwarf guardian reluctantly confessed that he snuck an item from Andarin's inventory when he was not looking. Linitus still looked perplexed and curious about what exactly his companion had taken. Peat sighed and told the elf to disregard what he was stating, though Marin already knew. She could discern what the dwarf meant. She told him that as consolation, he at least would put it to good use regardless of how he obtained the explosive barrel.

As the conversation transpired, a large humanoid figure wearing armor appeared from the smoke, along with two other remaining minions. This figure was a cave orc chieftain. He wielded a large, black broadsword and wore, of all things, an exquisite set of pitch-black armor. Linitus and Marin could tell and trace the origin and make of the weapon and armor as coming from Sanctum Novus, the capital of the Imperial Remnant. This heavily armoured cave orc was not interested in idle talk with these two strangers. The orc pointed his weapon toward the two heroes. Linitus stared and walked forward to place himself between his companions and the leader of the war party. The cave orc chieftain, still pointing his large broadsword at Linitus, shouted several curse words in orcish toward the elf.

Then, the cave orc, after he finished shouting, rushed and swung his large blade at the elf ranger. Linitus remained in a calm yet alert position. With his knees slightly bent, he quickly let go of his bow and unsheathed his long, curved blade while dodging his adversary's first attack. The orc chieftain brought his blade to swing back again in an upward diagonal motion, only for it to be at a standstill in locking against Linitus's blade. The cave orc pressed hard with his full force against the elf. Linitus, keeping his footing, used both his hands to hold his blade still at the hilt. Linitus strafed while letting the orc chieftain fall forward to lose his balance. As he regained his balance, the orc again swung but the width of his arc was short as Linitus struck at the same time using his right hand holding the blade all the while the elf ranger with his left hand pulled an arrow from his quiver. Linitus held the arrow by the midshaft and unexpectedly jabbed the arrowhead toward the jugular vein of his opponent. This daring maneuver had caught the orc chieftain off guard and surprised everyone else from the ensuing fighting. Immediately, the orc chieftain fell to the ground while bleeding to death.

The morale shifted. Though outnumbered still at least two to one, the remaining orcs, goblins, and two snow trolls fled back in the same direction they came. Behind this now routed and broken army, two figures mounted on dire wolves stared with disappointment and shock. Linitus had recognized one figure while pointing him out to the rest of his companions. It was the Nordling courier, Halkir, who had shown up again, only this time a goblin shaman accompanied him. The two figures, still in disbelief, became further struck with fear when the elf ranger pointed them. The goblin shaman and Nordling courier fled while riding on their mounted dire wolves back toward the Har-Fjell Mountains.

Meanwhile, realizing from across the distance that the staged ambush to draw the attention and overwhelm Linitus, Marin, and their Nebelheim allies had failed at least for the time being, the two Nordling chieftains decided they would send their combined retinue of armed bodyguards to attack them next before engaging in the actual duel. Though it was considered cowardly what they had done and were planning to do, both Nordling chieftains did not seem to care as long as they remained the rulers of their own settlements. With the bodyguards mounted on horseback charging away down the hill from the distance, Marin pointed out from observing that this was a deliberate trap by the two Nordling chieftains to wear them down before having the duel. Linitus nodded and devised an idea while asking Wyatt if he could teleport all the present company to the hill. Wyatt confirmed by nodding his head while looking at the hill and seeing how open it was with no major obstructions being present. Linitus then had the wizard execute a teleportation spell at the elf ranger's command, which he would do right at the moment when the enemy chieftain's bodyguard cavalry was far enough away from their lords to not have enough time return and interfere in the duel.

Only when these mounted Nordling bodyguards were within a hundred yards away from the Comradery did Linitus give the order. As soon as Linitus did, Wyatt teleported himself and all of his companions to the nearly lonely hill. Once teleported, the Nordling chieftains looked in shock at first at seeing that their adversaries had disappeared and then upon realizing with a voice calling from behind them that their challengers had appeared alongside with their companions.

Marin looked with anger and a sense of wanting to exact retribution for the deceit in staging the duel. The Princess Knight wielded a spear and shield while looking formidable in her legendary Golden Valkyrie attire. She called out to one chieftain and pointed her weapon at him. This was the chieftain of Frostburg, whom Marin had now intended to show no mercy for both his treachery and cowardliness in the duel that was expected to be held. Linitus pointed his blade at the other chieftain while saying aloud that it was time for them to finish this.

The two chieftains still mounted on their horses looked at each other both being visibly angered and disgusted at having to deal with these strangers directly themselves. Both chieftains gripped their spears in their hands and threw them at Linitus and Marin, the latter two of which anticipated the attack and dodged it. Not wanting to put up with any more of their cowardliness while seeming to give them a taste of their own methods, Marin and Linitus both looked at each other. They could read each other's minds on how to respond against their adversaries. The elf ranger and Princess Knight both dropped their melee weapons and suddenly concentrated in their minds while facing their adversarial counterparts several dozen yards away. The two heroes concentrating with their hands drew from their super divine-like powers and emanated with their hands bright flashing forms of energy shaped in the weapon that they both were familiar with using, Marin's being a throwing spear of light, and Linitus's being a bright bow of energy along with an arrow of light. Both heroes drew back their weapons and suddenly let loose the projectiles that darted quickly across the air and struck the intended targets as they were charging toward the two heroes. Immediately, the stricken Nordling chieftains fell down to the ground from their horses after receiving the fatal blow of these powerful supernatural projectiles.

As the Nordling chieftains lay dead on the ground, Peat, Wyatt, and their Nordling warrior allies that witnessed the quick duel, cheered and gave verbal praise to Linitus and Marin. Meanwhile, the retinue of bodyguards had already realized what had transpired from the distance. They turned around at full pace to head back toward the hill. Linitus and Marin looked at each other with straight faces ready to brace what was left of the enemy as Peat called out that the mounted bodyguards were closing in several hundred yards away. Linitus ordered the Comradery to ready their weapons but to not strike until the elf ranger gave the order. He could not help but release a slight sweat while wondering when these mounted Nordling warriors would stop.

Eventually, he sighed and caught his breath when he saw the mounted Frostburg and Shimmerheim Nordlings abruptly stop at least a hundred yards away while slowly dismounting. One of them assumed authority to speak on behalf of the rest of the former companies of the chieftains. This

Nordling warrior raised his hands up toward his shoulder while walking slowly toward Linitus. He spoke in a loud voice several words. Marin was in a state of surprise and disbelief from what he said. Linitus took notice and prompted to ask what startled her.

The Princess Knight recollected herself and turned toward her elven lover. She deciphered and translated well enough to convey to her elf lover that apparently the two housecarls (or house bodyguard) companies had recognized both her and Linitus's leadership after witnessing them best against their chieftains from trial by combat across the distance.

Linitus nodded while noticing that the Nordling representative of the two bodyguard companies next unsheathed his sword while proceeding to hold it sideways with both hands protruding outward. The Nordling next knelt before Linitus and Marin. The bodyguard spoke some more words in Nordling. Marin translated that the Nordlings of the two companies had now offered their service to the Comradery's cause.

Linitus nodded again while also observing the other dismounted Nordling bodyguards following suit and kneeling with their weapons being held in both hands as a form of submission. These bodyguards were formidable and though Marin would easily question the intentions of their now fallen chieftains, she had no signs of unease from trusting their bodyguards with their gesture and behavior seeming to be genuine and honorable by Nordling standards. Marin reported as such in affirmation when Linitus asked her thoughts about whether they could trust these now former housecarls. Accepting her answer, the elf ranger asked her to translate to which Marin nodded.

As Linitus spoke and Marin translated, the surrendering Nordling warriors who now offered their services to the prevailing victors were informed that if they would stay true to their pledge of fealty, they would have a purpose in aiding the cause of the victors and the Comradery. By joining with the Comradery they would hunt down what was left of the few escaping warriors of the goblin-orc war party and eventually fight alongside the Comradery's coalition to vanquish Helskadi and her forces. The Nordling warriors all nodded in agreement about the elf's proposition. Their speaking representative turned to verify their consent. Upon seeing it as unanimous, the representative nodded also and told the elf ranger that he would have each of them follow Linitus and Marin to the ends of the earth. Linitus was pleased after hearing Marin translate the representative's response. The elf then had Marin translate to tell the newly joined Nordling warriors to rise and follow the Comradery in pursuit of the escaping beastly creatures.

The Nordling warriors rose and cheered on unleashing sudden war cries before mounting again on their horses. Before taking off again Linitus instructed them that the creatures were likely heading back to where they came from which the spokesman of the mounted knights nodded in agreement while replying that this war party of beastly creatures likely came from one or more of the caves in the Har-Fjell Mountains. Linitus then told them to follow their tracks but not to engage them, at least not yet. The elf continued that he and his other immediate comrades would follow closely behind and that they would hunt the enemies down in their own lairs once they gave their positions away. The Nordling representative among the mounted warriors nodded before leading the rest of the cavalry to turn north by northwest toward the Har-Fjell Mountains.

Meanwhile, Linitus had Wyatt teleport their immediate group southward back toward the skyboat, which Andarin and Alvissan had used to prepare for loading the most vulnerable of the dyr townsfolk following the earlier failed attempted invasion by Helskadi's minions. After teleporting several times flashing in and out across the sandbars and river islands, Wyatt had finally teleported himself, Linitus, Marin, Peat, and the few remaining Nordling warriors from Nebelheim back to the skyboat, which was lowered onto the ground at the center of the dyr village. This sudden and daring act caught all the dyr folk by surprise, not to mention Andarin and Alvissan. Both respective dwarves sighed in relief that their newfound friends had prevailed and had now ended a potential disaster.

Without wasting more time Linitus explained in confirmation that they had prevailed and that there was no time to waste in which the skyboat now needed to disembark from the dyr village with any passengers to be offloaded so that the Comradery could use it to set sail in the skies above. They would use the floating vessel to track the few routed enemy survivors and their lair. The two sky-sailing dwarves that owned the skyboat nodded in acknowledgment. Within moments of offloading the dyr passengers, the skyboat had set sail again and departed from the dyr village. The dyr villagers were grateful for being potentially saved from losing casualties and possibly the entire village itself. To express their gratitude, the village elders agreed to send some of their best dyr warriors and even one druid priest to accompany the Comradery in the skyboat to help track down the retreating enemy survivors.

Before departing, one prominent village chieftain among the dyr folk had asked what happened to Alani-Aki. Linitus, using Andarin to translate, solemnly replied while holding back any tears from the thoughts of what happened, explaining that she gave her life to save the few of their company that had still survived. Ultimately, as the elf continued to explain, they defeated Wendigo at the cost of Alani sacrificing her own life to redeem the creature's innocence. The dyr folk that were present became saddened after they heard the elf ranger's account. The village chieftain replied in solace that it was perhaps necessary for Alani and the others who had fallen to fight for the same cause. Such sacrifices, according to him, were called for, so the rest of the living might still have a chance of finding a better life after the evil had been purged out of their lands.

Linitus once again still felt saddened in remembering the losses of those he led alongside Marin. He nodded silently before the dyr chieftain. He had no other words left to say and so he departed with the rest of the Comradery and their small, newly accompanied dyr folk warband. The elf ranger reflected on the friends he had met in this strange and hostile land. He thought about Alani-Aki, Arik, and some of the other Nordling warriors. The elf ranger only knew them for a relatively short period before they perished. He wished he would have known them longer. They were genuine, and it pained him to know at least in this mortal life he would long to see such unique ones like Alani and Arik.

Marin felt the same when hearing what Andarin had translated. She felt her elven lover's pain. Though they knew they would find no sense of permanent comfort, she still took it upon herself to put her hand over Linitus's shoulder. She reminded him that they had made it this far in which there was no turning back. They owed it to the ones they encountered and called friends to continue to fight for the cause that they each shared in freeing this land from the darkness with which Helskadi had planted it. They would undo it and ultimately undo her reign in claiming this cold, harsh, remote region. Linitus took her hand and kissed it while looking at her directly. He affirmed she was right and that they would finish this together before returning to their home in the southwest lands of the Kingdom of Swordbane.

As the two adventurers embraced each other, the skyboat ascended. The crew onboard each waved goodbye to the dyr villagers below before returning their attention at hand, in which Linitus pointed northwestward to the Har-Fjell Mountains. Once high enough above, the sight of the general landscape below became more visible. Linitus could see the fast-moving cavalry, who had recently sworn allegiance to him and Marin, now riding gracefully across the distance, but still within the horizon. He also could see something else further away, though faintly. The elf ranger pointed below at two tiny figures that were mounted on dire wolves from very far away. These mounted figures made their way at full pace toward the Har-Fjell Mountains. The mountains themselves stood high above the forest plain and hills. The imposing heights on which these mountains capped with snow stood perched above the various cloud formations were truly a sight to behold and marvel at. Very few mountain ranges rivaled these save for the ones that reminded Linitus of the mountains that lie just east of his forest city home of Salvinia Parf Edhellen.

Chapter Fifty-One

Unleashing the Winter Death Witch's Wrath

Deep within the Jotunn Mountains, at the giant citadel fortress city of Jotunheim, an amassed army grew as large as the eye of a storm, if not larger. It comprised various beastly creatures, jotunn giant folks, and snow dwarves. Among the beastly creatures numbered at least five thousand goblins and cave orcs, a thousand snow dwarves, over a hundred ogres, several dozens of snow trolls, and at least a dozen jotunn giant warriors. Among the goblins, a few hundred were also mounted on dire wolves.

Many among the elite ranks of the army were provisioned with the advanced dark black metallic armor and weaponry provisions that Helskadi's powerful Imperial Remnant ally from the south provided. Many of the other warriors still equipped themselves with simple yet crude weapons made of carved wood, flint stone, and obsidian. Still, some other warriors possessed basic iron and steel weapons that were looted from Nordlings that they had crossed paths in raiding against.

Helskadi looked downward at the amassed army from the top of her citadel tower. She felt impressed. It truly was an army ready to take over Shimmerfrost once and for all. Fornjotr, her jotunn male chief underling, stood by her side. Helskadi turned to him for consultation and updated reports on the various beastly creature and snow dwarf settlements that had reported being mustered. She would use these forces to unleash her wrath as a methodical campaign to ravage and bend all the Nordling and dyr folk settlements to submit to her will. Fornjotr spoke in a coarse, guttural jotunn tongue. He told his matriarch that all those summoned have reported, save for the beastly creature settlements along the Har-Fjell Mountains. He mentioned that Frostburg and Shimmerheim (the only Nordling settlements to submit to her will) also had not responded to her latest summons. Helskadi frowned mildly, with visible disappointment, though it was not unexpected. She counted on the possibility of the two respective Nordling settlements to hold back and wait. She knew they would only support her overtly once she had shown her power in dominating the only other major Nordling settlement that was not under her influence… Nebelheim.

Nebelheim, as Helskadi thought before many times over, was the prime target to unleash her wrath. She would make an example of it to demonstrate before all the other settlements in Shimmerfrost the price they would pay if they did not submit to her reign. As Helskadi thought about the aim of her conquest, she also thought about the means of carrying out that aim. She turned to her large amassed forces, and she raised her exotic, sharp-pointed staff. The Winter Death Witch delivered her speech to them. She told her forces that today would mark the first day of a new era. Her forces of darkness would march forth from the Jotunn Mountains to dominate all the lands and settlements of Shimmerfrost once and for all. Helskadi pointed her spear staff south to Nebelheim. The Winter Death Witch told her army of minions that this would be the first target among those who resisted her authority and her will. She then gestured toward Fornjotr while indicating aloud that it would be he who would have the honor to lead her forces.

Helskadi became delighted upon hearing a chorus of shouts, screeches, and howls of elation among her assembled army ring out in reaction to Fornjotr's promotion to lead her forces. She concluded that Fornjotr's dominating presence and reputation preceded well among the beastly creatures, snow dwarves, and also her fellow giant folks. Fornjotr had fought and won every major pitched skirmish in which he took part during his several hundred years of life. Only now he was eager to have the chance to show his potential to his matriarch. He hoped she would choose him as her formal royal consort, a title that no fellow male jotunn had ever been formally offered by her. This time was different, however. Helskadi recognized Fornjotr's desire as she looked at him. She told him loud enough that only the two could hear that she would give him this position of honor to be her consort. She would do so after he had proved himself worthy to command her forces while pacifying the whole of Shimmerfrost in her name. The male jotunn chieftain nodded and knelt before her. He pledged he would do so.

By this point, the mustered army had ended their drowned cheers of support for their dark queen sovereign. They waited for her chosen jotunn general to descend from the entrance of Helskadi's citadel to join and lead them from the front ranks. Fornjotr raised his massive war hammer in salutation to Helskadi. His jotunn matriarch grinned and nodded in acknowledgment. Fornjotr then raised his weapon again, pointing toward the south where Nebelheim lay before them. He unleashed a massive war cry while declaring for the army to march forth. All of them gave their own war cry once again before following their general on a path in which they intended to sow as much death and destruction as possible. They would reap their fill of bloodlust and potential loot that they would find along the way.

The marching army faded against the constant swirls of snow from the distance, surrounded by narrow winding paths, mountainous cliffs, and an endless ring of snow-covered mountains. Helskadi would wait patiently until she received updated reports from the goblin scouts on her army's progress in their destructive campaign. For now, her thoughts centered on the desires of how she would rule and impose her will throughout the entirety of Shimmerfrost once and for all. She was still upset about the loss of one of her most powerful lieutenants, Wendigo. It was hard for her to accept the news upon hearing the reports from a few snow dwarves that witnessed his downfall against a mixed group of Nordlings and dyr folk led by two unfamiliar figures. These two ever-increasing figures of notoriety she kept in mind in hoping her appointed jotunn general would cross paths to dispose of once and for all. She had warned Fornjotr before he departed to be aware of a mysterious elf-male creature known to be powerful with both his blade and bow. Helskadi also warned of an equally mysterious and formidable Valkyrie shield maiden. This Valkyrie was a living Nordling woman rumored to have slain the corpse of a possessed undead body, or draug, of the first king of Shimmerfrost. If there were any individuals that became a priority for Helskadi to single out in eliminating, it would be those two strangers she mentioned to Fornjotr. They were the same ones she heard of briefly in conversation with Lucianus and the spectral form of Decius. These two heroes were considered the biggest obstacles that the Imperial Remnant had faced in its rebellion and secession against the Kingdom of Swordbane. She became determined to not let them live long enough to stop her from shaping her destiny as a titan in becoming something more powerful. She became hell-bent on becoming the next chosen vessel or even becoming a fully deified being, no matter the cost.

Chapter Fifty-Two

Mutual Pursuits of Vengeance

The Nordling courier and goblin shaman hurried as fast as possible while riding on their dire wolf mounts and scaling the Har-Fjell mountain range. They reached the entrance of the goblin-orc cave they had entered and left roughly two days prior. Now, as tired as they were, they mustered every bit of strength and perseverance to press on inside the cave while encountering the goblin sentries.

The return arrivals informed the settlement goblin guards of what had happened while warning them they needed to prepare an ambush for when the pursuing enemies would enter the cave to still pursue the shaman and courier. The goblin guards nodded their heads while grunting and screeching. They expressed their eagerness to bait the strange enemy into their cave. Upon doing so, they would ambush the enemy pursuer with larger numbers, along with the cave orcs that shared the cave with them. The Nordling courier, however, cautioned them that this might be too risky, and he thought of a better idea, though it was also risky. The goblins asked (through the goblin shaman interpreting) what idea the courier had in mind. The courier smiled with an enormous grin. He looked at an angle downward toward the source of the large languishing noise he had heard earlier. The courier suggested instead that they set free the imprisoned creature provided he would agree beforehand to slay the enemy pursuers.

The goblins considered the idea along with the shaman. The shaman brought up a concern that this imprisoned jotunn titan was powerful and untrustworthy. His reputation preceded him even prior to his imprisonment.

The shaman asked the courier about considering the possibility that the imprisoned Wothunak would not renounce his word and turn on the beastly cave dwellers. He had as much reason to want to exact revenge on them compared to anyone else. The courier nodded. However, he pondered and asked if the goblins and orcs would abandon the settlement cave, at least until the danger was gone.

The courier proposed he would stage a pretense, in which he would act as a rescuer to aid Wothunak in escaping. The courier would also try to sway Wothunak to attack the Comradery. The courier would portray Linitus and his Comradery as allies of Helskadi who seek to dispose of Wothunak once and for all. After all, the courier reasoned, Wothunak had not met him before. The jotunn titan would have less reason to distrust him compared to the beastly creatures that tortured him for so long. The goblin shaman nodded and assumed leadership of the cave since the orc chieftain was slain. In taking control of the cave settlement, the shaman ordered the guards to send word for all the local cave-dwelling orcs, goblins, and trolls to abandon the cave settlement. They would take a passage through one of several tunnels to find the other network of goblin and cave settlements to embed themselves into.

This maneuver of abandonment and enabling Wothunak's escape was in both the shaman's opinion and the courier's the best ploy to come up with. They would frame their pursuers as Wothunak's enemy and would-be executioners. The only matter that still needed to be settled was for the courier to find access to going into the large secluded prison cell of Wothunak. It was secluded somewhere in the lower level of the cavern complex.

The goblin shaman, being familiar with the cave, knew the way and led the courier down a less-known pathway, which descended to the lower cavern level. There was a narrow strip of rock formation bridge that stood above the cave lake while connecting to the other end in which there was a circular island. Looming above this island was a large series of bricks that formed a wall, along with a thick metal wall cell door. Standing guard before the door were two large snow trolls and several cave orcs. All of them wielded large ox tail whips and blunt war clubs made of thick carved birch wood. The goblin dismissed the cave orcs and snow trolls, but not before calling in two cave orcs, which were inside the cell. These two orcs inside the cell took turns from time to time torturing Wothunak to their content. One of the snow trolls notified its other beastly companions that they were ordered to leave the cell by the goblin shaman. The two troll torturers grunted and nodded in compliance while exiting out of the cell and closing the cell door.

The two cave orc torturers became surprised upon exiting the cell to see who was before them and their troll allies besides the goblin shaman. It was an average-human-height Nordling donned in winter animal fur garb. The goblin shaman again assumed a position of authority. He instructed the snow trolls and cave orcs to follow him to evacuate the rest of the settlement while insisting they leave the Nordling courier to his own devices. The present company of trolls and orcs nodded. They left in procession behind the shaman. The courier himself waited a few more moments before deciding it was time to open the cell and convince Wothunak under a ruse that he was being rescued to prevent his execution by the Comradery under Helskadi's orders. The Nordling courier had hoped this plan would last long enough to at least fool Wothunak, the trickster titan himself, into believing in the courier's pretense. With luck, the courier would set up the Comradery in a battle against the male jotunn titan. If all went according to plan, it would distract them long enough for the cave orc and goblin settlement to escape from being further pursued.

The courier took a deep breath while feeling nervous. He then maintained a stern and serious face while slowly opening the heavy door of the cell to walk inside. Upon being in the cell itself, the courier noticed how bleak and damp it was. The cell was also very dark except for a few scattered wall-mounted lit torches bright enough to illuminate and show the imprisoned jotunn titan shackled against the wall in chains opposite the cell entrance. The jotunn giant was restrained in which he could barely move his arms or legs and he was fatigued, in which he seemed to be in a half-dazed state of near-unconsciousness. Upon hearing the noise of the cell door opening, the imprisoned titan asked what his troll torturers had wanted of him without realizing that the one who had opened the door was anything but a troll. The courier responded while slowly approaching the jotunn giant that he was not his tormentor. Instead, the courier claimed he was the opposite. He would be Wothunak's hired liberator. The courier claimed to be employed by someone who was concerned about Wothunak's well-being from being executed by a new group of tormentors dispatched by Helskadi.

Wothunak was in a deep realization of shock upon hearing what was said. After being imprisoned and tortured for so long, it finally came to this, he thought to himself. It seemed strange from his point of view that a lone Nordling courier out of all the creatures in Shimmerfrost would come to his aid. This was especially true at a time ironically, according to this Nordling stranger, when Wothunak's supposed executioners were also about to arrive to end Wothunak's life. Alas, the jotunn titan grinned with delight, knowing that soon he would no longer be imprisoned after listening to his newfound liberator. The Nordling courier meanwhile began to look into how to free the titan. The courier noticed that only two sets of cylinder pins had secured the jotunn titan to the wall with attached shackles. After releasing two of them near the giant's foot, the Nordling then looked about again and found a ladder which he scaled to the wall near one shackle that secured the titan's left hand.

Upon releasing the pin that secured Wothunak's left hand with the shackle, the titan let loose a grunt and then swung his left hand and body over to pull the last pin out of the shackle that secured his right hand. With his fingers being too big, the titan yanked his right hand free from the shackles while using his weight to face the wall to kick back against it. Eventually, it worked. His strength forced the shackled restraint to break apart and fling across the cell with tremendous velocity, along with the pin that had secured it. This display had intimidated the Nordling courier to flinch and cover his head, before looking up and realizing what he had done. He had helped to set free one of the most fearsome creatures to have ever walked Shimmerfrost, let alone the world of Terrunaemara.

Wothunak, for his part, looked about while shouting in elation that after so many countless years, he was now free. He now can resume where he last plotted in taking over Shimmerfrost all for himself. But first, he would also plot to take revenge against those who had been involved in his imprisonment. He turned to the Nordling in resuming what the latter had disclosed to him, the titan asked the courier of the whereabouts of those whom Helskadi sent to do her bidding to kill him. The courier pointed upward, away from the cell, stating the would-be executioners awaited him outside the cave.

Wothunak turned his attention and anger to leaving the cell. He made his way out of the cave to smite his would-be executioners. The courier, holding a lit torch, guided the giant to the cave exit, but as he did so, the titan stopped while realizing that something was afoot. The cave was empty and there were no slain bodies of goblins, orcs, or trolls. When the courier turned and realized that the titan had stopped, he asked Wothunak why he did so. The titan responded by pointing out the same observation while stating that the courier would be a fool to mistake this titan giant, not sensing trickery and deception when Wothunak himself was the embodiment of those aspects.

The courier was at this point dumbfounded on what excuse to say for his defense, and it seemed he needed to come up with some explanation before this terrifying giant would turn on him. Swearing aloud while noticing the goblin shaman had watched them from a distance, the Nordling called out to the shaman that the plan had failed and to send in the snow trolls. The giant titan laughed and then took notice of the Nordling's form. The titan, in a bright flash, somehow took shape and transformed himself to look like an exact copy of the courier, not to mention assuming the same size as him. This transformed titan also ran quickly next to the courier and took him by surprise to engage in a sudden physical scuffle. Both of them moved around a lot and rolled over on the floor multiple times. This sudden action confused the goblin shaman and also the four trolls that came to attack the titan.

Now there were two of the same Nordling couriers that the goblin shaman and the trolls struggled to figure out which one to attack. Both of the two Nordlings, the real one and the impersonator, pointed fingers at each other only in who the goblin shaman and the snow trolls should kill. The goblin shaman was uncertain and confused until one of the two images of the courier asked the shaman to ask each of them a question about the goblin's personal interaction with them. The other courier who was the impersonator turned and looked while complimenting the former about how good he was in getting the goblin and trolls to discern which one of the two was the impersonator.

Wothunak, with his ruse exposed, suddenly changed back into his real form as a tall, imposing giant while using his powers to summon his magical weapon, a large double sided war ax, which he threw toward one of the snow trolls before using his powers to summon the deadly ax back to his possession. Then the other three snow trolls still attacked the titan, only to realize that they still underestimated Wothunak's powers, with the latter using his hands to emanate and cast forth two lightning bolts, one in each hand, to strike two of the snow trolls. Now one troll remained. This one carried a large oxtail whip and used it to strike at Wothunak. However, the troll found and realized that the whip made contact only against the titan's enormous ax. Wothunak pushed with insurmountable strength against the troll. The titan then swung his ax and cleaved the troll's head. With the immediate attacking trolls now all slain by his hand, Wothunak laughed while noticing that the Nordling courier disappeared in a bright flash. Wothunak looked about in anger and some sense of insecurity over what happened. He saw no one else in sight and cursed aloud in the cave. The male jotunn challenged the Nordling and the goblin shaman to appear before Wothunak and face him as true warriors.

However, the cave was filled with near-dead quietness, save for the cold ambient windy air, which made its way through the tunnel. Wothunak could feel the wind and the direction which it came from through the entrance of the cave. The jotunn titan then decided to leave the cave and focus on more worthwhile targets than a petty Nordling and goblin shaman. Wothunak followed the trail of the windy air. He saw along the way an exit with a bright light that pierced through several dozen yards through the gaping mouth of the cave. Only two lit torches stood out in providing further illumination of the cave. Wothunak heard sounds as he saw several goblin sentries that did not hear him moving to react, but they reacted to the sound outside instead. The goblin sentries, numbered about a half dozen, guarded the cave entrance while buying off some time for the rest of the denizens of the goblin-orc settlement interior to evacuate and find other under-mountain settlements to join.

The mouth of the cave itself was large by human standards, with measurements being just over twenty feet tall. However, Wothunak was much taller than a jotunn titan. He would rather not bear the indignation of others in seeing him crawl as a jotunn to get through the passage. Instead, he recalled his powerful abilities and took advantage of the deception that he could unleash. He still remembered the appearance, shape, and size of the Nordling courier. Within moments, the powerful titan shapeshifted himself once again into that Nordling person of smaller stature and made his way through the mouth of the cave to the outside world.

Though Wothunak was a powerful jotunn, the brightness of the light outside still stunned him momentarily. He was still more accustomed to darkness since he had rarely seen much brightness aside from the faintly lit torches that were few in his mostly dark and damp prison cell. As he adjusted to the brightness, he quickly saw the ensuing fight between the goblins and a sizable party of humans, dyr warriors, and even some smaller creatures, including at least one dwarf and one halfling. Among the figures that stood out, was a lone male elf adorned in exquisite brown-orange light armor. This elf impressively slew two goblins in short order with his bow and arrows from a long distance of at least fifty yards away.

Wothunak's observation of the elf ended when he noticed one other impressive figure, a female warrior who appeared to be a Nordling human adorned in armor that resembled the Valkyrie shield maidens from long ago. This female warrior, after throwing an impressive spear of searing light energy that resembled the sun toward a fallen goblin, spotted and pointed at Wothunak while being disguised as the Nordling courier. Wothunak, now free from the physical obstructions of the cave, dropped the charade of his impersonation of the form he assumed and reverted in a flashing transfiguration to his natural form as a tall, white-bearded, pale, blue-skinned jotunn. This giant stood between forty and fifty feet tall. He had shocked everyone around them, including the elf and Nordling Valkyrie warrior. The titan jotunn himself became filled with mutual awe by their reaction. He asked why they did not attack him. He wondered who they were if they were not the executioners that Helskadi dispatched to do her bidding and slay him once and for all.

The various figures looked somewhat surprised. They found it difficult to believe both by what they had seen and by what they had heard. The elf, being the first to recompose himself, stated that if he, this jotunn, was an enemy of Helskadi, then they certainly did not come to slay him. Linitus took a moment to pause before asking this giant who he was. Meanwhile, the various Nordling and dyr warriors spoke in their own tongues in speculating who this was. Marin, knowing enough of the Nordling language—even in the variant spoken by those from Shimmerfrost—had a shocked look on her face when she made out who they thought this was. She said aloud that it could not be who or what she thought it could be. Once again, another legend of her maternal barbarian heritage was, in fact, true. She told Linitus that there was only one figure from the lore of her culture who was a jotunn known to reside in the Har-Fjell Mountains in which he was banished, with this place being his imprisonment. It was Wothunak, the jotunn titan and supposed claimant of being a partial deity who waged a war and lost against his rival sibling, Helskadi.

The titan laughed while hearing this and complimented her for being familiar with his supposed fame while telling her as a correction from his point of view that he did not lose fairly but was betrayed by his other jotunn vassals who turned against him while fighting his sibling sister. Now that they knew who this jotunn was, the giant demanded that each of these figures identify themselves in return.

The Nordling woman dressed as the Golden Valkyrie replied she was

Marin. Marin explained that she, along with her elf companion, Linitus, were the leaders of their order called the Comradery. Linitus then informed the jotunn that they were spearheading a coalition between Nordlings and dyr folk to end the dark reign of Helskadi.

Wothunak laughed and clapped his hands sarcastically upon hearing this. He paused while everyone around him looked startled and dumbfounded at what he would do next. The jotunn then questioned how they thought they would take on someone as powerful as Helskadi and her forces when he could not. Marin responded they would find a way and gather as many together as possible to oppose the Winter Death Witch and her forces. The male titan nodded while conceding that they were welcome to try, though it would be their own funeral in which no one would bury them.

Marin became angered after hearing Wothunak's insulting doubts. She replied in a sharp, witty manner that at least someone did not imprison her and her companions for a millennium, unlike Wothunak. The jotunn titan, being quick to anger, questioned her audacity to insult him and his own standing. Linitus even turned his head and asked Marin what she was thinking about in making the tense encounter escalate into an unnecessary brawl. Marin turned to her elf lover and winked at him. She told him to trust her and to be ready to use his powers to create a whirlwind. Linitus shrugged and nodded.

The jotunn titan meanwhile summoned his large double sided war ax while challenging Marin to a duel, which Marin said she would accept while also stating that to make it more fair, given her smaller size, her elf lover would fight alongside her. The jotunn laughed before nodding and replying, stating that they would get their death wish to share together.

Everyone else backed off and moved away as fast as possible, knowing that a massive duel was about to unfold. Linitus instructed Wyatt to teleport Peat and all the dyr warriors back to Andarin and Alvissan's skyboat. Marin also told the mounted Nordling warriors to ride back down the path they took to reach the mountain. Everyone knew this would be a duel in which no one would be safe from watching up close. After another moment in which everyone else fell back to a safer distance while still watching, Wothunak took a moment to laugh at his opponents, seeing them as puny and almost unworthy to slay, though he thought to himself they were at least of more impressive standing in demonstrating their ability to command compared to many of the non-jotunns he had encountered before. Little did the titan know that he had underestimated the full extent of the martial prowess of the two figures he was about to face off against.

Marin and Linitus stood with their arms against their waists after watching the colossus jotunn laugh. Both of them were unimpressed, and their facial and body expressions were evident. Wothunak realized this and became enraged when the elf ranger bluntly told him it was Wothunak's move to make the first strike. The titan emanated a large lightning bolt and threw it toward his two newfound challengers. Linitus and Marin both dodged while leaping forward on opposite sides, away from the lightning bolt that struck the snow-covered ground from where they both previously stood side by side next to each other. Marin got up along with Linitus. The Princess Knight, tapping into her divine supernatural powers, summoned a lightning spear that burned like the sun. She hurled it toward Wothunak.

Much to Marin's surprise, the titan expected the move after watching her previous demonstration of powers against the already-fallen goblin sentries. Wothunak caught the lightning spear and turned it to throw toward Marin. His aim was off, however, as Linitus used his own relative newfound powers to emanate and fire off an arrow of the same enchanted power and searing energy as Marin's. The arrow struck the giant on the kneecap. The strike caused the giant to lose balance as he hurled back the lightning spear toward Marin, the latter of whom strafed and leaped forward to tumble out of the way. Linitus told Marin to move back toward him while Wothunak staggered. The giant cast another lightning bolt. This time Marin used her exotic, Valkyrie golden shield and deflected the lightning bolt back to Wothunak. The deflection struck the titan's other knee and caused him to fall to the ground on both knees.

Linitus again called Marin to fall back, which she did. The elf ranger next concentrated his divine supernatural powers. He uttered several words of incantation while closing his eyes and concentrating his mind, in which he summoned a powerful whirlwind from the ground. This whirlwind centered on Wothunak and picked up the jotunn titan off his wounded knees. The jotunn levitated while not being able to have control. Only moments later did Linitus let go of his train of thought to release the whirlwind from being active, which it rapidly dissipated while causing Wothunak to make an abrupt hard vertical drop almost thirty feet in the air.

The jotunn titan slammed down hard against the snow and was

stunned. It was long enough for Marin to move swiftly and unsheathe her flaming sword to raise in the air near Wothunak's neck. The giant regained consciousness. He turned and looked to notice that the Golden Valkyrie warrior had the upper hand while she told him to yield.

Surprised by his reaction, Wothunak again as before laughed while stating that he had underestimated both his adversaries, though he intended to still beat them in the duel. Suddenly, however, Marin was in awe. The jotunn titan looked at her intently and then concentrated on shapeshifting his form to appear like hers. He instantly disappeared and reappeared in a bright flash of light.

As the light dissipated, Marin could not believe what she now faced. It was an exact mirror duplicate of herself. Even Linitus was in shock and unsure what to do while trying to trace the movements of the mirror duplicate to distinguish and tell it apart from the real Marin in her actual form. It became difficult when the two clashed using flaming swords and shields. The two figures of the Princess Knight clashed through several back-and-forth blows, with neither prevailing over the other.

Finally, one of the two Marins called out to Linitus to attack the other. The other Marin, however, told him not to, while indicating he would be attacking the real one and not the impostor. Linitus, unsure, asked how we would know which one was the real one. The last Marin that spoke out told him to be ready to use his whirlwind powers to save the real one and that he would know which one was real soon enough. Immediately, that same Marin who last spoke, facing the identical adversary, surprised the other Marin by taking a breath and shouting in a wail-like scream toward the latter figure. The intensity of the scream became like a powerful echoing sound wave in which the mountains behind the counterfeit Marin began to shake and tremble. Soon a larger noise from above emitted, and a descending large cascade of snow slammed down from the higher elevation toward him. The other Marin that had shouted ran toward Linitus, with the elf ranger recognizing she had to be the real one to still use her divine powers, which Wothunak likely would not have been able to know about since he had not seen it and even if so, likely did not possess the ability to imitate that with his own powers in appearing as a mirror copy of others.

As the avalanche descended, Linitus again concentrated and said another series of incantations while closing his eyes, in which he summoned a light-intensity whirlwind to appear under him and Marin to carry them upward. Marin at the same time closed her eyes and issued her own series of incantations to generate a large turquoise sphere of energy, which had encapsulated both her and Linitus as they embraced each other before ascending upward through the whirlwind funnel. Meanwhile, the power and intensity of Marin's wailing that had struck Wothunak directly still left him momentarily stunned. Upon waking up from his semiconscious state, the jotunn's form in the copy image of Marin had lost its shape, and now he returned to his natural state as an actual jotunn giant. Upon gaining full realization and consciousness, Wothunak looked in disbelief, seeing what Linitus and Marin had done while turning back from hearing the noise with a shocked face in seeing that the impending wall of snow had thrust itself over in smothering Wothunak.

Linitus and Marin became shielded while inside the enchanted sphere as they floated in the whirlwind, which rose high enough this time for the two of them to be above the top of the avalanche. Only after a few moments did the two comrades let go from using their powers. The whirlwind gently dropped them while the glowing radiant sphere that encapsulated them dissipated. Marin and Linitus looked at each other with relief while nodding and giving a quick embrace. They then turned their attention to the matter at hand.

The Princess Knight and elf ranger both saw Wothunak nearly covered in snow, save for his head and the part of his neck being exposed. The titan, unable to move below his shoulder line while under the heavy layer of snow from the aftermath of the avalanche, cursed at the two adventurers. Linitus turned to Marin. They both thought the same thing. They could finish it right now and vanquish Wothunak.

However, Linitus contemplated and had second thoughts. He told Marin he had a better idea. They would spare the titan's life in exchange for his service in partnering with them to fight and depose Helskadi once and for all. Marin, however, cautioned her elf lover to be careful not to be too reliant on Wothunak. He was known to be an untrustworthy deceiver as much as he was a symbol of power and might as a titan. Linitus nodded but told her it was important they pose themselves in not only having the upper hand against Wothunak (which they did) but also using their demonstration of prowess with the titan witnessing as leverage for him to stay loyal. Marin nodded and waited until Wothunak overheard them. The jotunn asked them why they should trust him knowing his reputation as well as why he should trust them also. Marin stated to the jotunn titan that he needed them as much as they needed him to dethrone and vanquish Helskadi. Wothunak nodded while grunting to concede that she was right.

Somewhat surprised but glad that it worked, Marin turned with a slight grin toward her elven lover and companion. Linitus smiled modestly in return while telling her that now they had to figure out how they would set free the titan since he was in a new predicament of captivity. The elf ranger took a moment to ponder. He soon thought of an idea, which could work, but would take some time.

Moments later, after signaling Wyatt's attention from the skyboat above, the halfling wizard along with Peat quickly teleported to the surface outside the cave, which was now completely sealed by the avalanche. The halfling wizard and the dwarf guardian could not help but laugh while noticing how helpless Wothunak was being covered up to his neck in the snow. The giant grunted while cautioning them how grateful they should be for not suffering his wrath for displaying such jeering insults.

Peat turned to Linitus and Marin, asking what they intended to do. Linitus turned while still smiling and shocked Peat by stating that they were going to set Wothunak free in exchange for his services in liberating Shimmerfrost from the darkness of Helskadi.

Peat's face quickly turned from optimistic enjoyment to a saddened and shocked frown. He rhetorically asked Linitus and Marin that they could not be serious. Marin nodded while stating that this titan was one of their best chances in reaching Helskadi as well as helping them defeat her. They had no choice, and as deceitful as Wothunak was, the titan would need to depend on them to be on the same side if he were to get his revenge against Helskadi.

Peat nodded while grunting reluctantly and turning to ask how they could get this titan free given his current restrained state. Linitus then turned to Wyatt while asking the halfling wizard if he had ever used his magic spell–crafting powers to create a constant burning stream of flames. Wyatt nodded while Peat overhearing was in further disbelief, asking that they still could not be serious. The elf ranger replied that both he and Marin were and that Peat was welcome to indulge in making wager bets with anyone on board the skyboat for how long this would take before Wothunak could break free from the melted snow and ice that currently held him stuck in place. The dwarf gave a loud laugh before nodding. Peat agreed, now that Linitus mentioned it, the dwarf would take his offer.

As the hours passed, Peat being back on board, the skyboat shared news of Linitus's plan while making bets with everyone on board for how long it would take for Wyatt to help set Wothunak free from his frozen imprisonment. Marin and Linitus looked cautiously and patiently as their halfling wizard companion, breaking periods of sweat, worked his magic spell casting in maintaining a constant state of burning flames around the base of the snow surrounding Wothunak's neck and shoulders. In time before nightfall, the snow would melt and weaken enough for the titan to break free with his shoulders and arms to get himself out of the layer of snow and ice caused by the earlier avalanche.

Meanwhile, as the sun started to lower and set, Linitus and Marin, standing alongside each other, discussed the next phase of their plans. They both agreed that they would stop by the same dyr village they had helped in averting a raid by the large goblin-orc war party. They would recruit as many dyr folk warriors as they could to join them in their cause while assembling more forces of Nordling warriors at Nebelheim before marching a short distance north in launching a frontal assault on Helskadi through the only commonly known entrance to her domain. It was a narrow mountainous path that ascended into the higher elevations and inner part of the ringed Jotunn Mountains. From there they would march to and launch a siege assault against Helskadi's fortress city, Jotunheim.

The plan seemed simple enough, but Marin pointed out to her elven lover that while they would have a powerful ally by their side to ensure greater success in taking out a mutually powerful foe, they also had to be ready. She did not rule out the possibility that Wothunak may decide to turn against them again. Marin did not trust the titan. She knew the folktales from her mother's people well enough to believe his treachery and deceitfulness. Linitus, for his part, nodded and agreed while going off Wothunak's recent behavior, in which it seemed he would only be trustworthy when those dealing with him had the upper hand or had enough leverage against him for the titan to consider what would seem is in his best interests for the time being. Still, the elf wondered how long they would be able to have this upper hand in which Wothunak would not turn on them. Nobody among the Comradery knew at the moment. What they did know was that they had to make the best of what they had and launch the attack against Helskadi before she would do the same to them and their allies in Shimmerfrost.

Chapter Fifty-Three

Triumph of the Lord and Lordess of the Infernal Plane

War drums beat along with a large stream of feet pounding the bleak upper plains of Hadao Infernum. Passing through the intimidating staring-eye mountain pillars of Sanctum Oculi Malum, the victorious army of Decius marched in a parade line formation. They were only a few miles away from the new undisputed sovereign hell lord's massive jagged ornate fortified palace. The palace itself still stood surrounded by lava, with the only exception being two well-placed drawbridges. Decius himself now rode on a makeshift chariot pulled by a dozen of his strongest imps. The sovereign lord of hell held out Orcus's severed head with Decius's sharp-clawed hand gripping one of the horns of the now-deposed former hell lord. Orcus was angry. He cursed several times. However, he could do nothing other than look with his eyes and speak. He no longer could move on his own accord and reviled at his victor for giving him a fate far worse than perishing in the flames of Hadao Infernum itself. Decius laughed while telling his former incumbent rival he got what he deserved for what seemed a near eternity in torturing all the denizens in hell. The new hell lord promised he would rule this fiery realm with a more fair-handed approach compared to his deposed rival predecessor. Orcus mocked and interrupted Decius mid-speech as the dux had not finished speaking. Decius responded by abruptly punching the deposed red-skinned hell lord in the mouth. The dux then threatened Orcus to know his new place as a permanent defeated talking severed head and object of mockery.

Orcus wanted nothing more than for his upstart victorious rival to be incentivized by ending it once and for all. Until his recent defeat, Orcus had not known to a deeper extent what pain really was. Now, the deposed red-skinned hell lord was ready for Decius to give him a quick and relatively painless death. Orcus knew, however, that his nemesis would not do so—at least not yet. They both knew that Decius would publicly taunt and belittle Orcus, with no near end in sight. And so, the former reigning lord of hell internally conceded his defeat while refusing to admit it outwardly. He closed his eyes. He refused to look and see his foes take pleasure or to receive his acknowledgment of his victor. Still, it did not stop all those present to spectate in awe, enjoyment, and jest of how Decius had bested Orcus once and for all.

Behind Decius's chariot was a small makeshift litter force carried by eight chained fallen succubi prisoners. Decius and Lucia punished these fallen demonic seductresses to the humiliation of traversing across the plains of hell while carrying an extravagant makeshift-looking litter. On top of the litter, Lucia laid herself back in a prone position. She held her scourging cat-o'-nine-tails in one hand while holding in her other hand a chalice filled with the blood of one of the fallen succubi in battle. Just as Decius received the title Lord of Infernum, he gave his eternal soulmate, Lucia, for her unwavering loyalty, the title Lordess of Infernum. If Decius was to rule as the undisputed sovereign throughout the infernal plain, Lucia would rule by his side. She was his infernal queen consort, and he would make sure that all the subjects of this hellscape would bow down before her as much as they would with him.

Behind Lucia's crude yet grandiose litter marched in formation five other succubi prisoners in chains. They were surrounded by a guard escort of armed imps and condemned warriors. This victorious army took turns as they marched shouting in war cries and screeches to celebrate their victory. Before the war, they never imagined fighting alongside one who would break the cycle of torment in hell while deposing its original ruler. Now they were ecstatic. They could only imagine and speculate what their future would be like under the rule of their new hell lord. Still, Decius, along with Lucia at his side, seemed to be genuine in wanting to make their subjects' lives in this realm more stable and tolerable compared to before.

As the parade celebration carried on, near the tail end of the procession appeared Decius's colossal werewolf avatar. This gigantic beast amazed the spectators among the various condemned and imps. The black werewolf gargantuan caused many in the crowd to tremble as the superimposing beast unleashed a large howl that was loud enough for all the infernal realm to hear. It was a form of expression by the avatar beast announcing the new undisputed hell lord's arrival.

After another passing moment, Decius's processional entourage had approached only a hundred yards away from the walls of his fortress-palace. Upon hearing the call by the dux's avatar, all the imps that were assigned to guard the dux's abode had come out to the upper ramparts of the fortress. They watched with glee to see that their master, along with their deployed imp counterparts, had returned victorious from his war against Orcus. The imps became further excited upon seeing Decius holding the head of his fallen foe. These imps could not help but screech loudly in a chorus that even the condemned became somewhat startled.

As the new reigning hell lord watched the drawbridge to his castle lower for him and his present company to be welcomed upon entering, Lucia leaped out of her makeshift royal litter. She flew to her soulmate. Lucia approached her lover while holding the chalice filled with the blood of fallen succubi. She told Decius it was only proper for them being of Citadellan ancestry during their mortal lives to observe the custom that Decius knew and understood. He knelt while allowing his lover to quench her hands in the same blood-filled chalice to paint his face red. This was done as a Citadellan reenactment for bestowing honor upon the leading commander during a victory parade. It was a sign of attribution of identifying with the essence, which Decius received from one of his chosen ascribed deities, Laran, the deity spirit associated with war and victory. Despite no longer having the same human form that they once had, the Citadellan customs still were strongly ingrained in the minds of Decius and Lucia. They had vowed to never forsake the culture in which they grew up from their former mortal human lives.

After Decius received the gesture by his lover in having his face painted in the blood of his enemies, he held Lucia's hand to signal their union. In his other hand, he held Orcus's severed head. Meanwhile, Decius had his avatar come to both him and Lucia. The gargantuan beast allowed both of them to walk on its open paw while it lifted them high above the air. All present, the crowd could see in awe the demonstration of the power that their victorious master possessed in controlling such a superimposing creature. The crowd of condemned and imps still marveled in awe while Orcus opened his eyes again to look in disgust. The deposed hell lord was filled with shame and contempt. The chained succubi captives from the surface below that looked above hissed and seethed with hatred in their newfound uncertain fate.

Looking about the multitude of infernal denizens, Decius howled once more to command silence. He then proclaimed before the crowd to bear witness to his victory against his fallen foe while displaying Orcus as now being only a talking head of insignificance that would cause them no further harm. The dux and now undisputed Lord of Hadao Infernum proclaimed that going forward in his rise to power would mark a new future for all those living in the infernal realm to no longer have to worry about the sadistic torment and torture coming from this now-defeated monster.

Unsurprisingly, the crowd burst into shouts of joy. The crowd believed that someone had truly led them in not only being a liberator but also ironically still worthy to maintain a sense of order in being the lord of hell. While the cheers continued, Decius waited while signaling for the condemned masses to come to silence in which the dux proclaimed himself as sovereign of all of Hadao Infernum. He then turned his gaze to his soulmate, Lucia, and raised her hand high in the air as a gesture. He declared her name before the masses. Per his decree, Lucia would rule alongside him as his infernal consort and co-sovereign of hell. Together, he asserted, they would govern over Hadao Infernum as worthy rulers fixed on their sense of justice for their subjects rather than torture for the sake of enjoyment when such punishment was not warranted. However, he had no reservations in passing on justice toward those enemies they defeated and captured, even in the form of torture and for his subjects to enjoy for the past vile acts Orcus and his succubi committed against them.

Upon Decius finishing his proclamation, both the condemned and imp congregants once again erupted in cheers and screeches of jubilation. It was over. Or at least the torment was over from the uncertainty they previously felt in being pawns of Orcus to be used at his leisure and pleasure, including the prospect of dying a painful last death.

While the celebration of the triumph was still loud, Decius turned to Lucia to consult with her on how she wanted to pass judgment, or rather punishment, against the captured succubi whom Lucia held much animosity for. Lucia's eyes and lips became filled with a strong sense of blood lust as she wanted to make those fellow demonic sirens pay for what they did to her. They had mocked her, whipped her, and even violated her. Lucia, after taking a quick moment to ponder, replied to her lover how she wanted to make a public spectacle of those who would wrong her and, by extension, her lover. She told Decius that she wanted to witness her enemy demonic siren counterparts have their batlike demon wings ripped apart before having the faithful followers among the dux's ranks assist her in impaling the succubi one by one on large stakes. She wanted to make them suffer as much as possible as retribution for the suffering these succubi had caused upon her.

After confining to her lover, Decius nodded and grinned. He complimented her in suggesting what he thought would be a fitting form of justice and punishment to dispense upon their captured enemies. Lucia, pleased and sadistically grateful by her lover's response, promptly gave Decius a brief kiss before inquiring what they would do with Orcus, or rather, what was left of him with his severed head. Decius shrugged. He stated he had given little thought on the matter compared to what she wanted to do to the succubi prisoners, save that he was content for the time being to make Orcus witness the beginning of their reign, not to mention to witness the punishment of the former hell lord's succubi followers. The dux then took some delight in expressing how much he wanted to see the reaction of how much fear and dismay Orcus would have in being treated as an insignificant token locked away from known sight in the darkest dungeon cell within the dux's fortress. Decius also imagined while sharing with Lucia an alternative arrangement of having Orcus's talking head on display near the hallway entrance of his fortified palace. The deposed hell lord's living severed head would serve as an object of mockery and shame so that any guests who entered the dux's abode to pay respects would remember well the example he had made of the last hell lord so that none would consider betraying the new lord of hell.

Lucia grinned and complimented her lover on his last idea, which she thought would be splendid. Orcus overheard, however. The deposed hell lord became visibly angered. He cursed and objected to the dux and the dux's consort's authority. Lucia decided to address this matter after sharing and drinking the last fill of succubi blood in her chalice with her infernal lover. The duchess and lordess of hell, without much warning, smacked the chalice toward the deposed hell lord's talking severed head, which Decius still held in one of his hands. Decius then warned his fallen adversary to stay silent lest he receive more pain from him or his wife. Orcus grunted before closing his eyes, not wanting to give any more attention to his enemies or himself in his new embarrassing and helpless situation.

As the triumph outside Decius's fortified palace ended, the dux ordered the condemned followers to return to their respective settlements after thanking them. For the imps, Decius commanded them to disperse back to their various scattered territorial brood dwellings. The dux still kept a small but sizable token force of his little horned red demon followers to stand guard at his fortress.

There was much to discuss and much to do as he looked forward to governing his new sole domain along with his soulmate. As the dux commanded his gargantuan avatar to put him and Lucia on top of the rampart of the gatehouse entrance of his fortress, Lucia turned and asked Decius what else he would envision next for them to do together in building his infernal empire and furthering his will. Decius took a moment to think and, looking at his lover's face, remembered that as they were a couple bound together in love, they had still a family in the mortal realm. He remembered again about their son that they had together.

It had now occurred to Decius that both he and Lucia needed to let their son, Lucianus, know as soon as the latter had performed a summoning ritual that they were both doing well and that Lucia was now safe and united with Decius.

In thinking that, while they still conversed alone with each other, Lucia expressed her views on how she and her infernal werewolf lover should address matters of the mortal realm. Once summoned by Lucianus or Agaroman, Decius and she would make sure to find out about their son's well-being. They would also follow up in ascertaining what the current political state was as of late for the Imperial Remnant. She and Decius would advise their son accordingly by conversing with him on how to run and manage the stately affairs of the Imperial Remnant. When Lucia had expressed that concern, Decius nodded, thinking similarly as well.

Despite no longer running the Imperial Remnant directly as they each had in their previous mortal lives in Terrunaemara, Decius knew all too well since being condemned in Hadao Infernum the importance that one could have in advising and having an influence on others. This was especially true when it came to his most fanatic followers in the mortal realm who commune with the dux when he assumed his spectral form upon being summoned to advise his summoners. Both he and Lucia would make sure to still advise their son to better ensure the latter's success. As parents, they both wanted their son to achieve what they considered the pinnacle of "cursus honorem," the Citadellan concept of the way of honor in climbing up the ranks of social and political prestige. Decius and Lucia both knew Lucianus would achieve that by establishing a reputation for himself as he had done so far in being the true dark lord successor, just as his father once was.

Chapter Fifty-Four

Nebelheim under Siege

After several days of flying in the air via skyboat, Linitus and the rest of the Comradery were eager to arrive at Nebelheim. Once there, they would take a brief rest and stock up on provisions before making preparations to take the war to Helskadi's domain. The mood of everyone aboard the skyboat was upbeat and cheerful. Even inside the skyboat's cabin, Peat and Andarin held dwarven ale drinking contests, with Peat encouraging Wyatt to take part. On the boat's topside deck, Linitus and Marin stayed outside to once again enjoy the view of the shimmering auroras. This was a common sight to still gaze at and marvel at night in this cold, far-off place despite being unknown in the southwestern Citadellan coastlands of the Kingdom of Swordbane. To an extent, they had finally felt at ease more so than ever before. They had felt that conditions were ripe in planning to make the first move against Helskadi's forces. The Comradery would use Nebelheim as a base camp and staging point to gather warriors from all the allied Nordlings friendly to Nebelheim and the dyr warriors.

However, their thoughts soon changed as they saw the conditions firsthand from traversing across the sky. They looked below and were horrified to see the outskirt rural dwellings set ablaze just outside the town settlement's walls. Even the port harbor and the Nordling longboats that were moored burned with intense flames. The Comradery saw all about the perimeter of the settlement, a large besiegement force of various enemy creatures. The bulk of the enemy consisted largely of beastly folk that numbered in the thousands. They included goblins, cave orcs, and a few dozen snow trolls. Fighting alongside them were at least a thousand snow dwarves and dozens of ogres along with several jotunn warriors.

Linitus and the rest of the company knew this large army was no doubt belonging to Helskadi. Linitus could not help but state bluntly Helskadi's forces finally did it. They had finally unleashed their forces in an open-pitched battle against one of the region's largest human settlements. Marin placed her hand over his shoulder to comfort him. She told her lover with a determined tone that it would be their job to help fight back and win this war. Her elven lover nodded while composing himself. Linitus then took command in directing Alvissan to change the boat's course back to the west. Once they did so, the Comradery would warn both Wothunak and the dyr folk warband on the surface about the impending invasion by Helskadi's forces.

However, a lone young scream emerged among the burning wreckage and debris of a carriage wagon from below. This changed the Comradery's haste plans in warning their allied forces of the new developments as well as going to the defending forces of the settlement's aid presumably near the inner walls that separated the chieftain's stronghold from the rest of the palisade wall settlement. It was near that sight of burning wreckage, just a few dozen yards past the entrance of the outer palisade walls, where Marin spotted the small young Nordling girl lying near the body of a slain adult woman, presumably the girl's mother. A group of goblins and cave orcs huddled around her while screeching and shouting war cries and insults toward the young girl.

The sight haunted Marin and enraged her at the same time. She instantly reacted by expressing aloud her natural reaction of being enraged. She wanted to deny revisiting what reminded her over thirty years ago of how she lost her own mother before her eyes. The young girl had reminded Marin of herself at that age in realizing the ugliness of war and being stripped of the innocence of childhood. Marin wanted no one else to experience it, but she knew there would always be those who would. Still, it haunted her to see this happening as an adult while reminding her of a relatable past.

Linitus looked toward Marin and knew just as much that this was a visible reminder of her past, which she took as personal. The elf ranger commanded Alvissan to have the skyboat come to a halt while Marin went inside the cabin to get Wyatt outside to teleport the girl to the skyboat. Marin went back out from the cabin interior with a somewhat gloomy face about her. This prompted Linitus to ask what was wrong. The Princess Knight informed him that Wyatt was drunk. Linitus gave a brief sigh of irritation, wishing he had ordered for all the boat's alcohol provisions to be dumped. Regardless, he knew they had to make do in getting Wyatt to do his best in staying functional and composed to use his magic spell casting.

Another moment with a loud burst and the cabin door flung out with Peat staggering while carrying out Wyatt, who could barely walk himself. The dwarf looked at Linitus and asked if the elf called for him. Linitus nodded while Marin took a sigh this time around, saying that they were going to need to pray to the five major Citadellan divine spirits. Linitus, trying to stay focused and maintain morale, pointed to the wrecked wagon in flames with the little human girl below, surrounded by a large gathering of a dozen goblins and cave orcs. The elf ranger told his halfling wizard to teleport the girl to the skyship. Wyatt nodded while struggling to take out his wand and motion with his hands to start his spell casting.

Within an instant, a bright flash emanated below and then onboard the skyboat. To everyone's surprise and the person being teleported, it was not the little girl but a small green goblin in ragged leather clothing wielding a spiked club. The goblin gave a grunt, followed by a shriek. However, the goblin stopped after receiving a lethal blow to its head from the smack of Peat's war hammer. The dwarf cursed aloud, regretting his earlier decision to entice his halfling wizard comrade to a drinking contest on the eve of a future battle that was now becoming the actual present battle itself. As soon as the goblin lay dead and motionless, the dwarf guardian picked up the corpse and unceremoniously threw it over the side of the floating skyboat. The lifeless goblin dropped on top of one of the other goblins below. Peat could not help but compliment himself on his aim being accurate despite consuming four pints of Frostburg ale and four pints of Nebelheim lager within an hour.

Soon it was enough commotion to not only have the attention of everyone onboard the skyship but also the enemy army below. They all looked up, trying to identify the source of their newfound disturbance. One of them found it while signaling to the other beastly creatures. All of them looked up while shouting obscenities and making threats to the Comradery looming above. Peat then looked below and shrugged his shoulders while saying "sorry but not sorry" sarcastically. Marin, looking over his dwarven friend's shoulder, told him she doubted they would understand one word he was saying, and even if she translated it in Nordling, they still might not understand her. Peat replied again while shrugging his shoulders, stating it was worth a try. Linitus sighed while turning to Wyatt and telling him to hurry in trying to teleport the little girl again. Wyatt tried harder this time around to concentrate and cast his teleport spell, only to find that another beastly creature had appeared instead of the little Nordling girl.

Marin was visibly upset while looking at Peat who could not help but release another expletive and then apologizing for getting Wyatt intoxicated. The cave orc was still in awe of making sense of his surroundings, only for Peat to catch the creature by surprise just as the dwarf did with the teleported goblin from earlier. Only this time around, Peat, using his war hammer, swung low and struck the cave orc in the groin area. The beastly creature moaned in pain while everyone on board gave a startled reaction, almost sympathizing with the pain that the enemy had endured from Peat. Once again, Peat, though struggling somewhat, grabbed the creature and rolled the orc off the side of the skyboat. The orc fell hard on the ground, but not before hitting another one of the beastly creatures during the creature's descent. The dwarf once again shrugged while stating an old dwarven figurative phrase: "Me fall on thee once, se blame is on me; me fall on thee twice, se blame is on thee." Linitus looked at the dwarf while admitting in agreement with what Marin stated earlier that these creatures did not know what the dwarf was saying and that it would not make them any more or less angry. Peat once again shrugged. He agreed but responded it was still the goblins and orcs' fault this time around for not learning to avoid being hit by their fallen comrades.

Marin meanwhile became more visibly upset in still being unable to come to the aid of the little girl. She shouted an expletive while indicating that they did not have time for this. Linitus nodded while devising a different idea, asking if the halfling wizard could teleport him, Marin, and Peat below to the surface along with the accompanied warriors on board. The wizard struggled but nodded. Peat cautioned that he did not think that this was a good idea, but nodded after Marin gave him a cold, angry stare. She did not have time to wait any longer. Within another moment, the halfling wizard motioned his hands and did his best to concentrate on casting his spell. Within an instant, it had worked as the halfling teleported Linitus, Peat, Marin, and three Nordling warrior survivors from the battle of Lone Pass.

After teleportation, Linitus and his landing party quickly made sense of their surroundings. They noticed that they stood halfway between an enemy contingent and the little Nordling girl, who still wept on the body of her presumably deceased mother. Linitus told the company to maintain a shield formation while Marin quickly tended to the Nordling girl. The Princess Knight placed her hand over the frightened girl's head. The girl looked up and became immediately startled. She nodded and became calm once Marin assured her it would be okay and that they were here to rescue her. Marin gave the girl her shield and told her to use it to take cover while they would protect her. The little girl nodded again. The Princess Knight, wielding her flaming sword, formed up next to Peat and three of the Nordlings to form a shield wall against any charging enemies.

Linitus meanwhile withdrew his bow and unleashed one arrow after another against the enemy in rapid succession. The beastly creatures steadily dwindled in number. Marin put down her flaming sword. She focused on harnessing her supernatural powers to create a lightning spear. Once she had done so, the Princess Knight threw the enchanted weapon across the air. The attack struck and impaled three goblins. The rest of the immediate remaining goblins and cave orcs quickly charged in the meantime. Peat held a dwarven beer stein in his hand. He drank several gulps of ale (only this time it was strong dwarven ale) before shouting an expletive and unleashing a quick burst of temper in which he broke from the ranks of the other three Nordlings. The dwarven guardian, in a sudden furry while holding his large golden war hammer, spun sideways in several circular motions of orbit while knocking down nearly every goblin and cave orc that came into contact with him and his weapon.

At this point, the group of enemy goblins and orcs had depleted from several dozens to just half a dozen. Peat noticed while starting to stagger and fall down from being inebriated. Upon falling down and passing out, the dwarf stated again sarcastically that it looked like the numbers now were more even. The remaining group of cave orcs and goblins cowardly retreated to the rest of their army after realizing that they had advanced too far with the bulk of the forces still outside the gates and palisade walls of Nebelheim. Marin and Linitus sighed in relief while looking at each other.

The little Nordling girl, still holding Marin's shield, looked up after noticing the ensuing brawl was over. Still sobbing, she dragged Marin's shield while walking up to the Princess Knight. The girl presented the shield while speaking in her Nordling tongue that this belonged to Marin. Marin in return nodded and accepted the shield back in her possession, while reminding the little girl that she would be safe. The girl nodded while crying that her mother was deeply wounded. Marin picked up the girl and walked back to the site where the girl's mother lay flat on the ground. The Princess Knight inspected the girl's mother but knew that she had already died. Marin did not want to be the one to tell her girl, but she knew she had to.

Linitus could sense how much this troubled Marin. Saving the expense of having Marin find some way to let the girl know, the elf ranger took it upon himself to say that he and his friends were sorry that the girl's mother had to leave this life and pass on to the next one. She would be in the afterlife with her ancestors to be at peace. Hearing the elf's words while processing it, the little girl cried some more but understood even though she knew as much as she did not want to accept it, especially since her mother did not make it. Marin held the girl harder in her arms to imagine feeling the girl's emotional pain. The Princess Knight wanted the pain to pass from the girl to her.

A few more moments passed. The only ambient noise that could be heard was the sound of war on the other side of the settlement. Large stones were hurled from catapults that Helskadi's army had used. These siege weapons were delivered to the Winter Death Witch by Lucianus's skybeast along with the armament and armor shipment. The catapult siege machines hurled stone projectiles that could be heard with the impact they made in battering against the palisade walls and various dwellings within the settlement. Other sounds could also be heard, including the shouts that the Nordling defenders gave from either being in pain or from war cries of defiance in holding back against the attackers.

The sounds were enough for Linitus to assess the situation in which he knew they had to return on board the skyboat. The elf ranger took his bow and readied one of his special flare arrows that he aimed high in the sky before letting loose. As he cast off the arrow, it sparked a bright streak in the sky. It was enough to catch the attention of not only the skyboat but also anyone else in the vicinity who could spot it. From the distance, the dyr folk warband that followed along the land could see the flare several miles away as they hurried to rendezvous with Linitus and his company. However, several of the enemy scouts and some of the beastly general infantry spotted it as well while making loud shrieks and war cries. Peat, with an alarmed face, looked at Linitus and questioned his course of action as being the most sane one. The elf ranger shrugged it off while stating that this was his signal as always to let Wyatt know to transport them whenever he and others were on the surface the halfling wizard was floating on a platform high above the ground. Linitus followed up by stating this was also a signal to let their allies know where they were. This should not be a surprise for Peat as he knew this before. However, Peat countered, indicating for the first reason that this time was different as Wyatt had become inebriated to the point he might even be passed out.

As another moment went by, Linitus and his present company on the surface still waited with eagerness to know what was happening on board the skyboat. Andarin looked below from the fly vessel after noticing. The dwarven pilot asked what they were doing. Linitus shouted back to have Wyatt ready to teleport them. Andarin looked down on the deck of the skyboat with Wyatt still passed out then turned to look down at Linitus and in a sarcastic tone asked if the elf knew whether the halfling wizard could teleport them from the surface while in his sleep.

Marin shook her head with some frustration and anger toward Peat in blaming him for enticing Wyatt to indulge in dwarven drinking habits that the halfling was not accustomed to. Peat shrugged off and sighed. The dwarven guardian indicated again that he was sorry for not knowing how much of a drink the halfling could handle and that it would not happen next time. Marin replied in a pessimistic and sarcastic tone that with luck, they will live long enough that there will be a next time to celebrate.

Within minutes, the Comradery could hear a loud stomp that grew louder with each step. It was the sound of jotunn footsteps. Marin turned to Linitus and asked if he thought it might be Wothunak. Linitus shrugged before realizing as the loud footsteps came closer in which they could see it was indeed a tall jotunn, but not the one they had struck a pact with. Instead, it was a tall, pale-looking humanoid giant that wielded a large wood and steel war hammer. This jotunn wore a massive chain mail armor shirt along with exquisite pauldrons, bracers, and boots that looked similar to dwarven-made armor except that it was not. This giant had a dark blonde beard and blue eyes. He also wore a helmet with multiple protruding spiked bones and two larger protruding animal horns. Behind this giant came another series of loud footsteps that made the earth tremble. There were three other jotunns who, though not as well equipped, were still imposing on their own accord. These three other jotunns wielded long blunt clubs from makeshift trees pulled from the ground. Then a wave of goblin shrieks and orcish war cries became more pronounced as several hundred of them approached just outside the palisade gate of the southern town's entrance.

The jotunn leader shouted out in a large guttural tongue, which Linitus did not understand but knew it was Nordling and in which Marin could decipher what the jotunn leader said. He had called them out for a challenge between him and their group's best champion. Linitus was ready to unsheathe his blade and answer the giant's challenge, but then Marin, placing her hand on her lover's shoulder, told him not to. It would be her challenge to accept to affirm the Nordlings with more conviction, who still considered her one of their own, to accept her legitimacy in leading them even if she would defer to Linitus whom she regarded as the better of the two in leading them.

Linitus then looked at Marin. He took her hand that she placed on his shoulder. He moved her hand toward his lips in which he gave a brief, subtle kiss before telling her to fight with caution. Marin nodded before turning and stepping out near the town gate entrance to face the jotunn general.

When the surprised jotunn leader saw who his challenger would be, the giant released a large laugh while holding one of his hands toward his belly. He spoke in Nordling again after taking another moment to compose himself. In response, he could not hold back from asking if that was the best that the Nordlings resisting the rule of Helskadi offered—a Nordling woman dressed up to look like a fake imitation of a legendary Valkyrie.

Marin's face became fierce and enraged while rebuking the jotunn's words. She told him he would find out soon enough just how real she was. The jotunn, still full of confidence, laughed again while replying if Marin knew who he was. Marin replied in a sharp, witty tone that she did not care, nor would it matter only that those bearing witness to their duel would know that soon enough he would be a dead jotunn. The jotunn, feeling insulted by her words, responded, stating that he was Fornjotr, one of the male chiefs of the jotunn folk and second only to his matriarch Helskadi in which he would receive favor from her after he is done smiting all those that resist the Winter Death Witch's power, including Marin.

Marin gave a visible and annoyed look. With a jest sigh, the Princess Knight refuted his pledge and she stated that as soon as she bested him in combat, she would go after his matriarch to send her asunder. Fornjotr, enraged, shouted curses in his jotunn tongue while charging at full pace with his large war hammer lifted. Marin, anticipating his move, quickly dodged just in time as the jotunn giant swung diagonally and missed. Meanwhile, the Princess Knight quickly seized the offensive in delivering a counter move of her own in which she quickly used her divine supernatural powers to emanate a spear of lightning in her hands. She quickly hurled the enchanted weapon toward her pale giant opponent. The enchanted summoned weapon quickly struck Fornjotr at the back of his leg joint. The jotunn ached in pain while nearly falling and barely able to maintain his balance. He turned around while limping and staggering, just to realize what had happened after he pulled the lightning spear out from his back leg only to realize the weapon disappeared out of thin air.

Marin caught her breath momentarily while realizing that she had not only angered her giant foe that she wounded but that he was perhaps more dangerous and certainly more angry than before. Fornjotr, while staggering over to Marin, raised his war hammer up in the air to strike harder upon Marin. Marin leaped back to dodge the attack. However, the tall giant quickly followed up with another vertical attack at a distance which Marin did not expect. Fornjotr used his massive war hammer to strike the ground in front of her. The shock and impact of the blow of his hammer had been noticeable and loud enough for those near to hear. The impact sent tremors across the surface, which forced Marin to lose balance and fall backward.

Temporarily stunned, Marin looked up while having her back against the ground. The jotunn chieftain laughed while raising both his hands, holding his war hammer high above the air. Before delivering the expected death blow, he laughed again while asking in Nordling if Marin, whom he referred to as the Golden Valkyrie impostor, had any last words. Marin grinned while stating that those would be his last words. Startled for a moment, the jotunn looked confused about what she meant while he lowered his guard before collecting himself to kill her. However, it was long enough for Marin to inhale and channel all her focus and energy to tap into her other divine supernatural ability. Before Fornjotr could strike Marin with his war hammer, the Princess Knight exhaled with a loud wailing voice a scream that had practically deafened the pale giant. It was powerful enough to have her adversary lose his balance and fall backward while moaning in pain.

Marin, seizing the opportunity to follow up again in another counterattack, quickly got up to her feet and with both hands holding her flaming longsword, she quickly slashed with as much ferocity as possible against the throat of the jotunn chieftain. Fornjotr bled to death while

Marin continued to slash viciously at the same spot. It was as if her rage for survival had taken over and she embraced that associated primal instinct and martial aspect of her Nordling heritage as she had time and again when her life seemed it was nearing its end, only for her to make a comeback to defy all odds. This time, however, she did not let go of her rage, not until she had severed the giant's head from the rest of his body.

The ferocity of her fighting spirit had captured the attention not only of her comrades and the Nebelheim defending allies but even the portion of the enemy army that had seen all that transpired from the duel. The witnesses among the enemy army were both mortified and enraged. She was powerful, and they had seen someone for the first time pose a credible threat to the forces of darkness. None of the beastly creatures nor the jotunn and snow dwarves believe such a sight would happen. Now, they knew a different aspect of fear, which they had themselves experienced rather than being the messengers of spreading to the innocent they preyed upon.

As the emotions of uncertainty of the creatures took over, a lone goblin shaman appeared. This shaman told the rest of the army to retreat and pull back. The beastly army sensed that this goblin shaman may have commanded enough authority and had a sense of prudence to look after their best interest after losing their leader. The rest of the beastly army heeded the acting goblin shaman's orders and routed back toward where they came.

Meanwhile, it was at this point by which the dispatched large warband of dyr warriors charged from the west going eastward to intercept and clash against the retreating army of Helskadi. The Nordling chieftain of Nebelheim had also begun to send a small warband of their own warriors from the various fortified positions of the settlement to pursue. The chase was on as the tides of the battle quickly shifted in favor of Nebelheim and their newfound allied coalition led by Linitus and the order of the Comradery. Only one thing surprised Linitus and those immediately close to him before they gave chase. The goblin shaman himself simply stood there and watched. It was enough to cause Peat to ask why he was not retreating with his other beastly comrades.

Linitus, however, understood and saw through this illusion. He quickly said aloud, stating that this was no goblin. Marin and Peat as well as everyone on board the skyboat who could hear from looking below were confused and startled at what he had just said and questioned if someone somehow did not put a spell on him. Instead, Linitus looked at the goblin that looked at him, impressed while suddenly clapping at the elf ranger and stating that he had done well. Linitus looked sternly and cautiously while receiving the acknowledgment and going forward in stating that the creative trickery was over and that Wothunak could return to his original form.

The same creature that had appeared as a dark holy goblin nodded before undergoing a rapid shapeshifting transformation to return to his original large giant form as the male jotunn titan that everyone in Shimmerfrost knew about from the folktales that passed on from generation to generation. Wothunak, towering high above everyone else save the floating skyboat, looked down at Linitus, Marin, and everyone else as far as the present company that was on the surface. The giant was astonished that he had still garnered their attention while the forces under Fornjotr's command had escaped as quickly as melted ice would drip to the surface on a warm spring day. The giant prompted them to ask what they were waiting for. Linitus, though cautious in discerning whether he and his comrades could trust this deceptive titan, ultimately chose to follow his suggestion while telling everyone else with Marin translating what he said in Nordling to charge forth and pursue as many of Helskadi's retreating warriors as they could catch up to intercept. Charging forth the now combined forces of the dyr folk warband along with the Nordlings of Nebelheim traversed the nighttime terrain while holding torches and weapons in each hand. Though they did not strike down all of Helskadi's warriors, they struck down several hundred of the enemy.

The remaining surviving enemy dark horde army (about half its original size due to the fierce ensuing fighting and fierce resistance by the defending Nordling allied force) escaped north back toward the legendary narrow gated pass known as Tor Jotunn Pass, or more commonly called Jotunn Gate in Nordling tongue, which led ultimately the path back to Helskadi's fortress domain farther north and nestled deep within the Jotunn Mountains. As it became midnight, Linitus called off the pursuit, not wanting to fall too far ahead of possibly being overtaken by a rallying counterattack with the enemy to overwhelm the allied coalition in spreading their forces too thin. Within an hour, the coalition of Nordlings and dyr folk warriors rallied outside the gated palisade walls on the northern side of Nebelheim. There they got to see the abandoned siege equipment that the predominant beastly army had deployed to attack the Nordling settlement.

Upon laying sight of what they saw, their faces were in awe. Nearly a half-dozen siege catapults have been left behind. These siege weapons were not only terrifying for the native forces of the region to see (as they had never seen before) but also for Linitus and the other original Comradery from Swordbane. These siege weapons were made of the same dark material that had been known only by the Imperial Remnant. Now, the Imperial Remnant had delivered the powerful arms and armament of Shimmerfrost while the young werewolf would want something in return. Linitus could not help himself but ponder for a moment what that would be specifically other than gaining a powerful ally from the far north to supply the Remnant's forces with more beastly creatures.

As the prevailing defending forces continued to muster outside the north palisade walls and gate of Nebelheim, Marin, along with Linitus, gave an impassioned speech in which she stated before all those present that together they had withstood the combined forces of darkness that hail from this region and that if there was a fighting chance to end the terror of Helskadi once and for all, that they must stand and march together against the Winter Death Witch and her forces deep in her own home territory. Linitus followed up by stating that if the dyr folk and the Nordlings continue to work together, more of their own people will recognize the merit of what they accomplish to join their cause.

Jarl Harleif marched out with his retinue of bodyguards. The Nebelheim chieftain then directed all his Nordling warriors to be under Linitus and Marin's command after being impressed by the display of leadership and surprise victory they achieved. Linitus and Marin acknowledged the chieftain's trust and bestowment in transferring leadership to them while nodding their heads. Immediately, Linitus informed the Nebelheim chieftain to have trusted couriers make haste and spread the word of the news of the victory throughout all the outlying Nordling villages to galvanize support and volunteer warriors in the area to assemble outside the gates of Nebelheim. Within two days, they would make haste to march north toward the mountain pass entrance into the interior of the towering Jotunn Mountains.

All the Nordling warriors, civilians, and even the dyr folk let out loud cheers of celebration throughout the night. What seemed impossible now became the reality in which they realized that they actually had a chance once and for all to stand up against Helskadi and her overwhelming army of minions.

As the many survivors celebrated the victory, Marin looked across the distance and still saw the same little girl that she rescued look back toward the direction in which she lost her mother at the south part of the settlement. Marin would go to the girl to comfort her again. She would see that there was someone to care for the girl and who would genuinely care about her.

Though the celebrations continued throughout the night, it was a sad and painful victory for the little surviving Nordling girl. Marin still tended to her while having empathy for the loss of the girl's mother.

Linitus realized this as well. He came to join Marin in comforting the girl as best as he could while assuring her they would give her mother a proper funeral under their Nordling tradition. As the night went on, the Comradery would take turns in shifts to rotate in helping the local town collect the remains of the fallen and hold a funeral in cremating the remains with makeshift pyres outside of the walls of Nebelheim. In due time, the skyboat would be ready in preparation to spearhead the coalition's next stage of the war.

Chapter Fifty-Five

Communing with the Infernal Lord and Lordess

  Lucianus was due to arrive back home to Sanctum Novus during the evening while traveling aboard his skybeast vessel. The dark brown and gray werewolf child planned to set about the following day to make future weapons shipment preparations. He would use the desert city's blacksmithing forges to prepare the next batch shipment of weapons and armament. Once ready, he would do as before and plan again to deliver the shipment to Helskadi on the next trip up north. Just as before, he would again seek to swap his shipment for more loyal beastly creatures that Helskadi could afford to trade.
  As far as the first shipment of beastly creatures that Helskadi provided for Lucianus, Agaroman advised the young dux where to have this mixed warband of irregular cave orcs and snow trolls to be used for raiding. Either the Nordling barbarian settlements along the interior (among those that have not already submitted to the Imperial Remnant) or the settlements belonging to the Kingdom of Swordbane near the border just west of the Remnant's territory would be prime raiding targets. It would also make retaliation difficult should the Nordlings or Swordbane discover the origin of these beastly creatures. Lucianus opted to raid the barbarian villages. Doing so, the young werewolf saw it as being more advantageous. It would weaken a potential ally for Swordbane in the future while providing for more potential barbarian slaves that the Imperial Remnant would use as

part of their labor force. Lucianus recognized a second advantage as well. He could use the conquered Nordlings as additional irregular auxiliary troops in service to the Imperial Remnant just as his father had done with the Nordling tribe of Barbarum Aries. In doing so, he would repeat a similar campaigning pattern as his father. Decius, during his mortal life, was renowned for his raiding against many of the mountainous interior and coastal Nordling settlements to gain their fealty and clientship by outright force. The prospect of repeating his father's prestige in such a feat was within the lucrative realm of consideration in Lucianus's mind.

This time was different, however. Lucianus, with Agaroman's advice, would have the Shimmerfrost beastly creatures assigned to Uruk-Kazaht temporarily. They would undergo training more thoroughly by the orcs and goblins of the high basin settlement before these new arrivals would be dispatched to raid their targets. These northern beastly minions would keep the same weaponry and clothing as they had before in their harsh, far northern environment. They could not wear or display any associated paraphernalia that would tie them to the Imperial Remnant. In doing so, this would make it harder for the coastal Nordling tribes or the Kingdom of Swordbane to place blame upon the Imperial Remnant. It was a shrewd and clever plan to conduct this type of raiding warfare using newly recruited mercenaries unknown in much of the western continent of Hesperion.

When the skybeast actually arrived, the vessel floated slowly above the brightly lit desert city's street oil lamps and near the top levels of the most prominent buildings. Lucianus along with Agaroman teleported to the main plaza and forum near the Temple of Laran, the senate curia building, and close to the dux's palace. The young werewolf dux, upon Agaroman's suggestion, would hold a celebration triumph at the main plaza and forum the next day. Lucianus would have his wizard advisor proclaim the young dux's victory against the Swordbane skyship crewed by the Comradery near Lone Pass in the far north. This proclamation with his soldiers as living witnesses would serve as a sign of Lucianus's legitimacy in claiming the title as the true heir and successor of being a dark lord. It would also be a reminder of the young new dux's resolve to carry out revenge for the death of his mother and father. Lucia and Decius were still revered throughout the Imperial Remnant's domain but especially in the desert capital city of Sanctum Novus itself.

For the time being, Lucianus along with Agaroman would proceed to the Temple of Laran. Once inside the main temple sanctuary, they would both perform the sacred rite of summoning Decius's spectral spirit. Lucianus would commence the ritual by giving an incense and libation offering before the altar dedicated to both Laran and Calu. Following as escort to the young dux was a small elite group of human Citadellan knights from the order of the Black Wolf, an orc war captain, and a goblin shaman. The young dux followed his father's precedent and included the latter two as honored senior members of the dux's council along with Agaroman. Lucianus had also dispatched a group of Black Wolf knights mounted on heavy dire wolves to notify Senator Diem of his grandson's arrival. Lucianus wanted to extend the invite to his grandfather should Diem wish to join his grandson in being present for summoning Decius. After all, they both wanted to find out an update on Lucia's well-being from when Decius last reported about her.

Lucianus would wait patiently for his grandfather senator's reply in which Diem eventually entered the temple after a half hour had passed. Lucianus, upon seeing his grandfather, ran toward him with open arms. The two embraced and exchanged customary familial kisses on the cheek while Diem informed his werewolf grandson that he had missed him and kept him in his prayers over the past several weeks.

Lucianus looked up to his grandfather. The young dux nodded. He stated that he knew and made sure he would come back alive to his grandfather. The young werewolf also let his grandfather be one of the first to know in the city that he had avenged the death of his mother by taking down the skyship of those he held accountable.

Diem nodded. He told his grandson that he was pleased to hear the news. Still, both of them knew that they still missed the one whom they loved and knew as daughter and mother, respectively. Lucianus sobbed only briefly before he acknowledged his grandfather was right.

The young dux then returned to the thought at hand about his mother. Lucianus signaled to his grandfather while pointing to the altar that it was time. It was time for them to do the summoning ritual to commune with Decius's ghost and find out how Lucia was faring.

Diem once again nodded while following his grandson's lead in walking toward the altar. The elder Citadellan statesman watched closely to observe his werewolf grandson usher several incantations. Lucianus also held a brazier. He slowly burned some incense and poured a cup full of red Citadellan wine on top of the incense. It served as an offering before a small statue symbolizing Calu and another for Laran.

Within moments, all those present became surprised by what they saw. Instead of being just the spectral ethereal form of Decius, they also saw the original dux joined by another figure who emanated the same hauntingly airy form of shade. All present were lost in words as well as mesmerized by what they saw. It was Lucia again in her postmortal ghost form standing next to her beloved soulmate. Lucianus and Senator Diem struggled to compose themselves. Lucianus recollected himself first, however. He knelt while asking his parents what happened and how Lucia was faring.

Decius and Lucia both nodded. The older, original dux told his successor son and all present that he had finally found and rescued Lucia while ending the infernal struggle once and for all. Decius proclaimed he ascended as the undisputed lord and sovereign of Hadao Infernum. Orcus, according to Decius, had been defeated once and for all.

Lucia took a moment to speak after Decius stopped responding. The ethereal succubus approached her werewolf son while extending her faded translucent ghost hand toward Lucianus's canine ears and jagged jaw cheek line. She wanted to embrace and hold her son, though she knew she could not physically feel him. Still, she had known this feeling before from the other end. This was when she was once mortal in human flesh and when Decius in his ghostly form tried to no avail to have physical contact with her. Regardless, the gesture of her motioning was understood by Lucianus. He tried to imagine the feeling of acceptance that his mother wanted to exude. At the same time, the young werewolf knelt his head and leaned closer toward his mother. He placed his hands around and through the translucent spectral form of Lucia. It was enough for the two of them to experience that sense of acceptance emotionally even if they could not physically.

Decius respected the bond between mother and son. It was a familial bond, which Citadellan culture had always revered since ancient times during the era of the original Lupercalian Empire. The ethereal werewolf hell lord waited another moment before he interjected in inquiring with his son on the status of the weapons shipment and beastly servant recruit exchange with Helskadi.

Once the new reigning infernal lord brought up the matter, Lucianus responded sharply with respect toward his father. Lucianus stood at attention in a postured form of military decorum. The young werewolf stated that the exchange went well and that he avenged the death of his mother Lucia and, by extension, Decius's death from ten years prior.

According to Lucianus, he had taken down the Comradery's skyship in a blaze using the skybeast, and foreseeably, everyone that was on board the Swordbane enemy vessel perished. Decius unleashed a howl of sadistic joy. He was pleased though somewhat skeptical. From his past experience, he knew his mortal adversaries had always found a way to evade death at his hands. Decius cautioned Lucianus to be aware and ready if they somehow survived the blaze from the skyship.

Lucia also commended her son with a wide gleeful demonic smile. At least from her point of view, if the heroes of the Comradery survived, they were left stranded in the harsh environment of the far north. Their chances of surviving, according to her, were far less likely than if they faced the Imperial Remnant as they did in their last encounter near the border by the Great Azure Lake.

Agaroman was eager to return to what he saw as the greater matter at hand. The bald wizard interrupted with a humbled and respectful disposition while addressing Decius as his lord. The wizard stated that Lucianus had done well in recruiting irregular beastly warriors from Shimmerfrost. These strange new warriors would be used to further the interests of the Imperial Remnant. They would be deployed as an unmarked reconnaissance force that would raid and pillage along the territories belonging to the coastal forest interior Nordlings that were friendly to Swordbane. Eventually, these warriors would be used to raid the outer territories of Swordbane itself from the coastal north. In doing so and by being untraceable with no identifiable markings associated with the Imperial Remnant, it would make it much harder for the Remnant's involvement to be proven and for Swordbane to consequently declare a justified war against the Remnant.

Decius howled from being impressed again while standing alongside Lucia. Lucia complimented both Agaroman and Lucianus in this shrewd plan. Decius then looked sharply at Lucianus. The specter of the werewolf hell lord walked up closer to Lucianus and stated how proud he was of his son's showing the first steps to be worthy of being called the next dark lord while succeeding his father. Lucianus nodded while stating he would do what was best in following his father's example. The young werewolf child strove to do so to bring further prestige not only for himself but also for the family names of both his parents (House Anici on Decius's family line and House Diem for Lucia's family line). Ultimately, Lucianus also did this because he believed in his father's vision. He believed what he did would be necessary to realize the reality that his parents sought in ushering the return of the next Lupercalian Empire in which the continent of Hesperion had not witnessed such power and prosperity in over a millennium. It was hard for them to not believe in it after all, considering Lucianus was born in a divine prophetic way as a Lupercalian when neither of his parents (being both human Citadellans) were werewolves themselves at the time, though Decius, being the progenitor of his son's werewolf identity, would himself eventually and unexpectedly transform into being a Lupercalian as well while discarding his human flesh during one of his last battles against the Comradery at the Swordbane capital a decade ago.

As the evening carried on, with Lucia's urging and Senator Diem's backing, the conversation shifted into a more casual direction. Lucia and Decius's specters would follow Diem and Lucianus back outside to the desert city plaza. They proceeded into the dux's palace, where they would share the remaining passing time together in the privacy of the estate's living room hallway near the atrium. Agaroman agreed to stand guard near the entrance along with a detachment of human knights from the Order of the Black Wolf. Senator Diem and Lucianus were both fascinated and yet somewhat horrified by the tales that both Decius and Lucia would tell them in their pursuit to overthrow the former sovereign of hell for Decius to take his place.

Eventually, within an hour, the effect of the summoning rite that Lucianus invoked began to wear. Decius and Lucia were slowly fading. All four of them as a family were aware while Lucianus's parents' shades continued to fade. Before departing, Lucia and Decius both reached out their translucent hands toward their son's shoulders while telling him they both loved him and to stay close to both his grandfather, Senator Diem, and his closest advisor, Agaroman, to heed their advice and follow Decius's path in becoming a great dark lord. Lucianus vowed to do so while telling his parents before disappearing that he would keep them in his prayers and continue to spend time with them as much as he could each night upon summoning them. The shades of his parents nodded while telling their son to always remember that they were family, along with Lucia's father.

Diem, feeling remorse for the life that his daughter chose, accepted and confided to her he understood why she did it. He understood that she truly was Decius's soulmate and exemplified the best of what a Citadellan husband could ask for from a wife such as her in having such devoted and unconditional piety in being so willing to follow her lover to the same path no matter where it led, even into hell. Diem still wished she would be united with the rest of their house family line in the afterlife heaven of Caelum, but it was closure to know that she found her happiness in being back together with the one she loved so dearly, no matter how bleak the place was. He understood that she and Decius were together and would face whatever challenges were set before them. Still, the aging senator asked Decius to promise him he would still do everything possible to look after Lucia's safety and well-being so she would never be in a vulnerable position as she was previously in being a prisoner of the now-deposed former lord of hell and torment. Decius nodded and vowed he would before his ghost spirit faded along with Lucia, the latter of whom expressed her love to her father before she faded out as well.

Lucianus realized that now in his own inherited estate, he was alone with his grandfather save for Agaroman and the few posted elite Black Wolf knights near the entrance that still stood guard. Lucianus approached his grandfather and simply hugged him. Senator Diem, feeling touched by the familial expression his grandson exhibited, returned the same gesture. Lucianus then looked up to his grandfather. The young werewolf dux told him that he would do his best to heed the elder's advice along with Agaroman. The young dark lord also confided that he knew what he had to do to carry out his father's legacy. Diem nodded at his grandson. The elder senator told his grandson that he trusted Lucianus as much as the young dux believed in himself to be a capable leader. The senator bid his grandson sleep well while leaving him outside his personal chamber room that once belonged to Lucianus's father.

Lucianus slept as best as he tried, but he could not hold back in his deepest dreams in aspiring to do what his father set out before him. He dreamed of the day that he would walk into the main street of Swordbane's capital, Citadella Neapola, as a conqueror with a loyal army behind him. Lucianus worked his way backward in his mind in how he would reach that outcome. He saw only the vile acts that he believed would have to be done to subjugate the capital of his most hated enemies. Still, there was a part of him that called out to be patient, to be different, to rule not by force but by a greater sign of power, which he did not yet know. He yelled out and demanded an answer of what that sign was. Still no reply other than an empty eerie voice that told him with patience and understanding he would one day know.

As soon as he heard that voice, he quickly sprung up from his bed with a violent sense of alertness until he realized there was no one else there. He was alone. It made him uncomfortable yet also challenged him to learn to adapt and be more accustomed to that feeling. Still, the voice he heard was unlike any he had heard before. It was a soft, feminine voice and one in which he wondered if he would hear again. Perhaps it was a portent into his future to pave the road he had yet to undertake.

For now, Lucianus was content to return to his slumber knowing the next day he would be busy along with Agaroman in making the next round of preparations to have another shipment of armament forged and tightly packed into the skybeast under his supervision before making plans to set off again to the far north. From there he would conduct another round of exchanging his weapons shipment for more far-north beastly warrior recruits. These irregular beastly warriors would be a key part of his plans to weaken Swordbane and the whole of Hesperion. It was a plan that Lucianus would see to make sure his vision would become reality one day.

Chapter Fifty-Six

Battle at Jotunn Gate

    A lone cloud loomed high above the sky. It remained separated from a cluster of many other clouds that filled the cold spring sky of Shimmerfrost. The unusual cloud formation looked over the dotted forest landscape below that stood before a narrowing valley and mountainous pass. One prominent feature stood out that blocked both ends of that pass. Though not as tall as the mountains that it stood in front of, this one feature still stood out as one of the tallest structures in the region. It was the legendary Jotunn Gate that was over several hundred feet tall. Both sides of the main gatehouse were adjoined by an enormous stone wall. The wall was built from an ancient, bluish-gray stone quarry that the jotunn folks and the snow dwarves mined from deep within the Jotunn Mountains. It was truly a sight for anyone to behold.

    Linitus gazed through the thick fog of the cloud while wearing a special pair of optical goggles in which he could see through the clouds. The elf looked amazed at what he saw below. So much so that Marin had asked with some impatience at her lover to describe what he saw. Linitus found no words to describe other than to show his wife and comrade what he had seen by handing the special optical goggles to Marin. When Marin saw and reacted in the same astonished manner, Peat gathered behind her, followed by Wyatt next in line. They were all impatient in wanting to see what the previous one had seen, only to be stunned by what lay before them. Once each of the four comrades had seen the sight of this formidable and superimposing barrier, they could not help but question their course of action. They wondered if the path they were taking would be the best one to take the war to Helskadi's domain.

However, there was one onboard filled with certainty that this was the best course of action. It was Wothunak, only that he had used his powers before boarding the skyboat to once again manipulate himself into looking like a goblin shaman. Linitus looked at him along with everyone else close to him to go over the plan one more time that the elf ranger had devised. If it was to work, it had to be executed with expediency and without too much of a delay.

Linitus with the optical goggles again looked through the cloud barrier and below at the majestic frozen-looking gated complex. He noticed it was guarded at the top of the ramparts with only two jotunn warriors covered in large fur skin, wielding heavy makeshift clubs made of quaking aspen. Next to these pale giants stood several smaller creatures. They were snow dwarves covered in crude leather and bone armor. They wielded crude shields made of red alder wood, sharp swords, and blunt weapons of various designs made of either forged steel or carved bones. These were terrifying foes that the Comradery would deal with using caution.

Linitus next turned his attention only a few feet away from them on the deck of the skyboat. In front of him, he stared at the little, green goblin shaman. Linitus asked if he was ready to be teleported below to the ramparts of the gate fortification. Wothunak, still assuming his guise as a goblin shaman, nodded while complimenting Linitus on his shrewd and cunning suggestion. Wothunak would use the same deceptive ploy as he had before to trick Helskadi's forces. This time, though, Wothunak would direct them not to retreat like the other dark forces did after their jotunn general fell in combat outside the walls of Nebelheim. Wothunak would sway these forces instead to come toward him. He would eventually alert and startle them into a false flag call of the gates being attacked from a distance.

Within moments, Wyatt, ready to enact his part of the plan, received the magical goggles from Linitus. The wizard wearing the magical goggles waved his magical wand while uttering several incantations. Wothunak in his imposture form soon teleported to the ramparts below.

Upon arrival, everyone in the vicinity at the ramparts was alerted to what they saw. Wothunak, in the guise of a goblin shaman, again pretended as if he had the magical powers to teleport himself. It was enough to convince the snow dwarves and jotunn guards. The goblin impostor warned them that he survived what was soon to be an impending attack on the gated complex. The shaman impostor ordered the guards to give the alarm and summon as many of the posted forces near the guarded gate. Within moments, one of the jotunn giants blew a large horn made of ram to issue the call to arms. Various jotunn and snow dwarves emerged from the mouths of two caves near the base of each side of the valley mountain ranges that flanked the border of the gate walls.

As the dark horde forces formed up on top of the wall, they soon looked about, wondering where the source of the impending attack would come from. The goblin pointed up toward the cloud while smiling before running and jumping over toward the edge of the wall. Within moments of noticing, Linitus surveyed with the goggles, then exchanged the goggles with Wyatt and called out for the wizard to teleport Wothunak in disguise back onboard the skyboat.

Meanwhile, the elf ranger also ordered everyone else on board the skyboat with haste to drop the ignited fuses of the explosive barrels to the surface below. As the rest of the crew complied, over a dozen large round barrels plummeted through the air. The defending forces of Helskadi looked still perplexed by what they had witnessed falling above from the sight of the large cloud that hovered above them. Only then did they begin to realize it was a trick of deception by the goblin impostor to bait them right where the falling barrels would fall upon them. A few of the guards tried to run upon realizing it. It was to no avail, however. The descending barrels within seconds impacted and exploded, causing loud and explosive bursts that wiped out everyone on the ramparts of the gatehouse. Not even the tall jotunn warriors within the proximity of the blast survived. Still, there were at least a hundred enemy forces that remained. Among them included at least a half dozen jotunn that did not make it to the ramparts and who had watched the unfolding carnage just above them. These enemy survivors unleashed loud curses and shouts of anger.

Peat, looking down below, laughed and mocked them from above. The dwarf guardian jested and told them they no longer stood as tall as him. They could not surpass his reach by causing so much death and destruction above. Marin and Linitus meanwhile looked at each other, lost for words after what their dwarven comrade had said. They both knew his words were not making the situation better, considering this preemptive attack had now stirred up more of Helskadi's forces to assemble. It also did not help that by this point, Wyatt's magic in creating a cloudlike mist surrounding the skyboat had dissipated and the enemy forces could clearly see the source of the attack.

Turning with a cold, serious, sharp stare at her elven lover, Marin asked if he had any other ideas. She knew after all that Linitus, being the natural leader in their group, would be the first one to find some creative solution to this. Linitus however, shrugged. The elf ranger then thought of one solution. He and Marin would use their powers from above. They would keep the stirred-up enemy forces occupied as long as possible, or at least until their morale faded as quickly as possible while the reinforcements from the main allied Nordling army coalition could help overtake the remaining enemy forces. Marin nodded while giving Linitus an unexpectedly subtle and brief kiss. She told him that among the reasons she loved him was his creativity in always finding answers. Linitus blushed mildly, nodded, and acknowledged the compliment while pivoting to the matter at hand in implementing his own suggestion.

The elf rogue ranger closed his eyes after gazing intently at the bulk surviving enemy army that clamored on top of the walls from which their fellow slain warriors still lay dead. Several retinues of goblins armed with bows let loose volleys of arrows toward the skyship. Most, however, were not within range of the floating skyboat. The vessel was high enough to only receive a few arrow shots at the underbelly hull of the skyboat. However, the jotunn giants also proceeded to scale the large stairway leading up to the stone gate rampart. These giants carried several large stones in hand. However, only when two shots of the projectiles were thrown and barely missed the skyboat did Linitus, with full concentration of his powers while uttering several incantations, summon a large destructive whirlwind. The whirlwind quickly engulfed the breadth of the rampart of the wall and part of the gatepost. Within moments, the ferocious power of the tornado had sucked in all present on top of the walls, including the jotunn giants. The bodies and any debris collided viciously before being let go in which they dropped hard on the ground just outside the gate walls on both sides of the gate. After letting go of his concentration, Linitus looked about in surveying the damage he had caused below. Marin too looked intently and pointed out that while many caught in the vortex perished, the jotunn giants, though hurt, could somehow get up. Everyone else onboard the skyboat cheered on but realized the danger was not over and became quiet for another moment. Marin asked Linitus if the elf could take a clear shot from above using his bow and arrows. Linitus assessed the windiness above and shook his head with uncertainty. He stated he would have to get to the surface below even if on top of the gate wall rampart to deliver more effective shots with his bow and arrows or use his supernatural powers to let loose a summoned enchanted arrow of light.

Linitus knew that he and Marin had supernatural powers in which they could take out the enemy jotunn warriors, not to mention Wothunak and possibly Wyatt, with his magic being able to do the same against these snow giants. The elf turned to his halfling wizard comrade and told him to prepare to teleport the four of them to the surface below. Meanwhile, Peat would be in charge of captaining the rest of the crew on board. The old dwarf guardian, however, did not like the idea of staying on the sidelines of an ensuing battle, nor did the rest of the crew on board. Linitus understood but he did not want to risk putting more lives in jeopardy in a battle as crucial as this. Still, the elf reconsidered after Marin realized that their dwarven comrade was right. She pointed out it was not the Nordling way after all with the two dozen allies they had on board, not to mention that dwarves like Peat were not ones to want to be left spectating from a battle in which they could actively take part. Linitus conceded her point and nodded. He realized that perhaps it was for the better. This was a cause in which everyone on board had a vested interest and it would help perhaps slow the tide of the enemy forces rallying by the gate to make them wary to the point of retreat.

After consenting to send almost everyone on board the skyboat to teleport and fight on the surface (save for Andarin and Alvissan who stayed behind to still command the skyboat), Wyatt teleported several at a time starting with Linitus, Marin, Peat, and Wothunak, still in his goblin shaman impostor form. Within moments upon arriving on top of the gate wall ramparts, Linitus and Marin hacked with their blades one of the two jotunn giants who was on his knees. Peat did the same to the other jotunn that was also on the rampart struggling to get up. Meanwhile, Wothunak unleashed a sadistic goblin laugh that changed into a more frightening superimposing voice as he assumed his natural gigantic snow giant form. The jotunn titan leaped from the top of the gate wall rampart toward the masses of enemy snow dwarves, goblins, and cave orcs. Wothunak summoned his deadly war ax. The jotunn titan hurled it in a downward stroke, taking out everyone near the path of his weapon. Wothunak made quick work disposing of each of Helskadi's minions while spotting several dozen yards away at least four more jotunn warriors who watched in anger while hurling insults to call the attention of Wothunak. The titan, also filled with rage, hacked his way through more of the enemy horde and charged toward one of the four jotunn. However, the enemy jotunn planned to use their strength in numbers to overwhelm the titan of deceit.

As they began to surround and encircle Wothunak, they patiently waited to see who would make the first move. Unbeknownst to them, however, a lone bright searing arrow pierced across the air and struck its intended target with one of the jotunn warriors falling on his knee while looking down and agonizing over the pain that was inflicted by the arrow striking behind his kneecap. Within a moment, however, the searing bright arrow dissipated. As this jotunn continued to moan in pain, another searing object struck him in the abdomen. This time it was an enchanted spear of light. The magical spear, like the enchanted arrow from before, also dissipated within moments after striking the giant. The severely wounded giant looked around while again moaning in even more pain. He looked about along with his other three giant companions. By the time the jotunns all realized who had struck one of their own, it would be too late for the particular severely wounded giant. They spotted the elf ranger alongside a human Nordling dressed as a Valkyrie across the distance. The elf ranger, concentrating on an aura of bright light around him, once again unleashed another one of his divinelike lightning arrows. This time it had delivered a final mortal blow to the wounded snow giant in which the deployed enchanted arrow struck and killed him almost instantly. The creature fell into his last mortal deep slumber while the other giants looked with disgust and horror at what they witnessed. It never occurred to them to imagine one of their own falling at the hands of their smaller enemies.

With the three surviving angry jotunn giants having their attention redirected to staring at Marin and Linitus, it became a moment of opportunity, which Wothunak quickly seized upon while taking his ax and hacking at one of the jotunn warriors. The other two surviving giants became angry once again. They both decided to split up, with one of them attacking Wothunak while the other would attack Linitus and Marin. The fighting became fierce as Wothunak and one of the two jotunn enemies took turns unleashing and blocking strikes with their own weapons. Wothunak, having his mind made up, unsurprisingly took his time while toying with the jotunn with ease.

Meanwhile, Linitus and Marin took turns evading and dodging attacks from the other enraged jotunn. Eventually, as the jotunn giant showed signs of fatigue, Linitus, harnessing his powers and concentration, quickly unleashed a supernatural arrow of light from his bow. The enchanted arrow struck the pale giant at his heel, causing him to stumble and fall on one knee. Marin quickly took the advantage to charge at the giant and use her own supernatural powers to emanate an enchanted spear of light, which she quickly hurled downward at the base of the giant's foot. The impact caused the giant to moan in pain while Linitus followed up, quickly charging toward the wounded foe. Linitus called Marin to raise her shield as the elf ranger kept charging at full speed. Marin, without hesitation, followed her lover's command and lifted her shield above her head firmly while Linitus quickly leaped high enough to bounce off the surface of the shield to propel himself high enough to land on the back of the giant. The elf ranger next scaled up quickly toward the giant's upper back and toward his head. Linitus then proceeded while unsheathing his curved katana-like long sword blade to plunge it into the giant's skull swiftly. Immediately, the giant fell face first in the snow a foot away from the stairs leading up to the gate wall ramparts.

Linitus and Marin took a moment to catch their breath. They both looked at each other to see physically how they were faring. Without nodding, they understood from each other's facial expressions that they were each okay. They both turned back to the current matter at hand. They looked on to see that Wothunak was also wearing down his fellow giant opponent. Within a few more blows exchanged between Wothunak and the other jotunn, Wothunak would eventually get the upper hand. The titan would overpower his foe by shattering the enemy jotunn's war club before Wothunak would follow up and deliver a ruthless slash toward the throat of the other giant.

Just as Linitus and Marin had done, Wothunak took a moment to catch his breath before turning to see Marin and Linitus victorious in their duel with the other jotunn giant. The titan giant complimented them while telling them that perhaps their next battle against Helskadi herself and her remaining forces would not be as difficult as thought. Linitus nodded while telling him they would proceed cautiously in striking Helskadi within her domain. Wothunak laughed while commenting on his amazement that this elf stood in stark contrast to the many creatures native to Shimmerfrost, including the Nordlings, who would not hesitate to charge head-on to confront their adversaries. Marin interjected, stating that perhaps that is why in part, until now, the Nordlings of Shimmerfrost had not realized victory in the way they now had against the forces of darkness. The jotunn giant grunted while conceding that perhaps indeed that was true. Before they continued their conversation, however, a loud horn from the skyboat sounded. Linitus knew that was Andarin and Alvissan signaling a matter of importance that had commanded the elf rogue ranger and Princess Knight's attention. Linitus turned to Marin and both of them read each other's mind to call out Wyatt's name. They would need their wizard comrade to teleport back to the skyboat and find out what the reason was for signaling the alarm.

The elf ranger and Princess Knight looked about and noticed that the battle near Jotunn Gate was still unfolding while Peat and several Nordlings guarding him fought fiercely near the mouth of one cave from which the hostile snow dwarves emerged in steady increments. Peat eventually planted an explosive barrel near the mouth of the cave and quickly lit it before running off. However, the fuse went out when one of the snow dwarves intercepted it. Peat looked from a distance and cursed a storm of words toward the particular snow dwarf before noticing a sudden burst of an enchanted arrow of light striking the explosive barrel and immediately triggering an explosion. Peat looked behind and saw his elven comrade holding a bow and giving a send-off gesture with his hand waving at the dwarf. Peat cursed again, saying that was supposed to be his kill. Linitus stated he was welcome while Marin told her dwarven comrade that he could add that to his tab for favors that Linitus owed him for taking his kill. Seeing the irony of her words, the dwarf laughed while pointing his war hammer and proclaiming that if it was not for her sarcasm, his life would have been less productive in smoking and drinking at some ill-forgotten inn in a backwash area like the Glens.

Linitus returned to the matter at hand. He quickly asked his dwarven comrade where Wyatt was. Peat shrugged while stating how he should know since the halfling was a wizard who teleported more times than the dwarf could count, not to mention that Wyatt was an evasive one at that. However, it would not be too long before looking at the other cave from the opposite direction in realizing what Wyatt was up to. It was there that Wyatt teleported in a series of flashes while the snow dwarves, goblins, and cave orcs, not to mention a few snow trolls, tried to intercept the wizard, only to fail and fall forward while losing their balance on the slippery snow and ice. Peat looked over toward Marin and Linitus. The dwarf guardian grinned while stating that he had told them so.

Eventually, Wyatt made his way toward the mouth of the other snow dwarf cave. The halfling planted an explosive barrel that he had borrowed from Peat. The halfling wizard carried the explosive strapped onto his back. After planting the barrel, Wyatt quickly cast an explosive marker trap, which it would set off as soon as any unsuspecting foe had been close enough in proximity to touch off the magical series of ember-looking glyphs on the floor.

The wizard would now wait until the next moment when one of Helskadi's minions would come to charge at him. Soon enough, several did, including two goblins, a cave orc, and a snow dwarf. The four enemies were within feet of the halfling wizard and had their weapons raised to strike at him. The wizard suddenly teleported as the enemies had enough momentum to make it difficult to stop without tripping the magical explosive glyphs. As they were within several feet of him when Wyatt flashed out, at least two of these minions had stepped on the glyph that activated in a sudden burst of flame while also triggering off the planted explosive barrel. This resulted in a large blast that caused the cave mine to collapse and take out everyone within the vicinity of the blast.

Marin and Linitus screamed in fear, however, that their comrade did not make it out from the blast, only to realize a flash of light appeared behind them. Emerging out was their halfling friend who now had laughed mildly, seeing how his companions reacted. Peat laughed as well stating that if anyone was a better trickster than him or the rest of the Comradery, it would indeed be Wyatt.

Marin and Linitus sighed a moment in relief. They both remembered again the matter at hand. The horn from the skyboat had sounded off several times. The skyboat, however, was nowhere near as high in altitude as it was before. Instead, it floated only a few dozen yards above the rampart of the fortified gate.

Andarin yelled out to everyone on the surface after he realized that the battle for control of the gate was over with the Comradery prevailing. The skyboat captain then responded they had more enemy company from far away south of the gate. These were Helskadi's assault forces that were routed after the failed siege of Nebelheim. They were now nearing their retreat close to Jotunn Gate. The dwarf captain went further to say that this gave Comradery and their allies the advantage to corner the retreating enemy army. The beastly horde was unaware that the gate was no longer under their force's control. Linitus nodded and understood. The elf knew that if they had seen the skyboat, it would give away their location and advantage in controlling the fortified gate.

It was now a race against time. The elf ranger, along with his lover Marin, did an impromptu muster of their accompanied forces on the surface. Though they took some casualties with a few fallen Nordling warriors, they had enough to form a small light contingent of archers. Linitus instructed the present Nordling warriors to salvage any bows and arrows that they could take from the fallen goblin corpses. There were enough bows and arrows for all the Nordling warriors to pick up and put to use. However, Marin pointed out to Linitus, archery was not something these Nordlings were well-versed in practicing. They lacked archery skill, much like their Nordling brethren in the forests and mountains south of Shimmerfrost and just north of the Kingdom of Swordbane's territory. Linitus nodded in stating that he knew as much also, but he reasoned that as long as the Nordlings knew the basics in using bow and arrow, they still stood a chance of holding control of the gatehouse and its wall ramparts. It would also help to corner and harass the retreating enemy army from escaping deep into the Jotunn Mountains since the gate was still closed.

As the dark horde army continued to advance toward the entrance of the gate, they noticed an unfamiliar large hairy jotunn giant signaling for them to come closer. The front ranks of the retreating army, though not familiar with this jotunn, continued to walk closer. It was not until at least two cave orcs recognized this figure that any hope of optimism in escaping to the Jotunn Mountains had diminished. The two cave orc warriors shouted in their startled tongues about this figure. They recognized this jotunn before as being an infamous prisoner condemned to one of the deepest dark cells in the Har-Fjell Mountains. This jotunn they had realized was not the portrayed ally they initially had fought.

Meanwhile, after the enemy caught on to his deception and trickery, Wothunak could not help but give a loud laugh. He announced with a thunderous voice in Nordling that it was now time to attack. Within moments of hiding under the obstruction of the gate wall rampart crenellations, dozens of Nordlings led by unfamiliar figures (an elf ranger and a female Nordling warrior donned in the image of the legendary Golden Valkyrie) let loose multiple arrows from the bows they held. Marin hurled an enchanted spear projectile through the use of her own supernatural powers. The various projectiles struck and fell many of the beastly enemies while the Comradery prepared to engage the enemy in melee combat. As this next phase of combat ensued, thousands of enemy warriors continued to pour out. They swelled in ranks despite the steady increase of casualties they suffered. The goblins tried to scale the walls of the ramparts with several succeeding. None of them, however, could gain control of the gatehouse and the wall ramparts as the now-defending group of Nordling warriors held off the enemy's attempt to recapture the gate complex. Many goblins that scaled the walls of the gate complex also got knocked down to their deaths by the defending Nordlings.

The tide of the battle continued to work in favor of Linitus and his Comradery. The few remaining acting leaders of the retreating enemy army decided that the next favorable course of action would be to fall back and retreat. They headed west toward the Har-Fjell Mountains, hoping to find refuge deep within the many caves of the heavily beastly populated area. Wothunak knew this much, at least from observing their movement patterns. The giant titan called out to Linitus and the rest of the Comradery of their plans and that they had to intercept them to make sure no survivors would escape. If they escaped, the Comradery risked later confronting an enemy relief army from Har-Fjell that would pose a credible threat to the Nordling–dyr coalition's army during its planned assault against Jotunheim.

Linitus nodded in agreement with Wothunak's assessment to hunt down every surviving enemy that retreated toward the Har-Fjell Mountains. However, the elf rogue ranger held some reservations. He knew that pursuing the remaining enemy forces on the surface away from the gate fortification carried a noticeable risk. It would expose his and Marin's present company of Nordling warriors from being overwhelmed if the enemy horde's army rallied and turned back to fight. Still, it was a chance they had to take to prevent enemy survivors from notifying Helskadi's Har-Fjell beastly vassals. If none of the enemies survived, Helskadi would have no way to realize in time or react in shoring up her defenses when the Comradery would lead the coalition forces of Nordling and dyr warriors against Jotunheim. This moment to decide on how to proceed still weighed heavily upon Linitus's mind. It was visible for everyone to tell.

Marin, looking to his side, understood her lover's dilemma and placed her arm over his shoulder, telling him that even though they would risk putting their own forces in harm's way to chase down a still larger enemy army, they had morale on their side and they would prevail or at least persevere, as they had always done. Linitus nodded and agreed with Marin.

Now that they were committed to seeing this through in pursuing the remaining enemy army, Linitus turned to Wyatt. The elf ranger told his wizard companion to prepare to teleport them and the rest of their Nordling allies as far as the halfling wizard could, to intercept the enemy army. Wyatt nodded while noticing that the enemy army had not yet reached the western horizon and that the most ideal position to teleport them was right at the western horizon point. Within moments, the wizard teleported one group at a time as quickly as possible.

Upon emerging from the flashing teleportation portal, Linitus, Marin, Peat, and three other Nordlings quickly assessed their surroundings. Linitus pointed out that the front ranks of the enemy army were several hundred yards away from them. The enemy army, however, was closing in fast. A few seconds later, however, another two groups of Nordlings, along with Wothunak and Wyatt, emerged from the final teleportation portal. Linitus quickly instructed the Nordling warriors to form a shield wall. They would use this shield wall formation to brace for impact against two dozen fast-approaching mounted platforms. These platforms were similar in concept to the Citadellan chariot. However, these platforms were still very different. Linitus looked somewhat puzzled until one of the Nordling warriors noticed and spoke, which Marin could decipher. She explained that these were snow dwarf war wagons powered by a combination of wheels and skis that acted like a sled when the snow was thick enough. The composition of these mobile platforms included a combination of thick alder wood, spruce wood, and animal bone. They were driven using native horned musk oxen as draft animals, usually two oxen per war wagon. Each of these wagons had protruding serrated scythe blades about two feet long from the center sides of the wheel spokes.

Even more terrifying, however, which the Comradery noticed was that these war wagons were each armed with a large ballista launcher. One or two of the crewed snow dwarves in each war wagon would fire off this mounted weapon while the wagon driver would focus on steering the wagon with the reins attached to the musk oxen. It was a harrowing contraption to see, but even more so to be susceptible to being targeted by these mobile platforms.

Linitus took careful observation of these mobile platforms of war and instructed the Nordlings to maintain their shield wall formation in front of him, Marin, and Wyatt. Peat, meanwhile, led the shield wall formation from the front center rank. His leadership, however, was not perfectly heeded as several Nordling warriors lost their composure and broke ranks while screaming war cries and charging toward the war wagons. The war wagons, however, trampled down on the Nordlings and severed body parts of some of the few Nordlings that exposed themselves as open targets.

The sight was gruesome for all those to witness, especially for Linitus and the small contingent of Nordling warriors that he led. However, he composed himself and yelled aloud for Marin to translate to the rest of the Nordling warriors. Marin nodded and translated as he spoke. He mentioned if their company had any chance to survive and break the morale of the enemy, then they had to hold their position. Linitus ordered the Nordling warriors to have their shields firmly planted on the ground while raising their spears in a forward stance. The Nordling warriors heeded the elf's words with devotion, knowing that he had already demonstrated superb leadership thus far along with Marin.

Meanwhile, as they held their position, Linitus quickly took out an arrow sabot receptacle packed with nearly two dozen arrows. Taking aim while pulling back his bow, he quickly let loose the container pod that deployed the many arrows toward the main center of the enemy war wagons. The arrows struck one war wagon, including both the draft animals propelling the chariot and three of its carried occupants of snow dwarves, including the driver. The attack caused the arrow-stricken draft animals to fall forward while the wagon driver, losing control of the reins, resulted in the war wagon assembly turning over to its side and flipping several times.

As this new standoff ensued, Wyatt cast several alternating spells of fireballs, thunderbolts, and magical explosive glyphs that would trigger upon contact. The wizard took out at least five enemy war wagons. One of the war wagons even lost control after triggering one of the explosive glyphs. The affected wagon collided with two other war wagons only a few dozen yards away from Linitus's company.

The wreckage from the enemy war wagons that had fallen was spread out enough to cause a curved barrier. Marin recognized the advantage their group would now have by advancing and taking. It would make it harder for more of the enemy horde army to outflank them. Marin called out to Linitus to point out this unfolding advantage. The elf ranger recognized the same advantage immediately that his lover had indicated. Linitus quickly called out to the Nordling warriors being led by Peat in front of them to charge forward and position themselves in forming a porcupine circular formation within the wreckage. The warriors acknowledged the order after Marin translated. While they marched quickly toward the wreckage, Marin spotted another war wagon turning about to intercept them. Using her supernatural powers, the Princess Knight quickly emanated a bright long spear of energy from her hands and cast it like a jolt of lightning toward the war wagon. It struck a powerful blow, causing the particular war wagon carriage to separate and fly through the air while its occupants fell out. The carriage landed near the other cluster of destroyed war wagons to give a small additional amount of coverage for the Comradery.

In a short amount of time, the advancing column of Nordlings along with Peat had made it to the small area of destroyed war wagons. They arranged themselves in a circular formation inside the surrounding wreckage with the debris acting as a natural barrier to shield them from being attacked and outflanked by the remaining war wagons. Linitus, Marin, and Wyatt also found themselves at the center of this circular formation that their comrades had formed. The present company gave more time for Wyatt and Linitus to use their powers and abilities. The halfling wizard and elf ranger then unleashed more deadly magical spell projectiles and arrow volley attacks respectively against the new contingent wave of enemy war wagons.

As the combat dragged on, the remaining war chariots, about four in total, retreated after the enemy forces realized they were at a clear disadvantage. Instead, several of the remaining jotunn elite unit commanders opted to use sheer force in numbers to attack in unison and overwhelm the Comradery while it was still holding its position near the wagon debris. Linitus knew the odds were very much working against them and that perhaps it was foolhardy to intercept the retreating enemy forces, to begin with. He could tell yet still hold back his facial expression of not letting it negatively affect the morale of his companions.

Marin, however, could still read Linitus's discreet facial expression. While he often took the more pragmatic approach to assessing the situation with as much optimism that can be afforded without sounding delusional, Marin still after all these years together was defiant as always even when the odds were against them. Her knightly pride and confidence, though tempered over the years since sharing her life with her elven lover, still was not forsaken. She clung to hope as much as her sword and shield with the attitude that she and her comrades could overcome the odds, as challenging as it may be. Marin called out calmly to Linitus. She reminded him as she did from time to time that they would find a way as they always had. They had been through more dire situations and this one to her was no different. Linitus nodded and knew that she was right. There was still hope, and he was only as limited as he would allow his mindset and abilities to be.

Then thinking about his abilities, Linitus recalled to himself with a positively new directed sense of resolution. They still had enough distance from the enemy infantry. He could at least concentrate again and summon a whirlwind. Though it would probably create a chaotic blizzard with the snow on the surface and the sky appearing murky, the elf would still do it just as he had done before while on the skyboat summoning a whirlwind to take out the enemy on the gate rampart before departing to the surface. Linitus told the rest of his companions to hold still and continue to once again maintain their ranks. He also told Wyatt to use his magic to cast several explosive glyph markers on the surface should any enemies come close enough to prepare to engage in melee combat. The wizard complied in casting multiple glyph explosive markers while Linitus looked intently at the main mass formation of the advancing ranks of enemy infantry that were mainly cave orcs and goblins followed by snow trolls and jotunn warriors.

As Linitus looked on, he uttered several incantations and concentrated with his eyes slowly closing. Within moments the elf ranger channeled his mental focus into summoning a slow but incrementally intense whirlwind near the center of the enemy army. The turbulent updraft had been powerful to suck in many enemy hordes. However, it became difficult to control the whirlwind as time went on, causing many of the surviving enemy army to run away from the whirlwind and instead divert their movements in going around it while still advancing more slowly toward the Comradery. Linitus eventually let go while feeling somewhat exhausted. Marin held him upright from losing his balance. She commended her lover on taking out as many of the enemy as he could. Still, he asked her if it was enough while he looked across the distance. Marin gave a faint half nod in which even she was hopeful but uncertain at the same time.

The surviving enemy army, now just under two thousand by headcount, was still rattled and persistent in charging toward Linitus and his companions. They were both equally determined to prevail against the other. Perhaps the Comradery's saving grace was Wothunak attacking the enemy with relentless brute force, particularly against the remaining few jotunn giants from their rear flank in order to keep them somewhat occupied. But it may not be enough, or so the elf ranger thought. He asked his lover Marin to kiss him one last time as he sought to recover his strength for the ensuing struggle. Marin nodded, knowing this might be their last moment together. As their lips embraced, the moment was only interrupted by a sudden blast of a horn which everyone recognized. From the distance charged another group of figures. It was difficult to make out until they came close enough for Linitus to pull out and use his spyglass to identify the then-unknown forces coming into the theater of battle.

The elf ranger could not withhold his expression of joy when he could identify who these fast-approaching figures were. They were dyr folk that came from the west. They numbered in the hundreds, with some charging forth on war wagons of their own numbered in the dozens and steered by domesticated caribou draft animals. It was a surreal moment to see before them. The dyr folk quickly charged and trampled with their war wagons many of the enemy infantry.

Even more shocking, however, was that as the enemy army changed movement and retreated back in the other direction toward Jotunn Gate, another loud blast from a war horn was sounded. This time the sound was distinguishable as well as the far distant war cries for Marin to make out and smile back at Linitus that this was the pursuing Nebelheim army. Though far away, they had enough distance to close in and force the dark horde army to fight on both flanks. The Nebelheim army, along with some dyr folk allies, numbered over three thousand and had enough morale and manpower to beat out Helskadi's retreating army, which was now just over half the size of the Nordling–dyr coalition forces by this point in the battle. The battle would be costly for the Nordlings of Nebelheim and, to a lesser extent, the dyr folk, but they all knew it would be worth the sacrifice of some of their forces in order to eliminate all the enemy dark forces that were still present outside Jotunn Gate.

Overwhelmed from various directions, the dark horde army crumbled quickly. Linitus and Marin made a haste call to further seize the advantage. The two of them had their accompanied Nordling companions, along with Wyatt and Peat, to charge forth out of wagon debris and venture into the fray of combat. Less than an hour later, the battle was over and none of Helskadi's deployed forces had survived. The snowy low plains outside of Jotunn Gate were littered with dead corpses, mostly of the enemy, with much blood that made the snowy ice look darkened red and black. None of the enemy survived to retreat to Har-Fjell or to Helskadi's fortress city of Jotunheim. The Winter Death Witch would receive no warning of the impending assault that this coalition of Nordlings and dyr folk led by a band of heroic strangers would unleash against her remaining forces and herself.

Linitus and Marin breathed heavily while surveying the battlefield. They both looked at each other with deep sighs of relief before turning again to see that many of the Nordlings and dyr warriors had survived. The elf ranger and Princess Knight witnessed before them the various allied warriors of Nordlings and dyr warriors lifting their weapons in the air while clanging against their shields and shouting in exaltations of their victory. The coalition army gathered around Linitus and Marin to pick the two of them up to raise high in the air. It was both the Nordling and dyr warriors' way of acknowledging the leadership and courage of the elf ranger and the Princess Knight in the face of such overwhelming odds.

Eventually, Linitus and Marin, the two revered heroic lovers, had the warriors that carried them to put them down. The elf ranger and Princess Knight then directed the coalition army to march toward the massive stone-built gate fortification. Wyatt would teleport Marin, Linitus, Peat, and himself back to the top wall rampart of the gate fortification while also teleporting Wothunak back to the interior side of the gate. Upon arrival, Linitus directed the jotunn titan that it was time for him to open up the gate while removing the large massive door bar that locked the gate from the inside. Wothunak nodded and complied. However, the titan thought to himself with some hesitance in deciding when he would have no further use for his partnership with these smaller mortals. He deeply despised the elf ranger and his Nordling companion lover princess clad in armor posing as the legendary Golden Valkyrie. However, the jotunn titan knew they were both useful and powerful to not yet turn against. He knew he would still need them as much as they needed him to overtake Helskadi. Wothunak would still wait patiently and bide his time in taking the guise that he was still a reliable ally to this coalition army.

The coalition army itself still became apprehensive and wary about Wothunak and his intentions. They had assumed a watchful disposition toward him. Many of the present Nordling warriors and even the dyr folk warriors wondered if they could trust this jotunn as he had a folklore reputation for being deceitful. Linitus and Marin, however, assured their coalition partners it was necessary to work together with this titan if they were to stand a better chance of prevailing in the last battle against Helskadi.

With Jotunn Gate being opened for the allied army to proceed in marching forward against Jotunheim, the awe and surreal suspense to see what was on the other side had captivated the minds of the Nordlings and dyr folk. Few if any among their peoples had ventured through the harrowing pass deep within the interior of the vast Jotunn Mountains. Before venturing, Linitus and Marin held council with the acting dyr druid leader and the acting Nordling commander in charge of the coalition forces. They discussed and plotted out their next phase of operations. Only several dozen Nordlings and dyr folk warriors would stay behind to cremate the dead using makeshift pyres. The ones that remained would also tend to the wounded while making preparations to return to Nebelheim to seek further aid in enlisting more Nordling warriors against the forces of the Winter Death Witch.

Meanwhile, in further planning out their next stage of operations, Linitus and Marin would lead the bulk of the coalition forces, still at least over two thousand strong, to march against Jotunheim. They also made sure they would have enough food supplies before venturing forth. They did not know for certain how many days and nights it would take to march out of Jotunn Gate to Jotunheim. However, according to Wothunak, they could do it within three to four days if the weather conditions were not too harsh.

On the next day by early morning, Linitus and Marin had stood from the top of the gate rampart to oversee the coalition army being deployed once again in its long march to Jotunheim. The elf ranger and his Princess Knight lover held hands to enjoy the view of the rising sun amidst the cold chilled air, with only a few clouds gracing the sky. It was a good sign for them. They took it as a divine blessing to proceed with the next phase of their war plans as they both readied themselves to go down the gate rampart stairway and march alongside their forces through the narrowing elevated mountain pass.

Chapter Fifty-Seven

Final Showdown at Jotunheim

On a chilly late spring day, the sky around Jotunheim was uneventful as usual. The many clouds in the area blotted out the sun and its rays from piercing the surface below. Still, the one noticeable feature that stood out was the majestic and imposing Jotunn Mountains that dotted in a circular pattern from afar around the fortress settlement. It was noticeable for all those within the vicinity of Jotunheim.

Helskadi herself took in the somewhat scenic and melancholy view of her natural surroundings. She sat on a makeshift throne chair she had installed on the main fortress tower wall walk. The Winter Death Witch would sit and wait patiently on her throne for hours on end over the past week. Only on rare moments did she move out of her seat while waiting for any word of her forces and their progress in the war against Nebelheim. The Winter Death Witch expected them to at least send a messenger to report on their status at least two days ago. Instead, all she saw were thick layers of foggy clouds that hovered low. These clouds obscured the narrow jagged path that led the road between Jotunheim to Jotunn Gate in the south. However, a small lone figure had emerged from the low-lying clouds. It was a mere goblin shaman. The creature ran in a frantic hurry. This goblin seemed as if it was being pursued and escaped with its life being intact through some miracle.

Helskadi saw this figure from a distance. She called out to her jotunn guards to stop blocking the goblin shaman from speaking about why it had fled to Jotunheim. The goblin shaman spoke back, telling her that the dispatched army led by Fornjotr had been beaten and now the survivors were retreating to Nebelheim. This creature went further to mention it had teleported ahead of the front ranks of the routing army to alert Jotunheim of the failed siege of Nebelheim. This goblin shaman also pleaded for Helskadi to have her guards open the gates that blocked the pass leading to the fortified settlement. The shaman explained further that the routed army could replenish its lost numbers to attack Nebelheim a second time after they regrouped in Jotunheim. The sense of urgency by the goblin outside the gate of Jotunheim was convincing enough for Helskadi to call out in a loud voice to her jotunn giant gate guards. She commanded them to open the gates with haste and prepare the forces of the settlement for receiving the beaten dark horde allies.

Two jotunn gate guards acknowledged while nodding. They lifted the door bar that locked the gate from being open and they pushed out the large stone doors to open the access to Jotunheim. As soon as they had done so, the goblin shaman called out above toward the layer of fog clouds saying that Helskadi was ready to receive their forces. Within moments, the goblin shaman ran to the other side of the fortified gate, and suddenly, he laughed. He then morphed into a large prominent jotunn wielding a large deadly ax. Before the jotunn guards had time to react to what they had seen, the transformed jotunn had struck and slew both of them. Much to everyone's surprise, especially Helskadi's, the creature had revealed himself as none other than Wothunak.

Helskadi was dumbfounded and could not hold back saying aloud to herself how impossible this was. Wothunak, however, laughed, telling her that her reign was over. Helskadi without hesitation ordered all the remaining armed jotunn guards and all those cave orcs, goblins, and the few snow trolls present to attack her fellow titan rival.

However, within moments, several arrows and an emanated bright spear of light had struck two jotunn giants closest to Wothunak. Helskadi turned and looked about with outrage at who had struck her fellow jotunn subjects. The Winter Death Witch spotted several figures standing across the distance from the top of one of the nearest round tower battlements within the fortress settlement. There Helskadi saw an elf ranger wielding a bow while readying another arrow. The Winter Death Witch also noticed next to the elf a Nordling woman with dark blonde hair clad in the legendary Golden Valkyrie armored attire made long ago. Next to them were two short creatures. One was a dwarf clad in dwarven armor wearing a three-pronged horned helmet. The other small figure wore green and black magical goggles and was donned in black and blue wizard robes. This short figure emanated an aura of magical energy with his hands while holding a silver wand. It was an odd sort, but one which she recognized as being the source of her ire and discontent the last several weeks. Helskadi called them out while stating she would make them pay for being a nuisance in her plans to rule over Shimmerfrost as its one true dark lord.

The Winter Death Witch pointed her spear staff at her newfound enemies. She called her forces to attack them on sight while Helskadi herself vowed to deal with Wothunak herself. Wothunak laughed, telling his female giant counterpart that they would see which of the two would deal the final blow.

Immediately at that moment, multiple goblins and cave orcs swarmed out from the entrance to the tower, which Helskadi looked down from below. She would have as many of her minions fight and die for her as it took before she would take it upon herself to fight the battle. Wothunak fought his way to the inside of the keep. Along the way, he carved a bloody path of fallen goblins and cave orcs to reach the top outside of the keep to confront his chief rival.

As the titan giant persevered against his female rival, Wyatt looked about where to teleport himself and Peat from one of the lower battlements. They would ascend upon teleportation to another higher point in elevation that was not well guarded. Meanwhile, Linitus and Marin would stay at the top of the lower battlement. The two of them would capture as much attention as possible to draw in Helskadi's forces. This would allow Peat and Wyatt to execute the next step of their plans. Within moments of arriving at the higher elevated battlement, Wyatt used his green and black magical goggles to see through the dense layer of fog that stood outside of Jotunheim. This was a magical fog that the halfling wizard himself had created to disguise and give cover to the amassed Nordling–dyr coalition army. Upon seeing through the dense fog, Wyatt spotted multiple warriors eager to wage combat against their oppressive adversary. Within moments, several groups of Nordlings and dyr warriors were transported, thanks to Wyatt's magic. The newly teleported allies became amazed at what had happened. Peat broke their stares. The dwarf reminded them they were in the middle of a war and that it was time for them to pick up their weapons to put to good use. Immediately from the top of the tower battlement, the

Nordling warriors engaged in melee combat using spears, axes, swords, and maces while staying in a loose formation. Meanwhile, the teleported dyr warriors fought at range and hurled bullets with their slings toward the fortified enemy. The dyr warriors also used bows and arrows to take out the masses of goblins and cave orcs below. Only the jotunn giants and the few snow trolls could withstand the force of the projectiles while showing some clear visible signs of pain.

Wyatt continued to teleport more groups of dyr warriors and Nordling warriors all about the various tops of the tower battlements in Jotunheim. As each wave of newly arrived Nordlings and dyr warriors arrived, Linitus and Marin called out to them. The two leaders of the Comradery commanded their allied warriors to continue to steel their resolve and press on in the fight against the Winter Death Witch's army. Helskadi became frustrated and even more furious. She ordered her minions to scale the stairways in the towers and take the fight to the enemy above. As the dark horde forces continued to scatter and disperse in attacking the nearest occupied towers, Linitus called out to Peat to signal the horn. The dwarf guardian did so and sounded off a loud blast. Immediately, the remaining Nordling and dyr warriors hidden within the veil of the thick cloud mist slowly emerged. They quickly charged toward the open gate entrance that separated the narrow steep jagged pathway from the settlement itself.

At this point, Helskadi's forces felt overwhelmed and uncertain in how to proceed. Some of them also showed signs of wanting to retreat out of fear in realizing their enemy was more persistent and determined than they initially thought. The brutal close-quarters fighting continued to take form throughout the settlement. There were skirmishes everywhere, from the gate entrance to the courtyard that separated the main fortress citadel from the rest of the towers. Linitus took note of it and called out to Wyatt and directed the halfling wizard to teleport the elf ranger and Marin to the highest tower. Wyatt, looking onward, nodded. He motioned with his hands and magic wand to cast his teleportation spell. Two sudden flashes emitted around Linitus and Marin. The two of them disappeared and no sooner reappeared on top of the citadel tower in which Helskadi was situated.

The Winter Death Witch turned around after seeing the bright flash's energy shine behind her. There she saw the same two figures that she had blamed for stalling her foreseeable conquest of Shimmerfrost. The elf ranger and the female Nordling donned in the Golden Valkyrie ensemble stood out. The Winter Death Witch went on to ask both of them their identities before she vowed to see to it in disposing of them. Linitus responded that their identities should be the last thing for Helskadi to be worried about. Marin followed up by proclaiming before Helskadi that the Winter Death Witch's reign would end today. Helskadi laughed while challenging them both on what they thought they could hope would be achieved and they would die failing. Helskadi assured them she was not only a jotunn giant but also a titan who could not be so easily killed, even if Marin was the prophetic embodiment of the Golden Valkyrie. Marin replied in a sharp tone. She let Helskadi know that she knew the extent of the Winter Death Witch's powers. Marin also revealed that the Nordlingdyr coalition made a pact with Wothunak in order to prevent Helskadi from prevailing.

It was at this point that Helskadi laughed again, somewhat dismissive of what Marin had said. Helskadi then asked in a rhetorical way what would give Marin and her elf companion any more reason to trust Wothunak over Helskadi. The Winter Death Witch did not hold back in expressing how Wothunak coveted getting as much power as she did. No matter who between the two of them prevailed, Shimmerfrost would be ruled by a power-hungry warlord. Helskadi pointed out that the key difference was that, unlike her male jotunn titan counterpart, she was sane enough to lead and not be clouded in her decision-making by bizarre delusions.

Upon hearing those words, Marin and Linitus both internally admitted that Helskadi may have been right about that, at least in part. However, the direction in which Linitus and Marin would proceed remained the same. They would both seek to depose Helskadi first before being left to determine Wothunak's intentions and if he would indeed pose a comparable threat to Shimmerfrost as Helskadi did.

However, no sooner did both think the same thing did Linitus ask Marin with intrigue about Wothunak's current whereabouts since they only saw him fight briefly outside before entering one of the towers in the fortress complex. Marin shrugged while stating that at least for the time being, he was on their side. Together the two now looked toward the giant Winter Death Witch while assuming a calm but determined fighting posture. Helskadi responded while wielding her spear staff to proclaim an incantation in a loud voice. She motioned one of her hands in which a large ice-looking globe emanated. This magical ball of energy was quickly hurled from her non-weapon wielding hand. The projectile darted toward

Marin, the latter of whom raised her enchanted Valkyrie round shield in time to block and absorb the blast.

Meanwhile, Linitus readied his bow and arrow while letting loose a shot aimed at the abdomen of the female jotunn titan. Helskadi, however, uttered a few words to cast an icy cold blue sphere around her that deflected the shot. Linitus was stunned but not deterred to find a way along with Marin to best this evil female dark lord of the far north.

Marin, meanwhile, concentrated her thoughts and emanated her supernatural spear of light which she hurled toward Helskadi. Helskadi, however, could barely dodge. As soon as the Winter Death Witch realized her successful evasion, no sooner did Marin charge toward her. The Princess Knight, also known as the Golden Valkyrie by the local Nordlings, wasted no time in sparing any opportunity to vanquish this cold adversary. Marin held her flaming sword tight in her right hand and carried her small, round golden shield in her left hand. She leaped toward Helskadi, the latter who still stood taller than the Marin by sevenfold, yet it still did not matter to the Golden Valkyrie. Marin aimed her blade and slashed toward the lower shin of the female jotunn titan.

For a moment it seemed to have worked. Helskadi was not fast enough to react and languished in pain while kneeling down on one leg. The Winter Death Witch, however, quickly used her large hand to swipe at Marin. This sudden instinctive attack caught the Golden Valkyrie off guard as she flung like a fly across the air by several feet while hitting hard against the tower crenelations.

Linitus, in shock with grave concern for his wife, called out in anger and desperation. He let loose an arrow not of his physical inventory but rather one of searing light, which he emanated using his supernatural powers. The arrow soared with uncanny speed from his bow as soon as he let loose. The enchanted projectile struck hard against the kneecap of Helskadi's other standing leg. The female titan wrenched in pain once again while unleashing another moan. This time she was immobilized, though only for a short duration. Helskadi struggled to get herself back up while still throbbing in pain. It was enough time for Linitus to come to Marin's aid and assess how badly she was hurt. Marin, however, was out of consciousness only for a moment. She expressed some aching pain, but it was enough to shake it off. Marin then tried to compose herself to get up while Linitus helped her to stand.

Meanwhile, a loud voice and vast shadow emerged from the stairway entrance of the fortress tower wall walk. The voice laughed. It was a loud voice full of sadistic pleasure. It was enough to catch the attention of both Marin, Linitus, and Helskadi. The figure lowering his gigantic head was Wothunak himself. He walked with a gaze of evil confidence and contentment. He held in his large hand a crystal-like ball, which Helskadi recognized. It was the same crystal ball that she had used to observe and communicate with those far away, including her contacts from the Imperial Remnant. Now, however, the female titan showed a sign of concern and fear. She seemed to be disturbed that this object was now in the possession of her male jotunn counterpart adversary.

Wothunak mocked Helskadi while asking in a rhetorical voice why she seemed to be in a state of fear. Linitus and Marin looked at each other with some perplexity. The two of them did not realize at first what this object was, which Wothunak had taken away from Helskadi's control. It was at this point, however, that the elf ranger and Princess Knight became suspicious of their jotunn ally's behavior. Marin and Linitus both began to question themselves that perhaps the Winter Death Witch was right after all. Perhaps their newfound ally who they met under dubious circumstances and had forged a temporary alliance with was too dangerous to be trusted after all. They had no way beyond doubt of knowing what power this crystal ball had other than being able to communicate to those intended far away.

Wothunak uttered several words in an ancient tongue of the jotunn language that only Helskadi would understand. As the male jotunn titan finished uttering the words, the crystal ball levitated in the air away from Wothunak's hands. The ball's radiance grew bright to where it became unstable. In another instant, it burst and shattered high in the air while opening up a bright flashing portal that seared with light.

Emerging from that portal grew the sounds of loud shrieking voices of what sounded like female Nordlings. Marin's face turned nearly pale while Linitus looked in awe and asked what it was. Marin barely composed herself. She struggled and managed to tell her lover that Wothunak had committed a sacrilegious act. He unleashed the Valkyrie shield maiden warriors, all of whom were covered in golden sparkly armor similar to Marin's. Linitus looked still puzzled. Linitus knew about some aspects of Nordling mythology but was still in shock when the little lore he had heard about the legendary female Nordling Valkyrie warriors descending from the heavens happened to be true.

Soon enough, the source of the loud voices emerged from the trembling portal where at least a dozen golden-clad female warriors with a goldlike skin appearance wielding bright weapons of light rode mounted on golden unicorn horses that soared through the sky with their wings. It was a sight to behold only that these supernatural shield maidens had been summoned by Wothunak to do his bidding and no sooner had they emerged out of the portal did they take to task in fighting off both Helskadi's forces and Linitus and Marin's coalition of Nordlings and dyr warriors. All about the sky the descending mounted Valkyrie female warriors trampled and fell upon both armies.

Wothunak laughed as he witnessed the carnage unfold before him. His enjoyment soon ended when Helskadi, in utter defiance of her male rival titan's power, shouted in rebuke of what she had seen. She declared her forces would fight for her even in a post-mortal state. The female jotunn titan waved her spear staff. She uttered her own magical incantations. No sooner than her forces and that of her enemy's fallen forces would rise in their undead state to fight back against the small but powerful summoned Valkyrie warriors.

Marin and Linitus now both realized while exchanging briefly their thoughts of how this battle had now descended into a chaotic situation that they had not expected. Only now did they learn the depth of Wothunak's true deceptive nature. Only now did they realize Wendigo was not the only one with the powers to summon the undead, but that his one-time master, the Winter Death Witch, in fact, had the same or at least similar powers as Wendigo had to command the forces of nature and the undead. One of them clearly had taught the other to use these dark necromantic powers.

It was terrifying to see. Two seemingly powerful and equal opposing factions each led by a jotunn titan would vie for power that they each wanted for himself or herself and that they would go this far to obtain it. As they did so, the summoned spirits of the mounted Valkyrie warriors continued to clash and fight against the summoned undead corpses all the more while the living for both Helskadi's army and the Nordling–dyr coalition were in awe before both realizing that they too had to resume fighting if they had a chance to survive and prevail on the side they represented. However, the fighting became intense and brutal throughout the courtyard of the fortified settlement as well as within the towers, the ramparts of the fortress walls, and even the top walkways of the towers.

Linitus and Marin, however, looked to themselves and agreed that they had to eliminate both Helskadi and Wothunak as soon as possible. The elf ranger and Princess Knight, however, realized the two titans may already have saved the heroes from the work of doing it themselves. Helskadi and Wothunak already had engaged each other in a vicious duel atop the main fortress tower walkway. Instead, Linitus and Marin called out for Wyatt to use his magic against the summoned Valkyrie spirits to see if it would have any effect. Wyatt saw his two companions and, with haste, the halfling wizard teleported them across to a lower tower. It was the same tower that Wyatt occupied along with Peat and several dyr and Nordling warriors. All of them fought as best they could against several waves of Helskadi's army that now consisted of undead forces as well as the living. The Comradery and their allies struggled as best they could to hold off against the enemy as long as they still lived.

Only when that moment seemed most dire did Marin realize again that this could very well be her last battle to fight alongside her closest friends, not to mention her soulmate and husband. The Princess Knight would also think about her father. She missed him dearly.

Linitus knew Marin well enough to read her face. He knew what she was thinking and she was feeling. The elf ranger held her hand. With a rare instinct and a voice that seemed to be not his own but rather the essence of the divine spirit of Silvanus, which was in part infused in him, it had called out. The voice, which only Linitus could hear, urged him to tell Marin what must be done, what she had to do. And so Linitus did. He told her to use the supernatural power of her wailing voice to be channeled and to call out for her father. Marin in disbelief asked what her lover had just said, to which Linitus repeated himself—to use the supernatural power of her voice and find a way to call out to her father. Marin, almost in tears, understood what her lover meant and though she somewhat doubted herself at first, she collected herself and conceded while nodding.

Marin took a deep breath. The Princess Knight looked toward the sky while facing the main fortress tower in which Helskadi and Wothunak still fought each other. Marin concentrated with all her strength and might while channeling her mind into thinking of her father. Then she unleashed her voice with everything she had in her to let out a loud, wailing shout of her voice. It was loud enough to make the snowy mountains and the sky above almost tremble. It was loud enough to catch everyone's attention, including Helskadi and Wothunak who both paused from their duel. Only after another quick passing moment when the ambient air was still and her voice ceased did something very loud echo back with the sound of a loud roar.

Radiating with a bright flash from above in the sky, another portal soon appeared. Out of the portal emerged a lone figure. It was a dark green half-man, half-dragon anthropomorphic creature that flew with its dragon wings. Surveying the chaos and battle from below, it became clear enough for the creature to make sense of what he had seen. Still, he looked about at the one voice who had summoned him. When he spotted her, he called out to her as his daughter. Marin replied loud enough to be heard to acknowledge her father, King Ascentius IV of Swordbane, and that she had summoned him in this time of need. Linitus followed up by interjecting. The elf stated specifically they had requested his intervention from what they saw as a violation of the summoned powers of other planes outside of Terrunaemara. This included Wothunak corrupting and calling upon the Valkyrie spirits from another realm to fight in service to him and Helskadi using dark necrotic magic considered to be outside of the mortal realm while she summoned the undead corpses to fight on her behalf.

Ascentius looked about the surroundings below him as well as in the air. He realized what his daughter and son-in-law had said was indeed true. Ascentius, the Dragonman King (as he was coined by his subjects with that nickname), still hovering in the air while flapping his dragon wings, turned to the two titans, both of whom stood lost in thought of what they had seen. Wothunak reacted first by asking who this creature was and by what authority he had to intervene in the affairs of Shimmerfrost. Helskadi was somewhat familiar with the identity of this new visitor after she recalled from her past discussions with Agaroman. The chief wizard consultant and advisor of the Imperial Remnant had mentioned this strange being. This creature was the king of Swordbane and formerly a human, but now had assumed an anthropomorphic dragon humanoid form. After Helskadi disclosed aloud her realization of who this was, Ascentius replied that he indeed is still that man as he once was in human form despite having a reincarnated body infused with the essence of the deity spirit of Sol Invictus.

Upon hearing such a proclamation, Wothunak burst into abrupt laughter. He struggled to maintain his composure after hearing what Ascentius revealed himself to be. The male jotunn titan expressed his doubts about such a divine claim by this flying half-man, half-dragon creature despite his apparent momentous arrival. Still, it mattered not to

Ascentius whether his newfound foes were impressed and intimidated by him or not. He told both the jotunn titans that their feud was over. They had misused their powers to disturb the natural order of the other portal realms to be corrupted in being used for corrupted and dark necrotic purposes. Ascentius followed up by stating in a pointed tone that both these two titans would stand judgment for their unsanctimonious transgression.

The two jotunn titans became angry. They both mutually agreed with each other to put their differences aside temporarily upon hearing this. They vehemently stood in defiance against Ascentius. Wothunak called upon his corrupted flying mounted Valkyrie to attack Ascentius. Helskadi continued to raise more of the corpses of the fallen soldiers from combat on both sides to attack the Nordling–dyr coalition forces. Knowing that these two titans would not surrender willingly, Ascentius looked down while hovering several feet above Linitus and Marin. The Dragonman King told his son-in-law and daughter that they would have to vanquish these titans directly since they would not surrender willingly. Linitus could not help but shrug and ask how. These titans were considered near-immortal. Ascentius drew upon the essence of Sol Invictus that was fused into him. He responded that there were other means to defeating them even if they were seemingly invincible. He told Marin to remember how she summoned him using her wailing voice and to use that same power to channel her mind and voice in summoning other creatures like him.

Stunned by what she heard from her father, Marin asked how that was possible and what he meant by that. Ascentius flopped his wings while hovering in the air. Before he flew off, however, he told Marin to have faith in what she could do and not give up hope just as she had before, including when she just called upon her father in a brief moment. Marin nodded with a determined resolve to heed her father's words. Confident in her daughter's response, Ascentius returned his attention to the matter at hand. He flew toward the extraplanar group of mounted flying Valkyrie to engage them in combat while allowing Linitus and Marin time to deal with Helskadi and Wothunak separately.

Linitus meanwhile had an idea while thinking back to how Marin earlier had vanquished Helskadi's chief lieutenant. When she had finished dealing the jotunn a fatal blow, she had severed his head as a trophy. Even if they could not kill the two other jotunns for being considered more powerful divinelike titans, they could sever and dismember them to the point where they could no longer pose a threat. Marin at first thought his idea was ridiculous, but then taking another quick moment to reflect, she nodded and agreed that he was right. It might be possible that they could deal with these titans in such a way if they could not kill them outright.

Ready to engage the titans, Linitus called upon Wyatt to teleport him and Marin back to the same tower walkway in which Helskadi and Wothunak still stood perched watching and directing their forces to overtake the Nordling–dyr coalition as well as Ascentius. Wyatt nodded and prepared to teleport his two companions. However, before he had done so, Linitus told his halfling wizard comrade along with Peat to do everything possible to keep the undead army at bay. Peat acknowledged while telling his elven friend that they would give them a good bashing.

In an instant flash, Linitus and Marin had flashed in and out of a teleportation portal. They found themselves returning to the main fortress tower on the walkway looking below the chaos of the still-ensuing battle. Helskadi and Wothunak both took notice and readied themselves to attack the elven ranger and the Golden Valkyrie. Marin told Linitus she would deal with Helskadi while letting Linitus deal with Wothunak. Linitus nodded and the two kept some distance from each other while Linitus drew his bow and let loose an arrow toward Wothunak's abdomen. The jotunn, though not fast, could absorb the impact. The arrow pierced him with only a slightly noticeable wound while he hurled his enchanted war ax in a wide horizontal arc toward Linitus before the weapon returned to the titan's possession. The elf ranger ducked under just in time as the magical weapon flung toward him. Linitus then readied another arrow and this time pulled back his bow and let loose while in a crouching position in which he rolled backward after firing his arrow. The projectile struck the titan near the kneecap. It dealt a strong enough blow, causing Wothunak to fall on one leg similar to what Linitus had done earlier in the battle against Helskadi.

For a moment this caught the attention of Helskadi herself as well as Marin. The Winter Death Witch, however, wasted no time in pressing her attack. She plunged her spear staff toward Marin. Marin in turn dodged and parried her adversary's attacks with her sword and shield. The two were at a back-and-forth standstill for some time with neither one gaining the upper hand.

The same, however, was not the case between Linitus and Wothunak, in which the latter struggled in desperation. Wothunak, already down on one leg by a crippling blow by his smaller elf adversary, swung in failed desperation toward Linitus with his enormous ax once again. Linitus strafed and, taking one of his arrows while holding the shaft, slammed the arrowhead deep into Wothunak's left non-wielding hand. The piercing blow caused enough agonized pain against the jotunn to languish loudly while trying one last time with his weapon-wielding hand to swipe his magical ax toward the elf. Once again Linitus dodged the attack and this time he went behind Wothunak. Linitus unsheathed his slightly curved, long silver blade. The elf used his weapon to slash the back bottom heel of his other uninjured leg. This caused the giant to lose his balance and fall forward face first.

Linitus wasted no time. He quickly ran atop the titan's body and readied his blade while doing a somersault flip. The elf ranger descended with full force vertically downward. His blade ran down hard against the back neck of the jotunn titan. The strike was vicious. It partially severed the giant's head. Linitus followed up and quickly slashed and hacked away with his blade. Wothunak found himself cut apart with his head rolling across the tower walkway, seeing the rest of his body lifeless and bleeding from the neck profusely. Though not dead, he was in immense pain. He almost wished he was dead while shouting in despair upon realizing and seeing what had happened. After defeating Wothunak Linitus quickly turned his attention to the spiral staircase leading to the wall walk. He could hear the creepy sound of several of the undead warriors approaching. The elf ranger with his bow drawn, started shooting his arrows to keep the approaching undead forces at bay while Marin continued to battle Helskadi.

Meanwhile the sight of Wothunak being soundly and swiftly defeated caught the attention of both Marin and Helskadi. The Winter Death Witch could not hold back her startled reaction to what she saw. She became filled with a mixture of fear, disgust, and anger at the sight of such a relatively small creature (compared to her size) who could best combat a fellow jotunn and titan. This was considered to be a reprehensible act for a jotunn to endure, even if Wothunak was once her sworn rival. Helskadi then became determined to make sure she would not suffer the same fate of her fellow giant adversary. She returned her attacks toward her immediate foe dressed as the Golden Valkyrie. The Winter Death Witch struck faster and with more fury using her spear staff against Marin. Marin evaded by strafing, dodging, and ducking under Helskadi's attacks. The

Princess Knight became patient during the unfolding melee to find the right moment of opportunity to catch the Winter Death Witch off guard.

Eventually, Marin pressed forward after strafing from a powerful lunge in which the female titan giant missed in impaling her smaller adversary. The Princess Knight tried to run up to the titan's foot and prepare to stab her blade with full force toward the base of Helskadi's boot. The hard strike connected in impaling Helskadi's foot. The giant female jotunn gave a brief loud moan of pain and anger. Marin took a moment to sigh and catch her breath at this point. She believed that the fight would be over very soon.

However, Helskadi quickly surprised Marin, who was briefly caught off guard. The female titan used her non-wielding hand to grab in her clutches the smaller Valkyrie-clad shield maiden. Marin struggled while her arms were tightly wrapped around the grip of Helskadi. The Winter Death Witch felt Marin's resistance and the throbbing pain the Princess Knight let out from her voice in feeling Helskadi's tight squeeze. Helskadi applied more pressure, only to see Marin throb even more in agony. Slowly the female titan moved her hand, holding Marin closer to Helskadi's face to look at the smaller human with utter scorn and a feeling of superiority. The sadistic female titan relished in the pain she inflicted upon her adversary while commenting on how weak Marin was to do anything about it. Helskadi continued to taunt the Princess Knight. The female jotunn told Marin that once she was done crushing Marin to death, she would do the same to Marin's elven companion. Helskadi would then set about redoubling her efforts to conquer Shimmerfrost with no further disruptions.

Marin, however, feared for her lover in what her adversary had said. Somehow the Princess Knight became consumed by both a manifested sense of rage and fierce determination. She thought back to what her father had said earlier in concentrating her powers and though she could not move her body outside the clutches of her giant adversary, Marin could still channel her energies into unleashing another loud powerful wailing shout, which she did, much to the surprise of Helskadi. The wailing noise was loud enough to send ripple effects by which Marin nearly deafened Helskadi with the sound of the former's voice. It was enough to cause the female jotunn giant to let go of Marin while Helskadi circled around in a daze before recomposing herself. By the time she did, Marin had hurled a radiant spear of light which pierced the right leg of the Winter Death

Witch. Helskadi was down to one knee again before realizing a more terrifying sight and sound, which Marin had caused. Soon enough, peering from the horizon, all present who could hear the sounds saw four large blue ice dragons that roared loudly while soaring across the sky, setting their sights dead ahead to Jotunheim.

The dragon roars continued to deafen the sky as the dragons came closer toward the jotunn fortress settlement. All four dragons circled about. They focused their sights on the source that had summoned them. Marin stared right back at them. She then pointed toward Helskadi before unleashing another wailing shout.

The Winter Death Witch became filled with an array of emotions, including fear, anger, scorn, and defiance. Helskadi refused to surrender. She yelled back, cursing the embodied Golden Valkyrie and her elf companion. Within moments, however, all four ice dragons heeded the signaled intent of their summoner. The dragons complied and unleashed a large series of ice blasts that engulfed Helskadi. Linitus and Marin quickly took cover near the far end of the tower walkway. Within moments, the Winter Death Witch, in an agonized kneeling posture, had now been frozen in ice. Marin wasted no time and rushed toward her frozen adversary. The Golden Valkyrie quickly used her flaming sword to hack at Helskadi, now in a frozen state. Marin ultimately delivered the final blow in emulation of what her elven lover had previously done to Wothunak. Marin severed Helskadi's head from the rest of what was intact of her frozen body.

By this point, the battle was finally over. The dragons swarmed around Marin, ready to serve at her next calling, while the surviving forces loyal to Helskadi quickly fled in fear, knowing the battle for their side to prevail was lost. The undead forces also had suddenly lost the summoned and channeled power that Helskadi maintained over them. The summoned corpses of the fallen now lay motionless on the ground. The spirits of the summoned Valkyrie had also disappeared in a series of flashes after Linitus defeated Wothunak. The remaining Nordling and dyr warriors looked about at what they had witnessed and cheered on loudly with shouts and war cries to celebrate their victory.

Marin looked at both Helskadi's frozen severed head and Wothunak's severed head, both of which still lamented in pain and showed signs of a faint life. The Princess Knight turned and looked next to Linitus. Marin shrugged, asking what to do next. Approaching from behind her, a familiar coarse and haughty voice replied that they should give the miserable wenches a final partying goodbye by dumping them over the cliffs of the Jotunn Pass leading down into what seemed like a dark endless abyss. At least nobody would dare to follow them again and whatever influence they would still have in their new dismembered state. Upon hearing the suggestive voice, Marin turned around upon recognizing it was Peat. She shrugged with casual indifference and agreed why not. He was right after all. If these fallen titans were discarded in an otherwise unreachable place, none would know or would dare to try to seek them out.

Marin looked at the four ice dragons that hovered above. Then she looked at her father a few feet above her, who was hovering in the air with his extended dragon wings. Ascentius seemed to have read his daughter's mind and knew what she thought. The king nodded in approval. Taking a deep breath, the Princess Knight unleashed another wailing screech. It caught the ice dragons' attention. Upon doing so, Marin pointed with her two hands at the severed heads of the fallen titans before pointing again to the endless abyss that lay beyond the near vicinity of Jotunheim and within the steep narrow interior pass of the vast mountain range that encircled the settlement.

The dragons glared and nodded back to their summoner. All four of the flying beasts unleashed a single wave of loud roars. Within moments, two of the dragons scooped one of each of the severed heads while the other two flying beasts scooped much of the remaining corpses of the now-fallen titans before flying off to the sky and dumping the contents that they carried down to the seemingly bottomless pit that lay between Jotunheim and the vast ring of the Jotunn Mountains. Wothunak and Helskadi (with her head thawed), both screamed endlessly for a time until their severed heads could no longer be heard.

The sight of what many of the surviving Nordling and dyr warriors had witnessed was considered by them as an epic for the ages. They would pass down this unfolding battle by song and oral campfire tale to countless generations among their kin. All of them that bore witness cheered on. They piled what seemed like endless heaps of praise for the two heroes that led them, Marin and Linitus. The victorious allied army also expressed praise to the one dragon humanoid who came in which was a sight to behold. The allied army was unfamiliar with this creature until this battle when he appeared. Now they knew who he was by which Marin had called the creature her father, King Ascentius IV of Swordbane, the Dragonman King. Truly many Nordlings felt that not only their nightmare was finally over, but that it was the start of a new golden age that Shimmerfrost had not experienced since the time of the first king that originally united the Nordlings in this region.

After receiving many cheers and war cries of veneration, Marin looked to Linitus, who nodded in acknowledgment of their achievement. The Princess Knight walked a few steps to embrace her elven lover. She then turned to see her father unleash a large dragon beast roar. The ice dragons from far away heard the sound and roared back. The flying beasts then soared through the air. They traveled due north from which they came.

Ascentius then slowly descended with his wings to the walkway of the main fortress tower. He looked at his daughter, who stood somewhat surprised, along with everyone else, at what he had done. Ascentius casually replied that the ability to command dragons ran in the family, and Marin was not the only one to have that ability. Marin chuckled mildly with some surprise. Still, she asked with curiosity why her father had finally come in their time of need so late in the hour when he could have come any other time earlier. Ascentius sighed with some sorrow and remorse. He conceded in part what she said was true but that deep down, she and Linitus both knew the answer if they sought to ponder deep enough in thought.

Linitus still held one of Marin's hands and nodded. The elf said aloud that just like Decius had once done in violating the tenets of chosen vesselhood, it was only in that sense in which Ascentius could also act when the two jotunn titans had unleashed and corrupted unnatural forces, including other realms sent to Terrunaemara by portals. In this type of circumstance, Ascentius had the authority to act. In this case, it was due to Wothunak unleashing the hidden power of the mysterious crystal ball, which he used his own powers to summon and command in a corrupted manner supernatural Valkyrie female warriors from another realm to deliver death to those the titan willed it upon. This was seen according to Ascentius as a violation of the ethereal shield maidens performing their intended duties in delivering the souls of the worthy dead to the afterlife which they, the Nordlings, ascribed to and called Val-Hifinn. Ascentius also mentioned that Helskadi was arguably equally as guilty since she used necrotic powers to possess the corpses of the fallen, which the divine spirits—as powerful as they are—were not able to detect this other act of supernatural desecration.

Marin, while lost in words, gave in ultimately while nodding and agreeing that she understood her father's justification for why he had acted at the time that he did. However, Ascentius reminded his daughter he would not have had to do so, had she not learned to tap into her inner supernatural powers and learned to summon him at the time she did in which she, Linitus, and the many allies they led direly needed his aid.

Ascentius reached out his jagged, green-clawed hand to his daughter. It was his sign that she knew that he missed her and wanted to embrace her once again. Marin could only hold back her tears for so long. However, she finally shed several droplets while reaching with both her hands and embracing her father. It was a sight that many survivors of the allied army could see. Everyone bearing witness was quiet. They knew that despite the appearance and aura Marin carried in being donned as the valiant and seemingly invincible Golden Valkyrie, she was still as human and capable of expressing her feelings with vulnerability to a creature that, as baffling as any had seen, could still recognize somehow was presumably her father, which he was (though originally in a different form from his past human life). This moment had truly captivated the Nordlings and dyr warriors. It was beyond words they could formulate into songs of great deeds, yet somehow they would strive to still do so and tell their kin again what they had seen.

After embracing her father, Marin held Linitus's hand as they approached the crenellations by the ledge of the main tower of the fortress complex. There they faced the main bulk of the surviving allied army below from the courtyard. Marin addressed them all as comrades and told them that the battle was over. The war against Helskadi was finally over. They now had a future in which they could live without being under the same yoke of fear and power of darkness that once took hold over them. She told them they would prepare a final rite for the fallen on both sides. They would salvage whatever materials from the giant settlement they could find to prepare makeshift pyres and cremate the remains of the dead. They would do this before finally departing this cold, barren place to make their way back south. There they would go through Jotunn Pass and return to Nebelheim to declare their victory before the settlement's chieftain and the dyr embassy in the hopes that they could start forging a new age together in prosperity and in the absence of the former darkness that once took hold over them.

After another day had passed, all the deceased remains from both sides of the battle had been prepared along with funeral pyres. Wood was gathered from various items and structural pieces found throughout the giant settlement. Once the funeral and ritual cremations were performed, Marin and Linitus organized their surviving allied army. They numbered just over five hundred. Together they would march in unison toward the gate of the settlement and back out through the steep narrow jagged Jotunn Pass.

However, upon marching out from Jotunheim, from a distance Linitus spotted and pointed out with his keen eyes a lone flying object from the sky. It was approaching them from the southern direction. It was difficult to make out at first, but the elf ranger knew what it was. He called out with excitement to the rest of the allied army that their friends, Andarin and Alvissan, had returned with their flying skyboat! The elf let loose a flare arrow high in the sky that sparked multiple bright flares, drawing the flying dwarves' attention. Within moments, the skyboat homed in on their location and descended to the open courtyard below.

After tethering the skyboat to the ground, the two captaining dwarves emerged from the side of the skyboat using a ramp plank and quickly ran to greet and hug Linitus and Marin as well as Wyatt and Peat. The Nordlings and dyr warriors cheered on after receiving the good news that Andarin and Alvissan had resupplied the skyboat with extra provisions to distribute to the surviving allied army. This included food and drink to the army, which they sorely needed as the food stores Helskadi had for her forces were somewhat limited unless being cooked on site. Though the reception had lifted the morale of the allied army that much more, they still had to traverse the long, narrow-winded path through the Jotunn Mountains leading to the entrance outside before making their way farther south to reach Nebelheim. Marin and Linitus commanded for the most severely wounded to be carried onboard the skyboat. This included those who still needed to recover even after Marin had used her supernatural powers to heal all those who were wounded in ways that Marin could not fully heal, including a few who were amputated.

After three days of steady travel, their forces had reached the Jotunn Gate, and within another three days of steady march, they would reach Nebelheim to deliver the news of their victory over Helskadi and her forces of darkness. Marin and Linitus had felt they could truly be at ease again. They would look forward to what they thought would be a promising future for the region of Shimmerfrost. Only then did they feel like they could confide to each other the relief in knowing that they had done enough to be content to leave Shimmerfrost and return home to the southwestern coastal lands of Swordbane. Still, the two lovers and celebrated heroes could not help but share in their own privacy each night along the way. They dreamed of what they would do together while finally being back home. It was the place in which they longed after many weeks of being so far away.

Chapter Fifty-Eight

Roadmap to Reunification

A week after their victory against Helskadi's forces at Jotunheim, the Comradery and the surviving veterans from the Nordling–dyr coalition army were within sight of Nebelheim. Linitus and Marin had sent word by courier ahead of their formation to notify the Nordling settlement of the victory against the Winter Death Witch. The town was eager to receive and celebrate the return of their defenders and champions, which they held Marin and even Linitus in such high esteem. Marin and Linitus could have easily taken the skyboat to make their grand entrance while traversing across the center of town toward the jarl's stronghold. Instead, they led a march on foot outside the settlement's walls. All those surviving warriors, dyr and Nordling alike as well as Wyatt and Peat, that followed Marin and Linitus into battle marched alongside the Princess Knight and the elf ranger. Marin and Linitus, after all, wanted the people to know that they were not the only ones to deserve the credit for liberating Shimmerfrost from the evil of Helskadi and also Wothunak, after his betrayal.

The march along the dirt-paved road to Nebelheim was a memorable moment. Marin and Linitus led from the front ranks while holding hands. They both considered themselves blessed to see a beautiful side of the far northern lands that they had not seen in such a way before as spring almost transitioned to summer. It was most noticeable as the sky was clear and the sun shined brightly on this late spring day. Wild purple and pink flowers on both sides of the dirt paved road stood out in being in full blossom. The ambient air struck a melody of sounds, from the chirping and humming of birds and small mammals to the loud sounds that could be heard from the town. The townsfolk knew they were coming and were eager to celebrate their victory. Right before entering the wooden palisade gates from a few hundred yards away, Linitus withdrew his bow and took a special arrow equipped with a small cylinder. With the bow fully drawn, the elf ranger pointed and aimed his bow and arrow upward before letting loose the bowstring. The arrow soared high across the sky before quickly exploding with an array of colorful sparks that glossed over the sky. The sight of such a rare display had captivated the townsfolk and local guards who saw from various locations about the town to cheer on what they had witnessed.

All the townsfolk and guards stood near the path from the main town gate leading to the chieftain's stronghold. The local populace continued to cheer on the small victorious parading army. Crowds of bystanders heaped various titles of praise upon Marin and Linitus. These local crowds also were in awe of not only seeing the skyboat flying from above but also the mysterious anthropomorphic dragonman creature that gracefully soared across the sky. The townsfolk did not know what to make of this creature.

Marin, however, quickly caught notice of their uncertainty. She dispelled any potential negative reservation they may have toward the unfamiliar creature. The ascribed Golden Valkyrie called loudly upon her father to request for him to remain by her side. Ascentius honored her request while slowly descending. Upon landing, Marin took her father's hand and raised it alongside hers while announcing as loud as those that can hear her that this person was her father and that he once walked the land as a human just like the rest of the Nordling crowd. The people, though somewhat in shock, still accepted the surreal claim she made about her familial relation with this dragon humanoid. After all, they reasoned, Marin had already proven herself to be a worthy hero to them in her own right. She was one who was full of many astonishments, which they had not expected, and now they would not dispute her claim about being the daughter of the Dragonman King.

It was at this point that the Nordling chieftain, Jarl Harleif, walked down from his stronghold toward the victorious coalition army. Harleif greeted Linitus, Marin, and Ascentius. The chieftain was in awe at first upon seeing Ascentius in his dragon humanoid form. The jarl struggled to comprehend Marin's claim of Ascentius being her father. Still, the jarl of Nebelheim accepted her claim as much as the townsfolk had. The jarl knew there had to be an explanation despite the physiological differences between Marin and Ascentius. There was no doubt in Marin's words of her familial relation with Ascentius, as she had been proven a trustworthy and honorable war maiden.

Once inside the stronghold, the chieftain hosted in his central hall a splendid feast to celebrate the Comradery and allied army's victory. Many tables and chairs lined up filled with various Nordling warriors and dignitaries. The dyr folk were also present at the feast as guests, including their warriors and several druid elders. All of them celebrated and discussed alongside the Nordlings various topics pertaining to Shimmerfrost.

The most important topic the Nebelheim chieftain brought up was the matter of going forward in how to unify the region of Shimmerfrost. He suggested Marin and Linitus could lead the coalition army to subdue by the use of force both Frostburg and Shimmerheim. In doing so, both the Golden Valkyrie and the elven ranger could rule the region as royal monarchs in a new dynasty to bring a new era of peace that the region had not experienced in a long time.

Linitus looked at both Marin and Ascentius. All three were apprehensive about the jarl's plan. Both Linitus and Ascentius were of the same mind, thinking it would be too much to interfere in the internal affairs among the inhabitants of this region now that they were free from the terror of Helskadi. Marin wanted to do more in unifying Shimmerfrost. However, with a restrained and saddened demeanor, she also knew the dilemma being posed if pursuing conquest of the region with means of force. It would be questionable to say they were liberators against the forces of darkness, only to become outright next-in-line conquerors themselves. It would impose a new order even if it was not one that sought to bring evil. It would still bring in a form of perceived tyranny in which there could be further resentment and resistance.

For Ascentius, he knew this lesson well enough. He considered this during his prior human life. To reclaim what once was would not always be welcomed if those that are brought under the name of unification, or reunification rather, were done by coercion or brute force rather than a genuine form of consent. The Dragon King interjected to let the Nebelheim chieftain know, with both Marin and Linitus nodding in mutual consent, that this request was one they could not do. Marin replied that if the chieftain wished to unify Shimmerfrost, then it would be best to do so by gaining the free will and consent of the remaining independent Nordling and dyr folk settlements in the region.

The chieftain was shocked. He displayed a sense of both mild resentment and feeling insulted. He rebuked what he heard by saying that this was not the Nordling way. Their people had only understood to follow the valiant and strong among them who led by force. How would they understand in any other way?

Linitus interjected calmly while pointing out to the chieftain to observe and consider how the Nordlings of his settlement had already gained an important ally. This was one far different from their own kin. The chieftain noticed and saw that at the many tables, the dyr folk feasted side by side next to the Nordlings. The elf was right, which the chieftain acknowledged. It took some effort, but even the dyr folk who had frequently fought against the Nordlings had sought a common cause to unite. Both groups realized the greater enemies that terrorized them were the forces of darkness.

The chieftain nodded while conceding that perhaps it was the better path to pursue unity, even if it lacked the glory of future warrior tales and songs to be sung from the actions of those who vanquish the defeated in battle. Linitus commented again, saying that at least such a song would not create resentment among those who survive on the losing side to resent and rebel. At least this lesser song lacking martial glory could still be sung for the roadmap to reunification. All those who heard such a song would appreciate its meaning and still be content. They would find no reason or past grievance to undo the unity that would be reestablished among the Nordlings in this region and also with the dyr folk.

A dead air of silence filled the dining hall. Every Nordling gasped at what they heard from the elf's mouth. It was unimaginable at first to think of such a praiseworthy song to sing about peace without war and great epic battles. The chieftain became amazed and in awe at what he heard from the elf. He took it to heart while placing his hand over Linitus's shoulder and thanking him for bestowing these words of wisdom. The chieftain admitted openly that even the most stubborn, battle-hardened Nordling must heed such profound advice if he was to lead and realize that a greater outcome could be achieved without bloodshed. Linitus nodded just before the chieftain motioned for the elf to stand up with him, which Linitus did.

The chieftain then stood and raised his tankard full of beer. He proclaimed that on this day going forward, the old ways of Nordling conquest in Shimmerfrost would have to make room for the new ways. He told his subjects and his dyr allies furthermore because of this elf, a stranger and foreigner in Shimmerfrost, even he, along with Marin, the Golden Valkyrie as the chieftain referred to her, and her father, the Dragonman King, he had truly learned what it meant to be a leader by both their example of deeds and virtuous words. The chieftain vowed to do all that could be done, even with patience, to unite the good people of this region by consent, no matter how long it would take.

Ascentius stood up to affirm the chieftain's vow. The Dragonman King stated it was the most noble and praiseworthy path to take. Even he, in his superimposing anthropomorphic form, had to learn once before that lesson what it meant to be a respected ruler while not overlooking the needs of his subjects. Ascentius invited the chieftain to send an ambassadorial embassy or to come in his own stead along with some appointed Nordling and dyr dignitaries as honored guests in the Kingdom of Swordbane to the south after the Nebelheim jarl unified Shimmerfrost through peace and consent of being governed by his leadership.

In a brief pause of quietness once again throughout the hall, suddenly a burst of cheers and clanking of ale-filled tankards erupted. All those Nordlings and dyr folk bearing witness became enamored and instilled with new vigor in a realization that they had not taken hold of before. The words they heard resonated from hearing it from their future king (who had been inspired by Linitus's words and example) as well as the Dragonman King. A new feeling of hope in the air had been realized.

Marin stood up next to say her own words, which she thought had to be said. The crowd of dinner guests all came to a quiet, still voice to hear her speak. The Golden Valkyrie told them that while she was honored to don the legendary armor, which was gifted to her, and play the role they had envisioned her to fill, it was no longer her place or role to play in their future. Just as she told the chieftain, she had also told the crowd that they had to want to fight for their own futures and even more so if possible to fight for it peacefully rather than through the use of force when possible. They had to not give up convincing their own countrymen in other settlements that peace had more meaning to celebrate. There would be no lives to lose. It would be a far better outcome than if she or Linitus had led and fought to slay countless lives that did not have to be lost in the name of unity.

All who listened were then silent and speechless once again from what she said in unison with the speeches Linitus and King Ascentius delivered in pursuing unity without force of violence. Marin then turned abruptly. She put down her golden winged helmet on the table in front of the jarl. Her dark blond hair now flowed more freely and her warm fair skin cheeks stood out less obstructed by the cheek guards of the helmet. Marin told everyone present in the jarl's hall that the Golden Valkyrie legend had fulfilled her role and that it was time for someone else to pick up the helm and outdo her not by how many lives could be taken in war but by how many could be saved through peace. The Princess Knight, as Marin now referred to herself again instead of the Golden Valkyrie, was ready to return home. However, she returned the helmet as a symbolic gesture to the chieftain as a symbol of her recognition of his pledge and her vouch for him.

The chieftain, in awe of what he had witnessed, was reluctant to accept. He stated to Marin that she had earned this helmet. The jarl questioned if she was sure of what she was doing. Marin nodded and told the chieftain to have every person who sought to be united under his authority in the name of peace to make their pledge before her helmet and only when he unified the region would she allow the chieftain to give the helmet to her again. The chieftain nodded and agreed with her wishes.

Immediately, a dyr druid, who was the most senior among the dyr folk, rose and slowly came to the chieftain. This druid slowly kneeled while placing his jagged palm on top of the Golden Valkyrie helmet that the chieftain now held. The elder dyr uttered a few words in his own language. Linitus understood the spoken words and translated them to affirm to the Nordling chieftain that on behalf of the druid's kin, the dyr folk would pledge their loyalty to him.

The chieftain, now viewed as a near-bestowed king in all but actual name, acknowledged the pledge of the druid's fealty. The jarl placed his gauntlet hand on the dyr druid and stated that he would accept his pledge and look out after the interests of the dyr folk with the same equal weight as he would with his own Nordling subjects of Nebelheim and all the other Nordling subjects as well as other sentient creatures of goodwill throughout Shimmerfrost.

Soon a line followed one by one in which all the other Nordlings and dyr folk would voluntarily make the same pledge of fealty as the dyr druid had to the jarl of Nebelheim. It was a moment of great joy and elation, in which Linitus and Marin embraced each other while standing and holding hands to witness. Even Ascentius was impressed. He quietly walked toward his daughter and son-in-law to tell them both how proud he was to bear witness to what they had done. They helped to forge a new beginning and a new hope for an emerging, vibrant kingdom. King Ascentius then took a moment to reflect on his reign during and after the Great Civil War unleashed by Decius just over ten years prior that fractured the Kingdom of Swordbane. The cause for the war was in large part due to the king's own general neglect over the actual needs of a wide swathe of his subjects in his kingdom. Ascentius hoped that in time when the jarl did become king in Shimmerfrost, he would not forget his subjects as Ascentius once had. However, the Dragonman King knew at least that life lessons could be learned and not repeated as they were in other places and eras of time. He would make sure before departing with the Comradery to pass along to the jarl his account of lived experience as a ruling monarch, including the choices he made and did not make as well as the consequences from those made and unmade choices he and his subjects endured throughout his reign so the jarl may benefit from the knowledge of kingship.

As the pledges of fealty and support ended with more festivity and celebration, Marin and Linitus found the opportune time to be discreet in excusing themselves. They headed toward the chieftain's honored guest rooms in his stronghold on the second floor to retire for the night.

Peat, meanwhile, did not withhold from his nature in being loud, haughty, and indulging in the consumption of alcohol. He danced on the table along with Wyatt. The dwarf had enticed the halfling wizard to drink a half pint of Nebelheim ale before taking away and consuming the other half pint from the tankard. In order to ensure his halfling comrade would not suffer the effects he had before from his last bout of beer drinking, Peat would take it upon himself to consume the remaining portion of the half pint. The Nordlings and dyr folk cheered on before all were passed out from drunkenness in the hall. The chieftain himself, knowing his stature had been effectively promoted to king, withheld from indulging in the consumption of beer as he normally would. He did not want to give the slightest impression of being a drunkard in order for his image to be taken more seriously throughout the region. Ascentius noticed this and took the time to have a more personal conversation as the former had planned to advise the jarl on his future expected reign as a king. After doing so, Ascentius went to one of the guest rooms to retire for the night. The chieftain meanwhile stood on his throne chair to sleep eventually while holding the Golden Valkyrie helmet and appreciating the significance this object held for not only his legitimacy and sovereignty but also in being the symbol to unite Shimmerfrost once again. He would take to heart the words of wisdom that he saw from three heroic legends and strangers to the region, for those words to him were wiser than that he had ever heard from among his own kin.

On the next sunrise, the heroes of the Comradery would depart along with King Ascentius to board Andarin and Alvissan's skyboat to take the long voyage back home to the southwestern coastal lands of Swordbane. Marin would wear the rest of her Golden Valkyrie armor while waving goodbye from the top deck of the skyboat alongside her elven soulmate, husband, and fellow adventurer, Linitus. She reflected and confided to her husband as the flying vessel departed about how strange, marvelous, and even dangerous this land was. Yet, she admitted to him, that this region was like the place they called home despite the differences in which this inhospitable land had tested them, shaping their character and endurance. She wanted to go back home earlier on various occasions, but she and Linitus both knew they had a role to play, and now it was time to move on. Now it was time for them to prepare for the long journey back home.

Linitus nodded after listening to what his wife had said. The elf ranger stated he felt the same. He told her, however, that since their time in this harsh cold land, she had surpassed him in many respects, in which he almost envied her.

Marin looked with a deep sense of gratitude and appreciation upon hearing those words from her elven husband and lover. Linitus was, from Marin's point of view, which she confided to him, always her role model for discerning right from wrong as much, if not more, than her own father. She admitted she had grown and attributed much of that to what she had experienced as well as what she had learned from him.

Linitus nodded with humility and gratitude but told her there was much in which he thought she had learned from herself and on her own. He was grateful to share his life with her and content to be a part of her life in seeing her grow. Marin, giving a brief surprised kiss, replied that he was her life and that they had become one in which she would never want to spend a day without being there with him. Linitus held her in his arms while telling her he felt the same way.

The members of the Comradery enjoyed the view while the sun shined in all its late spring brightness. Everyone on board the stern of the skyboat stood and looked back at Nebelheim one last time, facing the north. When it became far enough away to no longer see beyond the horizon, they turned and faced the bow of the vessel. They soaked in with appreciation and unwavering enchantment at the green forest-covered land interior that contrasted brightly with the sparkling waves that crashed into the elevated gray rock cliff fjords as the black orca whales farther away in the water splashed and leaped across the water. It was a long voyage home but at least with consolation: they could see the beauty and natural majesty in which the world of Terrunaemara offered from high above while departing the far northern lands of Shimmerfrost.

Chapter Fifty-Nine

Finding Closure

After nearly two and a half weeks of travel from Nebelheim and going southward, the Comradery had at long last made it to Swordbane's northern border. The border itself demarcated the boundaries between the Kingdom of Swordbane in the south from the coastal forest domain of the Nordlings in the north. It was at Swordbane's border settlement of Colonia Aldion (simply known as Aldion) that the Comradery made a brief stop. Upon arrival, the skyboat received new stores of supply. King Ascentius also dispatched the fastest horse couriers to deliver news to the capital of Citadella Neapola. Neapola was over 300 miles farther away to the south. The couriers could deliver the news within just less than a day while stopping along various horse-changing stations to switch between steeds.

The capital would be ready to prepare a special triumph and parade for the heroes' homecoming. King Ascentius and the Comradery were due to arrive within two days. It gave enough time for Linitus and Marin, along with Peat and Wyatt, to explore Aldion as they once had before. The four companions appreciated its beauty after not seeing the settlement for quite some time. It fared well if not better in its rebuilt state, just as Citadella Neapola had done in being revitalized after the carnage both places had received from Decius's rebellion and civil war over ten years ago.

The fortified border settlement of Aldion was also aware of the news of the disappearance of the Comradery from several weeks prior. Now, however, the townsfolk celebrated with great excitement. News began to spread with the word on the streets that the heroes of this elite order had now returned to the Kingdom of Swordbane. Crowds swarmed around them while cheering their names one by one. The townsfolk asked for the returning heroes to tell the tales of their latest adventures. Linitus and Marin both shrugged. They would leave the storytelling to Peat. They both knew their older companion would tell every detail, leaving no stone unturned. The dwarf would also add some embellishments to his own account, provided the listening recipients would give him at least two pints of beer to fill each of his two tankards. Wyatt would look on and nod. He enjoyed the contrast between Peat's accounts of unfolding events (especially after the dwarf had more than his fair share of drink) and the events that actually transpired.

It was at this point that Marin, and especially Linitus, preferred privacy over publicity. They did not want to draw as much attention from the crowds. Linitus and Marin waited a brief moment before signaling for their halfling wizard companion to teleport them back to the skyboat. Wyatt nodded and was happy to oblige in respecting his comrades' wishes.

This sudden arrival at Aldion was somewhat more subtle in comparison to the heroic reception the Comradery received from Queen Chieftain Helga when they stopped a few days prior at the Nordling coastal settlement of Aegir-Hafn. It was there that they stopped to deliver the news of their exploits in Shimmerfrost. Out of all the ones who originally left from the Nordling settlement to join Peat and Wyatt on the journey to Shimmerfrost, only two of the elite Banesmen berserkers survived along with the old fisherman who initially stayed behind in Nebelheim until the Comradery had finished their quest in vanquishing Helskadi. Now the returning old fisherman made sure to not come empty-handed. He fetched a large haul of Shimmerfrost salmon along with a newfound companion. It was a giant beaver. The old Nordling fisherman happened to also give the noble furry creature a new name, Harold.

Now, as the Comradery neared their final destination home, the skyboat departed after a mere one-day stay at Aldion just as they did at Aegir-Hafn. The flying vessel they traveled in would traverse at half speed. This allowed enough time for the couriers on the surface to deliver the message to the capital. It would also enable the city administrators to still have enough time to make their hastily devised preparations to formally receive the heroes of the Comradery and hold a triumph ceremony. King Ascentius intended to preside over the ceremony to confer and bestow honor to his daughter, the Princess Knight, and his son-in-law, the elven ranger.

Upon arrival at the capital, the procession of this triumph, unlike the previous ones that the Comradery had held before, would be much different. The Comradery marched with no prisoners of war or bearing any symbolic loot from a defeated foe. Only words of their deeds, along with Marin donned in her Golden Valkyrie armor, would bear any testament to what they had accomplished.

However, there was one other sign that Marin thought of in her mind to attest to the trials and tribulations that they had faced. It was one that she kept to herself, at least until she thought it was the right time to reveal that sign. As the triumph commenced, the Comradery marched their way down the long main street of the ancient seaport metropolis of Citadella Neapola on the day of their arrival. They would continue to march up to the steps of the city's ancient rostra, or ancient platform used for public speeches. It was there that Marin and Linitus, along with Peat and Wyatt, kneeled before Ascentius to receive the ceremonial silver laurels of honor. Marin, with an expression on her face, looked intently at her father. Ascentius could read her face and knew what she wanted. He granted her wish with a nod of his head. It was a show of sign, an omen of the future that would realize prosperity and survival as long as there was hope.

After looking toward her husband, Linitus, who also nodded in knowing what she intended to do, the Princess Knight held her breath. She then looked upward at the sky before finally unleashing a large, epic wailing shout. The power of her voice impressed the crowd, but even more so was the effect of the summons.

Within moments, a large roaring shout came back to respond to the one which had summoned it. It was the roaring shout of a large blue dragon that flew and soared high above the air. The creature came into visibility while roaring once again. It looked intently toward its summoner who had reached her hand in the air to signal her wanting for him to descend and be embraced. The blue dragon nodded and roared in a more subtle and obedient manner while slowly descending to the main plaza that surrounded the rostra. Upon landing, the creature slowly creeped toward Marin while lowering its long massive neck and snout to allow the Princess Knight to pet and embrace it.

The sight of what happened had now become the proof in which the inhabitants of the city, townsfolk and city guard alike, were mesmerized by what they had witnessed. Whatever tales that they had claimed to have undertaken could not be in dispute after seeing what they had seen.

Marin looked toward her father. Despite calling this place home, it was not the same as the calling of the wilderness. She realized the latter had become her other home. The same home in which she shared in adventuring with her elven husband and their two smaller companions. She pondered and asked her husband if they wanted to go on another adventure, which her king father acknowledged in giving permission. Linitus, like Marin, never rode a dragon before. Still, he smiled humbly and nodded.

The elf ranger and Princess Knight next turned to Wyatt and Peat. The halfling wizard, being excited, quickly teleported himself behind the dragon's back in which the blue flying reptile beast was surprised but also impressed by grinning at Wyatt's display of magic. Peat, reluctant knowing he would probably throw up the first time like he did when he first boarded a skyship in the air, shrugged his shoulders. He indicated he might as well, provided they stop along the way at an inn or tavern to have warm food to stuff his belly as well as another pint of beer.

All four of the Comradery grabbed a firm hold atop the dragon's back after all of them had mounted the gigantic winged beast. They motioned their farewell biddings to the king before flying off into the sky. All of the city folks were in awe once more. None of them had ever seen a person or even a small group of individuals before riding on top of a dragon, not to mention none of them had seen a dragon at all save for their king in his reincarnated anthropomorphic state of being a half-dragon, half-man. Everyone in the crowd motioned with waves of goodbye as well as displayed loud cheers of what they had witnessed despite still not knowing the full story of what had happened with the Comradery at Shimmerfrost. It would be a tale for another day, which Wyatt would eventually record in the royal archives of what had transpired during their travels in Shimmerfrost. For the time being, after finding closure from what they endured from so far away, the departed heroes were content to soar the vast skies, looking below for their next adventure while staying closer to home.

Chapter Sixty

A New Dark Ascendance

Just under a month after Helskadi's downfall, Jotunheim was abandoned and left in ruins. That was except for only two newly arrived wanderers.

They made camp and pitched their crude makeshift animal skin tent at the highest tower of the fortified settlement. It was the same spot, a large tower wall walk, where Helskadi and Wothunak were defeated. These two figures had set up a makeshift tent, lit a burning fire for nearly a week, and survived meagerly off small amounts of food that they would scavenge from the interior towers. They fetched water from a nearby well to fill their waterskins. They had used the campfire to set up a spit while cooking a dead snow rabbit they had slain and cured with salt before arriving at Jotunheim.

These two figures had been companions for some time, and they would converse in Nordling speech. In a short time, the Nordling courier, Halkir, and his accompanied goblin shaman, Knower of Many Tongues, made sense of what had happened. They deduced that the mysterious strangers, including the elf ranger and the Golden Valkyrie, had somehow vanquished Helskadi and Wothunak. It saddened the odd wandering pair to reach that conclusion. Helskadi was the only notable figure to lay claim to being the dark lord of this region. Now Shimmerfrost had become a power vacuum among the forces of darkness. There was no apparent logical candidate to contend with and fulfill her role from this region. Halkir and Many Tongues both knew this would allow Shimmerfrost, with its various

Nordling chiefdoms, the possibility to unite. Even worse, it could also lead to unity with the other sentient beings of goodwill in this cold region such as the dyr folk.

It was a future prospect that they did not look forward to. It was one in which the goblin shaman feared that the Nordlings and dyr folk would seek to hunt his fellow goblins to extinction along with other servant creatures of darkness. However, both the goblin shaman and the Nordling courier from Frostburg reflected on this while searching and consulting with each other for a resolution. There had to be a dark lord that could lead and aid the creatures of darkness.

Upon further pondering, they remembered Helskadi's powerful Imperial Remnant ally from the southwestern lands. It was a young werewolf adolescent who had made frequent transactions of weapon shipments in exchange for beastly creature conscripts. Halkir and Knower of Many Tongues both believed that this young werewolf from the faraway southwest high desert would be worthy to fill the power void. He would be worthy of the beastly creatures to proclaim as their new dark lord. He had the potential to bring a new era of dark ascendance in which Halkir and Many Tongues both recognized and agreed. The two of them had traveled for a short time on board the young werewolf's skybeast. Despite the little time they had known this one called Lucianus, he seemed far more suitable and pragmatic than Helskadi to lead the now-fragmented dark forces of Shimmerfrost. Lucianus would be perhaps the key to beastly creatures' survival in Shimmerfrost, even if the young dux had his own designs as a dark lord.

Perhaps even more that aroused intrigue was verifying if this young dark lord indeed had a connection with a rumored specter spirit of a dark lord from another plane of existence. Only since the arrival of a few goblins from the southwestern lands had the goblins from Shimmerfrost learned their counterpart's ways. They could use their magic and priestly abilities to conduct a dark ritual of prayer, libation, and incense offering to gain enough favor in summoning the specter spirit of this particular infernal dark lord.

Halkir and Many Tongues continued their conversation about these two respective werewolf dark lords. They pointed out the similarities, including that this infernal dark lord was one who in fact resembled in many ways the young, dark werewolf leader of the Remnant. The only difference was this summoned dark lord was an adult-grown black werewolf that burned with small embers throughout his body and when summoned, appeared in a spectral ghost form. This one went by the name of Decius. He had claimed to be the dark lord of the hellish realm known as Hadao Infernum.

The courier and goblin shaman concluded that there had to be a familial connection between the two respective werewolves. If so, by ensuring that the various beastly creatures of Shimmerfrost were in the good graces of both powerful werewolves, they would in this moment of despair and uncertainty realize a future in which the surviving dark forces of Shimmerfrost would perhaps thrive once again as they had previously under Helskadi's reign. The courier and shaman would wait a while longer. They had faith that the young werewolf dark lord would come to make his entrance with the flying behemoth vessel that he commanded. A few days later, during sunset, their faith and determination would pay off.

While circling in the sky and above the main fortress tower of Jotunheim, the skybeast vessel hummed in a loud tone. Then, two bright flashes emerged on the walkway of the main fortress tower. There, before the shaman and courier, appeared two other figures, both covered in black robes. One was a human who lowered his hood to reveal his bald head and clean-shaven face. They had seen him before. He was known as Agaroman, chief advisor to the dux and dark lord of the Imperial Remnant. The other figure also removed his hood. He was none other than the young dark lord heir werewolf, Lucianus.

Lucianus approached at a slow pace toward the shaman and the courier. The latter two both prostrated themselves before Lucianus. Lucianus and Agaroman, in shock, asked them what had happened. The goblin shaman and Nordling courier both explained the situation in which Helskadi had fallen to the visiting newcomers of this region. The dark forces of Shimmerfrost were now in disarray. Halkir and Knower of Many Tongues told Lucianus that they knew he would come along with the next weapons shipment. The courier and shaman both pleaded for the young werewolf to accept their services. They vowed to install him as their de facto leader among the beastly creatures of Shimmerfrost now that Helskadi's reign was over.

Lucianus, shocked and surprised, turned to Agaroman for consultation in which he knew his wizard advisor's feelings, saying no words, but just reading Agaroman's face and nodding in support. Lucianus looked at his new prospective followers. The young dux nodded. He told them he would lead them as their new dark lord sovereign and that he would do what was necessary to safeguard the well-being of his loyal subjects in exchange for their fealty and unwavering loyalty. He told his new followers to rise, which they did.

After Halkir and Many Tongues pledged their fealty to Lucianus, the young dark lord werewolf and his wizard advisor, Agaroman, looked about and surveyed the area from the high point of the fortress tower. They sought to further make sense of what had happened, as well as devising a plan to go forward. Though the jotunn fortress stronghold had fallen, there were many lairs in which the beastly creatures had resided throughout Shimmerfrost. Lucianus had considered before plotting with great attention to circumvent Helskadi's authority to recruit the beastly creatures native to this region directly to Lucianus's cause. Now, however, the circumstances have changed more quickly than the seasons of weather. Now Lucianus could travel wherever he pleased throughout the hinterlands of Shimmerfrost to recruit beastly creatures from their lairs as much as he wanted. He would transplant and use these beastly creatures from Shimmerfrost to the southwestern lands to raid and pillage Nordling settlements and the settlements of the Kingdom of Swordbane to the south. It was enough to cause the young dux to reveal his jagged wide grin with glaring eyes, delighted in thinking of such future possibilities.

After taking another moment to pause and reflect, Lucianus was ready to depart and return to the skybeast along with Agaroman and their newfound followers. Before teleporting, the young werewolf asked his newfound followers where the largest beastly settlement in Shimmerfrost would be. The courier responded while pointing his hand to the west. He stated that it would be in that direction within the many large caves that make up the Har-Fjell Mountains. Lucianus grinned again and told them then that is where they shall head and he will charge his two new followers to spread word about his arrival throughout the dark beastly lairs along those mountains and to receive their fealty as their new dark lord.

Within moments, the four of them were gone after teleporting to the skybeast. The behemoth vessel turned about in the sky while heading west. The trip from Jotunheim to Har-Fjell on foot would take two weeks or more. Much of the travel time depended on the weather near the passes through the Jotunn Mountains leading out to the open land that lies between that set of mountains and the Har-Fjells. However, the skybeast cut the travel time by at least tenfold. It would arrive at the Har-Fjells by the next sunrise.

When sunrise came, Lucianus wanted to make sure he caught the attention of all the beastly creatures in the Har-Fjell Mountains. He did so first by configuring the engines of the skybeast to initiate a sudden loud booming burst of acceleration. He then made a high-energy turn while steering the flying vessel. It was an impressive maneuver which the young wolfling learned from his mother, who taught him how to fly the skybeast with ease. Now Lucianus had the skybeast floating above the nearest settled cave lair that Halkir and Knower of Many Tongues pointed to below.

Upon teleporting to the surface, Lucianus, along with Agaroman and the young dux's two new followers who served as guides, made their way toward the cave entrance. Lucianus could see the many staring eyes that hid deep within the darkness of the cave entrance. The young wolfling knew they had observed and watched him moments earlier. He had made a strong impression to get their attention at the very least. Lucianus ordered his company to come to a halt. He sensed that these staring eyes were both goblins and cave orcs who were uncertain of his presence, though somewhat impressed. The glaring eyes, however, seemed familiar in gazing at Halkir and Many Tongues.

Curious to see how they would react, Lucianus unleashed a sudden large howl. It was terrifying yet also captivating as a dozen dire wolves rushed out of the cave lair. The wolves circled about the adolescent werewolf and howled before him in a crouching position with their tails tucked to display their submissiveness and obedience.

Then, with glaring eyes lurching in the cave's darkness, the cautiously observant figures finally stepped out. In full view, Lucianus could see along with Agaroman, Halkir, and Knower of Many Tongues the various armed goblins, cave orcs, and a few large snow trolls. The leader of the group was a large ornate bone-and-leather-clothed cave orc. He spoke in orcish tongue toward Halkir and Knower of Many Tongues about these newly arrived guests. Lucianus could understand and make out in the orcish tongue what was said. The young werewolf dux interjected before the present company. He stated when questioned about his authority that he was to gain their attention by being their new dark lord while telling them that their former dark lord jotunn matriarch had fallen.

Shocked to hear if this was true, the orc sentry leader looked at Knower of Many Tongues for confirmation of what was said. The goblin shaman nodded and admitted that it was indeed true. He told them that this recently ascended dark lord was not only powerful in his own right, but that he had the knowledge to commune with a more powerful dark lord in the infernal realm who was the father of this adolescent werewolf. The orc sentry leader was surprised once more by what he heard and doubted if it was even true. He questioned in the form of a challenge or ordeal that if this were true, then this new self-proclaimed young dark lord would demonstrate summoning this infernal superior dark lord as a trial for leadership of the beastly creatures.

Lucianus heard what the orc had said. The young dux could still make out the words while nodding. Lucianus stated he would do so and teach the other shaman in the region to summon his infernal father if they agreed to swear unwavering fealty toward him. The orc sentry leader nodded in agreement.

In a matter of a few moments, Lucianus prepared a makeshift altar and shrine. He displayed the miniature holy relic statue symbols of Laran and Calu. The young wolfling also carried a lit brazier full of incense. He then demonstrated his summoning call before all those beastly creatures that were present to bear witness. They saw the adolescent werewolf utter dark incantations as he poured some wine from a chalice into the brazier of burning incense. It was a spiritual and symbolic offering to the deity spirits of war and death as Lucianus finally uttered his father's name to request Decius's presence.

The air fell silent only for a moment. Then a large flash emitted with two ethereal ghostly figures emerging out from the portals. They were the spectral shades of Lucianus's parents, Decius and Lucia. For all those present who had not seen it before, it was a sight to see as the various dire wolves, goblins, and cave orcs along with a few snow trolls kneeled before Decius.

Decius and Lucia, in their spectral shade form, were in awe of what they had seen upon being summoned by their son. Lucianus could tell that from the look on their faces while quickly explaining to them that Helskadi had fallen presumably from the Comradery, which somehow survived. However, the young dark lord also explained to his parents a power vacuum had been left among the forces of darkness in this region. Lucianus had gained new hordes of beastly followers to serve him and, by extension, to serve the will of his parents.

Decius grinned with content as did Lucia. Both of them congratulated their son for exploiting the situation for what it was in the wake of Helskadi's downfall. Decius suggested to his son that should the Nordlings unite along with the dyr folk, a truce could be drawn to prevent further losses of the beastly creatures of this region if the goblins and cave orcs sent an astute emissary to convince the Nordlings to seek a mutual understanding of not attacking each other and to cease further provocations.

Lucianus, though just over ten years of age, could process and understand his father's reasoning. The young wolfling agreed to the suggestion. He commanded Halkir and Many Tongues to negotiate on behalf of the beastly creatures to forge a truce with the Nordlings and dyr folk of this region. Halkir and Many Tongues kneeled before their young dark lord while acknowledging that they would do as Lucianus commanded after they introduced Lucianus to the various goblin and orc settlements along the Har-Fjell Mountains. Lucianus nodded in mutual agreement.

Lucianus then returned to his conversation with his parents. Lucianus reiterated his plans to recruit, transport, and make use of these new beastly creatures to raid the Imperial Remnant's adversaries, now that Helskadi was no longer in a position to hold back the Imperial Remnant from recruiting beastly creatures directly in this region.

Decius and Lucia both being impressed, congratulated their son. Even Agaroman was impressed by the strategic understanding his young protégé and dark lord had developed. Truly, he thought if anyone had the potential to succeed Decius, it was Lucianus. He had at this point shown once again that he was indeed worthy to claim his father's title as the dark lord. Only time would tell how far Decius's son would go in setting out to achieve his father's legacy. Lucianus considered it his role to finish what his father started. When it would be his time, the young werewolf dux vowed to himself that he would wipe out Swordbane once and for all. He would restore the Lupercalian Empire as he and those who followed his father's vision had imagined it.

With the high winds starting to push against the mountains, Lucianus along with the shade of his parents and his chief wizard advisor signaled for the rest of the present company to rise. They did so and led Lucianus, Agaroman, and the summoned spectral spirits of Decius and Lucia into their mountain cave lair. Once inside, many goblin and cave orc clans were alerted. All of them assembled with haste outside their crude cave huts. They were anxious to see their newly welcomed guests. The young dux would introduce himself along with the ethereal spirit of his parents as their new dark lords.

Printed in the USA
CPSIA information can be obtained
at www.ICGtesting.com
LVHW040731280224
772933LV00006B/228/J